Murder on th

Lisa M. Lane

Also by Lisa M. Lane

Literary Fiction
Before the Time Machine

The Tommy Jones Mysteries
Murder at Old St. Thomas's
Murder at an Exhibition

Victorian Romance
A Heart Purloined

Academic/reference
H. G. Wells on Science Education, 1886-1896

Lisa M. Lane

Murder on the Pneumatic Railway

Grousable Books

Murder on the Pneumatic Railway

A Tommy Jones Mystery

Published by Grousable Books, Encinitas, California

ISBN: 979-8-9853027-6-9 (print)

ISBN: 979-8-9853027-7-6 (e-book)

Library of Congress Control Number: 2023903786

Cover illustration: Detail of image of the Battersea test pneumatic railway for mail, *Scientific American*, Vol. V, No. 14, October 5, 1861.

London 1870

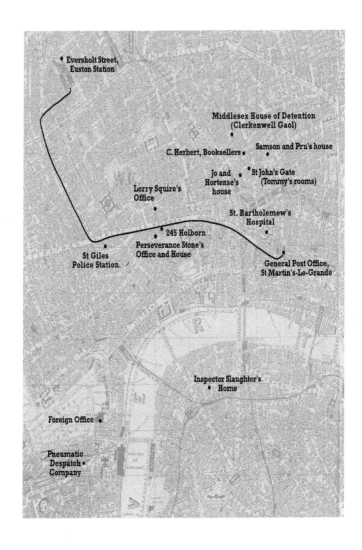

- Eversholt Street, Euston Station

- Middlesex House of Detention (Clerkenwell Gaol)

- C. Herbert, Booksellers
- Samson and Pru's house

- Jo and Hortense's house
- St John's Gate (Tommy's rooms)

- Lorry Squire's Office

- St. Bartholemew's Hospital

- 245 Holborn

- Perseverance Stone's Office and House

- St Giles Police Station

- General Post Office, St Martin's-Le-Grande

- Inspector Slaughter's Home

- Foreign Office

- Pneumatic Despatch Company

Durham 1870

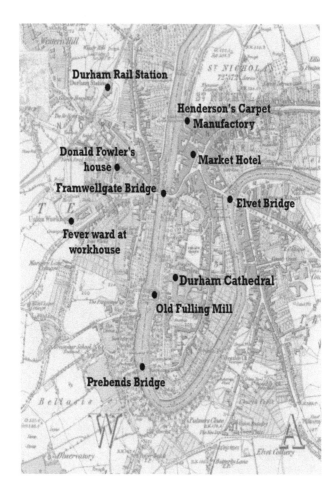

Dramatis Personae

Clerkenwell

Samson Light: surgeon/anesthetist at St. Bartholomew's Hospital

Prudence Light neé Henderson: bookshop worker, wife of Samson, formerly maid to the Slaughters

Fiona Harper: in Clerkenwell Gaol for forgery

Tommy Jones: young man, lives in St. John's Gate, formerly ward of the Slaughters

Mrs. Wren, Tommy's landlady

Jo(hanna) Harris: artist and illustrator, lives with Hortense at 54 Red Lion Street

Hortense Smith neé Miller: former telegraph worker, mother of Sally

George Smith: former Post Office worker, adventurer

The lawyers, the doctors, the government, and the plumber

Perseverance Stone: barrister, 6 Gate Street near Inns of Court

Mason: his butler

Lorry Squires: solicitor, Red Lion Square

*Arthur Otway: Under-Secretary of State for Foreign Affairs

Dr. Wallace: physician

*Mr. Thomas Spencer Wells: surgeon

*Thomas Crapper: Plumbing magnate

The Police

Detective Inspector Joseph Morgan: St. Giles police station

Detective Inspector Cuthbert Slaughter (retired): Palmer Street, Lambeth

The Post Office at St. Martin's-le-Grande

Horace Wright: Post Office clerk

Mr. James Henry: supervisor at the Post Office

Reginald: assistant to Mr. Henry

The Pneumatic Despatch Railway Company

*Richard Grenville, 3rd Duke of Buckingham and Chandos

V.G. Faber: manager and bookseller

Mr. William Wilson: secretary

Sam Jenkins: engineer

Durham and Darlington

Mrs. Treadwell: teacher and traveler

Donald Fowler: engineer

Maggie Fowler: tavern worker, daughter of Donald

Widow Hutton: owns boarding house

Callum: the man on the bridge

Simon Henderson: supervisor at fever ward building site

*Andrew Rutherford: river constable

historical figure

1

5 April 1870

He was lucky, Samson Light reflected as he sat in his small cell. His own water closet in the corner, a table, a stool, a hammock with a warm blanket, and a high window which let in the light. No prison clothing, either; he had the clothes he came with and could dress like the scholar and doctor he was. The food wasn't of the highest quality, that was true, but he had gruel, bread, and some meat every day, and perhaps Tommy would bring him something this afternoon. The bottle of beer from yesterday sat on one of the three triangular shelves in the corner, one of which held his microscope. Books were stacked on the top shelf all the way up to the ceiling. Visiting hours were from twelve to two every day but Sunday, and visitors could stay for twenty minutes, more if Moseley or O'Brien were on duty. *Just a few more weeks of this,* he thought, *before my trial.* The Seventh Session of the Old Bailey would begin the first Monday in May.

As one of the few prisoners with an education, Samson was respected at the Clerkenwell House of Detention. No one had pried into why he was here, although the charge was clearly stated on the paper stuck into the metal slot on his door: murder. That did not stop other prisoners from requesting his help when they were in their groups in the exercise yard. He had heard of horrible abuses taking place both here and at other prisons: hard labor leading to collapse, beatings, cruel warders. But he had experienced none of that during his stay. Just some cold, some loneliness, and occasional bouts of despair late at night as he wondered whether he would ever be free again. His books helped with that, too.

He was even permitted to shave. True, the blade and mirror had to be returned when he had finished, but they were reserved for him alone. Some men didn't shave in prison at all—they just trimmed their beard. Others were rightly fearful of infection. Lockjaw had killed more than one man who was careless about caring for his razor. But Samson preferred to shave. He felt it was more sanitary. And Prudence liked his face to be smooth.

He answered the knock on the door by pushing his empty bowl and spoon through the square hole. Moseley took it and peered into his cell.

"Good breakfast, doctor?" he chuckled, but not unkindly. "I'll have you out in ten minutes. You're wanted in the infirmary."

At least there would be something to do, thought Samson.

Little Sally knew she wasn't supposed to be in the kitchen by herself, but Mummy and Jo were in the other room and they wouldn't know. The big black box was sitting there as if it were looking at her, daring her to come near. It was a frightening creature, twice as tall as she was, with loud clanging doors, a voracious appetite for coal, and flames that shot out the top when you took one of the circles out. Sometimes it gave her nightmares, but Sally was determined to face her fear. Jo always told her "hot" and "be careful", but Sally saw how she and Mummy used the heavy cloth when they touched the big box. So she took the cloth and wrapped it around her small hand, then reached out and—

"Stop, young lady!" said Jo Harris, coming toward her. Sally froze, holding the wrapped hand up in the air. Jo never shouted, but she could be firm, and Sally wasn't taking any chances.

She felt herself being scooped up and turned to face the scowl.

"Now what exactly might you be doing in here on your own?"

Sally was still holding up her arm, and she looked up at her hand. Jo followed her gaze.

"Why you clever thing! You were wrapping your hand to touch the range?"

2

Sally nodded. She was absolutely not going to cry.

Jo hugged her and kissed her cheek. "That was the right thing to do, but for a reason I don't approve of. Little girls should not be touching the range. It's hot, almost all the time. Let's go over it again."

She set Sally down, and they approached the range together. Jo unwrapped her hand.

"Now, let's get close without touching, to see if it feels warm, yes?" Sally looked at Jo, her eyes wide, and nodded. Jo took her small hand in her larger hand, and they reached toward the door where the coal was put in. The closer they got, the warmer Sally's hand felt.

"I won't let you get burned," said Jo calmly, "but we're going to go closer so you can feel the heat."

Sally shrank back, her head turning into Jo's shoulder. Her hand was moved closer and felt warmer. It was soon uncomfortably warm, but Jo still held it close to the oven door.

"No, no, no," said Sally, her face muffled in Jo's blouse. Jo slowly pulled their hands back.

"That's quite right. No, no, no. If we touch something too close, too hot, it will burn, and that will hurt."

Sally sniffled and nodded her head so Jo could feel it.

"Now let's go find Mummy. She's got out the paper and the colors."

"Time to work?" said Sally, her serious face making Jo's heart leap.

"Time to work," said Jo. They went together into the parlor. The light was better here than in the kitchen, and the spring sunshine had that early evening glow. Hortense was at the square table, and the sunlight caught her blonde hair from the back, framing her head in straw-colored light. The impression of a madonna was unmistakable. Jo never tired of looking at her.

She put the child down, and Sally bounced over to the table, climbing up on her favorite chair, the heavy one that didn't tip. She grabbed for a large piece of yellowed paper.

"Steady," said Hortense gently. "We don't want it to tear, do we?"

Sally shook her head and reached for a colored stick. "Waxy red, waxy red," she demanded. Hortense handed her a stick of red pigment mixed with beeswax and oil. She knew the child's hands would be full of color by dinner time, but she had an oily rag nearby to wipe them first.

"I can make the meal if you'd like to color with her," said Jo to Hortense. "But I do have work to do this evening."

Hortense raised her head and gave Jo a grateful look. "Yes, I'd like to be with Sally for a bit," she said.

The kitchen was warm, and Jo set about checking the meat in the range and the beans in a pot on top. She chopped some onions and set them to fry in a pan, then got out plates and forks. Jo was no cook, and she surprised herself every time she entered the kitchen and came out with something edible. It was all very simple food, but hearty. She wanted Hortense to eat well. Her face was thinner now, and she struggled to keep on weight.

The infirmary at the Clerkenwell House of Detention was small, but unlike Newgate, there were usually enough iron bedsteads for the number of patients. The same surgeon, Mr. Thomas Warner, was assigned to both Clerkenwell and Coldbath Fields nearby, and on Tuesdays he worked at St. Bartholomew's Hospital. The result was that Mr. Warner stopped at Clerkenwell only twice a week, if that. The remainder of the time, the infirmary was staffed by warders and prisoners.

At twenty-eight years of age, Samson Light had been a surgeon for only three years, and his work at St. Bartholomew's Hospital had been sparse at first. The hospital had plenty of surgeons, thanks to its large size and its teaching branch. Samson had searched for a niche, a place where he was needed, and he found it in the administration of anesthetics. Most surgeons were enamored with the mechanical aspects of their art, the swift amputation or the meticulous removal of small tumors. Samson liked caring for the whole patient, and with anesthesia he could be responsible for both taking away their pain and making life-saving surgeries possible. He became adept at the dosing of chloroform (or ether if the senior surgeon preferred) and was content to limit himself to monitoring the levels of unconsciousness and the patient's breathing. This left the senior surgeon free to focus on the surgery itself.

Appreciation of Samson's medical talents were evident almost immediately when he arrived at the Clerkenwell House of Detention. Only the second night after his arrest, he had been resting in his cell, trying to get his bearings as his life had been turned upside down. The cell was quite cold, and he'd been wrapped in the blanket from his hammock, writing in one of the notebooks they had allowed him to keep. It was after midnight and sleep was elusive. He'd torn out a sheet and began to write:

> *My dear Prudence,*
>
> *I am so sorry to have caused you grief, and I look forward to your next visit. Would you please bring me the issue of the British Medical Journal I left in the surgery . . .*

He heard a loud groan from the cell across the corridor, and then another, then a shout. A warder came along and called through the square opening in the door.

"Are you all right in there, Mr. Franks?"

"No. No. Pain. My stomach!" Another groan.

Samson heard the warder sigh. There'd be no quiet duty tonight. "I'm off to get the other warder, Mr. Franks. I will come back in just a few minutes."

When the second warder returned, they unlocked the cell. Samson looked through his opening to see them help Mr. Franks, who was doubled over in pain, down the hall.

"Not sure what we'll do," said the first warder. "Better get him to the infirmary. Should we wake Miss Harper?"

"Dunno," grunted the other man, who had apparently taken most of the weight of Mr. Franks.

"I can help," Samson called down the corridor. "I'm a surgeon." He heard the other prisoners starting to stir in their cells.

The first warder half-turned. "Thank you, sir. I'll come back for you."

Perityphlitis. He knew it immediately. The abdomen was tender, his rebound touch on the right side causing extreme pain. The surgery wasn't completely new—the first one had been performed at Charing Cross Hospital over 20 years before—but few had been done, and he'd certainly never done it. The two warders stood there stupidly, one continually looking back to the corridor until the other sent him on his rounds.

"All right, Mr.—I'm sorry, warder, I don't know your name?"

"Conner, sir."

"Conner?"

"Yes, sir." Another groan from Mr. Franks.

"Mr. Conner, this man will die if I don't operate and remove his appendix from his abdomen. Is there chloroform in the cabinet?"

"Yes, sir."

"Would you be able to assist me?"

At that point, Mr. Franks, lying on the bed, turned his head and vomited into a pail, and Conner turned quite green.

Samson said, "Is there someone else here who has some experience?"

"Miss Harper, sir. She's some kind of nurse, in the woman's ward on a forgery charge. I'll fetch her, sir." Conner practically ran out of the room as Samson turned to his patient.

Miss Harper was a very good assistant, washing her hands with lye soap carefully as Samson instructed. She was unfazed by everything: the smell of the carbolic he had her spray over the abdomen, the fumes of the chloroform on the cloth frame over Mr. Franks' mouth and nose, the blood she helped mop up with a sponge, even the request to soak the sponge in potassium cyanide.

"Have you assisted in surgery before, Miss Harper?" he asked as he sutured the end of the intestine and began closing the wound.

"No," she said. "But it's always fascinated me. Do I need to give him more chloroform?"

"I think we're almost done, so he shouldn't need it."

Mr. Warner had called in the next day and hammered Samson with questions.

"Have you qualifications, sir?" Warner's wavy hair was half brown, half gray, and stood out from his head despite obvious efforts with bear grease. His beard quivered in restrained rage.

"Yes, sir. Medical degree from University of London, and I'm a surgeon at St. Bartholomew's."

"Hummph. Why the carbolic and the hand washing? Are you one of those young pups touting germ theory?"

"I tout nothing. Cleaner is better, that's all, whether it's miasma, dust, or germs. He'll have a better chance of survival."

After the interview, Mr. Warner shrugged, barked an order to the warder about laudanum to be administered for the next three days, and left for the governor's office as Samson was returned to his cell. Twenty minutes later, O'Brien came to fetch him out. It occurred to Samson that for a gaol, he hadn't spent much time in confinement.

He found Conner, the warder from the night before, standing in front of the governor's desk, looking miserable as he listened to the governor shouting.

"So your story is that you allowed a prisoner, a possible murderer"—Samson winced—"to cut open another prisoner?"

"He said he was a surgeon, sir." Conner was looking at his shoes.

The governor, a man in his sixties with a portly belly and a florid face, was about to shout something else when Samson cut in.

"It wasn't his fault, sir. I volunteered. If he hadn't let me do what I did, Mr. Franks would be dead. Now he might survive to attend his trial."

The governor looked at Samson, then at Conner, then at a file on his desk. He opened the file and ran his finger down the paper. He peered suspiciously at Samson.

"You, Mr. Light, are not even a Christian, as I understand it?" The governor's face was red, but around his eyes the lids were pale. Anemia, thought Samson. Probably eats more bread than meat.

"No, sir. I am a Jew. But I am also a qualified surgeon and anesthetist."

The governor looked down at the file again and took a deep breath, his pink jowls quivering. "I am much too busy for this sort of thing," he blustered. "Get out of my office."

Tommy Jones dashed to his room to change his clothes for the evening. He ran through the narrow doorway, up the circular stairway and into the storage room that had become his home. The floor was stone, but he had covered it with a rug Ellie Slaughter had given him when he left Southwark. The tiny window let in light, and he could see the traffic in the street. It was still pretty sparse, since the evening had only just started.

Soon the club men would be coming up and down the stairs. Tommy's room over the pub was next to St. John's Gate, and the old coffee room over the arch was reserved for the Urban Club. The stairs went right past his room. They'd be going up and down all evening, getting drinks and visiting the privy out back. They styled themselves the "Friday Knights." Tonight the occasion was dedicated to Club business. It was the most important planning meeting of the year, because April 23 was less than a fortnight away.

That was Shakespeare's birthday, a sacred day on the Club calendar. There would be the usual vociferous arguments followed by the usual grandiose toasts, and they'd be there till the wee hours. Tommy did not want to get in their way. Mr. Wickens loved having such a distinguished group of intellectuals at the Old Jerusalem Tavern. He felt it lent his place not only the cachet of literature, but a convivial medieval feel.

Tommy knew that the Middle Ages had nothing in common with the Urban Club members, who dined in comfort, looking out the glass windows from atop the gate. Well, perhaps it was medieval after all, thought Tommy as he grabbed his coat and changed into his better boots. The walls were certainly crumbling like an old ruin. An effort was being made to gather some money for repairs. But after all, the gate's derelict condition was why Tommy's room was cheap. That and his being willing to help downstairs when the beer barrels arrived.

He had spent the walk home from Bloomsbury hoping Susie would be out tonight. She was only seventeen, it was true. He was the older man, at nineteen. Quickly brushing his hair into what he hoped was an orderly mop, he bounced back down the stairs and out into the street.

Friday was Tommy's night off. It had been a long week so far, what with his tutoring two young people, his night class teaching at the Ragged School, and his work at the clockmaker's. But Tommy had always preferred multiple tasks. Tutoring rich children and selling clocks in the daytime, then teaching poor lads in the evening, gave a balance to his life that he enjoyed. *It's not what I want from life yet,* thought Tommy, *but it will surely lead to more, and it is far better than sweeping crossings and clearing up at the gasworks.* Less dangerous too. He could study a bit, work a bit, and go out and have some fun. Tonight he was off to the pub for dancing night, and Susie should be there already.

"We must get him a barrister, a good one," hollered Ellie Slaughter from the kitchen as she pounded the bread dough. The house in Palmer Street, although small enough for her and her husband to be comfortable, was fairly new and well-built; she had to raise her voice to be heard in the next room.

"Hmmm?" said Cuthbert, from the study.

"Samson Light," Ellie shouted. "He needs a good barrister."

Cuthbert Slaughter, retired Detective Inspector, folded his newspaper and took his pipe out of his mouth. So much for a quiet, rainy spring afternoon, he thought. He had been unable to concentrate on the article in the *Athenaeum*; he was having trouble caring whether Mr. E. M. Barry intended to use linseed oil, with or without added sulfur, to preserve the stonework at the Houses of Parliament. In truth, Samson Light's difficulties had been occupying his mind as well. He got up out of the wingback chair, his knee a bit creaky, and went into the kitchen. Warmer in there anyway.

"Yes, I've been thinking about that," he said to Ellie. "Perseverance Stone might be our man, or perhaps John Sims. He needs someone with experience in murder trials."

"His solicitor is bloody useless," Ellie swore under her breath.

Samson's solicitor was the somewhat bumbling Mr. Lorry Squires, a man with a good heart but a marked naïveté about humankind. Assuming the best of everyone was not a good characteristic for a solicitor, except when comforting the bereaved.

"How would we pay for it?" asked Cuthbert. "It could be fifty pounds or more for his defense."

Ellie nodded and pounded the dough harder. Her husband's police pension was just enough for the two of them. Tommy Jones, their ward, was living up at St. John's Gate and supporting himself now. She missed having him around. It was awfully quiet without him running in and out of the house, helping with the marketing, dirtying up the floor. But he was teaching now, and his education had been mostly through the efforts of Samson Light, his tutor.

"Yes, I know," Ellie said. "We'll think of something."

Cuthbert watched her continue to knead the dough on the large wooden table, admiring the way the gray light of the day made her hair look pale and whispery. Once, seeing her making the bread herself would have been a painful reminder that they couldn't afford a cook. These days he knew it was because she didn't trust purchased bread, which often contained things that didn't bear thinking about. Ellie had been to a great many scholarly talks in her role at the Women's Reform Club and knew more about London life than most.

"I'll go see Stone in the morning," offered Cuthbert. "His office is near the Inns of Court." Perhaps it would be brighter tomorrow, and his knee would enjoy a walk.

That night in bed, Ellie stared up at the ceiling. She considered herself a good judge of character and knew beyond doubt that Samson Light could not be guilty. It had only been six years ago that he had sat in her home, gratefully enjoying her tea and toast, teaching Tommy all about science. But he had taught more than science. Ellie had often overheard them discussing philosophy and morality. She had enjoyed having two serious young men weighing such issues in the comfort of her kitchen. Samson, even in his twenties, had a wisdom that many older men lacked, and a zest for learning that served him well in becoming a medical doctor. How had he gotten into this position, accused of murder?

Wrong place at the wrong time, she thought. He'd been seen arguing with the victim whose body had been found on the pneumatic railway. As far as she knew, there had been no other suspects. Surely it must have been an accident, or a coincidence. She was quite sure Samson could not be to blame.

Perseverance Stone was not a man to anger easily. Nor was he one to hold a grudge. But as he left the Old Bailey, he had to admit he held less than kindly feelings toward Judge Horton. No one, he thought, could look evidence in the face and come to precisely the wrong conclusion with more dispatch. And how could he possibly have resisted Stone's client? The accused had been, if not young, in the wholesome bloom of early middle age. She had been respectful in court, taking Stone's advice to look at Judge Horton modestly out of the corner of her eye. Her proper brown dress, discreet with hardly any bustle, had featured a dainty but inexpensive white collar that should have evoked the strongest sympathy with her case.

Despite his Quaker origins, Stone was headed directly to his favorite pub to order beer in hopes of washing away his failure. Well, not really a failure, he mused, avoiding a man in a tall hat who wasn't paying attention to where he was going. The sentence had been quite reasonable. Six months in Holloway was not bad, considering the amount that she had stolen from her estranged husband's family. Rather clever, that was, he thought, charging them rent on their own property. That might make a good story if he could think how to disguise the names.

Two hours and three pints later, he felt more positive as he walked from the Cheese to his office in Gate Street. The spring day was fine, with a light breeze that cleared his head as he took the greener route across Lincoln Inn Fields. He arrived at number six, where one of the several brass plaques declared "Perseverance Stone, Esquire." He marched up the stairs to his office. He had only just sat down behind his desk when he heard the door open behind him.

"Mr. Stone?" asked retired Detective Inspector Slaughter. "Are you available for inquiries?"

"I am!" replied Stone, coming back into the outer room to shake Slaughter's hand. "My goodness, it's been an age, Inspector Slaughter. How are things on the force?"

Stone really did look pleased to see him, thought Slaughter. That was gratifying, considering they had so often been on opposite sides in court. Perseverance Stone did most of his work defending clients against the evidence presented by the police. They had never, however, engaged in any personal animosity toward each other.

"I'm retired now," said Slaughter, taking the seat Stone indicated.

"Still living in—where was it?—Lambeth?"

"Yes, near Waterloo Road," replied Slaughter. "You're still practicing, by the look of it?"

"Yes, indeed. Just returning from court. Not as successful of a verdict as I would like, but we do our best. What can I do for you?" Stone pushed aside the papers on his desk as if clearing the way for a new venture.

"I'm afraid an acquaintance of mine is in some trouble."

"Arrested, eh?"

"Yes. The pneumatic railway murder. You might have read about it in the newspaper."

"Of course!" said Stone, leaning back in his chair to recollect the facts using his ceiling. "Dead man found in a car of the pneumatic railway. Hit once on the head and strangled, presumably in that order. Had the mark of some sort of chain on the front of his throat, probably used in the strangling. Extravagant pocket watch found on him. Some doctor was arrested, wasn't he?"

"That's Samson Light. He was a tutor to our ward, Tommy Jones. About five or six years ago."

"And you think he's innocent?" Stone's eyebrows puckered. Everyone was innocent, of course.

"It just seems so unlikely that he would harm anyone."

"Don't tell me: conscientious young man, well-liked, educated. Nowhere near the place, or near the place at the wrong time."

Slaughter sighed. Perseverance Stone had seen it all before, and fought on behalf of most of it. "Yes. And now he's in Clerkenwell awaiting trial and needs a barrister."

"In the Tench?" This was the street name of the Clerkenwell penitentiary, or House of Correction.

"No, in the House of Detention."

"That's a mercy, at least," said Stone sympathetically. "Nice place that, for a gaol. Visiting hours, proper food, mostly lesser criminals. And innocent detainees," he added quickly.

"So Ellie and I were wondering—"

"Yes," said Stone firmly. "I will go see him this week. Now," he said, taking out a fresh sheet of paper and a pen, "what is his name again?"

"Samson Light."

Stone paused. "Jewish name, is it?"

"Yes, I believe he's Jewish."

"But no one from the East End charities is taking his case?"

"I don't believe so. He was a student at the University of London and is now a surgeon at St. Bartholomew's. I don't know of his connections to synagogues or anything."

"Medical degree?"

"Yes, but he prefers the style 'mister' rather than 'doctor.'"

Stone nodded.

"Family?"

"His wife, Prudence, was our housemaid. I believe her father died at Coldbath Fields."

"Oh, that won't look good," mumbled Stone.

"I know. But Samson is respected at St. Bartholomew's. A good surgeon, if still young."

"How old is he?"

"Late twenties. Not sure exactly."

"Parents?"

"None, I don't think. His father was an apothecary and died several years ago. His mother lived in Birmingham, but I think she died last year or the year before."

"Children?"

"None that I know of."

"Solicitor?"

"Lorry Squires," said Slaughter.

Perseverance Stone looked up over his spectacles, then put the pen down. "So who might be paying for his defense?"

"Well, Ellie is pretty insistent that we do. And I agree," Slaughter added hastily, but he realized his reluctance was evident.

"I see," said Stone. Slaughter was a good man, a good policeman. An inspector's pension couldn't be very much. Really, they were on the same side, helping the cause of justice in a cruel, cold world. Perhaps it was the beer, or the challenge of the good fight, but Stone was feeling generous.

"You'll owe nothing if I fail to free him," said Stone. "And expenses if I do."

Slaughter tried to ensure that the relief didn't show on his face, but he knew it did.

"Thank you, Mr. Stone."

Tommy Jones awoke late the next morning with an aching head and cold toes. There were disadvantages to living in the gate, but he was happy to be up early. Drinking down most of the contents of the water jug by the bed, he splashed his face and got dressed. Bag packed with his books, he went downstairs to the tavern to find Mrs. Wren.

She was at the stove as he had hoped, taking buns out of the oven.

"Good morning, Mrs. Wren," he said, entering so he wouldn't startle her. She looked up with a smile.

"Och, there you are, young man. Came in late, did ye?" Wisps of damp gray hair peeked out from her cap.

"I did. But with all the singing and a lovely girl, it couldn't have been any earlier."

"Ah, to be young again," she said. "You'll be wanting a few of these for your Mr. Light, will you?"

"If you don't mind, ma'am," he said. "I'll buy some fruit on the way. They don't feed them well at Clerkenwell, Mrs. Wren, they surely don't."

"Well, mind you eat first yourself. I've got porridge in the pot and tea on the table."

"Would you like a cup, Mrs. Wren?"

"I would, Tommy, if you've a mind to pour."

The buns cooling on the table, Tommy and Mrs. Wren sat and drank their tea.

"So teach me something, young Mr. Jones," said Mrs. Wren. This was their morning routine, a bit of his knowledge for a bit of her cooking. "Tell me more about that Robert Boyle."

Tommy leaned back a bit in the chair, but without tipping it. Mrs. Wren was particular about her chairs.

"Well, Mr. Boyle was quite the character, they say. But he did amazing things with chemistry. Used all sorts of apparatus to separate and combine elements so we can understand what they do."

"Like what?" asked Mrs. Wren, as she sipped her tea from the saucer.

"Like his pneumatical engine, a kind of air pump. He discovered that you need air to make flame by putting a candle in his engine and pumping out all the air." Tommy thought it best not to mention that Boyle also did this with living animals, like mice.

Mrs. Wren frowned. "Was he a good Christian, then?" She did not like hearing about people who weren't.

"Oh, yes, indeed. He studied theology and wrote books about it."

Mrs. Wren nodded in satisfaction and got up to return to her work. "Boyle," she said to help her remember. "All right then."

"I'd best be off, Mrs. Wren. Thank you for the buns. I'm quite sure Mr. Light thanks you, too."

Mrs. Wren went back to her cooking with her head full of air pumps, humming a little tune.

2

On the first of April, three days before Samson was arrested, a man left his flat in Clerkenwell Close to walk to his job at the General Post Office in the City. His name was Horace Wright, and he was not a very important man. He knew this. Working at the Post Office was not a bad career, but he was aware that it matched his abilities. There were times when this saddened him, as when he visited his aunt in Brighton, and she spoke about the things he might have done if only he could have gone to university. He forgave her this. Aunt Mildred had married into wealth, which seemed to cause an almost instant transformation. She had come to believe that the lower orders of society, including the one from which she came, could pull themselves up. She had read Samuel Smiles, and like most people with just enough education to wholeheartedly believe a convincing argument but not enough to consider an opposing view, had adopted the ideas so completely it was as if she had thought of them herself.

Horace's mother had been a domestic servant before marrying his father. His parents had moved to London from Shropshire upon a job offer to his father from Uncle Thomas, who worked at Overend, Gurney & Company at its bank office in Lombard Street. The position had supported the small family for twenty-eight years, until the summer of 1866. The collapse of railway stock caused the liquidation of the bank, and the directors were brought up on fraud charges. Although they were acquitted of everything but taking bad advice, the bank's closing and the financial panic which followed had weakened his father's heart. He had died shortly before

Horace's mother also departed this world. Horace found himself thirty years old, living alone in the flat where he had grown up.

His childhood in Clerkenwell had been ordinary and respectable, and his schooling sufficient for his likely prospects. He wanted for little and grew up knowing that what was important in life was getting on and doing one's work as best one could. Work, his father had taught him, was what you contributed to society. To do it efficiently and well was to be a good and moral person.

What his father had not taught him, nor his mother either, was how to meet and persuade a good woman to share this moral life. Before they died, he had left the flat at the same time each day, wearing one of three versions of a similar suit, to go to the General Post Office in St. Martin's-Le-Grand, close to St. Paul's Cathedral. The large neo-classical building was imposing, but Horace loved the large room where he was assigned. The elongated space held rows of desks, tightly fitted next to each other, where the mail was sorted. This was where the chaos of London's communication became an orderly progression of messages from sender to recipient. Although he worked in the Inland room, he hoped some day to sort Foreign or Colonial letters. He believed in the empire, and in doing his part.

Things were different now, and not just because his parents were gone. The collapse of the Overend, Gurney & Company, which had led to his father's early death, also impacted his work. Under Sir Rowland Hill, the Post Office had become involved with a company building a pneumatic railway, which would connect railway stations, post offices, and docks. Hill and his colleagues had petitioned Parliament for permission to dig up streets and contract with the Post Office. But with the bank failures, construction was delayed and staff were shifted around. Horace was to be relocated to the basement in the south end of the building, to prepare for the opening of the pneumatic railway line. Instead of his morning shift in the large, bright sorting hall at the G.P.O., he would be in a basement with rails and all sorts of wiring for equipment. Instead of his evening shift preparing bags for the night mail coaches in the courtyard, he would be preparing bags to be carried by pneumatic tube to 245 Holborn, then onward to Euston Station. He knew that most of the business mail leaving London went out through Euston, and that the traffic on the roads slowed its passage considerably. But the importance of the job did not make up for the conditions. He'd already been down to the railway basement multiple times, preparing the various cubbyholes and tables that would be needed. The clatter of building and construction, the hammering and banging, rang in his ears all day. Lately the sound stayed with him at night, long after he'd left work. Increasingly, Horace felt like a coal miner, or a mole, doing his duty below ground for the greater good above it.

There were three separate railway lines involved in the project so far, although the plan was for many more in the future. The first, a small-gauge line from Euston Station to the North West Sorting Office less than a third of a mile down the road, had already closed about the time Horace was assigned to the new job. This small line had proved less efficient than using a cart on the street. The second tunnel ran two miles between the North West Sorting Office and the new central station at 245 Holborn, where the machinery was. It had taken a long time to construct this leg because it had to bend around the properties of the Duke of Bedford, who didn't want the streets dug up. The final section of a little less than a mile had been completed in the other direction between 245 Holborn and the General Post Office in St. Martin's-le-Grand, where Horace worked. This had been the most challenging section, as it dipped below Farringdon Street as part of the Holborn Viaduct. Horace had been told that when the cars began carrying letter bags on the new section, the G.P.O. would have more mail from around the world than ever before. But although the tunnel had been completed several months ago, shipments had not yet begun. All awaited some decision to be made by the directors. So Horace was patient and managed sorting in the cellar.

On this day in April, he arrived at the Post Office as usual, went downstairs to the change room, and put on his sleeve protectors. He arrived in the basement at ten, but heard no banging sounds. Perhaps there was a problem, or perhaps the work was at last finished. He had surprised himself by taking an interest in the construction of the line, the cars and their efficiency. He liked efficiency, and if the mail could be transported on a precise schedule, without interference from traffic, dying horses, and unexpected delays, so much the better. Despite his misery being downstairs, he had even conversed with one of the engineers, learning what he could. He went to see whether bags had already been loaded into the cars for a test run. He leaned over to peer into the first car, saw that it was still empty, and that was the last thing he knew before he knew nothing at all.

When Tommy Jones arrived at the Clerkenwell House of Detention, he found Samson's wife, Prudence Light, already there. He caught sight of her pale violet dress as he came down the corridor. She was in profile, smiling at Samson through the little door. Her cheeks looked flushed. Visitors were permitted for only the two hours, and Tommy didn't want to interrupt, so he waited half-way down the hall.

"Young man," a voice hissed next to him. Tommy turned to see a wizened face peering through the cell opening. The man's eyebrows were silver, and wispy white hair on his head and in his beard created a halo effect.

"Yes, sir?" Tommy said, respectfully.

He could see the man put on his spectacles before peering out again.

"Don't I know you?" the man said in surprise.

Tommy glanced at the card on the door: "Felix Tapper". Underneath was the charge: "Violation of the Pharmacy Act of 1868".

Tommy smiled. "Mr. Tapper!" he said. "Yes, you know me. Tommy Jones. I used to work with Sam Wetherby, at your hospital."

That had been seven years ago, but Felix Tapper remembered the lad. "Yes! I thought you looked familiar. It's been a long time. And poor Mr. Wetherby . . ." He shook his head sadly.

"Yes, indeed," said Tommy, wanting to change the subject. He glanced down the hall, but Prudence was still talking to her husband, her blonde side curls bobbing as she nodded her head.

"I'm sorry to see you in here," said Tommy. Felix Tapper was an apothecary who had always had rather loose rules about the distributing of opium. His generosity had been perfectly legal seven years ago, but the Act of 1868 said pharmacists could only sell to people registered and known to them.

"Yes, I'm sorry to be here. Third time, I'm afraid." His owl-like eyes blinked, and Tommy saw a bit of humor in them.

"Are you still in charge at St. Thomas's?"

"No, I'm afraid Sir Henry had to let me go. It was perfectly fair of him. I run my own pharmacy now, in Charterhouse Square."

"Will you be out of here soon?" Tommy asked. "I can come see you sometime."

"Oh, in a week or so, I expect. Just a matter of paying the fine. I've an old friend at the hospital. She'll send the money."

Tommy was pleased he would be released and wished him luck. He knew that Tapper was only trying to help people. Prudence must have finished her visit. She was coming down the corridor toward him with a smile.

"Tommy, how nice to see you!" she leaned over and kissed his cheek, and he heard a rustle of interest from several of the cells.

"Hello, Prudence," he said.

"Thank you so much for visiting Samson, bringing things and cheering him. I'm so grateful."

"Of course," said Tommy. "May I visit with him now?" He took out his watch, clicking it open. "I'm afraid there isn't much time left today."

"Of course," Prudence said, laying her hand on his arm. "But do you need to rush off afterward? Or could we have tea together?" He heard a low whistle from a cell across the hall.

"I'd be delighted," said Tommy.

"Then I'll wait out front," she said, turning to leave. Tommy thought that a woman waiting alone in front of the gaol might not be seen as proper, but Prudence tended to do as she wished.

"Hello, Samson," said Tommy. He looked in the door. Samson smiled at him but his eyes seemed tired, thought Tommy. This whole thing is ridiculous, he thought. Samson Light does not belong in gaol. He saw Moseley, the warder, and waved at him.

"Mr. Moseley, hello."

"Hullo, Mr. Jones," said Moseley, glancing at the bag Tommy was carrying. "Will you be wanting to bring the prisoner something?"

"Yes, I have some food. Would you like to take the bag with you to investigate?"

"No, sir, that's not necessary. Just let me take a look inside."

Tommy held the bag out, and Moseley looked, careful not to touch anything.

"That'll be fine, sir." He opened the cell door, and Tommy handed the bag to Samson. Moseley closed and locked the door again, leaving the opening uncovered for them to converse. He touched his cap and moved off down the hall.

"Have you been keeping busy, Samson?" Tommy knew that he wasn't Samson's pupil anymore, but he couldn't help the little boy tone from creeping into his voice.

"Yes, Tommy. I actually had to perform a surgery the other night." He explained as he curled up the bag to keep the buns fresh, putting them on the lower shelf in the corner.

"I would have liked to have seen that," said Tommy in amazement.

"Strictly routine," said Samson with a wry smile.

Tommy had been to see Samson twice in the last week. He knew his old tutor had been seen arguing with the dead man, but he assumed Samson was innocent as he claimed. The practical thing was to help with his confinement, Tommy had thought at first. But looking at Samson's pale face, and the medical books behind him on the shelves, he regretted his decision. He shouldn't just be providing comfort in adversity, he thought. This was beyond that. Samson could hang, and here Tommy was out there living his own life. And bringing buns.

"Samson, I really want to do something to help." He had said this before, and Samson always shook his head, looking at the floor.

"I'm not sure what you could do," he would say. Tommy always expected him to point out that he was only nineteen, but Samson never treated him like a child. He just seemed to despair of anyone being able to help.

But today was different. "You've got to get me out of here," said Samson in a low, urgent voice.

"Of course," Tommy said, "but how?"

"I can't do anything while I'm in here, to investigate, to prove my innocence. Prudence wants to help, but I don't want her in danger out there . . ." He trailed off.

"I understand," said Tommy. "I will help. I will find out what happened. I'll need names, dates, places . . ."

Samson had anticipated him. He held a small sheaf of papers up to the window.

"I've written it all down," he said. "I have everything I remember, all my movements for that day, the names of the officers who arrested me. I don't have a barrister yet, but I got a note from Inspector Slaughter saying he was looking for one."

"Is there a police inspector assigned to the case?" Tommy had lived in the Slaughter household long enough to know how the process worked.

"Yes," said Samson, "but I wasn't sure why—"

Moseley was at the cell door.

"I'm sorry, sir," he said to Tommy. "But the time has expired for today."

"All right, Mr. Moseley," said Samson through the grate, "but may I give Tommy these papers, please?"

The warder unlocked the cell again, Samson handed him the papers, and he relocked the door. Moseley shuffled through the papers, looking them up and down, before handing them to Tommy. Tommy was pretty sure Moseley didn't know how to read, but he didn't say so.

"Everything seems to be in order, sir," said Moseley. "Until next time, then."

As an artist at *The Illustrated London News*, Jo Harris knew that she was respected, and nowhere more than in the area of drawing machinery and engineering projects. Although originally hired to copy paintings and other artworks for the engravers, she had taken advantage of the many projects around London to provide greater opportunities, volunteering to draw the newest or most fascinating constructions. Given that she wasn't a draughtsman, her enthusiasm had caused some jealousy among the other illustrators, particularly the younger men. Jo often felt that if it hadn't been for the editor, Ann Little Ingram, she would never have had the confidence to undertake those assignments.

As she entered the studio provided for the publisher's illustrators, two of the men looked up to greet her. The younger was Herbert Cox, with his heart-shaped smiling face and curly red hair.

"Good morning, Miss Harris," said Cox. "You're here early for a Saturday. More machines today?"

"I believe so," said Jo, hanging her satchel from the coat rack. "I still haven't got that damned disc quite right."

Cox knew which damned disc she meant. The large disc that helped create the vacuum on the Pneumatic Despatch Company railway was difficult to draw from any angle. While Cox did not share Jo's ease with mechanical devices, he knew that the reading public was enamored with such novelties. He was very glad it was not his job to give it to them in pictures.

Jo sat at the table in the light. She was senior enough now to command the work area in the center of the front window, which looked across the Strand from the second floor. The page with the disc mocked her. It looked little different than it had the day before. The men and woman looking up at the machinery with admiration were portrayed well, but the machine itself seemed too small next to them. She began to work on enlarging the disc. Surely it was at least twice as big as the visitors? And its edge had been much closer to the ceiling.

In order to draw it, Jo had tried to learn how it worked. Somehow this disc, turned by a steam engine, created a flow of air that pulled or pushed the cars through a tube. This pneumatic tube had a track for the cars to ride on. But the cars, shaped like low horse troughs, had no means of locomotion themselves. Rather the disc acted like a fan, creating a vacuum that pulled the cars toward it, or was reversed to create a positive airflow that pushed the cars away toward the next station. The engines were loud, but the cars themselves traveled almost silently along their track. The idea was that the Post Office would make use of this throughout the city, communicating important messages of business at the heart of the empire. There had been so many inventions, so many schemes, but this one had an advantage in that an Act of Parliament had allowed the Pneumatic Despatch Company to tear up streets and lay the tubes. London needed faster, better communication systems.

Musing about communication made Jo think of Hortense, and not just because she thought of her much of the time. Hortense had worked at the London District Telegraph Company years before, when she had been a young woman. The District, as everyone called it, had not had the benefit of an Act of Parliament to get started. They were in competition with two other larger telegraphy companies, the Electric and the Magnetic. Instead of tearing things up, the District had politely asked building owners for permission to install telegraph wires, and strung them from building to building. Focusing on cheap messaging (only four pence for ten words), their system encouraged more and more people to send telegraphic communications around the city. Women had been trained as telegraphers from the day the company was started. Hortense has been one of them. Then she had met George Smith, a postal clerk, at the International Exhibition of 1862, where they had both been looking at telegraph equipment. They fell in love across wires and transmitters and had married just before Overend, Gurney & Company lost everyone's money, and Hortense was let go along with many others.

Jo had never met George Smith. She knew only that he'd had a reputation as a cheerful and able man. Now, when Hortense was very sad, especially during the long evenings of winter, she would listen to Hortense confide her previous love for George, and her shock when he had left her. Overnight he had changed from a reliable middle manager to an adventurer. He was off to South Africa, he declared, to make his fortune. He was sorry, he said, and he would of course grant her a divorce if she wished. A man only had one chance, and he was going to take it now, before it was too late. Hortense had not then told him what she suspected, that she was pregnant with his child. By the time she was sure, he had been gone a month, leaving her as much money as he could spare. A small inheritance from his grandmother spared Hortense the need to find immediate employment after his departure.

Instead she had cried for a solid week, then spent the remainder of her pregnancy remedying the gaps in her education. She began attending Unitarian-sponsored lectures at Essex Hall in the Strand, and there she had found a mentor. Mrs. Elizabeth Malleson was founder of the Working Women's College in Queens Square, Bloomsbury. She had encouraged Hortense to attend classes at the college. Although she had been nervous, Hortense had enrolled in art sessions and had become one of Jo's best drawing pupils. After the class was over, she and Jo began spending more and more time together. What began as friendship became much deeper, and Jo moved into Hortense's home in Red Lion Street to care for her and the baby. They had become a family.

Jo had enjoyed her first visit to the pneumatic rail station at 245 Holborn, but she hadn't had time to see everything. She collected her satchel again from the coat rack and left to take another look at the damned disc.

Tommy departed the Middlesex House of Detention, walking across the courtyard to the main gate, but he didn't see Prudence in the street out front. He went back to the courtyard, which had a small garden near the main doors. There was a tidy area for walking, with a circular path around a tree. Prudence was sitting on the bench, her gloved hands in her lap. She looked a bit pale, Tommy noticed. Having your husband in gaol couldn't be easy.

"You wanted to speak with me?" asked Tommy, sitting next to her. He was not yet accustomed to meeting her as a friend. Prudence was six years older than he was and had worked as a housemaid at the Slaughters' when he had been a child there. More than once she had ordered him to get his dirty boots off the floor, or forced him to come through the back door so as not to soil the carpets. She had made up his bed, the bed he never slept in because he always preferred a pallet by the stove in the kitchen. She ran a tight housekeeping ship on Mondays and Thursdays and didn't like being disturbed when she was blackening the stove.

But Tommy prided himself that it was because of him that Samson and Prudence had met. When Inspector Slaughter arranged for him to have a tutor, Tommy had been concerned that a male tutor not be in the house without Mrs. Slaughter having another woman there. It just wouldn't be proper. He had made sure that Samson's days tutoring him coincided with Prudence's days cleaning house. Gradually, Samson had begun walking Prudence to the omnibus stop, and a romance had blossomed.

Prudence did not look to be in the flower of romance at the moment, however. She was looking earnestly at him.

"Tommy, I want you to help Samson."

"I know," he said. "I've just promised him I'll do what I can. Inspector Slaughter is helping, too; Samson said he's finding a good barrister."

Prudence took a handkerchief out of her bag and dabbed her eyes. Tommy was surprised. Prudence was usually in charge of herself and everyone around her. He'd never seen her upset or even particularly worried about anything. She caught his confused expression.

"I'm sorry," she said. "It's not only Samson's case. There's my mum, you see."

"Is she more ill?" he asked, frowning. "I thought Samson had helped arrange for her to be in a sanitarium."

"She's at Dr. Graham's for now, in Sussex," said Prudence, "but if Samson goes to prison, there'll be no more money except from my bookshop job. And that won't pay enough to keep her there."

Tommy nodded in sympathy. Of course, a private hospital, even a small one like Dr. Graham's, must be very expensive. The clock on the church was chiming three o'clock.

"Are you hungry?" asked Tommy. "I have to be at the Ragged School by five, and I haven't had lunch yet."

Prudence rose to her feet and winced. "I'm so sorry. Of course. I asked you to tea, didn't I? There's a tea room around the corner."

The day was fine, if a little breezy. Wisps of blonde hair were peeking out from Prudence's bonnet. When they arrived at the tea room, Tommy opened the door, and the sticky sweet smell of tea cakes wafted out at them. Prudence stopped, turned a little green, and put her handkerchief over her mouth.

"Are you all right?" Tommy asked, concerned.

"I'll be back in a moment," said Prudence with a gulp, and disappeared into the alley beside the tearoom.

Tommy was unsure what to do, so he waited, politely opening the door for people as they came in and out. After a minute or two Prudence returned, dabbing the corner of her mouth. She smiled wanly at Tommy and went in the door.

There were no tables near the front, so they were seated along the side wall.

"What would you like?" asked Tommy.

"Now see here," said Prudence, more like her old self again. "I invited you. What would *you* like?"

Tommy laughed. "Tea and a sandwich, if they have one. And you, dare I ask?"

"Just tea," said Prudence, swallowing.

Tommy checked his pocket watch, but they were served quickly.

"He couldn't have done it, of course," said Prudence firmly.

"Of course not," agreed Tommy. He thought for a moment. Samson was simply not the sort of person to do such a thing; on the contrary, he was smart and conscientious. When he told the truth, would the jury believe him? And what could Tommy do about it, really? He wasn't a police detective or a constable. It could be said he was just a young man, working some jobs, having some fun, enjoying life. But Pru was counting on him, and so was Samson.

"Samson didn't even know this Horace Wright. He just happened to be walking by the Post Office," Pru continued.

"Right," said Tommy, removing from his pocket the papers Samson had given him. "I have his list of what he did that day, and how he doesn't recall having spoken to anyone on his walk to see his patient."

"A very ill-fated walk," Pru said wryly.

A nagging voice in the back of Tommy's mind said he'd never taken on anything really important. His whole nineteen years he'd just been bouncing in and out of situations, helping where he could, learning about things. He'd helped Detective Inspector Slaughter solve the murder at St. Thomas's by sharing ideas, and he'd helped Jo Harris with the murder of Mr. Pratchett in the art gallery by breaking a simple code on a list of photography customers. He was good at tossing around ideas and at making connections. Would that be enough? A man had been killed, and a friend wrongly accused.

"I'll go see the inspector on the case first thing Monday," he assured Prudence. "You said it was Inspector Morgan, at St. Giles?"

She nodded.

"I'll find out what he's discovered so far. You send me a message when you know that Samson has a barrister, and I'll talk to him, too. You can count on me."

As he said it, he wondered whether it was true.

With only three weeks remaining until Samson Light's trial, Perseverance Stone was annoyed at being interrupted. The note, sent by courier, said to report to the Foreign Office as soon as was convenient. It wasn't, but he went immediately.

"Mr. Otway will see you now," said the clerk at the desk of the new building in King Charles Street. Whitehall was changing rapidly, thought Stone. Gilbert Scott's "drawing-room for the nation" was an imposing classical building dedicated to diplomacy. He mounted the grand steps to the first floor.

"Proper legal advice, that's what I need," barked Arthur Otway, once Stone had been settled into his office and brought a cup of tea. As Under Secretary for Foreign Affairs, Otway was an important man. He'd been a barrister himself before taking this post two years previous.

Stone looked up from his tea in surprise. "Why, Arthur? Is something unusual happening?"

Otway put his own teacup down firmly and stood up from his massive desk. He could be an imposing man, with his broad face and sweeping curl of hair above his forehead. He had attended Sandhurst and had his father's Royal Navy bearing, but his eyes were hooded and he always looked like he was ready to spring into action.

"You understand I am not entirely at liberty to say," he began, as he came around the desk to pace behind Stone's chair. "But of course you must be aware that my focus for many years has been India. Reforming the government there in the wake of the Mutiny."

Stone nodded. The Liberals thought very differently about India than the governments before them, and had taken the Mutiny as a sign of the need for better treatment and more generous infrastructure in the subcontinent, rather than punishment.

"But now Mr. Gladstone is very concerned about the situation on the Continent," Otway continued, "and the issue of neutralization of the Black Sea. Russia's demands are increasingly being made clear, while Bismarck in Prussia is seeking to subdue France. And you, Perseverance, have quite a bit of background in international law. The Black Sea Clauses, man! You helped write them."

"That was many years ago, Arthur," said Stone, but he knew this was a losing argument. If Otway wanted his help, of course he would give it.

"Russia, France, and Prussia are involved in intense diplomatic relations at the moment. Russia is becoming a behemoth: the Crimean War was just the beginning of their perfidy, as we know from the January uprisings in Poland. France could be an ally if they didn't want our empire. But the Conservatives warn that the real threat is a united Germany. Prussia and France could be at war any day. Needless to say, there is some division about where Britain should place its support. Then there's Turkey!" He slammed his hand on the desk in emphasis then turned his hooded eyes toward Stone. "I need a legal scholar."

Stone sighed and put down his cup. "If you need my help, Arthur, I am only too happy to provide it. I do have criminal cases that are active now, of course. Shall I continue working on them, or do I need to find another barrister for them?"

Otway waved his hand impatiently. "Keep them, keep them. I should not need you more than a few hours a day."

Stone doubted that very much, but kept silent. Although he had not been directly involved in the Indian Reform Society, he believed that Otway had dedicated himself to it almost to the point of obsession. The European situation was more complicated, and he knew Otway would give it his full attention. Stone wasn't as young as he used to be, but he thought he could manage extra work for a few weeks if necessary.

As he returned to his chambers, he considered the case of Samson Light. He could not possibly do all the investigation himself before the trial, not if he was also working for the government. He'd need to think how to manage that.

3

"Here's my girl!" said Tommy Jones, sweeping a delighted Sally up into his arms. He'd found her, accompanied by Hortense and Jo, at the drinking fountain along the straight path into Regent's Park. There were many walkers there on a Sunday, but Tommy could always tell Jo by the way she walked: forthright, without artifice. She seemed not to notice that she was wearing skirts, and indeed had eschewed crinolines and other false shapes for a simple gown. Hortense had willingly copied her casual style, and the two of them together were unmistakable.

"How nice to see you, Tommy," said Hortense, reaching up to adjust one of Sally's pale curls. Tommy was Jo's friend, and had been for several years. Hortense liked the young man and enjoyed talking with him. He knew so much about so many facets of life; it made Hortense feel quite cloistered.

"And where are we off to today?" Tommy asked Sally, who twisted her head around, then pointed up toward the trees lining the long avenue. "Birds, then? Are we looking for birds?"

Sally smiled and nodded. "Bird-ey," she said.

"Bird-s," Tommy corrected.

Jo laughed. "Just don't tell her the scientific names of all the avian parts, please," she said to Tommy. "I'd rather she just enjoy their beauty."

Tommy gave a half-hearted frown. "I would never," he said.

"Of course you would," said Jo. Although she didn't say so, Jo was impressed with how Tommy had grown up. He'd been only twelve when they'd met, but he had been a streetwise, gentle, and intelligent lad. And even at a young age, he'd been a friend to her, helping her overcome the trauma of being nearly killed almost seven years ago. And then Tommy had helped her solve another mystery the following year, the death of a photographer.

After all the excitement, they had remained friends, although their lives were very different. Jo worried about Tommy, though. He supported himself now but was still doing several jobs and couldn't seem to settle. He hadn't found his direction.

"How is tutoring?" Jo asked him, as he carried Sally, who had removed his hat and was putting it on her own head. "Are you still trying to teach that wealthy young lady?"

"I am, I'm afraid. Wish she had the brains you do, little miss," he said to Sally.

"And what do you hear of Samson Light?"

"I visited him in Clerkenwell yesterday," Tommy said. "And I'm going to visit both the police inspector and the barrister, Mr. Stone. I'm hoping I can help. Maybe even do some investigating myself."

Jo nodded. "Sounds promising. You're quite good at investigating."

"I'm sorry," interrupted Hortense, "but would it be all right if we sat down over there?" There were seats lining the path to the Botanical Gardens across the grass.

"Of course," said Jo, taking her elbow. Hortense was looking pale again. "Let's take the one under that tree. There's still some sun there to keep you warm." It was not a hot day, and Hortense often felt cold.

Sally was not interested in sitting, and said loudly, "Bird-y! Bird-y!"

"Oh!" said Tommy, putting her down. "That was right in my ear, you little fox. Just for that, I will have to chase you!"

Sally squealed and ran toward the trees, her chubby legs pounding the grass. Tommy came behind, pretending he couldn't catch up.

"So nice that he takes an interest in Sally," said Hortense, pulling her shawl more closely around her.

"He likes children. He was something of a leader in the workhouse when he was younger, he tells me."

"It's so easy to forget he had such a deprived childhood. Do you suppose that's why he doesn't settle in one occupation?"

"I was just thinking about that, the way he hasn't found his calling," said Jo. Hortense was looking a little better now, but she was still a bit breathless.

"Does he have a girl, do you know?"

"I don't think so. He goes out a lot, dancing and such, penny gaffes, but I've rarely heard him mention a girl's name more than once."

She looked down the walk and saw Tommy sitting under a tree with Sally in his lap. They were both very still. Must have seen a squirrel or something, Jo thought.

"Well, there's plenty of time," said Hortense. "He is only nineteen, after all."

"Yes, it's easy to forget that. Imagine, a young man spending his Sunday morning in the park with two women and a child."

They both looked down the lane. Tommy and Sally seemed to be having a very serious conversation. Sally was nodding and listening, then she would talk. Tommy's head was bent toward her as if he were taking in some important information.

"It's good for her to have a man around, anyway," said Hortense. Jo's heart squeezed a little, but she said nothing.

After Tommy had left to go to the clockmaker's in Clerkenwell for his Sunday afternoon shift, Jo carried Sally down the path. Hortense tired again on the walk, and they took a seat for a few minutes before leaving the park for home. They had come by omnibus, but even that seemed like it might be too much for her.

"Sally's getting heavy," said Jo as they approached Marylebone Road. "Let's take a cab home."

Perseverance Stone knew himself to be an excellent barrister, and an excellent barrister is methodical and thorough. Accordingly, he felt it best to begin with Samson Light's solicitor. He had dealt with Lorry Squires before, and while he doubted there would be much information to be had, creating a cooperative relationship with the accused's solicitor was invariably helpful.

When he arrived at Squires' office in Red Lion Square, the noon sun was just starting to warm the pavements. It being a fine Monday, he was hoping to find the solicitor in his office, a below-ground suite of rooms. The door to the main building was locked, so he had no choice but to venture down the wrought iron stairs from the pavement and knock at the half-glass door. He waited. It was much chillier down here in the small basement area. He knocked again, and Squires answered, peering out into the bright light.

"Who is it? Oh!" said Mr. Squires, his round jolly face looking around the door-frame. "Mr. Stone! Come in, come in, dear sir. Let me find you a seat."

Stone stepped into the front room, noticing immediately the smell of cooked breakfast and moldy paper. It had been some time since he'd had cause to visit. The room had papers everywhere, brown folders stacked on every surface and filed longwise on the tall shelves. There was a door open into the pantry, where Stone could see teacups and plates piled in disarray on a counter. The carpet was thick, no doubt to keep the cold room warmer, thought Stone. He took a seat in the large double Windsor chair facing the desk.

"May I offer you some tea?" offered Squires, with a worried glance toward the pantry.

"No, thank you," said Stone. "I hope I shan't take up much of your time."

Squires looked relieved. His desk chair creaked as he sat, and he beamed across the desk at Stone.

"What can I do to assist you, Mr. Stone, on this fine day?"

"I have come to inquire about a Mr. Samson Light," said Stone, relaxing into the high back of the chair. "I have been asked to represent him in this matter of a murder charge."

Squires mouth opened, amazed, then closed again.

"Well, I must say," he said with wide eyes. "That's wonderful. I hadn't anticipated that Mr. Light could afford a barrister of your" —Stone thought he must be hesitating on the word *expense*— "reputation."

"Detective Inspector Cuthbert Slaughter asked my advice," explained Stone.

"Oh, I see!" said Squires brightly. Then he frowned. "Except I don't. He's retired, isn't he?"

"Yes, he is. But Mr. Light tutored his ward a number of years ago. A young man named Tommy Jones. The Inspector wants to assure himself that Light is well represented. I offered to assist."

Mr. Squires' balding head was bobbing up and down. "That's excellent," he said.

Stone pulled a small notebook from his pocket and flipped it open.

"I've been told that the murdered man is one Horace Wright, clerk at the General Post Office, and that he had been seen arguing with Mr. Light shortly before his body was found in a pneumatic railway car in Holborn on Friday, the first of this month."

"Yes, indeed," said Squires. "Quite unusual. Quite distressing."

Reviewing the details of the case didn't take long; Squires knew little beyond the inquest's finding of murder, the few details Samson Light had told him, and that a Detective Inspector Morgan was investigating.

"Morgan?" asked Stone. "He's out of St. Giles, isn't he? Clark's Buildings station?"

"Yes, he is. The body was found at the Holborn station of the London Pneumatic Despatch Company's railway; that's 245 Holborn, near the Music Hall. It appeared as though he might have been killed at the General Post Office, however, so that would normally be City Police jurisdiction. Somehow the case was assigned to Detective Inspector Morgan at Division E, perhaps because the body was transported to 245 Holborn? I tried to talk to Inspector Morgan, but as soon as he heard Samson Light's name, he wouldn't say much to me."

"Did that strike you as odd?" Stone was careful to use his most friendly manner.

"I suppose so. He's a rather gruff man at the best of times. Problems at home, I suppose," said Squires, putting his finger on the side of his nose and winking. Everyone knew that Detective Inspector Morgan had a lively young wife who was inclined to be most active in theatrical circles.

Stone rose to leave. Squires was a jovial man, but Stone had rarely found him able to retain, much less analyze, information. He really should be practicing in the country, thought Stone, handling simple wills and lawsuits over pigs wandering onto a neighbor's property. He said good day, and hailed a cab for the Foreign Office.

Although C. Herbert, English and Foreign Booksellers, was only a few minutes walk from Samson and Prudence's house on Wilderness Row, it took Pru a little longer than usual to get to work. She didn't want to be late. The shop in Jerusalem Passage was closed on Mondays, but she'd been asked to come in and help inventory a newly purchased library from an estate in Bromley. Her stomach, however, was not appreciating the early hour, and she'd only been able to keep down a bit of bread. Then there was the battle with her corset, toward which she had formed an animosity that had only become worse as her waistline expanded.

Mr. Herbert, she knew, would be delighted as always to see her. She could tell by his manner that he had never regretted hiring her. He had been expanding his business, especially against the competition of V. G. Faber, newsagent and bookseller. The advertisement in the *Publisher's Circular* had called for a young lady with one year's experience as a bookseller's assistant. Prudence had no such experience, and had instead spent several years as a domestic in Inspector Slaughter's home and a nurse for her ailing mother. But access to Inspector Slaughter's books had encouraged her to become a reader.

Her penchant for books had started innocently enough, Prudence remembered. She had been taught to read by her father when she was young. He may have been a criminal in later years, but he was a kind father and wanted his daughter to know more than he could teach her on his own. Her ability to read had helped her gain the position as maid in the Slaughter household, and over the time she worked there she'd been surrounded by books. Inspector Slaughter bought second-hand books, not only about criminality and justice, but about philosophy and theatre and science. There were stacks of them in every room of the house in Palmer Street. At first she had only dusted them, removed them from surfaces she was trying to clean, or tidied them in his study. But gradually some of the titles began to intrigue her. Inspector Slaughter noticed and offered to lend her books to read. *Great Expectations* by Charles Dickens had been difficult going, but she loved the way reading the story made the world disappear. Dickens seemed to know so much about what it was like to be poor and to strive for better. Harriet Jacobs' *Incidents in the Life of a Slave Girl* helped her understand African slavery; when she read it at night, she had trouble hiding her tears from her poor mother. The older works were much harder to understand. She found Marcus Aurelius utterly perplexing, and struggled to grasp Plato's thoughts on the ideal. She enjoyed poetry, although she thought Wordsworth used the word *O!* far too often, and she liked reading Keats' *The Eve of St. Agnes* just for the sound of the verse.

When she married Samson, however, she had little chance to read. She had managed the small household at her mother's flat in Gough Street while her husband completed his medical studies, and she continued as a maid-of-all-work at the Slaughters'. When Samson finished his studies and began earning some money, they decided to move out of the tiny flat. Her mother, although somewhat improved by Samson's ministrations, deserved the better care they could now afford. Samson heard of a place that had opened in Sussex, run by a doctor who wanted to help patients with consumption. Dr. Samuel Graham, whose own mother had died of the disease, had studied it extensively, relying on the discredited work of George Bodington, who had worked at St. Bartholomew's in the 1820s. Graham had become convinced that fresh air and gentle exercise, combined with inhaled substances to ease the lungs, could be provided in a healing establishment. Only a few doctors ran such small hospitals on the continent, but Dr. Graham had an inheritance that made it possible to create such a sanitarium in England. Samson had contacted him and arranged for a place for Mrs. Henderson.

The expense of Dr. Graham's sanitarium had been tolerable, professional courtesy being extended to Samson Light as a medical man, but the new home for the young couple had been more of a gamble. Wilderness Row was a new area of homes in Clerkenwell. The houses overlooked the back of the Charterhouse gardens. Although the gardens were unkempt, the builders of the homes had promised they would be reworked and provide an excellent view. Samson and Prudence had fallen in love with the smallest of the houses, which was fresh and new, and had devised a plan. They would live in the rooms on the first floor. Samson would have his surgery on the ground floor, but he would only use it on days when he wasn't at St. Bartholomew's. The other days could be let to other doctors. Their advertisement was quickly answered by an older chiropodist whose young partner had moved on, and a young physician who had just finished his degree. Both paid their rent on time, and the arrangement had worked out well.

But to afford the sanitarium and the house, and to give Prudence time for household management, a second income was essential. C. Herbert's bookshop had been a gift from heaven, a job Prudence enjoyed that was close to home. Selling books and taking orders was much easier than being a maid-of-all-work, even for employers as kind as the Slaughters. She also enjoyed the competition with V. G. Faber, who was opening bookstalls in rail stations, of all places. Mr. Herbert intended to keep his shop independent and personal, even as V. G. Faber became large and commercial, undercutting his prices. Prudence passed into St.

John's Road, turning into Albemarle Street then into the large, and this morning sunny, St. John's Square. The square was crowded with carts of goods, vegetables and fabric, clockwork pieces, artists' supplies, and tools. Barters were taking place in English and Italian, and two children ran in front of her, almost knocking her down. Without thinking, her hand had covered her belly as they pushed past. Turning away from the gate where Tommy Jones lived, Prudence passed the church and entered the narrow Jerusalem Passage. Her work in the bookshop was varied and interesting, if a bit dusty. And today, she thought, she particularly appreciated the old books. Samson was in gaol, in danger of going to prison, after all they had worked for. There was nothing she could do today to help him except earn some money. The antiquity of the books reminded her that time was malleable—it could be enjoyed and used or frittered away. And their smell was so much more steadying than the smell of food in her own kitchen.

Tommy woke early that Monday, determined to find Detective Inspector Morgan at the St. Giles station. St. Giles was only a half hour's walk, and the day was fine. Tommy knew his way almost everywhere in the city. The quickest way from St. John's Gate was straight to the new meat market at Smithfield, over to Farringdon Road, then along Holborn a mile or so until it became new Oxford Street.

The Smithfield market was a marvel. Only the City, with its separate traditions and institutions, could have created such a large and extravagant structure so quickly. Less than two years before, it had been a huge excavation, with deep pits cut into the ground for railway lines that would run to the basement stories. Even with all the glass to let in light, the iron structure was at least ten degrees cooler inside than outside, as Tommy could attest, having dashed in there to cool off on more than one hot summer day. The cattle carcasses, hanging in rows on hooks above the stall, disturbed him only when he thought of them as former cows. Thinking of them as Sunday roast made the whole thing much more tolerable.

And it was so much better than the old market. Tommy had been glad when Newgate Market was destroyed, even with the dust and construction. The screams of animals, herded through narrow streets, had been harrowing. London was growing, and the new throngs wanted their meat. The new market was larger and much better organized, and meat could now be moved by rail, so the slaughterhouses could be further away.

Turning onto Farringdon Road and heading downhill, Tommy took his favorite route so he could look at the viaduct from both below and above. He knew that the old Fleet River ran beneath his feet on Farringdon Road, and that the towers on the Viaduct stood above subways containing conduit for telegraph wires, gas lines, and the new pneumatic railway. The Holborn Viaduct itself, completed only a few months ago, was impressive, with its four towers and its bright red painted iron. But Tommy did not like to think about the bodies. When the wide, strong Viaduct was built, it had been necessary to move the bodies from the St. Andrew Holborn churchyard, which had been destroyed along with many buildings as Holborn was being widened. Tommy wasn't squeamish, but the idea of moving all those bodies seemed horrifying. All in the name of progress. He walked up the tower stairs to the Viaduct and across toward St. Giles.

St. Giles was one of the worst neighborhoods in the city, famous for crime and vice. But Tommy knew his way through the area, which alleys to avoid, and which shops sold the best food on the cheap. As he moved through, he kept his head down and walked purposefully, not meeting people's eyes. The police station was in the Clark's Buildings, which were quickly turning into tenements, with their low rents. There were women sitting in doorways, dirty children playing in the street, and the sound of a baby crying. He went up to the counter and asked for Detective Inspector Morgan.

Tommy could easily have been less confident walking into a police station had his life turned out differently. He had not had an easy childhood. His father had died in debtor's prison, and Tommy had been harassed by the police when he had witnessed a murder at the local gasworks. He'd lived in the workhouse and on the streets. But Detective Inspector Cuthbert Slaughter and his wife had requested guardianship, and had raised him as their own. He'd worked in many trades while living with them, and was now, at nineteen, his own man. Instead of avoiding police, he knew to seek them out when he needed help.

And now Tommy was trying to help Samson.

"You want to see me, lad?" Inspector Morgan was a large man, with a large dark moustache and woolly side whiskers. His eyes were sharp, and he did not look to be in a good mood.

"Yes, Detective Inspector," said Tommy, careful to use the correct title. "I've come on behalf of my friend, Samson Light."

Morgan's expression darkened. "And what might you be wanting? I am a busy man." Apparently the conversation was to take place at the enquiry counter. Two constables had moved aside, and Morgan had not invited Tommy back to his office.

Tommy knew better than to launch into a speech about Samson's innocence.

"I want to know what evidence you have to suspect him, sir."

"He was seen, young man. Arguing with the victim that very morning." Morgan's expression was mild. Tommy decided to try a different tack.

"Do you know why the man was killed? Have you other suspects, sir?"

"We are investigating," said Morgan warily. "Of course we are interviewing anyone who had contact with the victim. But the case seems fairly clear."

He came around the counter and shook Tommy's hand.

"Thank you for coming by, my lad. You're a good friend to Mr. Light."

Tommy could tell he was being dismissed but wasn't sure what else to say. What had he expected? That Morgan would take him into his confidence, tell him about the investigation? He'd just have to think of something else. Plus he was late to sell watches for Mr. Smith back in Clerkenwell.

Back at St. John's Gate before leaving to teach at the Ragged School that evening, he talked with Mrs. Wren. She was chopping vegetables with her large square chopper.

"Well, duck," <chop> "You can't expect an important inspector to talk to someone who comes walking in off the street," she said, shaking her head.

"Yes, I know, but he seemed—I don't know—reticent. And he was so gruff I got the feeling he was concealing something."

"Ah, you young ones. <chop> Always seeing deeper meanings than are there."

Tommy thought a moment.

"Well, I should at least try to find this engineer. See what he has to say."

"Good idea," she said, giving one last thwack to a cabbage. "'Cept no one at that place on Holborn is likely to know your Mr. Light. Might want to say as you're investigating, 'stead of just saying you're a friend."

Tommy left his least favorite pupil and began the late afternoon walk to the Inns of Court. Miss Fanny Templeton of Bedford Square did not take well to lessons. Her primary interests were fashion and gossip, and although she was intelligent enough to learn mathematics and science, she simply had no interest in them. This mid-day session had been an excellent example of the problem.

"So we've studied how the bones and muscles create motion," Tommy said. He had brought T. H. Huxley's *Lessons in Elementary Physiology* to help her learn anatomy. "So what's the difference between flexion and extension?"

"They're bending," she said, her dark curls limp on her shoulders and her eyes rolled up to the ceiling.

"Which one is bending?"

She tapped her teeth with her pencil. "I don't know."

What Tommy could not understand was how anyone who had the opportunity to learn could so clearly not wish to do so. Her surroundings, if not luxurious, were amply supplied with space and furnishings and good food. There were no distractions to keep her from learning. And yet she sat there, utterly bored.

It wasn't the subject, because it had been the same with each subject in turn. Tommy had only ever seen Miss Fanny take an interest in one topic, and that was the design of hats worn by women who walked past the study window on the way to the square.

"Give me your ribbon," he said, holding out his hand.

She looked at him sharply, then took the green, flat ribbon from her hair and handed it to him. He held it vertically between his hands.

"Say this is a man's leg—" Fanny sat up sharply, with a shocked look on her face. "Very well, a woman's leg." She nodded. *Good thing she doesn't object to me handling it*, Tommy thought.

"If the torso is facing this direction—" he nodded toward the window, "bend this ribbon as if it were a knee."

She took her finger and pushed the ribbon so it made an angle.

"Is that flexion or extension?"

"Um . . . extension?"

He snapped the ribbon straight. "This is extension, because the leg is fully extended. So what is flexion?"

She bent the ribbon. "Like this?"

"Yes, like that."

Fanny's attention had wandered to the window, where a woman in a frilly bonnet was walking across the street.

Tommy tried another tack. "So if you're in the park, and you see a lovely woman in a fashionable hat, and she nods to a gentleman on a horse, is her neck engaged in flexion or extension?"

Fanny perked up. "Flexion!"

"And if the gentleman is haughty and raises his head to put his nose in the air, his neck—"

"Is extended!"

And thus had the lesson gone. Every example from now on, Tommy thought, would have to relate to her own interests, however ridiculous and useless they might be. It was funny how concerned her parents had been that he was a young man in the house to tutor their daughter. The door to the study was always open, and one of the maids had the specific duty of walking past it and looking in every ten minutes. How anyone could think he would take a romantic interest in such a girl was beyond his understanding.

He walked past the British Museum, wishing he could spend more time in the Reading Room. He would daydream sometimes of walking in, requesting some esoteric material, and sitting at the tables doing research. He wasn't sure what he'd want to research, but it sounded like a mature, gentlemanly thing, to have the time and resources to study all day.

Arriving at Gate Street, Tommy looked at the directory inside the door at number six, then went up to the second floor. The door to the chambers was locked. He was just turning to find an office where he could borrow paper and pen to leave a note, when Perseverance Stone appeared behind him, the key in his hand.

"Good afternoon, young man," he said as he unlocked the door. "You are here to see me?"

"Yes, sir. I'm Tommy Jones, a friend of Samson Light."

Mr. Stone nodded his head. "Do come in."

The chambers were cold, with the window facing north. Stone moved to a small stove in the corner and set a match to the wood.

"It will be warmer soon," he said, taking off his coat and hanging it on a rack near the stove. "Do have a seat."

Tommy sat in the large wingback chair near the desk, perching himself at the front of the seat.

"Mr. Stone, Samson Light needs help. I was told you were taking his case."

Stone sat behind his desk and took a close look at the young man. He seemed a serious sort, but the slight wrinkling in the corner of his eyes betrayed a sense of humor. A clever, bright sense of humor, thought Stone, noticing the upturned corners of Tommy's mouth. His clothes were presentable, the collar fresh and the cuffs unturned, but he wore nothing expensive. A clerk, thought Stone. No, he has a candor in his eyes that indicates he doesn't work at a repetitive task. About twenty? Perhaps younger.

"Yes, I have agreed to do so. However—"

"You must help him, sir," Tommy said, leaning forward toward the desk. "He's been wrongly accused. Samson was my tutor, you see. I can vouch for him. He wouldn't hurt anyone, not anyone at all."

Accent just south of the river, perhaps Southwark, thought Stone, with a hint of uneasy street life. Expression very earnest, the sort of man you want testifying in the box. A jury would trust that open face, the gray eyes that seem to take in everything.

"I understand," said Stone, "and I will do what I can."

"I'd be happy to help in any way, Mr. Stone," said Tommy. "I know my way around the streets of the city and can find out things. We could share information. Here's what Mr. Light gave me." He took out the papers Samson had given him and handed them across the desk. Stone glanced through them, then raised his head and looked curiously at Tommy.

"Now that is an interesting thought, Mr. Jones," said Stone. "My problem is that I have somewhat limited time. I've just been called in to help the government, you see."

Tommy was impressed, but wary. He knew something of politics from his discussions in the Slaughter household. Under Prime Minister Disraeli, the Reform Act had expanded the voting franchise enormously, but the price of food had remained high because of protectionist policies. The new Liberal government seemed more promising, allowing in cheaper foreign goods. Gladstone was seen as an improvement by working people, but Tommy would have preferred a government that helped poor people more than either of the main parties was doing. Regardless, the government certainly needed help, thought Tommy, from either Stone or someone else.

"However," said Stone, taking out a small file of papers, "I can't know much until I get the particulars of the case in order. I should talk to any number of people, witnesses, police—"

"I did try to talk to the police," said Tommy. "Detective Inspector Morgan is leading the investigation out of St. Giles's station. He wouldn't tell me much of anything."

"I heard that he wanted to lead the investigation himself, rather than leaving it to the City police, since the man was likely killed at the General Post Office," said Stone. "Do you know anything about that?"

Tommy shook his head. "I don't, but I thought I'd ask about. I did feel he wasn't being completely honest with me, but why should he?"

Why indeed, thought Stone. A senior officer wants a particular case for himself. There could be all kinds of reasons.

"Was it your sense that he wanted to help Mr. Light?"

"Not at all. That's why I came to see you."

Stone looked through the papers again. "We have one witness who saw the victim arguing with Mr. Light, but I see nothing of that here in his notes."

"Perhaps it didn't happen," said Tommy.

"We need to find out."

The "we" wasn't lost on Tommy. "You'll let me help, sir?"

Stone thought for a moment. This was a professional decision. The young man was earnest, but he was also biased in favor of the accused. *Of course, so am I, or at least I should be,* thought Stone. Perhaps Jones could do much of the legwork, and Stone most of the thinking and planning, and of course defend Samson Light in court.

"I'll do one better," said Stone. "Have you the time and the means to do much of the tracking down, the questioning, the investigating, under my guidance?"

"I will make the time, sir," said Tommy, rising. "I have several jobs, but they can all be arranged around this. It's terribly important we free Samson Light, and that his reputation stands. And frankly, something doesn't feel right about this whole thing."

On even brief reflection, Stone had to agree.

Prudence's conviction that she could do nothing to help Samson lasted all of one day. She looked up from her work as it occurred to her she was literally surrounded with information in the bookshop. Any of it might be useful. Tommy had sent her a note saying he would talk to the barrister, investigate at the General Post Office where Horace Wright had worked, and try to visit the victim's home. Horace Wright, she considered, had been killed doing his job, something about an underground railway. No, a pneumatic railway that carried the mail, not passengers.

She went over to the section about railways, and began looking through some of the books. It would take too long to learn about railways from stories; she had read *Dombey and Sons* by Charles Dickens and knew he took a dim view of the impact of railways, but she didn't have time to go reading more novels. Facts. She needed facts. There were several books on individual British railway companies, but surely the organization of the railway business could be understood in a more overall way? She reached for the *Bradshaw's Railway Manual*, thinking it would have timetables. Instead, it had much information for shareholders in railway companies. She could find nothing about railways that carried mail, or ran in tubes. There wasn't much custom this early on a Tuesday and Mr. Herbert was in his office at the back of the shop.

"Mr. Herbert?" she asked, tapping gently on his door-frame.

Mr. Herbert's office was really just a small room that contained his desk and a bureau with stacks of papers. He sat in the only chair in the small space.

"Yes, Mrs. Light?" He was a kindly man, with a square face and thick round spectacles. Prudence had almost called him Mr. Pickwick when she first started working there.

"I know this has nothing to do with my job, but I'm trying to learn about pneumatic railways. We have books on railways here in the shop, but nothing on that sort of railway."

Mr. Herbert knew of the plight of Mrs. Light's husband. At first he had been worried that customers might consider her unsuitable to assist them and had momentarily considered telling her she could no longer work in his shop. But his own humanity, and the complete ignorance of his customers, had led him to feel pity instead. He correctly guessed that her interest had to do with her husband's arrest.

"The pneumatic railway is also called the atmospheric railway because of how it uses air pressure," he said, removing his spectacles. "I'm afraid we do not have any books about the mechanics of it, although I did see an article in *The Illustrated London News*. It runs on a rail and a vacuum is created in the tube to force the cars back and forth."

Prudence nodded her understanding. "How would I discover what person or company would manage the railway that goes from the General Post Office to a station in Holborn?"

Mr. Herbert hesitated. This was obviously to do with her husband's case, and she would no doubt need time to gather information. Was that a good idea for a woman to do? He didn't think so. But Mr. Herbert's own mother had also been a determined woman, and when she intended to do something, there was little anyone could do to stop her. He'd noticed the same tendency in Prudence Light. If she was going to leave work to investigate, better she do it now, at the beginning of the week, when customers were fewer than later in the week.

"There is only one company working on this business specifically, and that is the London Pneumatic Despatch Company."

"How would I find them?"

"I believe they are in Victoria Street, in Westminster." Prudence began to speak, but Mr. Herbert held up a hand. "No need to ask, Mrs. Light. You may have the afternoon to learn about the railway."

"Thank you, Mr. Herbert. You're a very understanding man." He was about to reply, but at that moment Prudence's stomach gave a lurch, and she needed to go outside.

Having been sick around the corner of the building, she took a deep breath, then she went back into the shop to take a last sip of her cold cup of tea from earlier that morning and fetch her coat. She went outside and thought about how to get to Victoria Street. It was well over two miles, and the clouds were beginning to gather. But Mr. Herbert had implied that the whole afternoon was at her disposal, and she would already be losing the money for that day's work, so walking was the only sensible way.

Walking down St. John's Lane past the back of the Friends' Meeting House, she wondered as always what went on there. It didn't look like a church, just a large plain building, and the windows that faced the lane were bricked up. She had heard that worshippers just sat or stood around until the spirit took one of them and they spoke. It sounded very different from the churches she had been in, even though she had to admit she had attended very few. She crossed over at Farringdon Station to get to Holborn and thought about the tracks that now crisscrossed the city. Her mother's generation had not experienced trains of various kinds running through London. Had they actually replaced any horses? As she continued down Fetter Lane to Holborn, the cart noise was deafening. It was more likely that so many people had moved into London that it balanced out the traffic.

The weather had changed, and instead of rain, the clouds had cleared and a cold wind had begun blowing down the streets. As Prudence walked past 245 Holborn, she shivered. This was where the body had been found. She was glad that Tommy would be asking the questions in this place; it would have made her sick to go in. She continued on, avoiding Seven Dials by taking Drury Lane to Long Acre, then St. Martin's, and was pleased to note that her stomach was calm, and she was feeling much better for the walk and the cool breeze. In fact, she felt positively energetic and increased her pace.

She could do this, she thought. She could work her job, and be with child, and help Samson too. Tommy would investigate, the barrister would do his work, and Samson would be released. She'd find a clue at this company, something that would help prove he didn't commit the murder. As if Samson could kill anyone. The whole idea was preposterous. She walked down the rest of the Strand, crossed through Trafalgar Square without noticing Lanseer's bronze lions, and cut along St. James Park to Victoria Street. She inquired of a constable on the beat and was pointed to number 6, where a small plaque by the door directed her to the London Pneumatic Despatch Company on the ground floor. She entered the small office, where a man with a trim moustache and pomaded dark hair sat working at a desk.

"Excuse me," she said, "my name is Prudence Light." It suddenly occurred to her she had no possible excuse for her visit. What should she say? That her husband had been accused of murdering a man who worked for the Post Office? She wasn't investigating for the police and could guess how she might be treated as the wife of the accused man. Thinking quickly, she followed with, "I'm a reporter for the *Illustrated Police News*. We're looking into the recent death at your company's station in Holborn."

The young man looked up, removing a pince nez from his nose so it dropped to hang from its ribbon. His eyes narrowed at the name of the magazine, and Prudence realized she should have chosen a more reputable publication. Instead, she stood a little taller and looked down her nose at him, as she used to do to workmen and vendors who came to the Slaughters' back door without invitation.

"And how can I help you?" he said. He had been the first in the office to hear of the killing and knew it was his job to protect the company and the members of the board. It wouldn't do to have it reported that the company had been uncooperative, but he had no intention of volunteering anything but public information.

"I am compiling some background on the company," said Prudence. "Have you a board of directors?"

"Naturally," said the young man. "I am the company secretary, William Wilson." His voice was reedy and thin, as if he spent all his time indoors. Prudence noticed his skin had a gray pallor, but his clothing and grooming were impeccable. He pulled a piece of paper from the top drawer of his desk and handed it to her. She read the names of two members of the aristocracy of whom she had never heard, several engineers, and, to her surprise, the bookseller V. G. Faber. She had not brought a pad of paper with her and felt it wouldn't be appropriate to ask for one. As she hesitated, the young man said, "You may keep the list. I have another."

Prudence folded the paper and put it in her pocket.

"Mr. Wilson, I would also like to explain to our readers how the pneumatic railway works. Would you be able to help me with that?"

The moustache turned down at the corners. "Other than the basic operation, I would not be able to help you. Why not talk with Mr. Brassey or Mr. Clark?" he said, waving a thin hand toward the list. "They would know more details."

"The basic operation would be a good start," she said. "I understand the train runs in some kind of tube? That it has cars that carry letters and parcels?"

"Yes, that is correct." His tone and his posture exuded a practiced patience, so she continued.

"Does it run on coal?"

Mr. Wilson's lips pursed, clearly indicating she'd asked a ridiculous question. "No. There are steam engines, but they are stationery and power the fan. The idea of an atmospheric railway is that it uses air pressure within a vacuum to move the carriages."

"How does it do that?"

"The doors are closed at either end of the tube, then fans are used to create the pressure to push the car forward along the rails."

"The air just pushes the cars on a track?"

"Not quite," Mr. Wilson said with a supercilious expression. "The carriages are the same shape as the tunnel and have India rubber flanges around them to provide a seal. That makes it possible to have positive and negative pressure in the tube, to move the carriage in either direction." He took out his pocket watch and checked the time.

Prudence could not understand how a vacuum and fan could move a heavy car, even with the seal that Mr. Wilson was describing. But perhaps that was less of a concern than knowing who was part of the company. She thanked him for helping make her story more accurate and walked back out to Victoria Road.

4

Tommy found that discovering the identity of the witness to Samson's argument with Mr. Wright had been a simple matter of asking. One of the sentries at the General Post Office helpfully gave him the name of Mr. Edward Teach, senior clerk. Tommy had never seen the Post Office building before and was amazed at its size. It looked like a Greek temple dedicated to the communiques of the empire. He found Teach sitting on a crate in the side yard, eating a sandwich. Nearby, a few carts and carriages were being cleaned after the morning mail run.

"I'm not sure what to tell you, lad," said Mr. Teach. He had a long lean face, and his graying hair was slicked with a bit of grease to keep the waves neat. "I seen what I seen." He told Tommy that he had witnessed a very upset Samson talking to Horace Wright. "Right over there, it was." He pointed over to the pavement along St. Martin's-le-Grande.

"How did you know it was Mr. Light?"

"I knew him because he's the one what gave me the ether when I got my little toe taken off at St. Bart's." Mr. Teach had a twitch that made his left eye blink disarmingly, which made him seem nervous. But Tommy thought that underneath, he really was nervous, and he wasn't sure why. Did this man know more than he said? Or did he just not want to talk about what happened?

"Did Detective Inspector Morgan write down your testimony?" asked Tommy.

"Morgan. Yes, Morgan. He did, lad, he did." Teach took another bite of his sandwich.

"Do you know what the argument between Samson Light and Horace Wright was about?"

"No, now that I do not. They were just both very angry." Teach lowered his head, saying quietly to his sandwich, "I thought they'd come to blows, I did, and that's a fact."

"How did they part?"

Teach's eye twitched erratically. "Um . . . yes . . . that Mr. Light just walked away. Quite angry, he was. Cursing, I think."

"Then Mr. Wright went into the building?" Tommy glanced back at the Post Office.

"That's right, young man. Working day, you know."

"Who did Mr. Wright report to in the Post Office?"

"That would be Mr. Henry, the supervisor." His concentration returned to his meal.

Tommy said good morning to Mr. Teach, then went inside and asked to see the supervisor.

"Mr. Henry isn't seeing anyone today." The clerk, a small spry man with a bald head and spectacles, shook his head at Tommy. Tommy realized that since he hadn't stated his business, the clerk assumed he was there to inquire after a position.

"I'm here investigating the murder of Horace Wright," Tommy said firmly.

"Are you with the police?"

Tommy was too honest to pretend. "No, I'm not."

"Then you'd better be off, young man. We are quite busy here today. Mr. Henry is working on getting the branch line of the pneumatic railway up and running." The clerk turned away.

Tommy thought a moment.

"I'm here on behalf of Perseverance Stone."

The clerk stopped and turned with wide eyes. He removed his spectacles, carefully bending the earpieces.

"Perseverance Stone, the barrister? The one who got the murderer of poor Mr. Briggs put away?"

Tommy recalled the case immediately. Mr. Briggs had been a banker, an older gentleman who had been murdered on a train two years before. Perseverance Stone had worked alongside William Ballantine, who had conducted the successful prosecution. The details had been in all the newspapers; even King William of Prussia had become involved, trying to get the execution of the killer postponed and failing. Tommy himself had attended the hanging of Franz Müller, a German tailor who had escaped to America then been returned to London for trial.

"That is correct," said Tommy importantly. "And I'm sure Mr. Henry will want to help Mr. Stone."

"I shall see if he's in," the clerk said, still awestruck.

But Mr. Henry, a large rotund gentleman sporting a large pocket-watch chain across his belly, had little to tell him. Horace Wright had been at work as usual for the evening mail run, then the next morning he didn't report for the morning shift and his body was found at 245 Holborn.

"What hours did Mr. Wright work?" Tommy asked.

"The usual sorting hours. Five to nine in the morning, then six to nine at night."

"Those are strange hours, aren't they?"

"It's a post office," said Mr. Henry impatiently. "The mail from across the country, and from the docks, arrives early in the morning. The night coaches leave at eight in the evening."

"Would it be possible to see the room where he worked?"

Mr. Henry twiddled his watch chain, perturbed. "I suppose. See the clerk." He turned on his heel and waddled back toward his office. Tommy heard him mumbling about watch chains, and what good were they without a watch.

"It's past the south end of the building," the clerk told Tommy helpfully, pointing to the end of the corridor. "Downstairs. You have to go across first."

Tommy went out the side door of the Post Office into an open courtyard, then across and into another building. It was a small building, and no one was there, but he heard the sounds of construction and followed them downstairs. Directly under the courtyard he'd just crossed were the tracks for the pneumatic railway, coming out from a small tunnel in the far wall. Desks and lamps were being installed, and Tommy didn't want to disturb the workmen. If there had been any clues to Horace Wright being killed in this space, there would be nothing left now, almost two weeks later. Since he had taken the day off from all his jobs to investigate, he decided the next stop was 245 Holborn.

245 Holborn looked like any other office building, and not at all like an engine station. Tommy opened the front door into a large room with very little in it, just a few tables, some drawings, and a desk. He walked through to the back, where a doorway opened onto a kind of bridge. Tommy had worked in gasworks, in the workhouse, and on buildings reclaiming bricks, but this place was different. The walls seemed to be exterior walls, but there was a ceiling above his head. Below his feet he could feel an engine running, vibrating the bridge he stood on. He looked below to see two tracks, parallel to each other, each coming out of a tunnel. The left-hand tunnel was open, the other closed. There were wheels embedded in the floor between the tracks.

Loading sacks into the car on the open rail was a man with a strong, stocky physique and a moustache that drooped below his chin. His dark eyebrows matched the moustache, and both were shiny with sweat. His white shirtsleeves were pushed up to his elbows, and his jacket hung on a hook near the far archway. Since there was no direct way down to the floor from the bridge, Tommy went back inside to find stairs, then emerged on the basement level where the tracks were. The sound of an engine was louder here.

Tommy waited until the man had finished loading the car and pushed it into the tunnel, then he spoke loudly to be heard above the engine.

"Are you Mr. Jenkins?" Tommy shouted.

Jenkins nodded and held out a sweaty hand.

"I am," he said loudly. "Who are you?"

"Tommy Jones," said Tommy. "I'm here investigating the death of Horace Wright."

Jenkins turned away toward the open tunnel on the left, closing the large metal barn doors and moving the handle to latch them. The lock clanged loudly in the large room, even with the engine running. He then motioned toward a small flight of stairs across the room that led to a platform with an iron railing. Tommy followed him. The sound of the engine became a little quieter.

"I need to start the train," explained Jenkins, moving a lever that rose from the floor of the platform. Tommy realized how round his eyes were when Jenkins laughed at him.

"Would you like to do it?" offered Jenkins.

Tommy, like many young men, was fascinated by machinery. He had been interested in the pipes and tubes at the gasworks but had little experience with anything that ran on rails. This may have been on a smaller scale than the railway locomotives he watched from Blackfriars Bridge, but it was nevertheless intriguing and the roar was impressive. He nodded and Jenkins stepped back, motioning for him to take the lever. Tommy grasped it with one hand on the red knob on top and the other on the shaft. There was only one way to pull it, and with a confirming look at Jenkins, Tommy pulled, then pulled harder. The lever hummed and trembled in his grip. The engine got louder and he heard a long low rumble, then a "whoosh" on the other side of the latched metal doors.

"Now pull it back," Jenkins shouted. "It's on its way to Euston."

Tommy did so and heard the engine begin to power down. His heart was beating fast. Jenkins was next to the lever at a Wheatstone telegraph machine. He tapped it three times.

"That was . . . exhilarating!" Tommy beamed

Jenkins grinned. "Glad you enjoyed it. I do that five times a day at least, and if it weren't so loud, I'd find it exhilarating, too. Now, what can I do for you, young man?"

Tommy took a deep breath to get his concentration back, but his mind was whirring. Maybe this was what he should be doing, becoming an engineer. What an extraordinary feeling of power.

"About Horace Wright," said Tommy. "You worked closely with him?"

"In a way. I ran the machines, and he managed the sorting and schedules. Helped load the cars now and then. Are you with the police?"

"No, I'm a . . . private investigator," said Tommy. He'd heard the term used to refer to Pinkerton, the man who'd created the agency that protected the American president. Not police, but hired for special tasks. "I'm working with the barrister, Perseverance Stone."

If Jenkins had heard of Stone, he gave no sign, just looked amiable. Clearly he was willing to talk.

"Did you discover the body?"

"In a sense," said Jenkins. "I came to work in the morning and was in the engine room. Fowler came in around ten, on the cart with the oil for the engines and doors. He started to work on oiling the tube door"—he pointed toward the archway on the right—"and he gave a shout. He called me over, and we could see a lump in the car. We brought the lamp over and saw it was Horace Wright."

"You knew him?"

"He'd come here once or twice, to look at the machinery."

"What did you do?"

"We pulled him out of the car and laid him down here on the floor, but we could see he was dead. No breath, no heartbeat."

"Any blood?"

"Not that I could see. Then I told Fowler to go up and find a constable, call the police. But he just froze. So I left him down here and went up myself. When I came back he was gone."

Tommy was confused. "Who was gone? Mr. Wright's body?"

"No. Donald Fowler. I'd left him with the body, but he was gone. Mr. Wilson at the company got a note from him later, saying he was leaving his post and would not be returning. He didn't even collect his last pay."

"Where did he go?"

Jenkins shrugged. "Somewhere up north. Durham, I think Mr. Wilson said. Had a job there, and family."

"Mr. Wilson?"

"The secretary at the company."

"That's very odd that he would just leave," said Tommy.

"Agreed," said Jenkins, stroking his moustache. "But not much we could do. Never understood Donald Fowler, really. Some of those northerners are hard to know, keeping to themselves. Not like the Welsh," he said proudly. "We are happy to talk to anyone, any time. I'm looking for another hand down here if you're interested?"

Tommy thought a moment. He was quite sure he'd love this job, at first. But he suspected the noise would become a problem, and his greatest pleasure was being out on the streets.

"Thank you, but I think I'd feel like a mole down here."

"You get used to it. And there are things that are better down here."

Tommy looked doubtful. Jenkins swung open the tunnel doors, cleared his throat and began to sing in a rich baritone voice: *Sleep my child, and peace attend thee, all through the night.*

His voice echoed through the tunnel and sounded like a church choir. Jenkins looked pleased with himself. Tommy smiled.

"Was there anything unusual about the morning on the first of April? Before Mr. Wright was found? "

"I've thought about that quite a bit," said Jenkins, looking up at the ceiling. "The car shouldn't have been here at all."

"Which car?"

Jenkins pointed to the car in front of the closed tunnel. "This car. It should have been at the General Post Office, at St. Martin's-le-Grande. This line was being tested, but the last test left the car out there."

Tommy nodded, thinking.

Jenkins pulled up his braces. "I'll be getting back to work, if you don't mind. Until the company hires a replacement, I have to move the bags and the cars."

"How do you move the cars without help?" Tommy was curious. The cars looked low and heavy.

"Like this," said Jenkins. He used the wheels embedded in the floor to roll the car from the right-hand track to the left.

"So wait," said Tommy. "This left-hand tunnel goes where?"

"To Euston Station. The other one goes to the General Post Office."

"So it's your job to switch the cars from one line to the other?"

"It will be, if we ever get this line open to the G.P.O. I don't know why that hasn't happened yet."

Horace Wright's flat in Clerkenwell Close was less than a mile from Samson and Prudence's house, and even closer to Tommy's room in St. John's Gate, but it was like another world. The street was lined with workshops and loud with carts delivering goods. Doorways on the road led back into buildings containing warrens of small rooms where men and women beat metal at small tables, painted clock faces with Roman or Arabic numerals, or drew wire for springs. A few had shopfront windows displaying clocks and watches, with rails and latched shutters to prevent thefts. One had been turned into a factory for making clocks.

Clerkenwell Close wound around the old St. James Church. As people passed him, Tommy heard many of them speaking Italian as well as English. He knew that many people had come from Italy to this area and that it was the center of the watch-making trade. At the second turn, there was an ice cream cart on the corner. Tommy bought a penny lick of strawberry, not expecting it to taste like strawberry but enjoying the bright pink color. He asked the ice cream seller whether Horace Wright was known in the area.

"*Si, si,*" said the seller, and pointed to the structure directly behind Tommy, number 42. It was a squat brick building, with a mostly buried basement and only two stories above. A woman was sweeping the small portico near the pavement. Tommy returned his ice cream glass to the seller, who rinsed it in a bucket of water for the next customer, and crossed the street.

"Excuse me, miss," said Tommy with a smile, removing his cap.

The woman's hair, a mix of black and gray, was done up in a tight bun under a white cap. She didn't look pleased.

"I'm not your 'miss'," she said. "Who might you be?"

"I'm Tommy Jones. I'm investigating the death of Horace Wright."

The woman's face paled, and she stopped sweeping.

"Whaddya mean, the death?"

Tommy's smile faded.

"I'm sorry, madam," he said. "Horace Wright has died. He's been killed down at the Post Office."

She stood with her mouth open for a moment.

"Well, I never," she said. "And him such a quiet, gentle man."

"You didn't know," said Tommy, with sympathy.

"No, I had no idea. Just got back today from stopping with my mum, who's been poorly. Haven't been here for almost a month now. When did this happen, then?"

"Almost two weeks ago."

"Well, I never," she said again. "Here I left him on his own, and look what happens." She stared down into the street.

"I'm sorry to disturb you, but would it be all right if I looked at his flat? We're trying to find out who killed him."

The woman stepped back and opened the door. It creaked on its hinges.

"Been meaning to get that done," she mumbled.

"May I ask your name?" Tommy said, as he followed her through the door and up the flight of stairs.

"I'm Madge Perkins. I own this place. Left me by my husband, may he rest in peace." The stairs creaked too, but seemed sturdy enough. The walls were nicely papered, if in a pale green design that had long ago gone out of fashion. The house was very quiet after the noise outside; Tommy could just hear some steady tapping through the wall. Likely a workshop, he thought.

"Did you know Horace Wright well?"

"Some. Knew him and his parents. They died, you know, some time ago."

"Do you have other lodgers?"

"Not now. I had a man in the other flat, but he's left now. Gone north, I think."

The door to Wright's flat was locked. Mrs. Perkins took out a key from her apron pocket and opened the door, stepping in. Tommy came in behind her and looked around. Under a layer of dust, everything in the flat seemed neatly laid out. To the left, the room with the window overlooking the street contained a table with three chairs, a china cabinet, a desk with a lamp, and a sofa with a matching upholstered chair. The bookshelves on the wall were full of books and various items of bric-a-brac: a china dog, a teapot of Japanese design, a vase with a tasteful arrangement of silk flowers in pink and red. To the right, past a small water closet, was a bedroom. The bed was neatly made, the basin clean, the jug holding just a couple of inches of clean water, the mirror spotless. The clothes-brush, hairbrush, and grooming tools were carefully laid out on the dresser, along with a pocket watch with its chain neatly parallel to the edge. The wardrobe contained four shirts, an overcoat, a beaver hat, and four pairs of trousers with braces. Collars and neckcloths were organized in one drawer, handkerchiefs in another.

The second bedroom contained a small bed, a washstand, and a number of boxes, all neatly stacked.

"He did that when his parents died," said Mrs. Perkins. "Packed up their things carefully and put them in boxes. Said he'd decide what to do later. But that was several years ago."

There was little in the flat that showed the personality of Mr. Wright, other than its cleanliness. The books were organized into sections on the Post Office, social conditions, and history. The few novels were of a nature one might call "improving." On their own shelf was a copy of Burke's Peerage from 1860 and an old Bible. The walls were papered in a floral pattern that had been popular thirty years before, and the floors were clean even if the carpets were threadbare. The small kitchen contained a wood burning stove and a pantry, and smelled of sour milk. A large and very beautiful clock hung on the kitchen wall.

"He bought that at the factory down the road," said Mrs. Perkins, taking up the old milk bottle. "If you are finished here, I should tidy."

Tommy thanked Mrs. Perkins and left. Walking down Clerkenwell Close to the Green, he turned past the Sessions House toward Farringdon Road, where the traffic was heavy, so he could hail a cab.

He reviewed his progress thus far. It didn't take long. He had interviewed those he could think of, seen the room where Wright had been killed, visited his flat. He had only a page or two of notes to show for it.

He needed to talk to someone who could help him get his bearings. Information was one thing, Tommy considered, but fitting it into a pattern was quite another. He had been confident that he could manage this, investigating and finding the culprit, assisting Mr. Stone in saving Samson. In previous times, he had felt sure that he had helped Inspector Slaughter with some of his cases, had been his man on the street, eyes and ears open to discovering clues. They had sat together at the kitchen table, or in the study, and shared ideas. Tommy had felt he had been of use. But perhaps Inspector Slaughter had only included him out of kindness. That would, he thought, fit the facts. The inspector and his missus had saved him from the workhouse, brought him into their home, cared for him as their own. He'd always been eager to contribute to the household in any way he could. But he'd just been a boy; his contribution might actually have been of little value. For a moment it occurred to him that perhaps Inspector Morgan was right, that he had no business getting involved.

But then Tommy thought of Prudence. He knew quite a bit about the facts of life and had not been fooled by her act of indisposition. Surely she was with child, and her husband was trapped in gaol. The best thing would be to put his pride and painful childhood feelings aside, go visit Inspector Slaughter, and see what he might advise.

─∞─

Jo walked with Sally along the tree-lined pavement in Marylebone as they waited for Hortense.

"Where mummy go?" Sally asked for the fifth time.

"Mummy went to see a physician. She asked us to take a walk until she is finished talking to him." Jo took small steps but was nevertheless tugged to a stop every few feet. Sally halted again and bent down to look at a daisy that had popped up between cracks in the pavement.

"Oooh, flow'r," said Sally.

Jo looked closely. "Yes, and that flower has a name. It's called daisy."

"Daisy," said Sally, and reached out to touch it. Then she grasped it around the stem.

"We need to leave it there so it can grow some more," said Jo, tapping her hand. "If we pluck it, it will stop growing."

Sally nodded sagely and walked on, her feet apart for balance. The day was dry, with enough of a breeze that Jo had put Sally's coat on her before they left the house. She held the little hand in hers when they crossed the road, but other than that let the child lead the way. Jo still thought it very odd that she was tending a child. She had no brothers or sisters herself, and as an adult had rarely been around children. The boarding house she had lived in catered only to single women. And after her friend and lover Nan had died, it had not occurred to her that she might someday be with someone else, and that the someone else would have a child. Domesticity was not a world Jo had ever considered, and it still amazed her that she was now settled with a family of her own.

But it had not been long before Hortense's physical weakness had become at first tiresome, then worrisome. She seemed to bleed more, and more often, than other women. Each month she recovered, but over time less and less fully. The midwife assured her that she had healed completely after the birth and had told her to buy nettles and red raspberry leaves and boil down a concoction, drinking three cups a day. This had helped some. A year later, Jo had asked the apothecary in Charterhouse Square for advice. He had given her a tonic for Hortense to take four times a day. It had helped some too. But now there were days when Hortense could hardly get out of bed, and the washing of all those towels was distressing. So, they had pooled their resources to consult this physician in Harley Street. Jo hoped there would be good news, or perhaps some stronger medicine Hortense could take.

"What's a fizzy-shan?" asked Sally.

"A doctor who helps people feel better."

"Mummy feel better?"

"I hope so, little one."

A fire engine could be heard in the distance, and Jo could tell it was headed their way. She picked Sally up and stepped away from the street into a portico. Sally's eyes got bigger as she heard the horses and the bell.

"Wagon?" squealed Sally, with her hands over her ears.

"Fire wagon," said Jo loudly as the red wagon came into view. The Metropolitan Fire Brigade was only a few years old, but everyone knew that Captain Shaw was making it the best anywhere. Jo and Sally watched as the wagon went past, the men in uniforms and shiny brass helmets that glinted in the sunlight. Jo had sketched a steam fire engine like this, and a few of the firemen, for a drawing in *The Illustrated London News* a few months before. She had spoken to the men. They had told her that the Tooley Street Fire, nine years ago, had caused the change. That fire had started in the warehouses along the river and spread through the wharves. The city's most respected director of the London Fire Engine Establishment, James Braidwood, had died when the wall of a warehouse collapsed on him. He had been a fearless leader fighting the fire, which had burned for a fortnight before it was completely extinguished. The insurance companies came to the conclusion that they could no longer afford to insure such properties. Parliament had stepped in and passed a law establishing a fire department for London, with Eyre Massey Shaw bringing in advances like this engine, which could go anywhere in the city.

"Did you know," Jo spoke into Sally's ear, "that the Brigade will go help anyone in London who has a fire? This one is probably coming from the station on Baker Street. Would you like to see the station sometime?" Sally nodded, her hands still over her ears to block the clanging of the bells.

Jo put Sally down, and they began walking back toward the consulting rooms of Dr. Edward Wallace. He had been Jo's choice. She had consulted with Samson Light and some nurses she knew from drawing their likenesses at St. Thomas's Hospital. Wallace's approach to womanly problems walked the line between dangerous intervention and deadly inaction. He was willing to conduct surgeries if needed for younger women to improve their lives and help them birth healthy children, but had definite ideas on hygiene and precautions to prevent infection. Jo knew a little about medical care and wanted Hortense to have the best.

"Mummy!" Sally struggled her way out of Jo's arms and went running up to her mother as she came down the steps.

"Such a fuss!" said Hortense, in a mock scolding way as Sally hugged her around her legs. "I was only away for half an hour."

"Will the fizzy-shan help you, Mummy? Was he a nice man?"

Hortense tucked an errant wisp of hair into her bun. Her clothing was still neat and trim, but her belt was a little askew. Jo was pleased that she had been examined. Some doctors only spoke to the patient, believing that a woman's sensibilities made a physical examination unbearable. It was an unhelpful approach, to be sure.

"Yes, darling, he was a very nice man."

"Oh good! Me and Jo saw fire wagon. Did you hear it?" Hortense shook her head. She smiled, but her eyes looked tired.

"Let's find a cab and start heading home," Jo said, "and you can tell Mummy all about it on the ride."

"I've laid it all out like you do, Inspector."

Tommy was at Inspector Slaughter's house. Ellie had fetched him a cup of tea just as she used to when he'd lived there, only this time he'd been invited into the study and she'd returned to the kitchen. Tommy got out his notes.

"I went round to the General Post Office in the City. Mr. Teach, a clerk, claimed he saw Samson arguing with Horace Wright the day before. Mr. Henry, the supervisor, had little to say and didn't like being bothered. Then I went to 245 Holborn, where Wright's body was found. I was able to see the tunnels and how they worked. There are two tunnels, one going to Euston Station and the other not yet open, but which goes to the General Post Office. Wright's body was found in a car on the closed line."

"Who discovered the body?"

"Mr. Jenkins and Mr. Fowler, both engineers." He wanted to tell Inspector Slaughter how he had pulled the lever and sent the train, but he knew that would be childish.

"Have you spoken to them?"

"Yes, I spoke to Mr. Jenkins. But the other engineer, Donald Fowler, left his post for some reason that very day. He left a note for the company that he was going to Durham, where he has family. He didn't even leave an address for his pay."

"Do you think he might be the killer?"

"I don't know. No one has seen him since."

Slaughter nodded thoughtfully, then walked over to his desk to fetch his pipe. It was late afternoon and the day had been warm, but Slaughter had his house slippers on. The clock ticked quietly on the wall above the desk.

"Would you like a pipe, Tommy?"

He had never been offered a pipe before, and the young man sat up a bit straighter before he realized that he didn't want a pipe. He had never acquired the habit of tobacco, and wasn't sure he wanted to start.

"No thank you, Inspector." He winced to himself. Should he still call him Inspector? He always had when he lived here.

"You may call me Cuthbert if you wish," said Slaughter kindly, "now that you're living on your own."

"Cuthbert." Tommy swallowed. "I laid it all out, Cuthbert, but I'm not sure what's best at this point."

Slaughter settled back in his chair and lit his pipe. The scent filled the room and reminded Tommy again of his years in this house.

"From what you've told me, you have very little information and no witnesses to the crime. Have you been to Mr. Wright's house?"

"Yes," said Tommy. "The landlady let me look around his flat. She told me his parents are dead, and he has no other relatives. There wasn't much at the flat that was helpful, except that he seems to have been a very clean and organized man."

"What does Samson say?"

"That he doesn't know Mr. Wright, that he was walking by the General Post Office on his way to see a patient in his home, but that he didn't talk to anyone, much less have an argument on the street."

"And the police?"

"Inspector Morgan was not helpful, and told me they would manage the case."

There was a pause as Slaughter thought, his head back on the antimacassar and his eyes closed. After a minute, he opened them.

"I see no alternative. You'll have to go."

"Go?"

"To find your witness, or the killer. Fowler, you said the man's name was?"

"Go to *Durham*?" Tommy knew that Slaughter could hear the panic in his voice.

"What else can you do? You have a witness who says he saw Samson arguing with Wright, but no one else to confirm that, and

Samson says it didn't happen. You have an engineer who discovered the body and then acted inappropriately. You have a useless solicitor, a police inspector who is being unhelpful, and a barrister counting on you. Fowler may provide crucial information. He was in the building when it happened and then disappeared as soon as the body was discovered. The question is why."

"But, sir," Tommy said, forgetting the invitation to manly informality. "I've never been outside of London."

"Then high time you went somewhere. Broaden your horizons."

"And I've heard about the north. They say the people there talk in unintelligible tongues, that you can't understand them."

"They speak perfect English, and the northern accent is quite delightful."

They were both silent for a moment, listening to the ticking clock and the sound of dishes in the kitchen.

"And," said Tommy, quietly, "how would I get there?" Tommy knew his way around London on foot, on the back of a bakery van, on the omnibus. He'd been born in London and had lived on its streets. But he'd never been north of Stoke Newington.

"Well, you should definitely take the train. Roads would be much too slow. Samson goes on trial in a fortnight. You must bustle."

Tommy stared at Slaughter, who was comfortably puffing his pipe. The inspector had bustled in his time, chased criminals, discovered murderers. But he was well-read, intelligent, educated.

"Would that I were as clever as you," Tommy said, "and that I'd read more books. You've always known what to do. You know why people do the things they do."

"You know what motivates people better than I do, Tommy." Slaughter sat up in his chair, removed his pipe from his mouth, and pointed the stem at the younger man. "The books are helpful, but the workings of the mind cannot be studied in an isolated way. You have had dealings with every sort of person in this city, from gas workers to stage actors to women who make a meager living selling their bodies. You know artists and reporters and policemen and bankers. You have an open face, a nimble mind, and the gift of conversation. You're charming to ladies and polite to gentlemen. And, above all, you have a sense of people. If Fowler's your man, you won't let him best you."

Tommy tried not to look surprised, but he felt pride growing inside him. Perhaps he had been helpful as a boy after all, for Inspector Slaughter to have this sort of faith in him. Tommy rose tentatively to his feet.

"Take my Bradshaw's—it's on the shelf there," said Slaughter, motioning to the books nearest the study door. He rose to go to his desk, unlocking the top drawer. "You'll take the train out of King's Cross or Euston. You'll need money." He took an assortment of coins from the drawer and gave them to Tommy.

"But Insp—Cuthbert," Tommy gasped, "this is almost five pounds."

"I was willing to pay Perseverance Stone more than that to help Samson, and he's not charging me yet," said Slaughter, settling back in his chair. "And Tommy?"

"Yes, Cuthbert?"

"Send word to me if you get into any trouble. And please, do be careful."

Tommy spent that evening studying *Bradshaw's General Railway and Steam Navigation Guide.* It wasn't an easy book to use. He looked up Durham, and there seemed to be three ways to go. Each was a different railway company: Great Northern, North Eastern, and Midlands. He tried following the charts, but without knowing the names of any of the towns in between, he had trouble seeing how the charts worked. No trains seemed to go from London to Durham, but rather to other places in between. This was much harder than just jumping on the next omnibus.

It was only nine o'clock, so Tommy went downstairs in search of Mrs. Wren. He needed to tell her he'd be gone for awhile, and he knew that in the evenings he could find her sitting in the kitchen. Her glass of whisky was her one indulgence, and she never missed it before bed.

"Tommy lad," she said as he came in, "come and have a wee dram."

"Thank you, Mrs. Wren," he said, sitting at the table. "I've come down to tell you, though, that I'll be leaving for awhile."

"You going out tonight? With that same girl?" Mrs. Wren winked and took a sip.

"Not tonight," said Tommy. "I'm leaving in the morning for Durham. I need to track down a witness." He did not mention that it was possible that Fowler could be the murderer, rather than just a witness. He knew she'd fret.

"A witness? That sounds important. Witness to what?"

"Possibly a killing, or maybe what happened just after the killing. I've been asked to investigate by Perseverance Stone."

"Who's he when he's at home?"

"A barrister. He's defending Samson Light in court."

"And you're helping?" she said, sitting up straighter. "That's very good of you, Tommy."

Mrs. Wren was obviously impressed. It suddenly occurred to Tommy that this venture was important, possibly dangerous, certainly necessary. While he wouldn't mention it to Mrs. Wren, he realized he was afraid. And perplexed. He took out the Bradshaw's.

"I've never been on a railway to leave town," he said, flipping the pages. "I'm not sure which train to take."

"Och, let me see the book," she said, putting down her whisky and holding out her hand. "I can tell ye."

Tommy was amused, but gave her the Guide. "It's very difficult to decipher," he said gently.

"Durham, you say? Now look here. You start with the list at the front. It shows two page numbers. Go to the first one . . ." She flipped through the book. "There you are. London to Durham. Have to change at Darlington to the other line. You're starting on the Great Northern, then changing to the North Eastern. Three minutes to change. You'll make it. Should be one platform over." She handed him back the book.

He was in awe. "How do you know all that?"

She smiled sadly. "My Mr. Wren, you know. He was a porter at Euston. Always left these lying around." She took another sip.

5

Tommy knew King's Cross rail station well, having sold newspapers there in the summer of '64, when he was eleven years old. He'd also been a runner, fetching forgotten items from the cloakroom, earning a penny or two from frantic travelers who'd left their coat or hat behind. This morning, however, he entered on the west side and just stood there, his satchel in his hand. He had never been here as a passenger before and felt an acute sensation of needing to fit in, to be part of the crowd. Much of his life had been spent moving cross-wise through groups of people, intent on his own business, fetching and carrying or helping others navigate the space. Now he was in the space himself and was expected to behave as others did. Looking around, he was relieved to note that the traveling clothes of many men seemed similar to what he was wearing: light woolen pants, clean shirt and collar, waistcoat and jacket. His cap, he knew, was not as elegant as the tall hats he saw gentlemen wearing. But he was going north, to be among working people, and did not wish to be overdressed. Besides, his cap had been part of him for as long as he could remember.

Mrs. Wren, having helped him decipher Bradshaw's Guide, had determined that his only option was the 9:00 Great Northern to Darlington, with a very quick change to the North Eastern company train. The ticket booth was on his left.

"One ticket to Durham on the 9 o'clock train," Tommy said to the agent. "Third class, please."

The agent raised a full head of white hair, stroked his moustache thoughtfully and said, "Ain't no third class, unless you're a cabbage. Or a piece of furniture."

"Sorry?"

"There's only first and second class. The rest of the cars are for goods."

"Oh," Tommy said, embarrassed. "Second class, please." He was not sure what the cost would be for second class. Inspector Slaughter had given him enough, he hoped.

"I can only sell you a ticket to Darlington. Then you have to change to the North Eastern."

"I'm aware of that," said Tommy, glad that he was, "At 3:27, I believe."

"Return?"

"Yes, please."

"For what date on the return, then?"

Tommy said nothing at first. When would he return? How long would it take to get to Durham, discover a place to stay, find Donald Fowler, and convince him to return with Tommy to London? A few days? A week? Two weeks would be pushing the edges of the frame, since the Old Bailey's next session would start the second day of May.

"I'm not certain. A week, perhaps, but maybe two."

"If you don't know the date, you can buy a tourist return. It's good for a month." Two people were now queuing behind Tommy, waiting their turn.

"I'll have that, then."

The agent tallied the numbers on a pad.

"Three pounds eight shillings, please."

Tommy stifled a gasp. If he spent more than three pounds now, he might not have enough to get to and from Durham. In fact, he might not have enough left to eat, especially if he were delayed. Shrugging to himself, he decided he'd worry about that in Durham.

"How much just to get to Darlington?"

"Second class?" The agent looked unsympathetic. The queue was getting longer.

"Yes, second class."

More tallies.

"One pound fourteen shillings."

Tommy counted out the money on the counter and took his ticket. He heard skirts swish behind him as the woman at the front of the queue stepped quickly into his place at the ticket booth. He glanced at the refreshment stand, and decided he couldn't afford it. For a single ticket to Darlington, he'd just paid out eight day's wages for a watchmaker. No wonder so many of the passengers were well dressed. Train travel was obviously a costly habit. And he didn't understand why there was no third-class carriage going to coal-mining country. He would even have been willing to take one of the old-fashioned open cars if he had to. But there was nothing for it now. At least his cap wouldn't fly off.

The departures platform was straight ahead, aligned under the westernmost of two huge glass vaults that made up the ceiling. The morning sun shone through the glass, the steam from the engines dissipating as it touched the arches. A large cast-iron clock hung near the wall. There were still ten minutes until the train left, so Tommy had time to walk along the platform. The carriages were clearly marked "First Class" and "Second Class." Most of the doors were open onto the platform, indicating there were empty seats inside. He chose one and stepped up into the car, then quickly took a seat to make it appear as if he traveled this way all the time. But he had expected wooden seats, and his "oomph" as his bottom encountered the padded seat gave him away. A gentleman in the seat across from him looked over the top of his newspaper with a smirk.

As the train pulled away from the station, Tommy tried not to look excited, but the rumble of the wheels beneath him were invigorating. Even before getting up to speed outside the city, the train felt like it was moving quickly along more than just rails. It felt like moving into the future, where people could travel faster than walking, faster than a horse. Tommy was riding backward and craned his neck to look out the window as the last few buildings of London passed by. At the edges of the city he saw pottery kilns, factory smoke, and brickyards piled with waste. The train passed a tannery where the smell was so bad that Tommy and his companion both rose at the same time to pull the window closed. Then gradually there was more grass, then greener grass, then fields and trees as they headed northward, the train gaining speed. The country seemed to open itself up to his view.

As the miles rolled by, green fields and blurred trees passing the window, Tommy fell asleep. When the train stopped and echoes of people, carts, and conversation became louder, he awoke with a start. Had he passed Darlington by mistake? The gentleman with the newspaper left the train, and Tommy stuck his head out the door to see the station clock. It was not even one o'clock, and he was at Doncaster. He sat back on the seat and took a breath.

A woman with graying brown hair and an unfashionable black hat bumped against the door and leaned her reddened face into the car.

"Is this right for York?" she panted, heaving her valise onto the floor.

"Yes, ma'am," said Tommy, grabbing her bag and almost staggering as he rose to move it into the compartment. "Ooomph."

She heaved herself and a large basket up into the car, her black bombazine skirts rustling around her, and collapsed into the closest seat.

"Oh dear," she said, taking a large breath. "That was quite the run."

"Were you very late getting started?" Tommy asked politely, wondering how else he could help. The whistle blew and the train began to move. Tommy leapt up again to close the door.

"Thank you, young man," said the woman. "Yes, ever so late. A funeral, you know, doesn't always go according to schedule." She took a handkerchief out of the basket and mopped her brow, then her cheeks and chin and neck, stuffing it into her bosom. Tommy had read his pupil's copy of *Alice's Adventures in Wonderland* and thought she looked a little like the Duchess in the Tenniel drawing, only with a much more pleasant expression.

"I'm sorry you've had a death," he said.

"Thank you," said the woman, and smiled wanly at him. "I'm Mrs. Treadwell."

"My name is Tommy Jones."

"Happy to meet you, I'm sure." Mrs. Treadwell hauled the basket up more firmly on the seat. "Are you hungry at all?"

It was well into the afternoon and Tommy had been hungry for hours. He had some coins but had been tentative about leaving the train in case it started to move again. "Only if you have some to spare, Mrs. Treadwell."

She took out a bread roll, cold joint, and cheese. Tommy's mouth started to water as she tore off some bread, then cut off a chunk of meat and a slice of cheese and handed it all to him. "Got plenty," she said.

They ate in silence as the train picked up speed across the landscape. After their meal, Mrs. Treadwell wrapped up the remaining food and put it back in her basket, belched as politely as she could, then leaned her head back and went to sleep. After a few minutes, her snoring combined with the sound of the wheels on the tracks. Tommy was still facing backward, and decided Mrs. Treadwell wouldn't mind if he sat beside her so he could look out the other side of the train. She snuffled a little and leaned her head against the wall.

The green color of fields and trees, the bright open sky, was a delight to Tommy. He hadn't realized how beautiful things were outside of London. Did the whole country look like this? He'd been in parks, of course, but this was field after field, the rolling hills dotted with farms divided by hedgerows that made a patchwork. Puffy clouds floated across an enormous sky.

When the train stopped, Mrs. Treadwell awoke with a start.

"Oh! I must have nodded off." She noticed Tommy beside her. "Good choice, lad. You can see more sitting this direction. Where are we?" She leaned toward the window.

"The sign says Huddersfield, but I don't know where that is."

"Then let's find my map," said Mrs. Treadwell, and began rummaging in the basket. "I know I put it in here somewhere . . . I always bring my map."

Samson had taught Tommy how to read a map. Mrs. Treadwell pulled out a folded paper and handed it to him. It was hand drawn, showing the towns and villages between Manchester and York. All around the map were drawings of flowers, sheep, and buildings.

"This is beautiful," said Tommy. "Did you draw it?"

Mrs. Treadwell sat up proudly. "I did, lad, for my pupils."

"You're a teacher?"

"I'm a teacher at The Mount School, instructing Quaker girls in drawing and geography."

Tommy was impressed. He had known a Quaker girl once, Isabella, the daughter of a flour seller. Every Thursday she would wait for her father outside the Southwark bakery where Tommy collected deliveries. She had taught him about how the Society of Friends had been persecuted in the seventeenth century. Tommy had been particularly enamored by their pacifism and their role in abolishing slavery. Isabella told him that Quakers had not been allowed to marry outside their community until 1860, but now they were, and that was when Tommy realized that the young lady might want more from him than conversation. Extricating himself from such topics had only been achieved when he began collecting his deliveries from the back door of the bakery instead of the front.

The train was pulling into Leeds. Viewing the platform and station with a newly experienced eye, Tommy decided the station was not as grand nor as interesting as others he'd seen along the route. As the train started moving again, two boys jumped up into the carriage, swinging the door wide and slamming it once they were aboard. Both wore rough homespun clothes and grubby caps, and they were laughing as they fell into the seats across from Tommy and Mrs. Treadwell.

"Hallo!" said the taller of the two. "Hope you don't mind if we sit here." The other one chuckled, removed his cap, and held out his hand to Tommy.

"I'm Archie," he said, shaking first Tommy's hand and then Mrs. Treadwell's. "And this is my brother Charlie. We're on our way back to York."

Mrs. Treadwell smiled stiffly but opened her basket. "Would you boys like a bit of bread and meat?"

"Oh yes, please," said Archie. "Sorry if we startled you getting on." He leaned forward as if telling a secret. "We haven't got a ticket, you see."

Tommy could see Mrs. Treadwell hesitate as she prepared the food, but she said nothing.

"You two live in York?" asked Tommy.

"We do! Well, not in York proper. None of our lot live in town. Out near the mine."

For the rest of the ride to York, Archie and Charlie ate Mrs. Treadwell's food, talking almost continually. They were coal mining boys who had been given a day off work because there had been an accident, a firedamp explosion that had killed another boy and an older miner.

"Everyone's gone to the funeral. We came to Leeds instead." Archie looked quite pleased with himself.

"Did you not know the miners who were killed?" Mrs. Treadwell asked. Tommy could tell she was shocked.

"Oh, we knew 'em, ma'am," said Archie. "But a funeral didn't fit with our phil-o-sophy."

"Your philosophy?"

"Yeah. You see, ma'am, wot's the idea of having a gathering after they're dead? Oughtta do it when they're alive, if you like 'em so much. Can't be there today, can they? Live life, I say. A day off to celebrate the dead don't make sense."

Tommy found himself nodding.

"So we came to Leeds. Never seen it. Got an uncle who lives here, so our mum will ask if we saw him, but we didn't. Spent the whole morning seeing what the city has to offer. We watched 'em laying rails for the horse trams, and got laudanum for our mum at an apothecary—he didn't even ask questions!—and saw the new town hall. " He grinned.

Mrs. Treadwell frowned, but Tommy found their mood infectious. He was at least half a dozen years older than they were but had spent many an hour just enjoying London. It was possible these young men, poor as they were, might have stolen an apple or two, but they deserved a day out. Mining was both a dangerous and tedious job.

The train was slowing into York. Mrs. Treadwell gathered her things and pressed her skirts to exit, but the bombazine became tangled on the door latch. Archie leapt up to help, opening the latch and getting out first so he could help her down onto the platform. Tommy moved back further into the carriage as Charlie lifted her heavy valise. Although Mrs. Treadwell's hat was almost dislodged by the carriage door-frame, she managed to get herself onto the platform. The boys removed their caps and bowed politely, waved to Tommy, and ran off down the platform.

Tommy settled back into his seat as the train started for Darlington.

Tommy knew he had only three minutes in Darlington to find the Newcastle train run by the other company, North Eastern. But when he jumped off the train in Darlington and looked quickly around, he spotted his train waiting on the other platform, steps away. He had plenty of time, and there was a ticket seller there on the platform, carrying his tray. Tommy reached into his pocket for his coins to buy a single to Durham, then stopped suddenly.

"Watch where you're going, dear," said a woman who bumped into him when he stopped. He tried his other pocket, then his shirt. His money was gone. It only took a minute for him to think it through before he realized the boys had taken his money. And probably Mrs. Treadwell's money too, he thought, though it was far too late to do anything about that. He chided himself for being too trusting, for assuming the lads were honest and just out for a bit of fun. Now it was a bit of fun with the last of his coins.

All right, he thought. I'm in a strange town with no money. It's half past three in the afternoon, so I have hours to get to Durham before nightfall. I wonder how long it would take to walk, or if I could ride with some conveyance going that way?

"Excuse me," he asked the ticket seller, "can you tell me how I can go to Durham from here? I have no more money for the train fare."

"Durham, eh?" The ticket seller looked over at the clock, then shook his head. "Last cart I know of left here at three, carrying furniture. I don't know of another. You could go out front of the station and see what else there might be."

"How far is it to walk?"

The ticket seller shrugged. "To Durham? Seven, eight hours. Depends how fast you go."

"Which way then?"

"Out here then up the row. Go left on Parkgate, across the stone bridge, up into the market, then out Northgate."

"Thanks very much," said Tommy, sorry he couldn't give him anything for his help.

Tommy left the station, grateful that the weather was mild. White clouds skidded across the sky, and so far there was no sign of rain. He turned up the row and walked along the fields to Parkgate, just short of the brickyard. As he approached the market, he could smell the tannery even before he saw it. Across the river, a narrow path led into the marketplace, past a huge church with a tall steeple. It looked clean and fresh, as if it had been recently restored. The market square was busy, and the smell of food made Tommy hungry again. In London, even without a penny, he could likely have found a pretty fruit vendor and talked her out of an apple. But this wasn't London. There were only a few carts in the square, the streets weren't fully paved, and something about the openness of the sky made it feel like the country even though Darlington was a sizable town. At least Inspector Slaughter had been right about the language; Tommy had no trouble understanding everything being said. The speech in the north sounded like music.

He walked past the tall clock tower toward the market hall, where more carts were loading up the last of the day's vending. Some had town names on the side, but he didn't see any that said Durham. An old man was checking the horse leads on a cart with old crates of vegetables, so Tommy approached him.

"I'm sorry, but would you know which carts might be going to Durham?"

The old man looked up slowly, then grinned a toothless grin at Tommy. "Yer not from around here, are you, boy?"

"No, sir."

"London, sounds like."

"Yes, sir. My name is Tommy Jones."

"Mine's Jonah. Whatcha want in Durham?"

"I'm looking for someone," said Tommy. The man looked uninterested but not at all in a hurry. Tommy explained. "My money was stolen at York, so I'll need to find work."

"Ah!" He perked up. "Yorkie lads caught you unawares, eh? Well, you don't look like a swell, but you do look out of place."

"I feel a right fool," said Tommy in agreement, shaking his head.

"I am not going to Durham, boy," said the old man. "But I am going to Aycliffe, about five mile north of here. Want to be a vegetable till Aycliffe?"

Five miles riding was better than five miles walking, thought Tommy, and jumped on the back of the cart.

"You can have anything you think worth eating," said the man, as the horse took them out to the main road.

Tommy was munching a cabbage leaf as they arrived at Aycliffe.

"Yer in luck, boy," said Jonah, pointing across the road. "That cart is Amos's. He's going north." Tommy eased himself off the cart and thanked the old man. Amos was younger and did not appear to be in a good mood. His cart had a large ram moving restlessly in his crate.

"Mind if I ride on your cart? Jonah said you are going to Durham."

Amos glared at Tommy. "Did he?"

Tommy tried to make his smile friendly, but not appear to be simple. Amos looked him up and down.

"You're not from around here, are you?"

"No, sir."

"Don't you 'sir' me," grumbled Amos. "Get on then, if you must." Tommy climbed up the back and squeezed himself next to the crate. "And don't rile the ram." Horns bumped the crate as the animal gave Tommy a suspicious look, and the cart began to roll northward.

Hortense told Jo what Dr. Wallace had said. The bleeding was due to something called fibroids that grew in the womb. She had probably had small ones for years, but the larger ones had grown since Sally's birth.

"What can we do?" asked Jo. They spoke in hushed tones. Sally was asleep, but in the evenings she tended to wake again. The days were growing longer, and the twilight made the kitchen seem gray and Hortense's face seem even more pale. The two women sat together at the square wooden table, which was scrubbed each day and was worn smooth. Jo had made Hortense a cup of tea and added just a bit of whisky to it. Hortense took a sip before she answered.

"He was honest with me. The options aren't good. If I do nothing, they will just keep bleeding, more and more over time, since I'm too young for the menopause."

"You'll run out of blood, then, and get even weaker?"

"Yes." She looked into Jo's eyes, and they both knew that she could die. "He said we could try leaching, but since I have no fever that would just make it worse."

"Can anything be done? A surgery?"

"Yes. Surgery." Hortense sniffled. Jo fetched a handkerchief from the drawer in the hall bureau and gave it to her. "They can remove the womb. But—"

Jo was absorbing the idea of removing such an important part of the body.

"But?"

"It's very dangerous. Most women don't survive."

Jo knew quite a bit about surgery. She had known nurses and doctors, talked with them, drawn their pictures. And of course she had been involved in the case of Dr. Morton's murder some years ago, which occurred at Old St. Thomas's Hospital. Many people who had surgery died, not from the surgery itself, but from infection. This had particularly been the case since the advent of gas anesthesia, because surgeons could take their time when the patient was insensible. Longer surgeries had often saved lives and made procedures like removing the womb possible. But with the body opened to the air that long, the chance of infection was high.

There were many theories as to why this was so, but the best success in preventing infection had thus far been Dr. Joseph Lister's carbolic spray and the hand-washing of medical staff. Washing hands seemed to prevent the spread of disease from corpses, used for dissection, to live patients. It had also helped prevent the spread of disease from patient to patient. The carbolic liquid, sprayed over the body cavity during surgery, also seemed to help. But such new methods were being continually questioned, dismissed, and reassessed. Some doctors were now claiming the carbolic, which was unpleasant for them to work with, made things worse. Meanwhile, the death toll was high. Jo was frightened, but she knew Hortense must be more so. She reached out and took Hortense's cold hand in her own. Hortense took a deep breath.

"He also said he could refer me to a good surgeon, someone who has done many of these procedures. A Mr. Thomas Spencer Wells. But he also gave me a warning. Mr. Wells often administers the anesthesia himself, but Dr. Wallace said it was safer to have a second doctor do it so that Wells could concentrate on the surgery."

"Well, there at least we have some hope!" Jo stood up to boil more water for tea, desperate to have something positive to do. "Samson Light must do the anesthesia. He's studied hygiene, and he specializes in putting patients to sleep for surgery."

"Jo," Hortense reminded her quietly, "Samson is in gaol."

Jo's eyes widened. In her satisfaction at finding some good in what was happening, she had forgotten.

"Of course," said Jo. "But he shouldn't be."

She set the kettle on the hob and turned to look at Hortense. The dark circles under her eyes were becoming more obvious, and she looked very tired. Her arms wrapped around herself as if she were cold. Tea would not be enough.

"I'm going to go upstairs and draw you a bath," Jo said. "You lie in the warmth for a bit, and then you should go to bed. I'll bring your knitting up. Don't worry about things down here. I'll tidy and lock up."

Hortense nodded and pressed the handkerchief to her mouth. Jo could see she was trying not to cry.

Upstairs, Jo checked on Sally, who was still asleep, and began to draw the bath. The boiler was loud, but if Sally woke, she woke. It was more important to keep Hortense warm and rested. There could be difficult times ahead.

Although Tommy arrived hungry and smelling like sheep, he couldn't help but wonder at the city of Durham. It seemed almost magical. Amos had left him at Framwellgate Bridge, and as he crossed the River Wear, Tommy could see the castle and the cathedral up on the hill to his right. The evening sun was just setting, and the brown river had a golden glow, with little white insects spinning above the water into the trees. He could hear the river below and smell the fragrant trees that lined the river banks. The bells of the cathedral began to toll in a tune, and he stood there rapt on the bridge listening to the clear coppery notes floating down to him. Instead of crossing upward into the main street, he took the steps down to the river to follow the sound. The path along the water was a bit muddy, but here the sound of the bells seemed to echo on the water as he walked. They must be practicing, Tommy thought, because surely there was no church service this late in the evening. Evensong would have been hours ago.

A building surprised him. Its sign said it was the Archaeological Museum, but a notice on the door said it was the Old Fulling Mill. He knew what a corn mill was, but what was fulling? Tommy wasn't sure he'd ever heard the term. After a time, the path took a turn back and began to edge upward, toward the side of the massive church. The bells stopped just as he climbed to the top, standing beside the stone walls. He walked around to the north side, across a small plot of graves, and onto Palace Green, where he looked up at the cathedral tower. *That must be where the bells are,* he thought. Across the green opposite the cathedral he could see the entrance to the castle, but the gate was closed. He walked past and down a cobbled street till he came out at Saddler Street. Pubs here were open, as was a bakehouse, and he could smell hot pies and warm beer. Workers and scholars were walking in the streets. He was passed by two young men in gowns, arguing something about Aristotle as they seemed to fly by. At the bottom of the hill, he noticed another bridge to the right and realized that the river had gone right round the cathedral and returned. The castle and cathedral, this street and likely others like it, were surrounded by the same river in a loop. Tommy had been taught a bit about medieval castles and military strategy and concluded that this place was in an excellent position for defense.

Saddler Street came down to the Market Square, where people were meeting and talking as the evening set in. An equestrian statue of a man in military garb, his tall feathered hat sticking up into the air, was in the center of the square. He seemed to be presiding over the merchant carts and wagons gathered at his feet, a cluster of temporary stalls. The church behind the statue, with its ambitious spire, looked new. Next to the church was an archway to a covered market with a sign saying "Saturdays Only," and next door to that was the Market Hotel. Even in London, the local pub was the place to find information, but Tommy had no money. He entered anyway.

At the table near the front window, overlooking the square, was a small group of men eating and drinking. Tommy tipped his hat to the friendliest looking among them and moved into the small room. Looking around he saw no bar for drinks, so he found an empty small table in the back and waited. Before long a girl appeared, holding a small notebook and pencil.

"What will you have then?" she said. She had dark straight hair escaping from her cap, and her eyes were dark too, and almond-shaped. When he didn't answer immediately, she looked at him, and the intelligence in her eyes held him spellbound for a moment.

"I'm not sure. I've never been here before."

She looked sharply at him and put the hand with the pencil on her hip.

"University student, are you?" she asked, taking in his appearance.

"No, no. Just looking for work," he said, thinking he'd need some coin before he began searching for Donald Fowler. The girl was frowning at him, but not in an unfriendly way. Tommy smiled his best smile at her, the one that left his face open and guileless. She smiled back, and he saw humor in her eyes as she cocked an eyebrow.

"You haven't any money, have you?" she said, and began tapping her pencil on her pad.

"No."

She looked over at the men in the front window, and he followed her gaze.

"Gerry?" she called, and the friendly man looked up. "Can you spell a man a meal? Sounds like he's here from London." She looked over at Tommy, and he nodded.

Gerry's friends laughed and one punched him in the arm. Gerry gently cuffed his friend's ear.

"Ow!" his friend yelped. "You gonna pay just cuz Maggie asks?"

"Ya," said Gerry, "just cuz Maggie asks." He turned back to Maggie. "Yes, I will. What's yer name, boy?" His voice carried easily across the small room.

"Tommy Jones," said Tommy.

"All right, Tommy Jones," called Gerry. "Have some mutton stew, but not too much, mind." And he turned back to his friends.

"Thank you," said Tommy loudly, "and if I can ever do you a favor—"

Gerry waved his hand over his head, dismissing the offer.

"Special friend of yours?" Tommy asked the girl. It was silly, he knew, but he was hoping Gerry wasn't too special to her.

"He's my cousin," she said. "Works at Henderson's. I'll get your stew." Tommy tried not to watch her as she went to the kitchen, but he couldn't help it. His heart was pounding. She was neither beautiful nor dainty, like any number of the girls he took out on the town. It was as if he had suddenly realized that beautiful and dainty wasn't what he liked in a person, that what he thought had been the attraction wasn't any longer. Samson had once told him that when he met Prudence, it was as if all other girls had faded in comparison, moving into the background of his life instead of the foreground. Tommy had not understood what he meant; it sounded like romantic nonsense. But right now it didn't seem like nonsense.

Perhaps this place is enchanted, he thought. A beautiful cathedral with magical bells and a castle, cobbled streets where workers and students mingled, all wrapped in the hug of the River Wear. And now this woman . . .

"Here you are," she said, and put down in front of him not only a bowl of hot lamb stew and a spoon, but also a pint of ale. She went over to the men at the front table and stood near Gerry, chatting with him and his friends. Tommy heard her laugh, a rich smooth sound, and smiled to himself. The man who had punched

Gerry's arm got up from the table and came over, taking the seat across from him. His eyes were hooded with a heavy brow, and the creases on his face were dark. His body was wiry, as if he worked hard at physical labor. Tommy thought he might be about 25 but that he looked much older.

"Maggie says you need work," he said. "Ever done any building?"

Tommy had carried and cleaned for bricklayers, among his many other tasks, and he said so.

"That's likely good enough," said the man. "My uncle is building the fever ward at the workhouse. They need more hands. Don't know what they pay, but it'll keep you in mutton stew."

"Thank you," said Tommy, holding out his hand. "I'm Tommy Jones."

"So I heard. I'm Bert." He leaned over in a confidential manner. "Me mum named me after the Prince."

Tommy leaned forward too. "My sympathies," he said quietly. Bert stared, then broke into a grin and shook Tommy's hand.

"Come to the building site in the morning, seven sharp," said Bert, pointing out the window and to the right toward Framwellgate Bridge. "Cross the bridge then bear left up to Crossgate and go on till you see the workhouse. Fever ward's being built at the far end."

As Bert returned to his friends, Tommy became aware how tired he was. The hot food and cool ale had made him content and sleepy, and he couldn't stifle a yawn.

"You got a place to sleep?" said Maggie at his elbow. He looked up into those eyes. She'd been so kind, and so had her cousin, but he couldn't bear her thinking that he was helpless or without resources. He nodded firmly.

"I do," he said. "But I certainly would like to see you again some time?"

She looked at him for a moment. "Are you courting me, Tommy Jones?" she said. "You don't even know me."

"I know your name is Maggie, and that you work at the Market Hotel, and have a cousin named Gerry who is a splendid fellow and just bought me my first meal in Durham City. And I know with great certainty that I like you very much." Tommy had never been this direct with a woman in his life, and he tried not to look as fearful as he felt. Had he said too much?

But Maggie just grinned. "Well, my goodness," she said, starting to collect his bowl and spoon. "One bowl of stew and he comes on all romantic. You just get a job and settle in, Tommy Jones. I'll see you another time."

It was dark when Tommy left the tavern, but the moon was rising and made the cobblestones shine. He walked purposefully across the square and down to Elvet Bridge, leaning on the edge to look into the water. He needed to find somewhere to sleep. He turned to walk back up the steep cobbles of Saddler Street, thinking there might be a place near the cathedral. He passed a small passage with stairs leading downward, and looking through saw it went back toward Framwellgate Bridge and the first part of the river's bend. He liked how compact this part of the city was, much easier to find one's way round than London. He went down the steps. The narrow passage would keep out the wind, which was becoming cold. He curled up against the wall and went to sleep.

"Isn't it odd, though?" Prudence said through the small window in the cell door. "That V. G. Faber would be on the board of the London Pneumatic Despatch Company?" The Clerkenwell Gaol corridors were crowded with visitors bringing their loved ones Good Friday wishes and gifts. The warders had been busy checking baskets.

Even with his limited vision through the bars, Samson could see that his wife looked pale and tired. He longed to take her in his arms and hold her, to tell her it would be all right, that she needn't worry. But that would not be the truth. Samson himself had been sleeping less, spending more nights pacing his cell, thinking. He'd rewritten the notes he'd given to Tommy, as much as he could remember. He had drawn the pavement in front of the Post Office, trying to bring forth memories of who else might have been there. He had written down ledgers of numbers, how much money he thought they had, how much Pru might need if he weren't there anymore.

"My darling Pru," he said. "You are working at the bookshop, and you look so tired. Whatever happens to me, you must protect yourself. Running about London trying to help me is very kind, but we have Tommy Jones and Mr. Stone and Mr. Squire—"

"Mr. Squire is bloody useless," said Prudence.

Samson ignored her language. "But Tommy isn't, and Mr. Stone is supposed to be one of the best barristers in London. I'm sure they'll discover why this horrible mistake has happened."

Prudence tilted her chin up. "You know as well as I do that lying around when pregnant is needless, and inactivity lowers the health of the mother. You told me so yourself."

He did not want to argue with her, although he wanted to point out that if she was still sick often, she was weakening herself.

She noticed that he looked weaker, too. There were dark circles around his eyes. She felt the tears come; she couldn't help it. Why was this happening? Samson was a good man, and he didn't even know this Mr. Wright. She wiped her eyes with her handkerchief as if dabbing away some dust. She could not afford to become weak if she was going to make it through the trial, and it wasn't fair to make Samson worry about her.

"It is an interesting coincidence, about Mr. Faber," Samson said, to return to her main point. "I cannot see what the company that makes the pneumatic railway has to do with the murder, but I could be wrong. How is Mr. Herbert managing his competition as a bookseller?"

Prudence knew that Samson was trying to introduce a different subject because they only had a few minutes left to visit. To oblige him, she chatted a bit about Mr. Herbert and his efforts to keep his shop as a place where customers felt at home, where they weren't rushed to make a purchase. Prudence was getting better at skimming books as they came in, so she could know what customers were asking for when they couldn't remember a title. That V.G. Faber was on the wrong track selling books at the rail stations. How could you look at titles when you couldn't hear yourself think? Samson smiled as she talked.

They heard a bell ring near the front entrance and a young woman upstairs start to cry. "Just another minute or so," said a warder as he passed.

"You get some rest yourself," said Prudence, "and be sure to eat what I brought you." She had been permitted to give him some hot cross buns from the batch she had made the day before, after she'd returned home from the bookshop. "And don't you worry. As soon as I hear from Tommy, we'll know more. And I'll write to him what I discover about the company"—Samson opened his mouth to speak, but Prudence put up her hand—"but I won't go running all over London and tire myself, I promise."

Friday in Durham dawned bright, early, and cold. Tommy was stiff from sleeping on stone. He walked carefully down the steps, then continued down Silver Street to Framwellgate Bridge. There were stairs just before the bridge leading down to the river and, having no other alternative, he went down quickly to relieve himself at the bottom of the steps, then came back up and continued across the bridge, tucking in his shirt. He had no money for breakfast, but he reminded himself that was why he needed to work.

Looking to the left as he crossed the bridge, Tommy saw the cathedral as a large shadow in the morning sun. The castle beside it looked cold and imposing, but the cathedral was starting to catch the light, and the tips of the pinnacles on the square towers almost seemed to glow. He heard singing, and saw a man ahead of him sitting on the ground, his back against the wall of the bridge. He was old, with a noble head and greasy ginger hair. Beside him was a dog, a big yellow dog with his head on his paws. The man was singing in a hearty voice:

> As me and my marrow was gannin to wark
> We met with the Devil; it was in the dark
> I was up with my pick, it being in the neet;
> And knock'd off his horns, likewise his club feet . . .

The man's left foot stuck out in front of him on the paving stones. It appeared injured or clubbed, and given the song, Tommy assumed a mining accident of some kind. He regretted that he couldn't put a coin in the man's cap, which was lying upturned on the ground in front of him. Tommy smiled wanly and touched his forehead in greeting.

"G'mornin', young man," said the old man, and when Tommy nodded back, he resumed his singing, his voice echoing off the walls of the bridge.

Tommy found the worksite easily, following Bert's directions and heading up Crossgate. The workhouse was a severe and imposing building, and Tommy felt himself shiver. He had spent much time in a workhouse in London, and the cheerful morning and novelty of the town still failed to overcome the feeling of dread. He walked past the main building to where timbers and bricks were stacked and saw a few men standing around. A cart was set up with a fire next to it for boiling water, and men were getting tea from the cart. Tommy, his stomach grumbling, looked around for Bert but didn't see him. A large man with a shock of black hair and pock marks on his face came up to Tommy.

"You Tommy Jones?" The man didn't look friendly, but Tommy nodded and swallowed.

"Good," said the man, planting his booted feet apart and crossing his arms over his ample chest. "I'm Simon Henderson, Albert's uncle. He said you'd be round this morning. Got any experience building?"

"Some," said Tommy, "but not much. Mostly I carried bricks for builders in London." He didn't think that Simon Henderson would be interested in his many other professions: crossing sweeper, gasworks boy, railway station fetcher, theatrical flyer runner, science tutor, or junior investigator to a police detective.

"Good," said Henderson again. "Ye'll be carrying bricks all day. The pay is two shillings for a 10-hour day, paid on market day, Saturday."

Tommy stood up tall. "Very good, but if I may ask a favor, could I have one shilling for today's work? I have no money to eat today." He tried to sound as if this were a normal state of affairs. Henderson looked him over, his eyes narrowing. "One shilling this evening, then. Get yourself some tea and a scone, then get over to that load of bricks with the other men." He turned away and walked to where two men were stacking timbers on the other side of the road.

Gratefully, Tommy rolled up his sleeves in the cool air, and joined the other men for his breakfast. As the day continued, he carried bricks and listened to the conversations of the other workers, getting accustomed to the way they spoke. He noticed he felt particularly well, even while doing heavy work. He was glad to be moving, and the air seemed so fresh and clean. Although he knew the London air was laden with smoke and fog, he hadn't realized how dirty it was. Here the town was smaller, certainly, and it had several industries. Yet the air was clean, even with the River Wear as brown and slow as the Thames back home.

At the end of the day he collected his pay from Henderson.

"Here you go, Tommy," said the big man, handing over two shillings. Tommy looked up in surprise. He had only expected one, with the rest paid tomorrow. "You do good work, and it's Good Friday," said Henderson. "And ye'll get two tomorrow if you work as hard."

"I'm grateful to you, Mr. Henderson," said Tommy.

"Simon."

"Simon. And might you be able to tell me where I could get a bed for the night, or lodgings for a few days?"

Henderson pointed back down toward Framwellgate Bridge. "Go back across the bridge, then through the marketplace, then down to Old Elvet Bridge on the other side. Keep going and you'll find the Waterloo Inn. It's for coaching, so it's a fair price."

⁂

Tommy opened the door next to the sign saying Rooms for Let. He knocked and called out, "Hello?"

The parlor was to the right, and he saw a threadbare but clean rug, a small table, a sideboard with a box of photographs and a stereoscope, a mirror over the fireplace, and three comfortable chairs. Since there had been no answer, he went down the hall toward the back of the house to find the kitchen.

A dark-haired woman in a black work dress was squatting in front of the large range, pushing at the vent on the oven door. She was muttering as she tried to force it to open.

"May I try?" asked Tommy. The vent got stuck at the Slaughters', too, and he'd help Prudence unstick it more than once.

The woman looked up in surprise.

"And who might you be?"

"I'm sorry," said Tommy, taking off his cap. "I'm Tommy Jones. Mr. Henderson at the fever ward building site said you might have a room for me."

She nodded and turned back to the vent.

"Right," she said. Tommy came up beside her, and she stood, her pock-marked face beaded with sweat. "I'm Mrs. Hutton, but everyone calls me Widow Hutton. Let us see if you can help."

She stepped back and Tommy opened the oven door, easing his fingernail around the edge of the vent and shaking the vent cover gently back and forth until he heard a click. Then he moved the vent back and forth to make sure it was eased.

"I hope that's better," he said.

"It is indeed. Now," she said, giving him a look of satisfaction as she pushed the stray damp hairs off her forehead, "let's find you a room. From London are you?"

Tommy's room was small and on the top floor, so the ceilings tilted in, but he didn't mind.

"Privy's out back," said Widow Hutton, pointing down into the yard. "And there's no bath in the house. But you need one before you sleep in my bed," she said, looking at the clothes he'd slept in for his night in the passage. He undoubtedly smelled bad too, after all the traveling and a day hauling bricks. "The wash and bath house is across Elvet Bridge. Stay left by the river and you'll get there."

Although he had enjoyed having use of an inside bathroom during his years at the Slaughters' in Southwark, he had both used and cleaned backyard privies at the workhouse, and taken baths in tubs in the kitchen. As he crossed Elvet Bridge, he could see the public bath house on the banks to his left, and he followed the river. The sign said Durham City Swimming Baths. He happily paid four pennies to damp brush his clothes and wash himself in warm water.

After Tommy had given Widow Hutton a shilling for the week and settled into his room, he came downstairs and asked for paper to write a letter. Widow Hutton looked surprised.

"You read and write then?" Tommy nodded. She had gone into the parlor, where there was a small desk in the corner.

"In the desk," she said. "There's ink there too, and a blotter. But you'll need to do your writing here. No ink in the rooms."

Tommy quickly wrote several short letters. The first was to Samson, telling him of his arrival in Durham to find Donald Fowler. The second was to Perseverance Stone, with the same message, that he had arrived safely. He also wrote a short note to Jo Harris, saying not to expect any meetings in the park for awhile, and explaining why. Then came the notes to his employers. Mrs. Ernestine Templeton of Bedford Square, Miss Fanny's mother, explaining that he had been called away on business and should return in a fortnight. Mr. John Smith, clockmaker in Northampton Square, apologizing and explaining. And lastly, Headmaster Mr. Griffith at the Ragged School.

Widow Hutton told him where he could post the letters next day, at the post office in Elvet Bridge. Bidding her good evening, he walked back across the bridge. He found himself heading for the Market Hotel. There were other places to get a meal, he was sure, but he was hoping to see Maggie. As he entered, he steeled himself. He'd been thinking about her all day, which he knew was foolish. His face would surely show his interest, and he would likely be made fun of, if not worse, by the men in the pub. Nonetheless, there was a feeling of beginning something as he stepped inside.

Just like the night before, there was the group of men at the front table. He recognized Gerry and Bert.

"There's the London lad," said Gerry, smiling. "Gonna pay for yourself this time?"

"Oh yes," said Tommy. He had planned to get his own table, but Gerry moved over and patted the bench beside him. At Tommy's hesitation, he laughed.

"Look, boys," Gerry said to the others. "He's here to see Maggie!" The others laughed too, and there was a general shaking of heads as a burly man in an apron approached the table.

"What will you have?" he said gruffly to Tommy. The hair on his muscular arms stood out thickly, and the apron was dirty and stretched tightly across his ample stomach. Tommy looked over at Gerry and raised an eyebrow.

"He'll have a beer and the chop," said Gerry, leaning over to Tommy to add, "You don't want the whiting." The gruff man nodded and went back toward the kitchen.

"Maggie doesn't work here on Fridays," said Gerry.

"But you can hear her from here," Bert said, raising his eyebrows in a way clearly designed to indicate deep meaning. There was silence for a moment, but all Tommy could hear were the bells from the cathedral.

"I don't hear anyone," Tommy said.

The men laughed.

"All the way from noisy London, and he can't hear anything! Can't you hear the bells?" said Gerry.

Tommy nodded.

"Maggie pulls the bells. Right good ringer she is, too."

The men nodded and drank their beer.

"Then she goes home to cook a late supper for her father."

The burly man arrived with the chop and the mug of beer, waiting for his money, then glowered when Tommy handed him his second shilling. The man sighed and reached into his greasy apron, mumbling something about how people pay. He handed back a sixpence and two pennies. Tommy hadn't realized how hungry he was until he smelled the food. It was clear the others had already eaten. He took a bite. The meat was hot, salty, and greasy, absolute heaven.

"Better tell him about Maggie," mumbled Bert into his beer.

"So, London lad," said Gerry, leaning his elbows on the table. "About Maggie. She's a wonderful lass, and everyone in town—well, every man not related to her—has tried to catch her eye. But she's got ambition, that girl, and she won't have any of us, nor anyone up at the mines either. Got a mind of her own."

"Aye, that she has," grumbled an older man at the end of the table. "Gets it from her father. Clever and stubborn."

"Her father's a good man, make no mistake," added Bert.

"What's her father do?" asked Tommy, taking another bite of the chop.

"Engineer up at the mine, working with that crazy man John Marley. They been sinking a shaft down to the Busty Seam."

"Bad idea," said a younger blond man. Tommy noticed his fingers were torn and scarred. "Everyone knows that seam is done."

"Where's the Busty Seam?" asked Tommy. He was completely ignorant about coal mining but didn't want to appear uninterested.

"Up at the Littleburn Colliery," said Bert. "Southwest of here. Marley thinks he's gonna get rich, but most of us think his company will fold." There were nods around the table.

"So there's no coal down there?" Tommy asked.

"Oh, there's coal," said Gerry. "But it's perilous hard to get out. Since it's John Marley, though, he's got investors."

"Marley could talk a man into anything," said the blond man.

"They do everything better down in Darlington," mumbled Bert.

"So Maggie's father is engineering the project?" said Tommy as he finished the chop.

"Yeah, they brought him all the way up from London. Hey!" said Gerry. "Maybe you know him, seeing as you're from London too!" There was hearty laughter around the table as the men drained their mugs and got up to go.

"That would be odd," said Tommy, shaking his head and rising with them. They went together out into the marketplace. The full moon was up and the night was chilly. The church steeple was glowing against the northern sky, and all the buildings around them were quiet as the group broke up. Gerry walked with Tommy down to the bridge.

"Maggie's a wonderful woman," said Gerry. "But be careful. Not only is she stubborn, but her father doesn't like young men hanging about her."

"That must be hard on him," said Tommy. His mind was already determined that at some point, he would be talking to her father.

"Yeah," said Gerry, heading off up Silver Street. "He won't like anyone distracting his Maggie."

6

There was hope, thought Samson as he sat in his cell. He had received a note from retired Inspector Slaughter earlier in the week saying he had retained Perseverance Stone, a reputable barrister. Samson knew the money for that could not have been easy to come by, and he had promptly written a note in gratitude. He had also written to Prudence, hoping it would relieve her mind somewhat that he would have good representation. Dear Prudence. She had looked so frail when she visited him.

The key clanged in his cell door, and Conner stood in the entry.

"Ready for infirmary duty, sir?" he asked.

"Yes, indeed," said Samson. He took one of his books off the corner shelf, *The Science and Art of Surgery* by John Eric Erichsen, and stepped out into the main hall.

It always surprised him, the hall. It rose to three stories, with dozens of cells along the walls. A spiral staircase at each end led to the open walkways on each side, and light came in from windows on the ceiling. His own cell was on the ground floor, so he had never been up to the other levels. The walkways were lined with identical cell doors, each with its covered window at head-height. The prisoners were not allowed to talk with each other except when they worked together.

And now Miss Harper was working with him on Saturdays, their in-house infirmary days. After they had operated together on Mr. Franks, Samson had requested of the governor that she be assigned infirmary duty if she so wished. She had, and they had become something of a medical team on the days when Mr. Warner wasn't there.

Today she was cataloging supplies. He handed her the book.

"You may already have read this," said Samson, "but in case you haven't, you might enjoy it."

Miss Harper looked at the flyleaf. "I have not," she said, "but I have heard of it, of course." She began flipping eagerly through the pages. "This is the textbook the medics are using in the American war, I've heard."

"Yes. And Mr. Erichsen lectures at University College Hospital. Perhaps one day you can attend one of his talks." Miss Harper was a woman of few words and fewer social graces, but her interest in surgery was evident, and Samson wanted to encourage it.

"That would be most satisfactory," she said, setting the book aside. "May I borrow this for awhile?"

"Of course," said Samson, "That's why I brought it." He could tell she was pleased, although her face remained impassive.

Conner looked at them, and Samson caught a glimpse of a smile.

"A quiet day, it seems," said Samson as Conner left to make his rounds.

"Nothing wrong with that," said Miss Harper.

Samson looked at the determined face, the set jaw.

"You don't seem happy today, Miss Harper," he said, hoping he wasn't being intrusive.

She looked over at him. Her eyes were a steel gray.

"I've had a letter from my brother," she said.

"Not bad news, I hope?"

"Not exactly. Tales from home, which girl the postman has his eye on, how much milk the cows are producing. But it's evident from his tone that he thinks I should be here, that I deserve to be punished for what I've done."

Samson wasn't sure what to say. He knew she was accused of forgery, but they had never discussed the charges that had brought them to Clerkenwell Prison.

She sniffed and busied herself with counting bandage rolls.

"I'm sorry," he said.

There was silence as he went over to the cabinet and checked to make sure the stethoscope was still there. Things from the infirmary tended to walk off on their own.

"It's so unfair," he heard her grumble. "You'd think I was doing it all just for me. I've taken care of all of them, him, mother, even little Jimmy. And he has the nerve—" She stopped and seemed to get herself under control with a sigh.

"If you'd like to talk about it—" he said.

"No, thank you," she cut in, with a clipped tone. "I'll manage."

Conner was back with a prisoner in tow. The small man looked miserable and had his hand to his cheek.

"A tooth for you, sir," said Conner, and left.

"How can I help, Mr. . . . ?"

"Brown, sir. Mortimer Brown. It's my tooth, sir. Hurts something awful."

Samson knew there were only two things that could be done with a bad tooth: cloves for pain if it could heal itself, or removal. But he sat Mr. Brown on the stool to take a look.

Victor George Faber, known as V.G. to almost everyone, awaited the others for the meeting of the London Pneumatic Despatch Company board of directors. He was earlier than usual. His role as a Member of Parliament for Westminster (Conservative party) had taught him the value of being the first person in the room. One controlled the space, which was important for negotiating. Like Viscount Palmerston, whom he had supported as Prime Minister even though he was Liberal, strategy was more important than stultified party loyalty. Faber had disagreed with Palmerston, however, about Germany. Faber knew Bismarck was a threat, but Palmerston seemed blind to the newer ways of the world, of politics and diplomacy.

Faber smoothed his side whiskers, which made wide lines of white hair down the sides of his face. He knew that with his balding head, his mutton-chops made him look even more distinguished. This railway company venture was important to him, as a man of the future. The empire was held together not just with blood and men, but with machinery. Innovations like the pneumatic railway may seem inconsiderable, toys to carry messages from office to office. But they represented far more. The post was not just for family news and a few business orders. The mails tied the empire together, as did the telegraph and the railways. It had been genius, he congratulated himself, to bring literature to those bankers and merchants traveling the rails by selling newspapers and books at railway stations throughout the country.

And now Faber had helped assemble a company to guide investors toward developing atmospheric railways, which used less coal and could move more quickly, away from the traffic of carts and coaches. Having at least one aristocratic member was important to any venture's success, and they had Richard Grenville, the Third Duke of Buckingham, who enjoyed the friendship of Benjamin Disraeli. Not all dukes were helpful, of course; that damned Bedford had forced the pneumatic tube to go all the way around his holdings in Euston and Holborn. He had refused to allow their tunnels. The company had been forced to dogleg the track. But it had worked.

The door opened and Thomas Brassey came in, greeting Faber with a nod. Brassey was one of the more useful members of the board, thought Faber, an engineer who knew all about railways, a man of vision. He was accompanied by Mrs. Rachel Bond, a stout and reliable investor who had guided her husband's importing business before he died. Faber stood as she entered the room. Mr. Brassey and Mrs. Bond took seats across the table from each other.

"I'm afraid His Grace is unable to attend today," said Faber to the newcomers, "but he did send me his instructions."

Mrs. Bond was about to reply when the door opened again, admitting Edmund Clark, the hydraulics specialist, and John Horatio Lloyd, the barrister.

"Good afternoon, gentlemen," said Faber, "I was just explaining that—"

The door opened again and Mr. Wilson, the secretary, came in with his notebook, quietly taking a seat.

"Thank you, William," Faber said to Wilson. "Although His Grace could not be here today, he sent me his instructions." He resumed his seat, and smoothed his side whiskers as he took out his pen.

Business commenced with the financial reports, including the expenditures and investments. When the meeting turned to the opening of the railway line to the General Post Office in St. Martin's-Le-Grand, Faber leaned forward. "His Grace's instructions are to open the line as soon as possible."

Mrs. Bond, looking down at her notes, raised her pen. "Mrs. Bond?" asked Faber.

She stood to address the others. "As you know, I had deep misgivings about the construction of this line to the G.P.O.," she said in a calm but determined tone. "I continue to have them. The construction cost a great deal more than we approved, and we still have no indication that any money will be saved using the cars. In addition, I have heard that there has been some objection from the Post Office itself. Is that true, Mr. Faber?" She sat down, looking placidly at him.

"I can report that we have been engaged in deep discussion with the Post Office," Faber said, rising. "They have indeed been somewhat uncertain about the time saved by using the line, and are naturally cautious. However, His Grace has honored the company by stepping into the negotiations personally. I can assure you that the Post Office is now ready to initiate the use of the new line."

Mrs. Bond raised her pen. Not looking up, she said, "I continue to lodge my objections and would like my position indicated in the notes."

Faber turned to William Wilson and gave a nod. "Please do so, Mr. Wilson." He looked benignly around the table. "Is there any other discussion needed on this issue?"

"One question," said Mr. Brassey, raising a grease-stained finger. Faber nodded and Brassey rose to speak. "The murder," he said, with a brief glance at Mrs. Bond. "I wonder whether the death of a Post Office clerk, and his presence in a pneumatic railway car, has in any way affected the investors or the opening of the line."

Faber sounded confident. "Thomas, I have the assurance of Detective Inspector Morgan at St. Giles that there will be no obstacle to opening the line as early as next week."

Mrs. Bond spoke. "But a man is dead. And we don't even know why."

"Likely it's the result of some personal affair. I'm quite sure that Joseph Morgan will sort it all out."

John Horatio Lloyd, adjusting his spectacles to his large brown eyes, looked confused. "But surely the postal worker was killed at the General Post Office in the City, not 245 Holborn. Why is St. Giles involved and not the City Police?"

"We have had the good fortune that Detective Inspector Morgan took an interest in the case and has taken over the investigation," said Faber. There was a silence.

"I'm afraid I don't understand," said Lloyd, blinking.

"Your inquisitive lawyer's mind is an asset to the company, John," said Faber, "but in this case we're just happy that it's Morgan instead of some City functionary, with their authority within an authority. City Police know about banks and finance, embezzlement, that sort of thing. This is business. And murder," he added hastily. "Shall we take our good luck where we find it and open the line?"

He looked around the table at the men's heads nodding, and adopted a paternal expression. "We are about to prove the usefulness of the pneumatic railway to mankind," he said. "This is an extraordinary opportunity. Once the G.P.O. is connected to Holborn, and thus connected to Euston, we will be part of the mail service that runs Her Majesty's Empire. Our machinery, our vision, will be part of the larger operation of the finest empire the world has ever seen . . ."

As Faber continued in this vein, Mrs. Bond stopped listening. His Grace the Duke of Buckingham and V. G. Faber made an ambitious pair, but she had wondered even before her husband died about the wisdom of the scheme. The telegraph she understood—there was an invention that could connect the world. Wires, impulse signals, a universal code, sub-oceanic cables—these were the way of the future. A new central telegraph office was being rightfully annexed to the G.P.O building, and she had willingly invested in that project. But an underground rail system for letters and parcels? It seemed to her such a small segment of transportation for such a large investment. It was already an overly expensive venture, with such complex machinery, and seemed destined to lose money. Perhaps men like the Duke and Faber were just afraid of losing face after all the publicity over the last decade. But she thought the London Pneumatic Despatch Company was doomed to failure.

Visiting Samson in prison was vital, and Perseverance Stone had little time to spare. The note from Tommy Jones explaining why he must travel to Durham had arrived at his office that morning. While pleased at Tommy's initiative, Stone wanted to be sure that nothing was being overlooked, and that Samson Light still wanted his services given the time limitations.

It had been a taxing morning of work at the Foreign Office, and now this afternoon, even the weather was frustrating. The wind was gusting, the rain was cold, and his umbrella was useless. He had been lucky there had been plenty of cabs in Whitehall.

Visiting hours at Clerkenwell were restrictive. He managed to arrive only minutes before two o'clock, but Moseley recognized him and allowed him to shake off his wet overcoat and proceed to Samson's cell.

"Mr. Light?" Stone asked at the window in the metal door. No one answered.

"I'm sorry, sir," said Moseley from behind him. "Mr. Light must be in the infirmary. If you'll follow me, sir?"

One never really got accustomed to gaols, thought Stone, although he had visited plenty of them. Clerkenwell was unusually pleasant, particularly compared to its neighboring prison, but the sense of confinement was unnerving. The two men walked along the hall until they came to the open door of the infirmary. Stone was impressed that they allowed this prisoner such liberties. Moseley put his head in the door.

"Mr. Light?" Samson and Miss Harper sat at the examination table, their heads together as they leaned over to look at a book. Satisfied that his duty was done, Moseley turned to Stone, tapped his cap, and headed off down the hallway.

Perseverance Stone found his attention captured, not by Samson Light, but by Fiona Harper. He knew her immediately from the Foreign Office Christmas festivities that winter, to which Otway had invited him. He had seen her talking to one of the representatives before the dinner. Reginald Spalding of the War Office had pointed her out, explaining that she was much admired in diplomatic circles. Harper had recently returned from Kashgaria, where she had posed as an archaeologist while actually spying for the British government. She had helped secure the release of the explorers Robert Shaw and George Hayward from the clutches of the warlord Yakub Beg the previous spring.

Stone was confused to see her here. Why was she in Clerkenwell Gaol? And what was her relationship with Samson Light? Surely he couldn't know she was an international spy? Stone cleared his throat and both of them looked up.

"Excuse me," he said with a bow. "I am Perseverance Stone, Mr. Light's barrister."

Samson rose at once to shake his hand.

"Very pleased to meet you, Mr. Stone," he said. "May I introduce my assistant, Miss Harper?"

"Pleased to meet you," said Stone, holding out his hand. Her grip was firm as she looked him in the eye with a friendly smile. She closed the book, marking the place with a slip of paper.

"If you'll excuse me, gentlemen," she said, "I'll leave you to your business." As she left, it occurred to Stone that her manner was as if she had been at a dinner party in Kensington rather than in gaol in one of the lesser parts of London. Quite a woman, Miss Harper.

"I apologize for not having been to meet you sooner," said Perseverance Stone, as Samson motioned him to take a chair next to the desk. "Is it all right if we talk here?"

"I think so," said Samson, glancing toward the open door. "I have about ten minutes before I have to return to my cell."

"I shall be brief," said Stone. "I have read your report, and been in consultation with young Tommy Jones. Due to certain demands at the Foreign Office, I have been forced to ask that Jones do some investigation on his own in preparation for your trial."

"I know Tommy well," said Samson. "I was his tutor."

"Yes, indeed. I also want to make sure that you do not prefer to consult another barrister. I had not anticipated the conflict with my Foreign Office duties when I agreed with Inspector Slaughter that I would take your case."

Samson frowned. "Are you saying that you will be unable to do an adequate job defending me?"

Stone looked into Samson's face. It was a young man's face, but with a determined set in his jaw and the intelligence of an older man in his eyes.

"I believe that with Jones's help I shall be able to mount a defense, but I am aware we haven't much time. Tommy has gone north, to Durham, to find Donald Fowler. He was the engineer who ran the pneumatic railway cars at the 245 Holborn, the central station. It is likely he was the last person to see Horace Wright alive. He disappeared right after the murder. Tommy has already interviewed the witness, a Mr. Teach who works at the Post Office. He says he saw you arguing with Horace Wright the day before he was killed."

Samson shook his head and looked at the floor. "That is what I find stranger than anything about all this," he said. "I never knew Horace Wright, and I certainly didn't argue with him, that day or any other day."

"But you were in the vicinity of the General Post Office?"

"I was, but quite by accident, Mr. Stone."

"What do you mean?" While he did not know Samson Light at all, Stone prided himself on being an excellent judge of character. He had defended guilty men, and he could tell they were guilty even when they insisted on their innocence. His instinct was that Samson Light was honest and forthright. He would certainly put him on the witness stand if it came to that.

"I received a note that morning at the hospital—"

"At St. Bart's?"

"At St. Bartholomew's, yes. I was working there very early that morning, going over a case I was operating on that afternoon. The note was from a patient who had left the hospital the week before, the last week of March. He had requested that I visit him at his sister's home in Friday Street, near where St. Matthew's church used to be."

"Did you walk or take a cab?"

"When the weather is fine, I always walk if I have time. So, I walked."

"So, you would have walked right past the front of the General Post Office on St. Martin's-le-Grande?"

"Yes, and I did. I visited my patient, Mr. Thirsk, in Friday Street, but it was getting late. So I caught a cab back to the hospital."

"What time did you pass in front of the Post Office?"

"It must have been around half past eight."

"Did you see Horace Wright as you passed the building?" Stone asked.

"I have no idea, Mr. Stone. I didn't even know what he looked like. I suppose it's possible, but I'm quite sure I didn't speak to anyone."

Stone caught a cab outside Clerkenwell Gaol. It was still raining, but now more of a cold drizzle than a real rain. As he returned to the Foreign Office for his four o'clock meeting with Arthur Otway, he thought about the peculiarities of this case. A victim found in a railway car for a line that was not yet in operation, an engineer who quickly resigned directly afterward, and an accused man who happened to be in the neighborhood of the murder scene. He was hoping to hear from young Tommy Jones again very soon. In the meantime, he pondered the presence of Fiona Harper in Clerkenwell Gaol. What was she doing there? Did she need help? Should he offer his services? And why was she working so closely with Samson Light?

After a full day of hauling bricks at the fever ward, Tommy was exhausted. He had spent his lunch time running back across the bridge to post his letters in Elvet Bridge, and had only been able to eat a penny loaf and a bite of cheese from a vendor in Market Square before returning for the long afternoon. But his agitation kept him going. He had discovered from Henderson how to find Donald Fowler. He lived in Neville Street, which was close to the work site, up a street just before the bridge. He'd been told that Fowler, if he was out at the Littleburn Colliery, was sure to return by seven that night. The two-and-a-half miles to town were covered by a cart owned by John Marley's company, the North Brancepeth Coal Company Limited. The cart carried the coal miners to the villages north of the mine where they were sinking the new shaft. Fowler was an engineer, Henderson told him, but he preferred riding in the cart with the miners to riding in a private carriage.

"He's not a gent and he's not a miner," Henderson said with some admiration, "but something in between. A working man, just with a bit more schooling than most of us." Hardly the profile of a murderer, thought Tommy.

At six Tommy had collected his two shillings and returned to the boarding house across the peninsula, washed, and changed his clothes. He was hungry and begged a bite of bread and cold meat from Widow Hutton.

"I only have you down for breakfast, young man," she said. "But I have hot cross buns from yesterday, since a lad needs to eat, even in Holy Week."

He'd eaten quickly and crossed back over the peninsula, down Crossgate a short ways and then down Neville Street to number seven. He knocked but there was no answer. A woman with a basket passed him, and he tipped his cap to her. She lowered her eyes and passed on. Three working men also passed him, heading for what he assumed was a pub near the bottom of the street. Maggie must be at the Market Hotel, since Saturday was a busy night. Many workers were paid on Saturday evening, and liked to celebrate the end of the week. Tommy waited patiently, thinking what he was going to say. He was nervous, but it wasn't like he could just blurt it out, ask Fowler if he was a killer or a witness. There wasn't really a good way to play this, as his old actor friend Cyril would say. Just say your lines plainly, speaking clearly. First, introduce yourself, then . . .

Tommy saw a man in a gentleman's hat walking slowly up the road with a black satchel over his shoulder, eyes to the ground, bushy black eyebrows drawn together in concentration. It occurred to Tommy that evening was drawing on, and he didn't want to appear like a footpad waiting for his victim. The pavement was narrow. He decided to stand a bit in the road so he could be seen clearly as Mr. Fowler approached the door.

"Mr. Fowler?"

Fowler looked up. His countenance was bland, but his brow was furrowed as if he'd been thinking hard. His mouth turned down at the corners as he answered. "Yes, young man?"

"I'm sorry to come upon you in the street, but I've come down from London to see you."

Fowler looked quizzical. "You mean up from London, surely."

"Oh," Tommy was embarrassed, "I was told that London was always up, because of the railway timetables."

Fowler frowned and took out his key. "Best come in then, whether you're up or down. I need to get my tea." He opened the heavy door and stepped over the narrow sill, pulling off his bag and putting it behind the door. The houses on Neville Street were all in a row, and the entrance was between the lower ground floor and the first floor, where Tommy assumed the bedrooms were. Considering for a moment, Tommy looked up the street to make sure there were people about in case he had to shout for help. It seemed a busy enough street. He was also fairly sure that he could defend himself if necessary. Fowler walked straight through to the kitchen, waving Tommy into a chair at the kitchen table. He then went through a door to the small yard out back, and Tommy heard rats scurry away from the rubbish bin. He saw a particularly large one go over the wall to the house next door, and shuddered. He thought rats were large in London, but up here in the clean air they seemed to grow huge.

Returning with some kindling, Fowler started a fire in the range and put the kettle on the hob. He opened the larder door and began making a plate of bread and butter, cheese, pickle, and cold ham. Tommy was surprised. He thought Fowler was just getting himself some tea.

"Looks like more than tea to me," he said in a friendly way, pleased that his voice held no obvious concern. "You must be hungry."

Fowler looked at him, and gave a sound between a grunt and a sigh. "London," he said with a scoff, "where tea is a drink. Here it's a meal, and yes, I'm hungry. Long day."

"I'm happy to wait," said Tommy, as Fowler put a china cup in front of him.

"Well, you'll have to. Goin' out back for a minute." Fowler went back out to the yard and across to the privy. Tommy looked around the kitchen, with its bright yellow curtains, scrubbed sink, and worn flagstone floor. There were little items on the shelves with the crockery: two small ceramic milkmaids with their cow, a thimble with blue flowers painted on it, and a tiny sheep made of wood with a real wool fleece. In the front room, there were three comfortable chairs arranged around the grate, and the carpet was thick and new. A vase of flowers was arranged on a table near the front window, next to a silver-framed ambrotype of a woman smiling kindly at the camera. Tommy looked closer and noticed she looked like an older version of Maggie.

In addition to the flowers, there was a candle next to the photograph, an envelope sealed with a wax "F", and a small silver ring. Tommy realized he was looking at a family shrine to Maggie's mother. She must have died very young, Tommy thought.

He turned back to the kitchen as Fowler returned, tucking his shirt into his trousers and going over to the sink to pump water, then wash his hands and face.

"I see you've found my dear Emmy," he said. "Died only two years ago. My daughter Maggie put those things out."

"Yes, the place has a woman's touch," said Tommy, coming back to sit at the table as Fowler poured the hot water into the teapot. Should he mention that he knew Maggie? It didn't seem the time for that yet.

"Would you like something for your tea?" Fowler asked, pushing the plate toward the middle of the table.

"No thank you. I ate my din . . . tea already." Poison seemed unlikely, but one couldn't be too careful. Fowler used a knife to butter a slice of bread, put a piece of ham on it, and took a bite as he looked at Tommy. About forty, Tommy thought. Strong, with a quick mind, but slow to speak, and perhaps slow to act. He looked at you like he was trying to figure out how you worked. He recalled Inspector Slaughter saying he had a sense, that he could tell what people were. This man was a hard-working family man.

"Right, lad, you didn't come up from London to watch me eat my tea. What do you want?" It was not said unkindly, but it was clear that now that he was ready, Fowler wanted to get to the point.

"Yes, sir—" Tommy began.

"I ain't no sir," said Fowler. "My name is Donald." He rose, poured the hot water over the leaves in the teapot, and brought it to the table.

"Donald—Mr. Fowler. I have come up from London because I have a friend, Samson Light, who is in trouble, and I think you can help."

"How could I help a friend in London?" Fowler's eyes narrowed.

"You see, he's in trouble because they think he killed Horace Wright, a clerk you might have known from the Post Office."

Fowler stopped chewing for a moment. His brow furrowed again, and then he nodded.

"They do, do they? Who's they?" He poured tea for himself and Tommy, then went back to eating. Tommy waited till Fowler took a sip from his own cup first.

"Well, the police. And a witness, who says he saw Horace arguing with Samson on the street the day before he was killed."

"What time?"

"About half past eight in the morning."

"Then that's wrong. I was at the Post Office that very morning because I was helping prepare the tracks at that end. I was out in front of the Post Office at half past because I was waiting for the cart to arrive with the grease and wax for the flanges. I didn't see any argument," Fowler said.

"This witness, Mr. Teach—"

Fowler scoffed so forcefully he almost choked on his bread. "Teach? He'd say anything to anyone. Weak-willed, Teach is. Always watching people to see if there's advantage to him. He should be more careful. The things I could tell you about Edward Teach!"

"You and Mr. Jenkins found Horace Wright's body in the rail car later that morning, is that right?"

"Yeah, that's right. Had to go back with the cart to 245 Holborn. It had brought the wrong delivery. Started oiling the door on the G.P.O. tunnel, and there he was in the car."

"Jenkins says he went up to report, but when he returned you were gone. He said the company got a letter saying you had gone here, to Durham."

For several minutes there was just the sound of Fowler chewing. He stared at Tommy as he ate, and Tommy fancied he could see the works going in his head. He was thinking what to say, how much to say, whether to say.

"I had work up here," he said. "Better work than London. Real engineering work."

"You weren't able to get real engineering work in London?"

"No." He looked down at his food. "Did it the wrong way. Got a degree at London University. Thought I'd be a degreed mechanical engineer, then I could set my own terms, and send money up to help Maggie."

"What happened?"

"The world didn't want my degree. They wanted men who had begun as boys, as apprentices, and learned the trade within the trade. Men who were sons of engineers. My father was a gamekeeper."

Tommy took a gamble with a direct question. "What made you leave right after Horace Wright was killed?"

Finished with his meal, Fowler rose to put the kettle back on. Then he stared out the window over the sink into the yard, his hands turned and pressing on his lower back.

"I was afraid I would be killed too if I stayed," said Fowler. "So I returned to Durham."

Tommy could see that Fowler had closed his lips and pursed them, as if he would say no more. He decided it was best to change the subject.

"When you decided to leave London, did you have a job waiting here?"

"I did," said Fowler. "I had been looking to leave, to return to Durham. The pay was good at the Pneumatic, but it was no true use of my talents, and living in London was too expensive. Saw an advertisement in the *Railway Times* for an engineer at Littleburn

Colliery and knew I could return to Maggie and make a decent living." He glanced over at the photograph. "Never did like leaving her here alone. Oh, she's fine at Mrs. Hoggett's—that woman could defend her boarders against anything. But it's Maggie . . . "

He paused and looked down with both pride and sadness, shaking his head.

"What about Maggie?" Tommy asked quietly.

"She wants more. Well, of course she wants more than she has," said Fowler, his palms up. "I mean she wants more than to be a good working woman, and a good wife someday. She wants—" he looked around as if someone might be listening, then lowered his voice and leaned in toward Tommy. "She wants to run her own tavern."

Tommy knew the surprise showed on his face. Widows ran taverns, but a young woman?

"I know, I know," said Fowler. "But why shouldn't she, if she wants to? She's got a good business sense, better than a lot of the men in this town."

He finished his tea and rose with a yawn.

"I'm off to bed, lad. It's been a long day."

Tommy had to agree. He felt sure Fowler wasn't a murderer, but he wanted to tell him he needed to come back to London to testify. He wanted to explain about Samson, and how much it mattered that he come. But the man was obviously exhausted, and there was so much more to discuss. Tommy had never been the sort to rush people; if you gave people the space to be kind, if you talked to them until they came upon the idea for themselves, people would go out of their way for you. If you pushed and poked, they would curl up and refuse to help. He still had time to talk with Mr. Fowler, and he needed the time anyway to earn enough for train fare back, for both of them.

Tommy said goodnight and left.

"If Sir Rowland Hill hadn't retired, hounded by those traditionalists, this might have been much easier," Faber grumbled to Wilson. If we'd been able to do what we promised ten years ago, Faber thought, this would have been easier too. When the company began selling shares, it had promised a pneumatic line running from St. Martin's-le-Grande. That was to be the first line, guaranteed to show that the entire idea was profitable. A decade later, that line was only now ready to open.

Dealings with the Post Office had been an unexpected and continual struggle. Although originally men of merit, the aristocrats serving as Postmaster General over the last decade had benefited from the office while doing little work. Sir Rowland, who had originated the penny post and was a man of vision, found it impossible to make improvements. He had extolled the virtues of connecting the communications systems of the nation, and had plans to do it, but they were ignored. The Duke of Bedford's refusal to allow the pneumatic line to run through his estate in Holborn had forced a costly detour, and the small first line between the Northwest Sorting Office at Eversholt and nearby Euston Station had saved neither time nor money before it was closed down.

"Naturally," said Faber, "it is an issue of class. Sir Rowland was the son of a schoolteacher, and had a mechanical bent. He worked at the assay office in Birmingham."

Wilson tried hard to look attentive, sitting at his desk with his pince-nez in place. He had heard all this before. Faber began pacing in front of his desk, his new boots tapping on the wood floor, as he warmed to his theme.

"The man invented the postage stamp, for heaven's sake. Rational, orderly development of knowledge resources—that was Sir Rowland's business. He won the Albert medal, what, six years ago? He was knighted! If those damned Conservatives—"

"But Mr. Faber," Wilson felt obliged to cut in, "several of the postmasters were Liberals."

"The wrong kind of Liberal, I tell you! Even my father couldn't have foreseen how the railway would change everything, but it has ..."

Wilson didn't need to hear the rest. He had worked for Faber for years before the Pneumatic Despatch Company, keeping the records for the vast network of newsstands and book stalls as Faber expanded his father's business. The secret of success, Wilson knew, was virtue. He respected that. Sir Rowland had been a virtuous man, hounded out of the job he did best. He must now be gardening or beekeeping or something in that Georgian house on Hampstead Green. And now Faber, who had combined a desire to sell books with a desire to eliminate the immoral volumes that sold so well on street corners, was trying to bring worthwhile books to the masses. He'd stocked cheap paperbound books with distinctive black and white covers to make sure the reading public had something morally uplifting or amusing to encounter on their way to Birmingham or Edinburgh. Wilson himself had a copy of *The Adventures of Mr. Verdant Green* hidden in his desk and was enjoying it immensely. His admiration for his employer was great, but that didn't mean he enjoyed the tirades. He found them rather self-important.

"Well, never mind," grumbled Faber. "The company shall continue. We shall open that line. Please send a note to Mr. Henry at the General Post Office. Ask that he be prepared to start the engines within a fortnight. It's time we got that line opened."

"Yes, sir. Shall I have the boy wait for a reply?"

Faber grimaced. "No, no. We're telling him, not asking him."

"There was someone there, Jo," said Hortense quietly as they rode home in the cab after Easter service. "I'm sure there was."

"And you think he was watching you?" Jo whispered. Sally's head was in her lap, and she was fast asleep.

"I could feel it. I didn't see anyone, but . . . I don't know how to explain it."

Jo reached over and patted her hand. Hortense looked so lovely today in her Sunday best, the deep blue dress setting off her golden hair. No one could see the padding underneath, where she had tied the cloths against herself. Jo had designed the undergarment for her, in the shape of an hourglass with ties on the side that were easily concealed at the waistline.

Was it possible that loss of blood could cause delusions? Jo wondered. Hortense had been a little nervous lately, but she assumed that was because of the decision she needed to make. The question of whether or not to have surgery could certainly occupy the mind. But a few days ago, Hortense had mentioned this feeling of being watched, and Jo was becoming worried for her state of mind.

"There were so many people at St. John's for the services," said Jo, trying to sound reassuring. "And surely everyone was watching everyone to see what they would be wearing." Sally had certainly been entertained by all the different styles of dress: the older women still wearing crinolines, the young women with hanks of hair looped over their ears, the new styles with the skirt scooped up into a bunch at the back, and the soft spring colors for jackets and hats.

When they arrived home, Jo put on the kettle for tea while Hortense carried Sally upstairs to continue her nap. The afternoon was warm, and Jo took off her cotton jacket and hung it on the peg, then began tidying the kitchen. The water boiled, the tea was made, but Hortense had not yet come down. Jo went upstairs and found Hortense, her hat removed but still in her Sunday best, lying next to Sally on the bed, fast asleep. Jo gently removed her shoes and crept back down to the kitchen.

She had just sat down at the table with her tea when there was a knock at the kitchen door. It couldn't be a tradesman on Easter Sunday, she thought. Outside stood a large man with blond hair and a round, eager face. His cheeks were red, and his full lips wore a gentle smile as he stood with his hat in his hand.

"Excuse me, miss," he said to Jo. "I've come hoping to see Mrs. Smith—Hortense—if I may?"

"She's asleep," said Jo. She was unsure whether to invite him in or ask him to return. "May I tell her you called?"

The man grinned, puffing out his chest and hooking his thumbs in his cherry-red braces. "Yes, miss, tell him her husband called. Name of George Smith."

"Oh!" said Jo, her hand flying to her chest.

The man looked sheepish and wiped his palms on his shiny frock coat. "I don't want to wake her, and maybe it's best she's asleep, so you can tell her I'm back from Australia. I can return this evening to speak with her, if that suits?"

Jo swallowed hard. "Yes, that would be fine. Later."

"I'll return at seven o'clock. But, miss, may I leave something here? I have to go back to St. Katherine's Dock, and I think the poor creatures could do with some quiet." He leaned over to the side of the door and took up two wooden boxes with handles and wire screening on the sides. Jo could hear shuffling sounds inside them.

"You have cats?"

"No, miss. They're not cats. They're Australian animals," he said proudly. Jo said nothing, but peeking into the smaller box saw a furry animal with white spots.

"Have you a bit of cold meat, by any chance?" Smith asked, putting the boxes down on the floor.

Jo found a piece of cold mutton in the larder next to the sink and gave it to him. He pushed it through the wire of the smaller box, and she could hear the animal eating.

"What is it?" Jo asked quietly.

"It's a quoll, miss. But don't let him out. Sharp teeth and claws, he has. Doesn't like being awake like this in the daytime. This one," he said, pointing to the larger box, "is a quokka. Don't worry about her—I put some grass in there with her."

He picked up the boxes again.

"If you just put them under here" —he put them under the table in the corner—"they'll be fine until I return."

Jo realized she was standing with her mouth open for several minutes after he left.

It was Easter Sunday, so much of Durham was at the cathedral. Tommy, embarrassed that his Sunday clothes were quite scruffy, arrived early.

In London, it had always been Tommy who wanted to go to church. At first, Inspector Slaughter and his wife Ellie had taken him, hoping to instill some religious morality after his years of living on the streets and in the workhouse. His father had been in prison then for stealing opium to help his mother, who had died when he was four. They knew his parents weren't criminals, and even if they had been, neither believed that such traits were passed down. But they also knew that Tommy had lived a life deprived of stability and a familial moral code. Although not regular churchgoers themselves, they took him to services to help him adjust to his new life.

It had been utterly unnecessary. Cuthbert and Ellie Slaughter quickly learned that Tommy had a strong sense of right and wrong, and his moral judgements were sound even at nine years old. But Tommy had loved going to church. He felt uplifted by the ceremony and the words, hearing them said and repeated by those around him. Whenever he'd felt bad or unfocused, he had taken himself to a service and felt much better.

The cathedral service was no different from other Easter services, but the surroundings were extraordinary. The Slaughters had attended Christchurch in Southwark, a building with two stories and a tower. While it had been large and impressive to a boy, it was small and cramped compared to the space enclosed by Durham Cathedral's carved pillars and pointed windows. You could drive a dozen carts down the nave, Tommy thought as he walked down the side aisle. It wouldn't begin to fill the space. He'd arrived early to walk around the building. The canon seemed surprised when Tommy asked permission.

"Of course, young man," he said with an open smile, "just walk quietly near St. Cuthbert's tomb. There are people praying there." He had pointed toward the far end of the cathedral, behind the altar. Tommy walked back that way, marveling at the stonework and the light that fell softly through the windows onto the curved arches and stone floor. He crossed the transept and walked past the effigy of a bishop until he came to a small flight of steps leading up to St. Cuthbert's tomb. He stepped in quietly.

A silken blue cloth covered the tomb, with bells on its edges. Tommy assumed they would make a lovely sound when the cover was removed. The floor was green stone, and there were two women and an old man kneeling and praying, the old man holding his staff to keep him steady. If Tommy had been a true believer in God's intervention, he might have prayed too, because the mood in the space was deeply spiritual. Instead he appreciated the calmness, sanctity, and beauty. If there was a divine presence, he thought, surely it was here. He walked through quietly and went down the steps on the other side.

When he got back around to the nave, the canon was directing worshipers to take a seat, and he chose one on the aisle. Tommy could see a priest in the transept pulling on bell ropes, but he couldn't hear the bell itself deep inside the stone cathedral. The clergy and choir entered, and the service began, with songs of praise and the glory of the resurrection. Tommy's favorite part had always been the Glory Be:

Glory be to the Father, and to the Son, and to the Holy Ghost;
As it was in the beginning, is now, and ever shall be, world without end.
Amen.

He loved the idea of a world without end. Tommy knew many of the hymns, although the tunes were somewhat different than he was used to, and as he listened, he looked at the people in the rows in front of him. He saw rough-looking men with pale faces who were obviously miners come into town. There were gentlemen in elegant coats with their wives and well-dressed children. Most of them rose when it was their turn to go up the nave to take communion. Tommy shuffled out of the row to let them pass but did not go up himself. He knew what communion was supposed to be but had never participated. With his strong belief in science and rationality, he considered himself worthy to witness but unworthy to take the wafer.

When the service was over, most worshipers headed for the big doors, but several groups were leaving by the side door into the cloister. Tommy followed them and was stopped by the beauty of the space. The cloister was a square of green grass, surrounded by perfect arches. He could see the tower of the cathedral above, and could now hear the bells. To the right at the end of the walk was a doorway. Clergymen were leaving through there, so he assumed their dwellings must be that direction. Instead he walked all the way around the cloister, noting the shift of the light. He sat for a moment, reflecting. He had been here three days now and had not yet told Donald Fowler what he needed to tell him. Would he come with him back to London? He didn't seem a fearful man, but the risk to his life could be real. And what about Maggie? As Tommy watched the rays of light come into the cloister, he imagined her face. It showed her strength and her humor, and the more he thought about it, the more he knew that he wanted her. Not like the girls he'd been out with for an evening or two in London, but in a different way. He sighed. How could love come upon one so quickly? It didn't seem possible.

The cloister was quiet now, and he re-entered the cathedral, crossing by the baptismal font to go out onto Palace Green. The bells were still pealing, and groups of people were crossing the Green, some going downward toward the river, others into Durham Castle, which was now a university college. Most were heading down Owengate to Saddler Street. By now Tommy knew this was the way to Market Square, so he followed them. At the bottom of Saddler Street he looked up toward the square and saw Donald Fowler coming down the hill toward him. Now was the time.

"Hello, Mr. Fowler," said Tommy, "and a happy Easter to you."

"And to you, lad," said Fowler. "Would you like to have a beer together?" His usually taciturn face held an open, happy expression, and Tommy suspected he'd had a beer or two already.

Tommy agreed, and he assumed they were going to the Market Hotel, but Fowler continued to walk down the hill toward Elvet Bridge, and Tommy turned around to follow. They walked in silence across the bridge to Old Elvet, passing by people strolling in their Sunday best clothes, a market stand selling hot cross buns, and several pubs before they arrived at the Dun Cow Inn.

"No better place on Easter Sunday," said Fowler. "The race is tomorrow, and it's the closest pub to the racecourse."

They entered to find the pub full of working families, many of them arguing over horses. Tommy saw a woman drawing a horse on a piece of paper, trying to convince her companions that the length of the nag's neck meant it didn't have a chance. In the corner a group of men in top hats were conferring over listings.

"Odds, betting forms, calculations," shouted Fowler to Tommy over the din. "Getting ready for tomorrow. I never get to go, but oh—the excitement!"

There was a passage through the pub, and Tommy followed Fowler to the back garden where there were quite a few people but a little less noise.

"You stay here," he said, pointing to the only empty table, "and I'll be back."

Tommy sat unnoticed and listened to the people talking around him. What was the best way to tell Fowler what he needed him to do? Just explain the problem, he heard Inspector Slaughter say in his head. Give him a chance to be helpful.

Fowler returned with two large glasses of beer, and put one in front of Tommy.

"I'm on my own today," he said. "So I'm happy to buy you one. Most of the men I know as friends live near the mine, so I'd be quite lonely here if it weren't for Maggie. Glad I ran into you."

Tommy saw his opening. He took a sip and said, "Yes, friends are important."

Fowler took a large gulp and nodded. "Always know where you stand with friends. You must have some in London."

Tommy nodded. "I do. I have a very special friend named Samson. He was my tutor. I think I mentioned him to you before."

"Oh, that's right. You told me about him. The one accused of killing Mr. Wright." Fowler looked thoughtful, his brow furrowed. "What's going to happen to him?"

"Well, he'll hang, I expect. Unless someone comes forward with evidence."

"What sort of evidence?"

"Testimony. For example, the fact that you didn't see the argument they're saying happened between Mr. Wright and Samson."

"Can't testify about something I didn't see," Fowler pointed out.

Tommy nodded, took a sip, and sat quietly.

"I do think Horace knew something, though," said Fowler. "He was worried about the carriages."

Tommy's mug stopped halfway to his mouth. "Why was he worried?" He tried to sound casual, as if this were just a normal conversation.

"The seals. They leaked, he told me. The system wasn't going to work. The railway couldn't go fast enough because you couldn't get a proper vacuum where the car attached to the track. He asked if I could solve that."

"What did you tell him?"

"I told him the truth. There wasn't a way to solve it with that design. It would always leak. And the managers didn't care."

"You told the managers?"

"No, Horace did. He told Mr. Henry, for one. Henry told him not to worry about it. I didn't worry myself, because by then I knew

this job was here for me and I'd be leaving. Then when he was killed
. . ."

"You thought you were next?"

Fowler nodded, slowly, looking down at his beer.

"Can't prove anything, mind. It seems ridiculous, my foolish fancy. Mr. Henry couldn't kill anybody."

"Perhaps," Tommy said carefully, "if you came with me to London to testify . . ."

Fowler looked up at him. His bushy eyebrows moved up and down as he considered the situation. Then his eyes narrowed. "That's why you're here," he said. "You want to bring me back to London."

Tommy waited a moment. Some people at the next table were laughing over the prospects of one of the horses in tomorrow's race.

"I do, Mr. Fowler," he said earnestly. "It may be the only way to save my friend."

7

Hortense awoke with a start, her arm numb from Sally sleeping on it. If she'd slept for less than an hour, she'd be able to help Jo prepare dinner. She sat up, then stood and groggily made her way into the bedroom to change out of her Sunday clothes and into a more practical day dress. The clock said it was only four. At least she hadn't slept the afternoon away.

After some time in the bathroom to clean herself up and change the stained cloths, she came down to the kitchen. From the doorway she saw Jo putting the turnips in the oven, opening the range door slowly. It was obvious she was trying to be quiet. Hortense shuffled her feet a little so as not to startle her.

"Oh good, you're awake," said Jo.

Hortense could tell something was wrong. Jo's expression looked like it did after they'd had an argument: proud, angry, and frustrated underneath a smooth exterior.

"What's wrong?"

Jo harrumphed, blowing strands of hair upward off her face.

"Let me get you some tea," Jo said, pulling a chair out, "then we can talk."

Hortense sat down, noticing the boxes. "What are those?"

There was a scratching sound inside one of the boxes, then it stopped. "I'll get to that," said Jo, fixing the tea.

Hortense waited patiently as Jo moved assuredly about the kitchen. She brought over the teapot, milk, and sugar, then shoved one of the boxes over with her foot so there was room to sit at the table. There was a small snuffle of protest from the box.

"Take a sip first. For fortitude," ordered Jo. Hortense did as she was told.

Jo then told her about George Smith, watching Hortense's eyes grow rounder and rounder. She finished by explaining the content of the boxes.

"So they both start with a Q, but I can't remember the names, only that the one in the big box eats leaves and doesn't drink much water, and the one in the small box has teeth and claws and eats meat."

Hortense didn't even glance at the boxes. She had not caught up to Jo.

"George was here?"

"Yes, he was here."

"Is he all right?"

"Yes, he looked all right to me. Of course, I've never met him."

"Did he say what he wanted?"

"Only for us to hold the animals until he returned this evening."

A minute passed. Hortense took another sip, then looked up, her eyes moist.

"Oh Jo," she said, "whatever will we do?"

Jo had been thinking about that, and what they could do, in a practical sense. They could tell him to go away, but he had a legal right to be there—he had been away less than seven years. They could hide that they were a family now, but Sally was there and he'd have to be told he was her father. They could pretend Jo was the maid, or just a friend. The very idea made Jo furious and, she admitted, frightened. While Hortense had slept, she had come to the conclusion that all that mattered was what Hortense wanted.

"What do you want to do?"

Hortense sat still for a long time, not speaking, sipping her tea, then she said, "Please fetch me the mending."

Jo brought the mending basket and put it on the table. Hortense took the sock off the top of the basket, got out the darning needle, and prepared to darn the sock. Doing something with her hands always helped Hortense to focus. She darned and thought, darned and thought. They sat together, listening to the rustling sounds in the animal boxes and the further sounds of footfalls in the street. Hortense finished the first sock and looked up at Jo.

"What I want is for everything to stay just as it is. You, me, and Sally are a family. I loved George once, but he left. If he's returned a reasonable man, I'll just have to make him understand he isn't wanted. Or that he is wanted, but not as my husband. And I won't tend to strange animals."

Jo was about to answer when she heard Sally's voice. She was singing to herself upstairs.

"I'd best fetch her down," Jo said, and went up to Sally's bedroom.

"Come on, little one. Time for tea." Sally blinked, her cheeks pink from napping.

"Cake?" she said. Jo sat Sally up, removed her church dress, and pulled on the pinafore and apron that was hanging on the bedstead.

"No cake. Too close to dinner. But you may have an extra lump of sugar in your tea if you like."

Jo helped Sally negotiate the stairs. She thought it was better for the child to practice steps, rather than be carried up and down. Sally immediately saw the animal boxes and rushed over to look at the bigger of the two. Jo grabbed for the hand that reached toward the screening.

"No touching, young lady," she said. "Those are special animals, and they bite."

"Hot?" Sally asked, her face serious as she looked up at Jo.

"Hot," Jo nodded. Sally put her hands in her apron pockets and sat next to the box, looking in. The quokka raised its head and looked back at her, curious. Jo put Sally's cup of tea next to her on the floor, moving her chair so she could keep an eye on the child.

"Do you want me to be here when he returns?" Jo asked Hortense. "I could take Sally out for a walk, if it's still light out."

Hortense blinked. "I'm not sure. Did he seem angry?"

"Not at all. He seemed quite amiable, to judge from his expression. A bit puffed up, a bit pleased with himself. But amiable."

"That does sound like George," Hortense agreed.

They had their tea, Sally's plate with bread and butter put on the floor so she could watch the animal. Jo had turned the smaller box away from Sally, just in case, but Sally seemed quite content watching the quokka. She was whispering to the animal, and they could overhear "You're good kitty, not hot."

After dinner, they stayed in the kitchen as the light changed to lavender and the street became quieter. They could hear the clock ticking in the parlor, and several times Hortense got up to check the time. Shortly before seven, there was a knock at the kitchen door. Sally scrambled to her feet. "Knock, knock, Mummy."

Jo got up to open the door. George stood there looking a little more tired but with the same smile. He looked over Jo's shoulder and saw Hortense, and his grin widened. He took off the satchel he was carrying over his shoulder and put it on the floor near the door.

"There you are, love," he said. Jo opened the door wider and gestured toward the chair. George scraped his boots and came in.

"Your friend here," he looked over at Jo and she nodded, "told me you were sleeping." Then he saw Sally. Jo had thought his smile couldn't get any bigger, but she'd been wrong. Instead of taking a seat, he crouched on the floor next to Sally, careful to keep some distance so he wouldn't frighten her.

"I'm George," he said quietly, and held out his hand.

Sally looked over at Hortense, who gave her a little smile.

"I'm Sally," she said, and took one of his big fingers in her hand, then pulled it back. "Ruff," she said.

"I'm sorry, Sally. My hands are rough because I do hard work. I've been on a ship."

Sally looked puzzled. "A big ship?"

"A very big ship." He stood then and looked at Hortense. "Is she . . . ?" Hortense nodded. George sat down rather harder than he had intended.

Rule number thirteen at the Middlesex House of Detention was that all prisoners were to attend Divine Services regularly, unless excused. Any prisoner not a member of the Established Church could be visited by a clergyman of their own faith on Sundays.

Samson had chosen not to exercise the option. He was not a member of any synagogue and did not know a rabbi. He had married Prudence in the Clerkenwell Register Office, so they hadn't had to worry about such things. She had lived in Clerkenwell with her mother long enough that the waiting period wasn't burdensome, and the cost had been minimal. They had not been to church together before. But there had been rumors that the Easter Services in the gaol was special, and that all were expected to attend, the men's service at 10 a.m. and the women's at 11 o'clock. Unusually, each prisoner could invite one family member to attend the services with them, so Prudence had arrived early, well before 10 a.m.

Since all prisoners walking through corridors had to maintain strict silence, family members were awaiting them in the chapel, which was situated near the governor's office and other staff rooms between the male and female wings. Everyone was given only a few minutes to greet their loved ones, then the service began. Warders kept a close eye on the impromptu congregation from the aisles.

Samson and Pru sat with their hands clasped, the Book of Common Prayer in Prudence's lap.

"Any news?" asked Samson in a whisper so quiet that even those seated next to them couldn't hear.

"Tommy is trying to convince Fowler to come to London, but other than that, no. Here?"

"Perseverance Stone came here yesterday."

After they stood to participate in the creed, Samson continued.

"I told him about how I visited Mr. Thirsk in Friday Street, and that my walk that morning was the only time I was in front of the Post Office."

"So why would anyone say you argued with this man if you didn't?"

Samson shrugged, then they bowed their heads for silent prayer.

As the sermon began, Prudence whispered, "I need to go talk to this supposed witness."

"No!" said Samson, rather too loudly. The couple sitting next to them said, "Shhh!"

"Pru, it could be dangerous," he said more quietly. "You mustn't."

The priest continued his lecture. "Now for those of us here today, resurrection is close to our hearts. We must cast aside the elements that connect us to wrongdoing, and vow to do right. For the innocent, this is a test, and God will prevail. For the guilty, a chance to confess and repent—"

Samson had uncharitable thoughts, wondering whether the sermon was designed to elicit confessions from the prisoners.

"What does it mean that Christ is risen? Does it mean that we are all to be made immortal, as He is? No, it does not. His divine gift, his sacrifice, was to make it possible for men to see their sins forgiven, to be at the hand of God after they have left this world."

Prudence whispered again. "I must do something. I could at least find out what this Inspector Morgan knows."

Samson shook his head vigorously and heard a harrumph of distaste from the pew behind them.

"Stone will see Morgan this week," he said. "He told me."

The sermon was concluded and the congregation rose for the hallelujahs. Samson could not help thinking that in a literal sense, the resurrection made no sense. The dead could not rise. The important thing was to keep them from becoming dead in the first place, a goal to which he had dedicated his life.

As the service finished, the governor rose and gave instructions. All prisoners were to say goodbye quickly and return to their cells in silence after being checked by the warders to make sure they had not been given anything untoward by their family. All visitors were to leave by the front entrance. The usual visiting hours of noon till two on weekdays would continue in force.

Samson grasped Prudence's hands and looked into her eyes. "Pru, for goodness sake, don't put yourself in any danger," he pleaded. "Stone will help, Tommy will convince this Mr. Fowler to come talk to the police. But I couldn't bear it if anything happened to you."

"All right," said Pru, wanting to quell the worry in his eyes. "But may I go to see Perseverance Stone, to talk with him?"

"Yes, of course," said Samson, considering this a safe option compared to encountering anyone at the Post Office or police station.

As she left the House of Detention with the other family members, the sun was just coming out from behind clouds that had threatened rain that morning. Pru decided to consider that a good omen.

Perseverance Stone sat by the fire in his study, trying to think before going up to bed. If Tommy was unable to get Fowler to come to London to testify, he would need much more to help Samson Light. Unable to find time to lay out the case on paper, Stone was well aware he had not been able to do so in his mind. This would not do at all.

"May I fetch you something to drink?" Mason asked.

"No, I don't think so," said Stone, staring into the fire.

Mason was familiar with his master's moods. He knew the work for Otway had been difficult and absorbing, but something was clearly causing consternation.

"Would it be Mr. Otway's work on your mind, sir?"

"No, Mason, it wouldn't." The two men knew each other well. Mason had been assigned to Stone's childhood home as a footman when both of them were sixteen. Mason had served the household, and Stone had little contact with him unless he was home from boarding school. As they had both gotten older and Stone had undertaken to study law, Mason had ascended through the household. But the household butler was also young, in his thirties, so there was no room for Mason to advance. It was decided that he should become valet to Perseverance Stone once he began his law practice, and he had become attached to Stone's new home in Gate Street. When Mason later fell in love with a stage actress, Stone's family was shocked, but Perseverance had encouraged Mason to marry if he wished and create a life of his own. The couple had lived happily together for a decade; Mason had worked at an agency, interviewing young men seeking positions in service. But Elizabeth had died giving birth to their first child. The baby had not survived either, and when the request for a butler from Mr. Perseverance Stone, Esquire, came across Mason's desk at the agency, he interviewed for the position himself. Stone had been delighted. As confirmed bachelors, the arrangement suited both men perfectly.

Certainly an outsider might be critical. It was unusual for a manservant to have as many days off as Mason enjoyed, or the opportunity to educate himself, which Stone had encouraged. The second-best bedroom in the house was his, rather than a servant's room. Unusual also was that all other staff, including the cook and housekeeper, lived out. Stone preferred a calm and quiet house, and Mason enjoyed cooking. While they had maintained many of the typical formalities between servant and master, personal boundaries were crossed more often than would be comfortable in many comparable homes.

Stone nodded toward the other chair, encouraging his butler to join him by the fire.

"I've had a letter from Tommy Jones, Mason. He has found Donald Fowler, but the man refuses to come to London to testify. He's hoping he can convince him, since there is still some time."

"Yes, sir. This is the man who found the body in the pneumatic rail car?"

"Yes. And according to Tommy, he did not witness any argument that morning, nor had he ever seen Samson Light. The prosecution's line will likely focus on that argument. Fowler also called into question the veracity of Edward Teach, the witness who saw the argument. And he's mentioned Horace Wright was worried, something to do with the pneumatic railway mechanism."

Mason listened and thought for a few moments.

"I assume there is an investigating police officer handling this case?" he asked.

"Yes, Inspector Morgan at St. Giles."

"But surely the body was found in the City?"

"Morgan has taken a special interest in the case. I've no idea why."

"Has he discovered anything helpful?"

"If he has, he has not informed me. In fact, now that I think on it, he has not communicated with me at all. It was Tommy who went to see him before he left for Durham."

"I've seen nothing in the newspapers either, sir."

The crackling of the fire was becoming quieter, and Stone was getting sleepy.

"Perhaps you should eschew some of the services you're providing to Mr. Otway, sir, and consider a visit to Inspector Morgan."

"Yes, you're right. Thank you, Mason." Stone rose with resolution, stretching his back as he stood. "Remind me in the morning to send a note to the Foreign Office. I must go see Inspector Morgan."

After he had gone upstairs, the butler broke up the fire so it could die down, checked the draperies, then went down to make sure the kitchen was in order for morning. He secured the front door and took himself off to bed.

Shaking his head slowly, George Smith was smiling as he looked at little Sally sitting on the floor next to the quokka's box. Jo glanced at Hortense, then at the food cooking on the range, and raised her eyebrow, receiving a barely perceptible nod.

"Mr. Smith, would you join us for dinner?" Jo asked.

George looked up from staring at Sally. "Well, that's very kind, miss, but are you sure you have enough food?"

"Quite sure. And perhaps after we eat, I can take Sally for a walk so you two can talk." Hortense gave Jo a grateful look.

George agreed readily and helped pull out the table from the wall to make room for four.

"Sally, love," said George. "Come sit at the table with your mum and Jo. Then we can all eat together."

Sally considered for a moment, then her blonde curls nodded as she got to her feet and went over to the tap at the kitchen sink. She turned to George, raised her arms and said, "Up?"

George lifted her so she could reach the tap and helped her wash her hands, then set her down and washed his own. He sat down with a quick smile to Hortense, pleased to be helping out. Jo saw the expression on Hortense's face, a look that combined exasperation with resignation and a bit of humor. It was the look of someone who knows the other person well, their foibles and their triumphs. Jo felt a lump form in her throat as she served the ham, turnips, and greens, cutting up Sally's portion into small pieces and separating the three different foods on the plate. There was a scratching sound from the larger box. Sally's eyes got bigger, but Jo just smiled at her.

"So, George," said Hortense, "How is it you have these animals?"

"Well, I'll tell you. I was in Australia, about starving to death in the Gold Fields. There were so many men there with knowledge and equipment, and some of them were right vicious. My fortune would not be made there. I was in Walhalla, a growing town in Victoria, and it had a Free Library. So I went there to read the newspapers and look through the books. Trying to decide what was best." He chewed thoughtfully.

"Did you find anything?" Jo asked politely.

"No, not at first. But I met a man there, doing the same thing. Small man, with spectacles. He read in the newspaper about Charles Jamrach, who'd been bringing exotic animals to London for menageries and the zoological gardens. You may have heard of it, the one in Regent's Park?"

Hortense and Jo knew the zoo well. Jo had been escorted there by Dante Gabriel Rossetti when they first became friends, and she and Hortense had taken Sally twice.

"So this man, Mr. Green, figured that might be the way to make a fortune, find exotic animals and bring them back. We'd seen a few outside of town, strange birds and jumping wallabies up in the rocks above the town. Mr. Green knew another man, a naturalist, who was collecting for some rich people back home. The three of us formed a partnership and began finding animals."

Sally wasn't listening but was quietly glancing at the animal boxes, which had been placed near the sink. After they had finished eating, Jo cleared the dishes and asked Sally if they shouldn't get their coats to go for a walk.

"Raining?" asked Sally, wrinkling her nose. She did not like the rain.

Jo looked out the window over the sink. "No, just a lovely sunset." Sally nodded and got down off her chair by turning her belly to the seat and hanging her feet down until they touched the floor. Jo took her hand and they walked upstairs to get their coats.

Out on the street, the spring light was fading, but it would be a while yet before dark. They walked hand in hand, slowly.

"Jo?" Sally asked, "Is that man a fizzy-shan?"

Jo was perplexed. "A what?"

"A fizzy-shan, like when we saw the fire wagon."

Jo realized that Sally thought that since they'd left her mother alone with him, he must be a doctor.

"No, he's not a physician." She was at a loss to say what he was.

"Will he make mummy feel better?"

"I'm not sure, but that isn't why he's here. He's a friend from before I met your mum, from before you were born." Sally's eyes widened to think of a time so long ago. "So," Jo said, "they have much to talk about."

They walked along in silence. A couple passed them, saw Sally, and smiled at Jo. They think I am the child's mother, thought Jo, and in a sense I am. She picked up Sally to cross the busy road toward Clerkenwell Green, a space large enough to have staged workers' protests. Then they walked together to the church, with its tall square tower. As they often did, they found a spot to sit on the steps to watch the people in Clerkenwell Close. But even with her nap, Sally soon tired of their outing, and Jo carried her most of the way back to the house.

She was trying to decide whether to knock or make some other noise at the kitchen door before entering, but Sally wriggled down and pushed open the door. Hortense and George were sitting where they'd been before at the kitchen table, but now their heads were closer together as they talked quietly. When Hortense raised her head to welcome them, Jo saw a glassiness in Hortense's eyes, as if she were about to cry, but she was smiling.

Sally ran up to her mother and crawled up in her lap.

"Jo," said Hortense with a catch in her throat, "thank you for taking Sally for a walk."

Jo bristled a little at that, as if she didn't always take Sally for outings, then felt she was being petty.

"How did you two get on?" she asked, trying to keep her voice even and friendly.

Hortense didn't answer the question. "Jo, I'd like George to stay with us for a little while. He's in a bit of a fix with accommodations at the moment."

Jo opened her mouth, then shut it again. A bit of a fix? That didn't sound like Hortense. George caught her expression and rose.

"It will be all right, miss," he said with a gentle smile. "I won't be any trouble. It's just for a fortnight, perhaps less. You see, I brought the animals all this way, and then Mr. Jamrach . . ." Jo heard little of his explanation, something about bringing the animals but the dealer had not yet returned from India, other animals and birds were housed somewhere near St. Katherine's Dock—she didn't catch it all.

"And I've gotten some temporary work. I went up to the West Central Post Office to see if they had any jobs, and an old friend there told me the Pneumatic Despatch Railway Company needed a man. So I'll be at 245 Holborn and bring in a bit of money, then I'll get paid for the animals, and it will all be all right."

Jo doubted very much it would all be all right, but Hortense looked calm and not in the least put out.

"I'll make up a bed in the parlor," she said, and retreated from the kitchen as quickly as she could.

"What on earth is Fiona Harper doing in Clerkenwell Gaol?" asked Perseverance Stone. He was in Otway's office after a particularly difficult meeting with the Prussian ambassador. The room was damp, but the fire was helping and so was the brandy.

"Damned confusing, talking to Bernstorff," grumbled Otway, pacing in front of his desk. "My secretary doesn't know how to address correspondence. Is he the North German Confederation ambassador, or the Prussian ambassador?"

"I don't think he knows himself, Arthur," soothed Stone, seated in the leather wingback chair. "When he criticized Bismarck last year, we thought we were going to lose his company altogether. You've worked well with him and should be glad he's still in the position, whatever that position is."

"True, true," conceded Otway. "Treaty of London and all that. But even agreeing to the independence of Luxembourg does not mean that Prussia doesn't intend to create a larger and greater Germany. It does, or certainly Bismarck does. He's got the Kaiser eating out of his hand. They might be a threat to us, or they might be our best bulwark against Russia. There's the rub."

Stone stifled a yawn. Despite his willingness to help the government, he was not a political man. Both Germany and Russia seemed likely candidates to threaten Britain, but he had every confidence in the navy to prevent any incursion on British soil.

International relationships seemed to involve a great deal of sharp practice, in which Stone had little interest. He sipped his brandy and tried to return Otway to the subject.

"Fiona Harper. I was asking you about her."

"Oh yes," Otway waved his hand as if she were a secondary consideration. "She's working for us, of course. Well, the War Office anyway."

"In Clerkenwell? Are there foreign influences at the gaol? The Fenians again?" Three years ago Irish republicans had created a gunpowder explosion, blowing a hole in the wall at Clerkenwell in order to free the imprisoned Richard Burke. He'd been remanded for arming Fenians in Birmingham and was awaiting a trial for treason. Even now some referred to the incident as the Clerkenwell Outrage, and the result had been popular feeling against the Irish.

"No, no," said Otway, waving his hand again. "Damned Fenians. That's all done now." He looked up as if suddenly realizing Stone was still there. "Can't talk about her current mission, I'm afraid. Sorry, old man."

Interesting, thought Stone. He didn't necessarily expect to be taken into Otway's confidence, but he had hoped for more of a hint than that.

"I'd like to help her with the forgery charge, after what she accomplished in Kashgaria. That Yakub Beg was nothing more than a warlord, plain and simple."

Otway stared at him for a moment, then guffawed, a loud sound in the quiet room.

"Attracted, are you? Good man. Means you're healthy." Stone sat up a little straighter, pulling his waistcoat down and trying not to look perturbed by Otway's suggestion. "Dinna fash yourself, as the Scots say. We'll see that she gets what she deserves."

On the way back to his home, Stone began to worry about Tommy Jones. He had been gone awhile. It occurred to him he should have given him some money, but Tommy had left before he had the chance to offer. An enterprising lad, thought Stone. He might make a good lawyer. Stone lived next door to his office in

Gate Street and was just about to put his key in the door when Mason opened it for him.

"Good evening, sir." He took Stone's hat and coat. "A mild evening, sir."

"Yes, I suppose it is. I hadn't noticed."

"You have been occupied. I have hot stew on the stove, and your smoking jacket laid out on your bed. Your correspondence is on your desk." Mason bowed only slightly, then went back toward the kitchen.

"Thank you," mumbled Stone, his head still fuzzy from one too many brandies with Otway. He went upstairs, splashed some water on his face, and changed into his slippers and house jacket. Mason insisted on calling it a smoking jacket even though Stone didn't smoke. It was, Stone thought, an unpleasant habit, both for the smoker and those around him. Goodness knows there was enough smoke in London already.

His desk at home was small and tidy, particularly when compared to the one next door in his office. Three letters lay on the blotter. The first was from his sister, informing him of a garden party she was planning for June. He was expected to be there, and he hoped he wouldn't have to disappoint her again. The next was a bill from his tailor, along with an apology for the tardiness of the cravats he had been making. The third looked like a letter, but was actually an advertisement for a stationer's shop. Clever that, thought Stone.

"I can't leave Durham now," said Donald Fowler. Tommy had greeted him again on Neville Street that evening and was again seated in his kitchen. The races were over, but neither had been able to attend with Fowler at Littleburn Colliery and Tommy working at the fever ward. "It's the miners, you see."

"Something is happening with the miners?"

"Yes. They are just starting to organize into the Durham Miners' Association. Met up in the Market Hotel last November, and now we have members from twenty-eight collieries."

"What kind of association?"

Fowler nodded. "It's a co-operative, or a workers' union. The wages have gone up the past few years, but the work is more dangerous."

"Why more dangerous?"

"More and more digging into seams that appear to have tapped out but have more underneath. Deeper shafts with more flooding. More firedamp."

He said the word in an ordinary tone to see whether Tommy understood, but he didn't. "What's firedamp?"

"It's the gas that builds up underground. The smallest spark will ignite it, causing an explosion."

"The Davy lamps don't help?" Samson had taught Tommy about Humphrey Davy in one of their lessons. Many knew him as a flashy showman for his lectures at the Royal Institution in the early years of the century. But Samson explained he had been a brilliant thinker and experimentalist in chemistry and galvanism. He had also invented a lamp designed to prevent explosions in coal mines by using wire gauze to enclose the flame.

Fowler smiled. Oh, those London ways. "They're not Davy lamps here, young man. They're Geordie lamps, designed by George Stephenson himself. They go out on their own when the gasses get too high. They don't rust like a Davy lamp and are brighter too. Much better than what they're using down south."

"Do they help?"

"They do, somewhat. But you can still get a spark on the ground from your shoe, or from the crackling in your hair when the air is dry."

"Have there been many explosions?" Fowler could tell Tommy was fascinated by the subject, so as they drank their tea, he detailed several recent mining disasters. There had been one in early March, at the Astley Deep Pit in Cheshire, where nine men were killed and almost two hundred were "benumbed", deafened by the explosion. Fowler had heard it might have been caused by a venting problem. Before that, in Wales in February, there had been several explosions down the shaft of Morfa Colliery. At first caused by firedamp, the explosions were particularly deadly because gunpowder was stored below as they were deepening the mine. Thirty men had died.

But firedamp wasn't the only cause, Fowler explained. That same month an explosion at Pendleton Mine in Lancashire was caused by someone firing a shot inside the mine. Nine men died, three of them under the age of seventeen.

"I assume they punished the man who fired the shot?" Tommy asked, horrified. He had seen accidents at the gasworks, but nothing at this level.

"Jonathan Chapman," said Fowler quietly, staring into his cup, his full eyebrows hiding his expression. "My cousin. No need to punish him. Died of his burns." He thought of his sister, who had seemed to age ten years after Jonnie had died.

Before Tommy could respond, Fowler stood up to clear away the tea things.

"None of that's going to happen at Littleburn," he said with force, his brow clearing. "John Marley wouldn't allow it, and I won't either. We have the knowledge, and we'll follow the law."

"The law?" Tommy rose to help.

"Passed ten years ago. Proper ventilation, proper lamps. Not everyone follows the rules, but we do at Littleburn."

Tommy was about to say he thought that a very good idea when the door opened and Maggie came in. She stopped when she saw Tommy, and Fowler saw a blush creep over her cheeks.

Now Maggie, he knew, rarely blushed. In fact, he hadn't seen her do so since the teacher had praised her sums to him during a school visit. She was tough, his Maggie, and he'd been proud of her strength and independence. She'd been avoiding unwanted attentions since she was eight years old. And now here she was blushing when she saw the young Londoner.

"Slow night at the tavern?" he asked her.

She nodded. "Everyone's out on the street, grabbing shoe buckles off the girls."

Fowler caught Tommy's perplexed look. "You don't know about our Easter traditions?" He laughed. "Well, on Monday the men try to steal girls' shoe buckles, or a whole shoe if they can get it, then ransom 'em back for a kiss or a favor. Tomorrow the women will grab the men's caps for the same thing."

"Interesting tradition," said Tommy, smiling at the thought.

"No one's settled down to eat yet, so I thought I'd come home and cook your tea." Maggie glanced at Tommy.

Fowler got up and fetched his hat off the rack near the door. "That's very generous—thank you. While you do that, I'll go down to the shop and get us a bottle of something." Tommy rose to accompany him. "No, no, lad. You stay here and keep Mags company. I'll be back directly." And he left.

Maggie went into the kitchen to fetch an apron, filled a pot with water, and put it on the range. She got out a knife and began to slice a turnip.

"What are you doing here, Tommy Jones?" she asked, her eyes on the turnip.

"Talking to your father," said Tommy, coming up beside her and putting his hand gently on the knife. "I can do that," he said.

She allowed him to chop the turnip while she started on the cabbage, then a piece of salted pork.

"Why are you talking to my father?" Maggie asked, still not looking up at him.

"I haven't had the courage to tell him yet, but I need him to come back to London with me."

She looked up, surprised. "Good heavens, why?"

"To testify. He's a witness to the murder of Horace Wright, who worked at the Post Office. If he doesn't come tell what he knows, an innocent man will be convicted of the crime."

Maggie stopped slicing and stared at him.

"And the innocent man is someone you know," she concluded.

Tommy nodded. "My tutor. And more than a tutor. My friend, and the husband of another friend."

She began slicing the pork. The water was almost boiling now, and she motioned for Tommy to add the turnip.

"I see. And this other friend, the wife. She's special to you, I suppose?"

She was trying to look like she didn't care, and Tommy's heart gave a leap. She liked him. He just knew it. In his mind's eye he saw her cooking, just like this, with him beside her, in their own home. He saw himself being helpful, being a companion, protecting her from harm, kissing her brow at night . . .

He had a sudden impulse. "Come to London with us," he said.

"I'm off to visit Inspector Morgan, Mason," Perseverance Stone hollered toward the kitchen as he put on his boots in the hall. He felt anxious because he'd meant to go the day before, but had been held up by yet another request from Otway to review documents.

"I certainly do appreciate your attention to these matters," Otway had said as he had prepared to leave late again, after six. It had been too late to go to St. Giles Police Station.

"Happy to do it, Arthur," he had said as graciously as he could manage. "I do need some time, however, to prepare for my cases. I shan't be in tomorrow till late afternoon."

"Absolutely, Pers, absolutely. You've been so very generous with your time. It should all come to fruition early next month, and we couldn't have managed without you."

Stone had returned home that night, his eyes bleary from examining old, faded, handwritten documents in an effort to support a tradition of control over the North Sea. He knew this was important as a negotiating point with Germany, and he knew also that such paperwork was his strong point. Otway had been most particular in praising these abilities. Stone could get to the heart of the matter in a document obfuscated with diplomatic or fanciful language. He could tease out of a stolen communication the relationship between the parties at either end of the letter. His knowledge of human nature was almost as much help as his legal prowess.

But now he must find out where Morgan stood in the investigation of Horace Wright's murder. It was less than a fortnight till the trial, and despite Tommy's periodic missives, he felt lost in creating a defense of Mr. Light. Some days it seemed like his loyalties were being torn between Arthur Otway and Cuthbert Slaughter. Both were old friends, but of different worlds. He worried that he was neglecting the ordinary world for that of high politics, since he had always prided himself on being a defender of those who had fewer resources with which to defend themselves.

It was less than a mile due west on Holborn to St. Giles station in the Clark's Buildings, and the sky was promising a fine day. But even if it had been raining, Stone suspected he would have walked. He was building up a head of steam, as the engineers said, to encounter Morgan. While he had no reason to believe the Inspector would be obstructive, the fact remained that at no time had Morgan contacted him to convey information about the investigation. But he wasn't just angry with Morgan. He was angry with himself. He had not questioned his own client thoroughly, had been slipshod in his record keeping, and had left much of the work to a nineteen-year-old young man with little experience.

Stone had not been to St. Giles in some time but was not surprised that within a mile of his own home was a place this downtrodden and ill-kempt. He nevertheless felt a sense of sorrow as he passed the dark doorways, the windows broken and patched with paper, the shoeless children playing with sticks in the muddy streets. An occasional daisy or patch of green appeared in a crack in the pavement, but for the most part the area was gray with poverty and despair. He did not envy Morgan's officers on the beat.

He came up to the desk at the station, but a young woman was ahead of him, so he prepared to wait patiently.

"My name is Prudence Light," he heard her say, "and I am here to see Inspector Morgan."

"I'm sorry, ma'am, but the Inspector is very busy at the moment. If you would please have a seat, I will inquire whether he is available?" The young constable was pale, as if he spent much of his time in this office, and his chiseled face was sympathetic but determined. He had obviously dealt with hostile people before.

Stone saw the woman's back, in her pale blue dress, tense as if she were about to say something more, but instead she sighed and took one of the two seats against the wall. So this was Mrs. Light. She looked pale, too. Perhaps the gas lighting, necessary in this gloom even during the day, made everyone look pale.

"I am Perseverance Stone, barrister, to see Inspector Morgan." He realized he was using his courtroom tone, one which forestalled refusal. The constable complied.

"Yes, sir," he said. "I'll be back directly." He turned and went down a corridor toward what Stone assumed was Morgan's office.

Stone turned toward Prudence and held out his hand. She was looking at him already, having overheard his name.

"I'm Perseverance Stone, Mrs. Light. I am so sorry that we have not met before." He was not going to make excuses; he truly was sorry. This was the accused's wife, and she looked like she'd recently been ill, although he could see the strength in her face.

"Mr. Stone," she said, not rising. "Perhaps you can help me—"

At that moment the constable returned and opened the small gate beside the counter.

"Mr. Stone?" he said, gesturing that he should come through.

"Remain here, Mrs. Light. Allow me to speak to him first."

Prudence took in his smart suit, his muddy boots, and his determined expression. She decided to wait.

"Mr. Stone," said Inspector Morgan gruffly, gesturing him to take a chair. "I have very little time this morning but will naturally help you in any way I can."

Stone observed Morgan's gentleman's suit, the neat stacks of paper on his desk, the dirty tea things on a tray in the corner, and the dark hair plastered down with macassar. This man was a contradiction, but Stone wasn't fooled by his offer. The inspector had little intention of being truly helpful.

"I have come to request information on the present state of your investigation into the death of Horace Wright." He forced his tone to be off-hand, as if such a request were routine.

"Are you the barrister for Samson Light?" asked Morgan.

"Yes, I will be defending him in court."

Morgan rose and began pacing the few steps behind his desk. "I see. As you know, Horace Wright was found dead in a railway car at 245 Holborn, site of the pneumatic railway station. He was murdered by strangulation, possibly by some kind of chain, after being hit on the head. Mr. Light and the victim were seen by a Mr. Edward Teach, senior clerk at the Post Office, arguing outside the afternoon before."

"And what have you discovered thus far?"

"The witness reports that the argument was heated and that it looked like it would come to blows. Two engineers, one named Jenkins and the other Fowler, found the body in the rail car. The car was on a track that had not yet been opened. The body likely traveled from the Post Office to Holborn. Jenkins said he saw nothing, and Fowler left his job immediately, heading up north."

"Have you tried to contact him?"

"Of course we have! Do you think we don't know our business? We've been unable to locate him."

Stone debated whether to tell Morgan he knew where Fowler was and decided not to reveal that for the moment.

"Was there any physical evidence? The chain that was used, for example?"

"No. His pockets contained"—here Morgan leaned back to a small shelf behind him, took up a file, and consulted it—"a clean handkerchief, a key, six shillings, and an old but fancy pocket watch."

"Anything else?"

"That would be of use to your client, Mr. Stone? No. Mr. Wright seems to have been a neat, decent man, dedicated to the Post Office. We are at a loss as to motive."

"That is all you have?" Stone tried not to look astonished.

"That is all I intend to share with you," grumbled Morgan. "Now if you don't mind, sir, I have an investigation to conduct."

Stone could not afford to get angry.

"Are you aware that the wife of the accused is waiting for you at the front desk?" he asked mildly.

"Yes," said Morgan. "We have no need to speak with her."

"All the same, I would like to bring her in. In case she has any questions or information that might be helpful."

Morgan glared at Stone. If he said no, he would look not only churlish but incompetent. Saying yes would complicate his day and was not likely to improve his mood.

"Very well," barked Morgan. "But as I said, I have only a few minutes."

Stone stepped out briefly and asked the constable to bring Mrs. Light back. She peered around the edge of the office door.

"Come in, Mrs. Light," said Stone kindly. "Detective Inspector Morgan will speak with you now."

Prudence's eyes narrowed, but she politely said thank you. Although not invited to be seated, she took the chair directly in front of Morgan's desk, seating herself as if she were making calls and intended to stay awhile. Morgan's eyebrows raised but, not wanting to stand when a woman was seated, he was obliged to take his seat as well. Stone chose to stand by the door.

"Yes, Mrs. Light. What can I do for you?"

"I want to know what you are doing to clear my husband's name, Detective Inspector Morgan. He did not commit this crime."

Morgan sighed. "Mrs. Light, we are doing all we can to ascertain the truth about what happened. We are not interested in either clearing or slandering anyone."

Prudence seriously doubted that was true.

"What have you discovered so far?" she asked.

"Madam, I have just told all the particulars to Mr. Stone, so perhaps he could enlighten you. I must get back to work."

"If I may say so, that's rather callous, Detective Inspector," said Stone quietly from his place by the door. "Mrs. Light believes her husband to be innocent and has the same interest in your information as I do."

Morgan stood behind his desk. "I'm sure you're aware, Mr. Stone, that in such cases the police work most closely with the prosecution, not the defense. It is our job to provide the evidence we find so it can be openly used in court."

"And it doesn't matter whom you convict?" Stone was getting angry now, despite his earlier warning to himself.

"That is inexcusable, sir," Morgan's face was turning red. He took a deep breath and turned to Prudence. "I am sorry I cannot help, ma'am. Good day to you both." And he left his office and marched down the corridor, leaving them alone.

"That could have gone better, I suppose," said Stone once they were outside the station, "but I did not get the sense he intended to be of any help."

"Neither did I," said Prudence. The smell on the street was making her feel ill.

"Allow me to find a cab," said Stone, offering his arm as they headed up to Holborn. "You look tired, and no wonder. Where can I take you?"

"Jerusalem Passage, near St. John's in Clerkenwell, please. C. Herbert Booksellers. It's closed today, but we're taking stock."

As the cab rattled down Holborn, Perseverance Stone realized he had missed something. Tommy had told him that Horace Wright's pocket watch was laid out on his dresser, left in his flat. And yet an old, fancy pocket watch had been found on his body. Surely a man of Wright's income couldn't have two pocket watches. Something was nagging at his mind about a pocket watch, but he couldn't place it. Suddenly, Prudence said, "Mr. Stone, do you think my husband is guilty?"

"No, Mrs. Light. I have seen nothing to convince me that he is. Inspector Slaughter has given me an idea of his character, and I have visited your husband myself and talked with him. He is an earnest and dedicated man. It seems very unlikely he is a killer of anyone."

They rode in silence for a few minutes.

"So do you think Morgan is just an officious little bastard, or does he have it in for my Samson?" Prudence said suddenly.

Stone couldn't help but laugh, at her language and her spirit.

"Oh, Mrs. Light. I am sorry to laugh, but that is a very good question put very well. I think I shall spend some time investigating it. Perhaps Morgan does have some reason to dislike your husband, or some reason to take Edward Teach's word without question. I spoke with Mr. Squires—"

Prudence scoffed.

"—and he said that the case should have been taken by an inspector with the City police, but that Morgan took the case for himself. That confused me, but now that I've met Morgan, I want to make sure there wasn't anything personal. I've certainly met grumpy, overworked inspectors before, but his manner seemed unusually hostile. That might be explained by me being a barrister for the defense, but one would expect his attitude to have softened when he spoke to you, a distressed woman."

Prudence thought that if she hadn't been feeling poorly, she would have given Morgan a piece of her mind that would have distressed him plenty. She was turning decidedly green as they pulled up to the bookshop. She took a gulp of air as she stepped down and thanked Stone for the lift.

"You're welcome, Mrs. Light. I shall send a note as soon as I find out anything, I promise."

She smiled weakly up at him and turned to go into the shop.

It was later that night, and Maggie had agreed to walk with Tommy along the river path.

"The miners won't let him go, you know," she said. "They need him too much. He's the only one with a university education. Who knows when the next explosion might happen?"

Tommy had explained to both Maggie and her father that time was important, that the trial was scheduled for May 2.

"That's a fortnight away," she said. "Why don't you stay here in Durham for awhile?" She glanced at him out of the corner of her eye, and Tommy felt his heart leap. He heard the river flowing, and the wind rustling the leaves in the trees by the riverbank. He knew the castle and cathedral were up above them on the hill, immovable. At that moment, he wanted nothing more than to stay in Durham for a very long time. But he had to return to London, with Fowler in tow.

The problem wasn't only the miners. Tommy still didn't have enough money for the train tickets. He had not worked on Sunday and had only two shillings from this day's work. He could not ask Donald Fowler, much less his daughter, to pay for their own fare. He had his return ticket from Darlington to London, but nothing for Durham to Darlington. And from there to London and back he knew cost one pound, fourteen shillings. So, for two people from Durham to London and back, he would need at least four pounds. That would take forty work days to earn. He didn't have forty days. And anything other than the train would take even more time.

He still had a few days to sort it all out. The moon was just coming out from behind the clouds.

"Did you know," said Tommy, taking Maggie's hand as they walked, "that the moon is waning?"

Maggie laughed. "Now there's one I haven't heard before," she said. "And yes, Tommy Jones, I know that it's waning, and that it's a gibbous moon, and I know why."

They walked along hand in hand, silently, listening to the night sounds. An owl hooted up in the trees, and the moon's bright light was shining on the river, making it look silvery.

"I think I love you, Maggie Fowler," said Tommy quietly.

They kept walking until they came upon a stone building by the side of the river.

"Do you know what this is?" asked Maggie.

"It's the Archaeology Museum," he said. "I walked here before. But the sign on the door says Old Fulling Mill."

Maggie nodded. "Do you know much about fulling?" she asked.

"Nothing at all. I confess I don't even know what the word means."

"Durham makes carpets now, but for many years we produced woolen cloth. You know how after wool is spun and woven, it becomes cloth?"

Tommy nodded as they continued their stroll. The leaves crunched beneath their feet along the path.

"Well, after it's woven, the cloth smells of lanolin. It isn't waterproof, and it's itchy. Not something one would want to wear. Fulling mashes the cloth in a liquid to mesh the fibers."

"What kind of liquid does that?" Tommy asked, curious.

In the shadowy moonlight he could see the humor in Maggie's eyes. "Urine," she said. "All the boys would come down here and help fill the fulling stocks."

He hoped she wasn't fooling him about this; it seemed ridiculous. At the same time, it made scientific sense. Urine had a lot of ammonia.

"And then what?" he asked.

"Then it's stretched on tenterhooks, sheared, roughed up with teasels, then sheared again till it's smooth and lovely. Some of it might be dyed in between."

"I never knew," said Tommy.

"Before the mills, they used to do it in flat baths lined with stones, on the ground, walking the cloth with their feet. And if you know anyone named Fuller, or Walker, or Tucker, that's what their family did. They call them tucking mills in Scotland."

Tommy stopped walking and took both her hands in his.

"How," he asked, looking into her eyes, "do you know all this?"

"We're a town of industry," she said, looking into his eyes. She licked her lips. "We have many different types of mills—"

Tommy leaned in and kissed her mouth, gently.

"—and we produce many different things. Cloth, grain—"

He kissed the side of her neck and heard her breath quicken.

"—um, beer—"

She sighed, took his head in her hands and kissed him back. She wrapped her arms around his neck and held her body against his. He held her close, feeling her heart beat and wishing the world would stop.

They heard the sound of laughter and footfalls coming closer from Prebends Bridge. University students, Tommy thought, probably the worse for drink. They pulled away from each other and began walking back.

8

On Easter Monday, George Smith rose from his makeshift bed in the parlor in Red Lion Street, grateful to have had such a comfortable place to sleep. As it came back to him that he was a father now, and that his wife and her friend were upstairs, he decided he should be the one to make breakfast. It was half past seven, and the light outside the kitchen window was a morning gray. He found the coal scuttle, searched for matches in drawers until he saw the box attached to the wall, and started up the fire in the range.

The pantry cupboard held eggs and a loaf of bread. George had loved to cook before he left England, but the gold fields had offered little opportunity. Mutton had always been available, but unless you were lucky enough to have a garden plot, little was fresh. He'd had a bout of dysentery within weeks of his arrival and had needed his precious bottle of Dr. Eadie's sarsaparilla pills more than once. But potatoes were cheap to buy, and he could make damper bread over an open fire if he had to. He noticed a pot of herbs in the window and cut off a bit of chives.

On the shelf in the corner he saw Hortense's old copy of Eliza Acton's Cookery book. He remembered her bringing that from her parent's house when they had wed. He didn't want to touch it; he decided to keep things simple. Fried bread? No, an omelet. Except he'd want some milk. When he opened the front door, there was nothing there. Outside the kitchen door, there was a bottle of milk. All right, he thought. The only problem was he shouldn't start before someone was awake; omelets cook fast. He laid everything out, then sat down at the table, listening as Sally crossed the landing into Jo and Hortense's room. He'd thought about that last night. There were two bedrooms upstairs, one for Sally and one for them. When he'd gone up to use the toilet before going to bed, he'd peeked in and seen there was one bed in their room. Not unusual, he thought, for women to sleep in the same bed.

Hortense appeared at the kitchen doorway, disheveled in her dressing gown, with Sally on her hip. George thought she looked beautiful.

"Jo's still asleep," she whispered. "Would you take Sally for a moment? I'll be back directly."

He took the child, who was still rubbing her eyes. George had been the eldest in a family of four children, and the trick to holding her secure on one side while he used his other hand to cook came back to him easily. Sally looked blearily down at what he was doing. "Egg," she said.

He hummed to her as he cooked, keeping her well back from the stove. Sally yawned. "Kitty?" she asked, looking around for the boxes.

"Yes, you can say good morning to the quokka," George said, and put her down near its cage. But instead of sitting, she walked over to the cabinet and pulled out the top drawer.

"What are you looking for, little one?" George asked.

"Pay-pa. Cway-on." He looked in the drawer and saw a stack of paper and a box of waxed crayons. He hoped it was all right to let her use them and handed her a sheet and opened the crayon box. "Which color?" he asked. Sally pointed at the animal box. Figuring the quokka was brown, he gave her the brown stick, and she went and sat on the floor next to the box, putting her paper in front of her.

He could smell the first omelet was brown on the bottom and he flipped it as Jo came into the room.

"Oh, that's kind of you," she said, going over and filling the kettle. "Smells delicious."

She saw Sally on the floor and smiled. Perhaps the child would be an illustrator, like herself, or a famous artist. Or perhaps, she told herself, she would just enjoy drawing. That would be all right, too.

The four of them had a quiet breakfast. Jo tried to appear as though she wasn't watching every exchange between Hortense and George, but she couldn't help it. She began collecting the plates to scrape them. The morning light was shifting, but it looked like it would be a gray spring day.

"I have to take the animals out back to clean their cages, and feed them," George said. "Then I must get to the dispatch room in Holborn. I'm due there at a quarter to nine."

Once he had tended to the animals and left for the day, Jo began to collect her things for shopping.

"Are you well enough to have Sally for a few hours?" she asked Hortense, noting the dark circles under her eyes.

"Yes, I think so." Hortense looked over at Sally, who'd gotten back down on the floor to draw some more. "Jo, is it really all right for George to be staying here?"

Jo hoped her firm nod was convincing. "Of course," she said. "He does get on well with Sally, doesn't he?"

Hortense smiled. Jo got the basket and her list, plus the cloths for wrapping any fresh fruit or vegetable she decided to buy. "We need washing powder, too," she said, looking in the cupboard. "I'll see what they have in Clerkenwell Close, but I may need to go further afield. You're sure a few hours is all right?"

"Yes, Jo."

"Is that all right with you, Sally, if I go out?"

Sally nodded. "I draw Mummy next," she said, not taking her eyes from her work.

"Jo, are you working today too?"

"Not today, or at least not at the *News* office. We should be able to manage without a full week's wages. I'll make up the time near the end of the week. There are a few illustrations from Ireland I've been asked to tidy up on Friday, and the side-striped jackal I sketched at the zoo won't be needed till Monday after all."

Hortense started to say something, but Jo kissed her quickly and hurried out the door. She had already decided what she was going to do: shop quickly and meet George at his work. She wanted more than a few words with him, and she could bring lunch.

Perseverance Stone worked on foreign policy documents in the morning, knowing that Otway would not be in the office until the afternoon. He had been given his own desk in a small room that overlooked St. James's Park. It was a much nicer view than his own home and office in Gate Street, which just looked out onto the street. Here he'd sometimes look up from the documents to see ducks flying up from the lake, or elegant couples walking on the pavement below. It was most pleasant.

Too pleasant, thought Stone. He finished the paper he was working on, then arranged everything out on the desk, as if he'd just stepped out for a moment. But he planned to step out for longer than that.

As a barrister of long standing, Perseverance Stone knew some people who could be useful, including an older constable at St. Giles Police Station. Brian Acker was a career constable, one of those men who chose not to rise up for promotion despite his abilities. When he was younger he had preferred the beat, and St. Giles was safe enough for him with his large build and deep, booming voice. Once he got older, he was happy to work the enquiry counter, assisting the public with his solid, authoritative demeanor. Stone had been able to do a favor for him once before. Acker's brother had gotten into a spot of trouble with the law, stealing a case of bottled beer from a pub so he could offer hospitality to his friends. Unfortunately, in removing the case from the basement, a pipe had been broken, causing water to fill the ground floor and damaging the woodwork. When it went to court, Stone had defended the brother, who had amply demonstrated when on the stand his complete ignorance of plumbing. Although he had been found guilty, Stone's intervention had commuted the cost to a few pounds.

When Stone approached the enquiry counter at St. Giles, there were only two people sitting in the waiting room. A young constable came forward.

"May I help you, sir?"

It was the same constable Stone had impressed when he'd visited Inspector Morgan.

"Yes, constable, I'd like to speak with Constable Acker, if I may. I'm Perseverance Stone. I believe we've met."

"Yes, Mr. Stone," said the young man. "Constable Acker is having his lunch, sir. He's in the mess room, down that corridor."

"Thank you," said Stone.

The mess room was small, but Acker was alone, eating a cold lunch of cheese and pickle with bread. He rose when he saw Stone, his gray moustache rising at the corners as he smiled.

"Mr. Stone, sir. How good to see you!"

"And you, Acker, and you," said Stone, sitting at the table across from him. "Do eat your lunch. I'm working on a case and thought perhaps you could help me."

"Happy to do so if I can, sir. What's the case?"

"It's Samson Light." Acker nodded. "You know about it?"

"I know that poor clerk, Horace Wright, was killed in some sort of rail car," he said.

"Yes, and my client is accused of killing him. But my concern is about Inspector Morgan's involvement in the case."

Acker thought a moment. He knew on which side his bread was buttered.

"Understood, sir. I wonder, have you ever tried the Museum Tavern up in Bloomsbury? It's nicely done up now the last few years, and is only a few minutes walk from here. They serve a nice chop. I was thinking of going there myself after my shift, around five o'clock."

"It does sound good," said Stone, rising from the table. "Thank you for your time, Constable Acker."

There was time before five for a visit to the General Post Office, which would require a cab to get to the City. As he left the station, two grubby children came out from the open doorway of one of the shabbier flats in the Clark's Buildings.

"Please, sir," they said, holding out hands so dirty they were almost the color of coal. "Spare a coin, sir?" They looked like brother and sister, both underfed, with hardened eyes, but their hair had been brushed till it shone in the gray light. They couldn't have been more than seven. Stone found two pennies and a two-penny piece in his pocket, and split the four pence between them. They ran back into the flat without saying a word.

Stone was glad to leave St. Giles and caught a cab in New Oxford Street. Traffic along Holborn was heavy as always, all the way across the Viaduct and into the City. He alighted in front of the General Post Office, a place which always reminded him of the British Museum, trying to imagine where an argument might have taken place. Then he went inside to the counter, where a bald, bespectacled man asked what he required.

"I would like to see your supervisor, please."

"That would be Mr. Henry," said the clerk, "I'm afraid he's not available at the moment. May I take your name, please?"

"Perseverance Stone."

The clerk looked taken aback and his hand came up to check his collar.

"Oh! Mr. Stone. Yes, sir. May I say congratulations, sir, on your conviction in the Briggs case? Mr. Müller deserved to die. We can't have people being unsafe in railway carriages, can we?" He paused for breath. "I am a great admirer of your work, Mr. Stone."

Stone's mind churned. The case had been six years ago, and at the time he had been quite sure that Müller had been guilty. Since then, he had considered the case several times, never comfortable with the execution. Müller had been an unpleasant man, and a foreigner, but there had been no motive. And while the victim had been robbed of his watch chain, which played a major role as evidence in the case, money had been left in his pocket. Train travel was less common then, and it was in everyone's interest not to have people terrified of getting on a train. Stone was no longer sure about his role in the drama.

"Thank you. Might it be possible to speak to Mr. Henry?"

"Certainly, sir. Allow me a moment," the clerk said as he bustled back toward the office.

Stone waited, looking around the room. There was no question that the building was impressive, and there were many people about. Anyone could have walked in, intent on making mischief.

"Come this way, sir?" said the clerk. Stone followed him to an office near the rear of the building. The room was quite opulent compared to the public areas at the front. There was a carpet, a large oak desk, and two comfortable chairs in front of it. The room was paneled in a honey-colored wood, and the large window let in light that shined on an aspidistra in a Chinese pot, displayed on a marble-topped stand. There were colored drawings on the walls, most of romantically depicted carriages and trains used to move the mail around the country. Mr. Henry stood behind the desk and motioned toward a chair.

"Good afternoon, Mr. Stone. I'm afraid you have quite shocked my clerk with your celebrity. Do sit down and tell me how I can be of assistance," he said, settling his round body into his desk chair.

"I have taken the case of Mr. Samson Light, who is accused of killing Horace Wright."

Mr. Henry fingered his watch chain. "I see. And you wish to talk to me about that morning, I assume?"

"I do."

"Then let me ask for Reginald to bring us in some tea. No use talking without some tea." He rose and went to the door, leaning out and barking to someone in the corridor. Then he returned to the desk.

"Well," said Mr. Henry, settling in again, "I did tell Inspector Morgan everything that happened."

"Yes, I am aware that the body was discovered at 245 Holborn, but that Mr. Wright was likely killed here?"

"That does indeed seem possible."

"Wouldn't someone have seen it happen?"

"Quite possibly not. Mr. Wright was preparing the room where the pneumatic railway terminates. It's in a basement that was dug directly to the south of the building, but is accessed only by walking across the courtyard into the annex. I checked my records upon the Inspector's request, and it seemed that the builders were up in the courtyard taking tea at the time."

"What were your thoughts when the Company contacted you that morning about the body being found there?"

Reginald entered with the tea, and Stone noticed there were three cups on the trolley.

"Ah, thank you, Reginald." Henry turned to Stone. "You don't mind if Reginald joins us, Mr. Stone? He is the one who keeps things organized around here."

"Of course," said Stone. Some men, he knew, felt lost without their retainers, their assistants, their butlers. As he would without Mason. Reginald began serving tea.

"It really is a shame about poor Mr. Wright," said Mr. Henry, shaking his head. "Has anyone discovered why he was killed? Was it simply some sort of quarrel?"

"I'm not sure, but I was asking, Mr. Henry, about the Company contacting you that morning?"

Henry glanced over at Reginald.

"The Company can be quite demanding," said Reginald.

"What do you mean?"

Mr. Henry said, "Surely you've seen what they've done to our streets? What all these companies do? Do you recall trying to travel on Holborn while they were building the Viaduct? The whole thoroughfare was just a monstrous ditch." His face was getting red.

"It's disruptive, certainly," agreed Stone.

"They tunneled right under the courtyard of this building. Made everything shake. Then I was told I must staff the basement, tolerate the noise of their engineers and builders, manage everything."

"It has been quite a trial," Reginald murmured.

"I see," said Stone. "And how did Horace Wright come to work on the railway? Did he have engineering knowledge?"

"Good heavens, no," said Mr. Henry.

Reginald quietly cleared his throat, and added, "Mr. Wright was moved from upstairs because of his sorting skills, to prepare the room for sorting. I don't think anyone asked about his engineering knowledge."

"And who is this Edward Teach, the man who saw the argument?"

Another glance at Reginald. "One of our senior clerks," said Henry. "Been here for years."

"Reliable?"

"Certainly."

Stone was shown the railway terminal annex by a clerk, but there was not much to see beyond a room with two tracks. The flooring and paint were all new. He left the General Post Office knowing little more than he had before. Since it was only three o'clock, and he was to meet Acker in Bloomsbury anyway, Stone decided to take the cab only as far as the British Museum.

He always found it soothing to walk through the Assyrian Reliefs showing the elites hunting lions. They were on the ground floor and occupied two long rooms. Stone was not an admirer of violence, of which he saw plenty in his profession. But he was fascinated by King Ashurnasirpal standing in his carriage with bow primed, killing lions who had clearly been brought there in cages for his amusement. Power and authority, he thought, is so often staged, as if it were a theatrical production. The lions were real, but the "hunt" was not. It was just for show. He also enjoyed the lion's tail, which had been carved one way then erased and carved along a better line. The artists had been told what to portray, but paid servants or not, they had valued their work and wanted to do their best for the King. Loyalty. There was loyalty in that tail.

Acker was waiting at the Museum Tavern; Stone saw his reflection in the bar mirror as he entered. He was ordering a beer, and Stone offered to buy them both. They found a small table near the wall.

"I'm sorry if I caused you any trouble at the station," said Stone.

"It's all right, sir. Just thought it would be best to talk about some things elsewhere, is all."

"How is your brother doing?"

"Very well, sir, very well. Has a small house in Chiswick, he does, with a wife. She's quite a harridan. He deserves her." He laughed. "So, you want to talk about the Inspector."

"Yes. I am curious why he took over the case. Given where the body was found, shouldn't it have been investigated by the City police?"

"He wanted it himself, and he outranks everyone at the City station nearest the Post Office. So he simply took it over."

"Have you any idea why?"

"I might, but I hate to cause suspicion if it's unfounded." Acker sounded thoughtful.

"I understand. I assure you I will only use the information to understand, not to judge."

Acker thought for a few moments, looking down into his beer. A waitress came over, gave Acker a cheeky smile, and asked if they would like something to eat. Acker looked over at Stone, who nodded.

"Two chops, Mary," said Acker. "Yer best, please, for Mr. Stone here."

Acker watched Mary as she headed back to the kitchen. "Young enough to be my daughter," he said ruefully. "But a cheery face on a chilly day."

"About Morgan . . ."

"Well, I've been at St. Giles for a long time. Used to be on the beat. Morgan worked his way up, same as me. I knew about his family, and that he doted on his daughter, Patsy. Three years ago she was killed, about the same time he was promoted to Detective

Inspector. Hit by an omnibus. They tried to save her at St. Bart's, but couldn't. She was only twelve."

"That's horrible," said Stone, shaking his head.

"It was. Then a few weeks ago, when Morgan heard Mr. Light was arrested, that was when he took over the case. When they brought Mr. Light in to St. Giles, he said he worked at St. Bart's. I thought it was strange that the case came over to us like it did, with Inspector Morgan so insistent. He'd never done that before, so far as I know. So I went and asked at the hospital and found out that Mr. Light had been one of the doctors who tried to save Patsy."

"And you think he blamed Light for his daughter's death?"

"I didn't think so at first, till I saw how he was treating you and Mrs. Light, telling me to say he wasn't in when he was, telling the other constables to do the same if anyone came asking about the Horace Wright murder. That's why I wanted to meet you here," said Acker, raising his head as Mary arrived with the chops. "That and the food, of course."

In addition to a small repast of bread, cheese, and pears, Jo had brought her shopping and her sketchbook to 245 Holborn. It was almost one when she arrived, and her load was getting heavy. There was no one on the ground floor, so she tucked her baskets by the archway at the back of the room. Jo heard the whining of an engine coming to a stop. She stepped out onto the bridge-like gallery overlooking the tracks. The metal doors to each track were open, and George and Mr. Jenkins were moving cars back and forth across the wheels half-protruding from the floor, then oiling the wheels that squeaked. Beyond them stood the large platform with the controls. Jo was familiar with the room, having been through here to the engine room to draw the giant disc. She leaned over the gallery until George looked up and saw her.

"Miss Harris!" he said. "I didn't expect you to come here."

"I'm sorry, Mr. Smith, if I'm interrupting your work. I was wondering whether perhaps you might spend your lunch time with me? I brought some food."

George looked over at Jenkins. "It's after one, George," said Jenkins, with a knowing smirk. "You go on then."

"Oh, Miss Harris," said George, remembering his manners. "This is Mr. Jenkins. He's the engineer here."

Jo and Jenkins nodded at each other. "Would you like to join us?" she asked Jenkins, hoping he would refuse. Jenkins caught her tone.

"No, thank you, miss. I have my lunch with me."

As they went upstairs, George said quietly, "I'm glad you've come. I forgot to bring anything to eat."

Once she'd collected her baskets, George suggested they go out back into the old Bull and Gate yard, where there were some crates they could sit on. The weather was mild, the sun deciding it could spread some warmth in Holborn. Jo took out the bread from the basket, tore off a piece, and handed it to George. "Allow me, miss," he said, and began serving the rest, the two spreading the cloth serviettes across their laps. He smiled at the two bottles of beer, handing one to her and reaching in his pocket for a knife to open them.

He took a few bites, then smiled at her. "I don't think you're interested in pneumatic railways, so I assume you've come to talk with me?"

"I have, Mr. Smith."

"Call me George, please." She had been trying not to look too closely at him at home, but now she began to study his face, the red cheeks, the guileless smile, the twinkle in his eye. She would like to draw him, should the opportunity present itself. He reminded her a little of a proud red rooster. It was certainly difficult to consider him a threat. The life she had with Hortense was important to her, however, and a threat he certainly was. Her mind went through the various approaches. Being direct had often been her downfall, but at times it could be useful.

"Of course. George. Well, George, I want to ask you about your intentions while in London."

"My intentions, Miss Harris?"

"Yes. Do you intend to stay long? Have you moved back permanently? And what are your plans for Hortense?"

He looked at her closely, but his voice was non-committal. "To be honest, miss, I don't know."

"Do you intend," Jo said, no longer hungry, "to resume your marriage?"

George looked uncomfortable, and Jo noticed his cheeks became even redder. "I feel I need to explain to you what I told Hortense last evening, while you were out with little Sally," he said, taking a sip of beer. "Has Hortense told you why I left, three years ago?"

"She told me you were off to seek your fortune."

"That's very true, Miss Harris. Very true. I couldn't manage that with a wife, and I'm afraid we should never have married. She's a home sort of person, God bless her, and I'm a go off sort of person. So I had to go off, to make my way in this world. I intended South Africa, but then heard the gold fields were best in Australia. I suppose," he said thoughtfully, "I had a young man's dreams."

"An unmarried young man's dreams."

George looked contrite, but continued. "I left to make my fortune, as I said. And I haven't quite found it, you see."

"But the animals?" Jo was confused.

"Ah, yes, the animals. That's the problem. In Australia it all seemed like such a good idea. We were able to capture the animals, find a man who made wooden crates for them, and arrange for me to travel to London to sell them. I left Victoria with two kangaroos, four wallabies, over a dozen birds, two quokkas, a Tasmanian devil, the quogg, a goat, and two koalas." He sighed, and she noticed his eyes were getting red around the rims. "I arrived with two wallabies, ten birds, one quokka, and the quogg."

"Good heavens," said Jo. "What on earth happened?"

"They died on the ship, miss. There was nothing I could do. We had tried foods the locals had told us about before we left, and when some wouldn't eat, we thought they just weren't hungry. I kept giving them trays of water, but they didn't touch them. And on board ship, I had brought the goat for her milk, but they barely touched that either."

"What about the birds?"

"They were easier, since I had brought seeds and nuts. But even so, two died and I don't know why." He sniffed and took up his serviette to wipe his nose. "I didn't realize. It wasn't that I liked them so much, or got attached to them. But they got so sick, and just shriveled up, and it was because of me, these poor animals—" And George began to sob.

They were alone in the yard, so no one witnessed the poor man crying. Jo decided that waiting patiently, as she did with Sally, would be best.

"The koalas," he sniffed as he calmed down. "Losing them was the worst."

"I'm so sorry," Jo said. It sounded horrible, poor frightened animals on a ship, starving to death.

"So then I arrived here. We had contacted Charles Jamrach from Australia, and he had written that we could house the animals at his warehouse in St. Katherine's Dock, where he had keepers to care for them. I'd have to pay for their care for the first day, until he could come and purchase them from me. I was met at the ship by one of his workers, with a cart. But when we got to the warehouse, I could see so many animals, crowded in cages. They had ten wallabies in one crate, and the birds were jammed so close together they could barely eat." He stared off into space, seeing it again in his mind, the horror in his eyes.

"I could not carry them all myself, so I had to leave some of them there. As the man was unloading them, he told me that Jamrach wasn't in town, in fact wasn't in the country. He was in India and would be back in a fortnight, and until then I'd have to pay daily for the care of my animals."

George then explained how he'd taken the two crates he could carry, his satchel of clothes and necessities on his back, and gone to find a place to bathe. Once clean, he'd found out about the job at 245 Holborn and was hired immediately on a temporary basis. Then he'd tried to find Hortense, but she wasn't in the old house, and he'd asked around until he found the house in Red Lion Street.

"They told me at the market in Clerkenwell Close," he said. "I came to the house to leave the animals, then had to go find my friend Rex to borrow some money to pay the warehouse. But he knew I was good for it, because I had this job."

They didn't speak for a few minutes, eating their lunch quietly.

Jo spoke first. "I'm still not sure what you intend for Hortense."

George sighed deeply. "Miss, now that I know I'm a father, I'm aware my priorities should change. I didn't know when I left, and I thought I had done right by her, giving her my grandmother's money. And little Sally, she's so sweet—"

Jo did not want to be uncharitable, but she looked around, sincerely hoping he wouldn't start crying again.

"I should be the responsible father, I know," he said, his voice beginning to sound desperate. "I know I should resume our marriage, as you put it, and be a good husband. But miss," he said, and reached out to grasp both her hands in his. "I have found a way now to make my fortune, don't you see? And I must follow that dream."

Jo kept hold of his hands. "What is that dream?"

"Bugs," George said.

At first Jo thought she had misheard, but he was looking directly into her eyes, an earnest expression on his face, and he had said "Bugs."

"Bugs?" Jo asked.

"Chinese bugs. There's a huge trade in insects right now. All sorts: beetles and spiders and crawling creatures of all kinds. And I could go get them. And if some die as I'm bringing them back, my heart won't be broken. Go to China, that's my plan. As soon as

Jamrach pays me my money. I realize," he said, trying to convince her, "that it sounds insane."

It did, but Jo could feel her heart growing larger, both for this man of dreams and for what she hoped this must mean—that he wouldn't be coming back into Hortense's life. She was terrified she might say something to break the spell.

"Jo—may I call you Jo?" he asked. Jo nodded. "Jo, I can see how you care for Hortense, and for my little girl. I see how you are so considerate of her ways, much more so than I could be. It's asking a lot, but perhaps you care enough for them to watch over them? So I can go do what I need to do? Would it be asking you to give up your life, your dreams?"

"Hortense and Sally are my life," she said. She could hear her voice sounded husky, and felt as though she might be the one to cry now.

George nodded, then looked down at their hands, still clasped. "Then you must tell me—is Hortense ill?"

He deserved to know. For the next few minutes, Jo explained to George about Hortense's illness, blurting out all the options for the surgery. It was a relief to say it, especially as George nodded his understanding with a concerned look on his face.

"There's a surgeon we want, to do the anesthesia," she said. "And it happens to be Samson Light, the man accused of murdering Mr. Wright."

"That's the man who worked in the Post Office?" Jo nodded and explained as best she could about the accusation, and her friend Tommy trying to find Mr. Fowler, the witness who had left employment.

Lunch time was ending, and they started packing up the basket together.

"All right," decided George. "I'm going to help in any way I can. I think right now I need to ask some innocent questions round the dispatch office. And that surgery—well, Jo, I don't know much about doctors and medicine and the like. But if you and Hortense think it's best, I can help with Sally if I'm still here in London."

Jo walked back down Holborn to catch the omnibus home, her steps much lighter than they'd been that morning.

Tommy knew Maggie was right—there was still time. He'd been there a week now and had been unable to convince her father to go back with him. The miners were raising money; they'd paid out a lot on petitions to Parliament, and talks with John Marley and the managers were about to commence. On Saturday they'd get their officers organized.

He'd written again to Perseverance Stone and to Samson, saying he'd found Fowler but was having trouble convincing him to come to London, and had found work in the meantime. Maggie herself had been called up to Chester-le-Street to care for her Aunt Clara's daughter, who was giving birth to her seventh child. He missed her.

The other thing he was missing was money, and Tommy sat by the river near Prebends Bridge, thinking what to do. There wasn't enough, and his calculations indicated there wouldn't be, even if he worked as hard as he could hauling bricks. He could borrow, possibly, but how could he promise to return it if he borrowed here in Durham? He might never come back. Looking across at the old fulling mill and the cathedral, he felt a sadness at the idea.

Tommy heard the creak of a door, and a man came out of the mill house with a scowl on his face.

"You there!" he shouted at Tommy. "What are you about?"

"Sorry?" Tommy rose and put his cap on his head. The man was raking back his ginger hair to put his hat on. It looked like a constable's hat, tall and black with a sturdy brim.

"What are you about here?" the man asked again. On closer inspection, each seemed to decide that the other was not as much of a threat as they had originally thought. The man took in Tommy's youth and working clothes, and Tommy saw the lines of humor around the man's eyes.

"Just resting here, thinking on what I'm to do next," said Tommy. "Is that your house?"

The man took a deep breath, as if the walk to the river had been an exertion.

"Yes. Well, no. I'm Andrew Rutherford, the river constable. I patrol this area, for the city."

"I'm Tommy Jones. It's a very nice house," said Tommy.

"Yes," nodded the man, turning to look back. "It is. Rebuilt just a few years ago. Used to be a mill house—that part's the mill there," he pointed toward the large side of the building nearest the river. "No one's used it for thirteen years now. But they made the house large, more suitable for a man of my station." He pulled himself up to his full height, which was still half a head below Tommy's, and looked him up and down.

"Yer not from round here," he said.

"No, I'm from London. Here to do some work and find the man I was sent to find."

"London, eh? Thought so. Who were you sent to find?"

As Tommy explained, the two moved to the river bank, and sat together watching the light change to the pale tan of evening. Insects were skimming above the water, and ducks were coming by, flapping toward the weir.

"The trick," said Andrew, "is to do the very best you can. You're a lucky young man. You have friends, and people who count on you." Tommy nodded as the two men looked over the water.

"And you could do more jobs, you know. Plenty of work round here. You're working at the fever ward site, yes?" He pointed behind him, up the western bank. "So, you need night work. Could do night soil, couldn't you?"

Tommy supposed he could, but the very thought made him uneasy, especially in his stomach. Nightsoil men went around the town, emptying cesspits and privies, loading up the waste for hauling out to the fields. The smell was horrible, even worse than working at a tannery. But it did tend to pay well.

Rutherford caught Tommy's expression. "How about a baker's, then? Start around three in the morning they do, some earlier. William Gowland's a baker. His shop's right over there at Framwellgate, next to the shoemaker's. I hear tell he could use some help."

Tommy smiled. "A very good idea, thank you. I'll talk to him in the morning—early morning!"

"Then," said Rutherford, warming to his idea, "there's the evening hours . . ." He stood and walked a few steps away, then back again. "I have it! The *Durham County Advertiser*. They set their print on Thursday evenings for the morning paper, up on Saddler Street. That's not every evening, but it's something."

The light was starting to fade, but Tommy could see Rutherford's face, now flushed with eager helpfulness, his thumbs in his braces as he rocked back on his heels in satisfaction.

And he could well have found the answer. "Thank you so much, Mr. Rutherford."

"Andrew, please! Off with you, then," he said, dismissing him with his hand. "Don't lose hope. Farewell."

Tommy considered himself dismissed by the constable. He walked up past the mill house to South Street, where the newer, richer houses were. People liked the view of the cathedral. Lamps hanging by front doors were just being lit as he passed. A baker's, the newspaper, maybe something else on other evenings. He could do this.

He turned to cross the Framwellgate Bridge and saw the old man sitting on the ground with his dog. Tommy dug in his pocket for a penny and tossed it in his cap.

"Evening," he said to the man.

"Evening, young man," nodded the beggar. He was eating a piece of bread, sharing bits with the dog. Tommy was glad he had something to eat.

———

William Wilson, personal secretary to V.G. Faber, alighted the cab quickly at St. Martin's-le-Grande in the afternoon light, his heels clicking on the pavement. In his wisdom, Faber had decided that on the following Friday, the 29th of April, the main line from Holborn to the General Post Office in St. Martin's-le-Grande would finally open and begin operations. The board of the London Pneumatic Despatch Company had not been so sure. Summoned that morning, they felt they had not been truly consulted and were annoyed at being called to an unscheduled meeting. Thomas Brassey, the engineer, had to cancel a suspension bridge contract consultation in order to attend. John Horatio Lloyd, the lawyer, had been in Cambridge on business and had to hurry back. Mrs. Bond had to miss an important meeting of her philanthropy club, where they were to decide how to disburse funds for helping orphans. Richard Grenville, Third Duke of Buckingham, sent his regrets as usual, and Edmund Clark was in East Anglia on a hydraulics project and could not come to town. Added to the inconvenience was a downpour of rain, which had made transport to the company office in Victoria Street difficult from all directions. The atmosphere in the room was not propitious.

Mrs. Bond had lodged her protest immediately, again voicing her objection to the amount of the investment and the dim possibility of return. John Horatio Lloyd felt she had a point, particularly since there had been no resolution of the murder. He demanded to know when Inspector Morgan would solve the crime.

"I'm sorry, John," said Faber, "but you know as well as I do that justice cannot be rushed."

Faber then explained that orders had been issued to prepare the line, and all would be in readiness. He would like to contact the press immediately, as soon as they had voted. The vote went in his favor, with only Mrs. Bond casting a nay. Faber's expression did not change, but he rose to thank them, offering the gentlemen a drink nearby at The Albert. Mrs. Bond gathered up her things and left the room immediately. The meeting had not taken long, so perhaps she would be in time for final decisions at the philanthropy club. Tomorrow she would contact her banker about withdrawing her investment.

Wilson opened the door for her and courteously said goodbye, although he received no reply. He had not been invited to join the gentlemen for a drink, nor had he expected to be. There was much work to do in the office now that the vote had been taken. He was just starting on his list of reporters to contact when Brassey, Lloyd, and Faber fetched their coats from the rack. He jumped up to open the door for them.

"Thank you, Wilson," said Faber. "You will be contacting *The Times* and the journals?"

"Yes, sir, and I will write to His Grace, and begin a list of people to invite to the opening. I assume you would like drawings prepared for *The Engineer*, and an artist requested from *The Illustrated London News*?"

"That would be excellent, Wilson. We had such good press back in '65."

"We did indeed, sir."

"But I'm afraid I must ask you to go talk to Mr. Henry first. Let him know the vote, but try to soothe his feathers. He's no more supportive of our efforts than Mrs. Bond."

"Yes, sir. Good afternoon."

Wilson understood the board's reticence but had been sure that Faber would prevail. The urgency was understandable, and Wilson was pleased to think that his employer had confided in him. Faber had felt pushed by what was happening elsewhere, especially the proposed Channel Railway. Just last month, Mr. J.F. Bateman had presented the idea he had developed with a French counterpart: a railway tunnel running along the bottom of the English Channel. While by no means the first to propose the notion, this railway was pneumatic. With a cast iron tube thirteen feet in diameter, and fans ensuring good air throughout, it would use ordinary railway carriages. It would be fast, with the time in the tube a little over an hour, or even less for express trains. The trip from London to Paris could be made in only eight hours, with multiple trains each day in both directions. It would be a vast undertaking. The joints between the ten-foot sections of tube would have to be absolutely watertight, since twenty-two of its thirty-mile length would be under water. Bateman claimed the machinery to lay the sections was ready to use.

Such a proposal not only made the Post Office railway seem small by comparison, but it spoke to how quickly development was happening. The Company could easily be left behind as newer, flashier ventures were proposed. It was crucial that the main line to the General Post Office be opened as quickly as possible, and that it be efficient. Another failure, like the first line to Euston, or another delay, was unacceptable. Faber's mood had become increasingly irritable as time went on. He was responsible to shareholders, certainly, but it was more than that. He prided himself on knowing what people wanted and being a man of vision, as he had proven with his bookselling. At times, Wilson thought Faber may have questioned the wisdom of becoming involved in the pneumatic railway scheme, but it wasn't his way to declare failure. Dogged persistence had gotten him this far, and the railway would be no different.

"The Channel Railway will take five years," Faber had told Wilson, "at a cost of seven million pounds. But it may capture the imagination in a way that smaller railways don't. We need to move quickly."

As he walked, Wilson thought how best to soothe Mr. Henry, who would certainly be most annoyed by the order to prepare the line for opening. There were no arguments of loyalty he could make: the Post Office had no deep ties to the Company. Money was similarly useless, as Mr. Henry would get paid the same whether he cooperated or not. Wilson would simply have to be diplomatic.

"I sympathize, Mr. Henry, I surely do," he said, once seated with Henry and Edward Teach at the General Post Office.

"Do you indeed, Mr. Wilson? Or have you just come to make sure we are working hard to prepare in time?"

The last few hours had not been easy for Mr. Henry. The receipt of the "fortnight note," as he called the order from Faber, was not well taken.

"How on earth can we be ready to transfer all the mail processes?" he had fumed to Edward Teach, his watch chain quivering in fury across his ample belly. "Why don't they understand it isn't just the trains, the machinery?"

"I'm sure I don't know," said Teach, his long face sad, and his left eye twitching ever so slightly. "Human nature, I suppose."

"What do you mean?"

"Faber doesn't care about us, only his own business."

"True," said Henry, calming somewhat.

"He's loyal only to his own idea, not to other people."

"Yes," said Mr. Henry, "we do know about that, don't we?"

"We do. Sometimes it doesn't lead to a good end, does it?"

"It does not," said Henry, looking down at the plans on his desk. "Well, no one is going to murder V. G. Faber, so we had best look at how this could be done."

And he had, working out schedules, moving two men to different positions, arranging for an additional cleaning woman to make sure the terminus room was ready. All in one afternoon. And now here was Faber's lackey, come to move him along.

"I assure you, Mr. Henry, I have not come to check your progress. I merely want to send Mr. Faber's regards and his regrets at the rush, but we had no choice. The board voted just this morning. They are in quite a hurry to get things going, as you know."

Henry knew nothing of the kind, nor did he care. Teach, glancing over at him, decided to intervene before Henry's dangerously unanchored watch chain started bouncing again.

"Mr. Wilson, we appreciate your visit, but we have things well in hand. Are we to assume that visitors and the press will be invited? We have been making the station ready in case."

"Yes, indeed. It would be a shame if the Post Office did not benefit from the publicity. We all hope that the public will be even more willing to entrust their letters and parcels to the Post Office, knowing how speedily they will travel."

Mr. Henry seemed somewhat mollified by this line of thought.

"Again, Mr. Henry," said Wilson, "I do apologize for the rush. But your office has a reputation for being at the forefront of invention and forethought, and the board was absolutely certain that if anyone could manage such an inconvenience with grace and efficiency, it would be you. The public acclaim will be well-deserved. It is entirely the Company's fault that this has been delayed so long."

Wilson watched Mr. Henry decide. The death of Mr. Wright must have been a blow to the office, and the opening of the line would provide an excellent distraction. The Post Office could use this opportunity, as could the man's career. Mr. Henry gracefully acquiesced.

Samson Light set the letter on the infirmary table and continued wrapping bandages.

"How are you doing, Doctor?" asked Fiona, coming to sit on the bench near the infirmary door.

"Oh, very well, Miss Harper, very well."

"A note from your family, then?" she asked, with a slight smile.

"No, from Tommy Jones."

"He's the lad going up north to find your witness?"

Samson nodded and looked up from the bandages. Fiona reached across the table and took one, rolling it slowly.

"It must be nice to have someone looking out for you, on the outside," she said wistfully.

It was a quiet evening on the wards, and the sole candle made the light flicker, causing Miss Harper's hair to shine like gold. Samson noticed the curve of her cheek and her long lashes as she looked down at the bandages. His blood quickened for a moment, but then she looked up and Samson found himself wishing they were Prudence's eyes.

"No one is watching out for you, then?" he asked her.

"Oh, somewhere, I'm sure," she said. Samson remembered her anger at being accused.

The warder came by. "Time to close up, then, Doctor, miss. Back to the cells with you."

Samson spent a peaceful night, although he did dream. In one, he was arguing with a man in front of the General Post Office. The man was yelling at him, but the words were indistinct. Then he saw a shape behind the man and realized he was growing wings, great dark wings that became larger and larger until they lifted the man up above the pavement. He looked and saw the man's head hanging at an awkward angle as he hung there in the sky. He woke with a start, and as his heart slowed, he realized it was morning. He relieved himself in the pot under the metal bedstead. When O'Brien came with his breakfast, he asked if he might go to the infirmary.

"I forgot to make notes on Mr. Jarvis," he explained. Jarvis had come in several times because of sleeplessness and pain in his elbow. Samson had prescribed henbane drops but had forgotten to record the examination and diagnosis in the infirmary book.

It was very early in the morning, and as he passed the cells he could hear most of the inmates eating, forks clanging on plates. The infirmary door was closed, but it opened quietly on its hinges when he turned the handle. He could see Fiona Harper, her back to him, searching through the cabinet. He stood quietly watching as she took out and read the labels on several of the ridged bottles, selecting one and putting it in the pocket of her apron. Samson closed the door quietly, then opened it again, clearing his throat and making more noise.

"Oh!" he said, pretending to be startled. "I didn't know you were in here today."

"Good morning, Mr. Light," she said easily, as she moved toward the table. "Yes, I wanted to take a look at the notes from yesterday."

He noticed that she had deliberately moved away from the cabinet, but she did not blush or stammer.

"Is there a problem?"

"Yes, a woman named Susannah was up in the night with griping pain, lower abdomen. It passed, but I would like you to see her today if you can."

"Shouldn't she wait for Mr. Warner on Tuesday? Or do you think it's more urgent than that?"

"I do think Tuesday would be a long time for her," said Miss Harper. "Perhaps we could help her pain, and then she could see Mr. Warner?"

Pain was an ongoing problem in medicine, Samson had to admit, and gaol conditions did nothing to improve it. Most older inmates had rheumatic pain, aggravated by damp and the lack of fresh air. Active men had various pains caused by inactivity. And many prisoners had stomach pain because of the food. The best remedies were opium, of which they had only a small amount, and henbane, which was better because it didn't slow the bowels. But he had to be careful, because there wasn't much of that either. Orders to the apothecary were strictly limited.

"Of course," said Samson, "let's see her this morning."

He decided not to mention the bottle Miss Harper had taken, and to look in the cabinet privately later to see which one it was. The ridged bottles were for poisons or substances regulated by law. He was beginning to suspect that neither Miss Harper's evident skill nor her availability were accidental.

9

It had been another tiring day at the fever ward, but the work was progressing, so Henderson was happy and Tommy had more coins in his pocket. As he walked, he thought about Maggie. She'd only been gone a couple of days, and although he'd tried to talk to her father the day before, Fowler had been busy with the Association. Widow Hutton had told Tommy that morning she would be spending the evening with her sister out in Claypath but would be back for church on Sunday. He started across Framwellgate Bridge, tapping his forehead to the beggar sitting with his sleeping dog. Tommy put three pennies in his cap, and the old man wished him a nice evening.

But it wasn't really a nice evening. Clouds were gathering and moving quickly over the river, and it looked as though it might rain. Tommy did not feel like going to the Market Hotel, where the Miners' Association was meeting; Maggie wasn't there anyway. Nor did he want to go back to the empty boarding house. He was edgy even though he should be exhausted. He'd taken Rutherford's advice and had helped set type on Thursday for Mrs. Duncan at the *Durham County Advertiser*, and he was working the ovens on Tuesdays and Saturdays at Gowland's bakery from four to seven in the morning. Both had been glad of the help. Even though Tommy had been awake since three, and his muscles ached, and his jacket was only moderate protection against the wet, he found himself on the steps down to the river again.

He was walking where he and Maggie had walked, toward the old fulling mill, thinking about what had passed between them. He didn't know how he was sure, but he was sure about Maggie. He knew enough biology from Samson to realize that the mating instinct might play a part, but his feeling for her ran much deeper. He had begun imagining in his mind asking her to marry him, and he could feel his heart twist at her possible refusal. He could just see her eyes crinkle at the corners, and hear her say something like, "You want to marry me, Tommy Jones? I have my own life, I'm going to have my own tavern, and here you're coming on all romantic."

Twilight was darkening into night as he approached the mill, when he heard the sound of feet, men's boots coming toward him from Prebends Bridge.

"Ah, there you are, Londoner," said Gerry. As they got closer, Tommy could see that Bert and three of the other men were with him.

"Evening, Gerry. Bert."

"'Evening', is it?" said Gerry. Tommy noticed the tone was not friendly. None of them looked happy to see him. As Gerry approached, he could smell drink on his breath.

Tommy's muscles tensed as he scanned his surroundings. He was accustomed to keeping alert as he walked the streets of London, always aware of doorways and small alleys, knowing where they went in case there was trouble. Here there was the hill up to the cathedral on one side of the path, and the brown slow river on the other. He began reviewing in his mind the moves that he knew. Most of them were intended to escape rather than engage. He knew he was strong, and all the brick carrying had made him stronger. But he was only one next to these five, three of whom were, he noticed for the first time, rather powerfully built.

"Well, it is evening, isn't it?" he said heartily. "Where you all headed? Are you celebrating?"

"No, we ain't celebrating," said Gerry. "Wanna talk to you."

"Of course! What about?"

"My cousin Maggie. You been seen with her, and we don't like it."

Tommy scanned their faces. They had all been drinking, but Gerry and the two smaller men looked like they were the worse for it.

"I'm sorry, Gerry. Maggie makes her own decisions. You told me that."

Gerry stopped for a moment with his mouth open, then his eyes narrowed. He tried another piece of his mind.

"You Londoners, with yer fancy ways. Think you can come up here and take our women." The other men mumbled in agreement, and Tommy thought he heard Bert growl.

Even in his situation, the irony was not lost on Tommy. In London, he was considered pretty low in the ranks of society, although his job as a tutor had elevated his station somewhat. But he certainly had nothing that could be called fancy ways.

"Now, Gerry, I'm not taking anyone," Tommy said. Then he spoke to the group. "You all know why I'm here, don't you? I got a friend in London, in gaol for a murder he didn't commit. I'm getting help from Mr. Fowler." The men looked at each other, confused, but Gerry took a step forward.

"You bin seen, Mr. Jones, manhandling my cousin." Gerry swung his fist out. Tommy took a step back, leaning to the left. Gerry lost his balance and fell onto the path. Two of the men hoisted him back up, as Bert went around them and landed a punch on Tommy's jaw. Gauging his balance, Tommy mustered his power in his shoulders and pushed him. He could hear a few coins fall from his pocket as he fell. There was a low roar of thunder from above the castle, but he heard Gerry grumble in a low voice, "He's mine, boys."

Tommy could see him lower his body to ram him and tried to sidestep to the left, but the side of Gerry's head caught his hip and he went sprawling. Deciding this was not a fight he could win, he started to run back toward Framwellgate Bridge, the men following behind and yelling.

As they neared the bridge, they heard a clatter, like metal on stone. Tommy ignored it and ran for the steps, then dashed up the hill into the dark before reaching them. He clung to a bush, willing himself to breathe more quietly, then he heard female voices on the bridge.

"There you are, boys!" a bright voice said loudly. "Such a night as this, where have you been?"

Tommy heard the men's boots stop and figured they must be looking up at the bridge.

"You fellows been fighting already?" The other woman's voice was brassy, a confident sound that rang out from the bridge. "Why didn't you bring it to us first, then do your fighting?"

"You know I don't like a dirty man," the other woman said, with a laugh.

Tommy could hear the men murmuring to each other, then Gerry yelled up. "We got men's business, Kath. Gotta get that Londoner."

"Oh, really?" said the brassy woman. "What's he done, then?"

"Molested our Maggie," shouted Gerry. "My own cousin. Damned Londoner."

"Aw, Gerry," cried the other woman. "You know Maggie knows her own mind. But she's no whore." The other men were murmuring agreement.

"That's what we're here for!" laughed Kath.

"And he's a good lad, you oafs," said the other woman. "Been keeping company with Widow Hatton, helping her out, the poor thing. And giving pennies to the bridge beggar."

"And quite the lover!" added Kath. The two women laughed heartily.

"Not better than me, Kath!" hollered Gerry, his drunken voice threatening, carrying to the other side of the river.

"Well, no," Kath considered, "not better than you. But I wouldn't know," she said consolingly. "It's Pamela who's had 'im."

"Pamela?" Bert's voice rose up, sounding more sad than angry.

"She's just teasing," said Pamela, and Tommy heard Kath say, "oomph" as Pamela kicked her.

"Kath," Gerry said, his voice lustful now, "I'm coming to get you."

"No, not tonight, Gerry. We've got company tonight."

"Now, Kath. Tonight."

Tommy could feel himself blushing. Some street-wise Londoner, he chided himself, embarrassed at the ploys of ladies of the evening.

"See here, gentlemen," said Pamela in a firm tone. "We'll have you up for a private party, won't we? But we want a promise."

"What?" said Gerry doubtfully.

"We won't tell Maggie you made a scene over her, and we'll give you a shilling discount for the lot of you, but—" She paused dramatically, and Kath picked up the thread. "But you leave the Londoner alone."

There was a moment, and the rain began to lightly fall on the assembled group. Tommy could hear the men whisper and a few coins jangle in pockets in anticipation.

"And you won't service the Londoner," barked Gerry.

Tommy heard a rustle of clothing, as if the women were moving their skirts.

"And we won't service the Londoner," pouted Pamela.

Tommy held his breath as he heard the men's boots pounding up the steps to the bridge, and the women laugh as the group walked up Silver Street together to the narrow entrance into the dark passage by the castle wall. Two of the men were singing together; it sounded like someone named Cushie Butterfield was *a big lass and a bonnie lass and she likes her beer*. A woman opened a shutter above the street and yelled at them, "Oy! People sleeping! Quiet!" but there was no quiet until they were up the alley and inside somewhere. Tommy, ashamed but grateful, then made his way up and over to the boarding house.

Perseverance Stone said goodnight to Mason and went up to bed. It had been another exhausting day of meetings at the Foreign Office, and hours reading documents about Prussia: munitions estimates, reports from a man working for Bismarck but actually employed by Otway, a draft of a treaty that would likely never be enacted.

The paperwork was interesting, but Stone was becoming a bit confused by Otway's behavior. He seemed only vaguely interested in what Stone produced and the opinions he gave. As Under Secretary for Foreign Affairs, Otway was clearly a busy man, and there could be no argument that the work wasn't important. To his knowledge, however, few others who worked for Otway were being given the same sort of access or complex tasks that Stone was assigned. Was this because Arthur trusted him so much? Certainly Stone would like to think so.

"Are you never worried that this man of yours will be exposed?" he had asked Otway over their brandy and cigars (or, at least, a cigar for Otway).

"Oh, yes, of course, of course," Otway had replied, looking deeply into his glass. "But it's the future, isn't it? The governments of this country have only become organized about espionage once before. A couple of years ago. The Earl of Derby, you know."

Stone knew that Edward Smith-Stanley, the 14th Earl, had been Prime Minister of minority governments several times during crucial events. The Great Mutiny in India had occurred on his watch, and he had wisely ended the practice of the East India Company acting as a government. He'd also presided over the passage of the Reform Act, as a new Conservative. And he had been known for provoking the Irish, and making inspiring speeches. But spying?

Otway nodded. "Little known, this," he said quietly. "Derby established a Secret Service Department. All about the Fenians, for a start. It lasted less than two years, but I always thought it a good idea. Like India, disparate actions with the same goal need organization, a government umbrella." His voice was rising dramatically. "We can't have assassins running around trying to execute Napoleon III, and loyalists infiltrating the Irish republicans, without some sort of controls!"

Stone had stifled a yawn.

Otway gazed at him through his cigar smoke.

"Yes, you must be tired," he said sympathetically. "And I've taken you away from your case, the one about . . . what did you say the case was about? Some post office clerk who was killed, you said?"

"Yes. I have a young man working on some leads now."

"How is he getting on?"

"Not as well as I expected. Oh!" he said suddenly. Otway raised an eyebrow. "Money!" said Stone. "I meant to send him money."

"All young men need money," said Otway, nodding. "Look, I am sorry, old man. And very grateful for your help."

In the cab on his way home that evening, Stone thought about the tasks he'd done. As grateful as his friend was for his assistance, any competent lawyer could have done the work. He enjoyed Otway's company, but he hadn't called on Samson in over a week, nor worked on his defense beyond a few pages of notes. It was almost as if he were being pulled away from the case, distracted by international affairs.

But as he went to bed, he realized he was thinking like a politician instead of a barrister. Everyone is distracted by international affairs, he thought. War could happen at any time, and no one wanted Britain involved. Well, no one sensible, anyway. And were the Fenians really done, as Otway had said? The Irish were not becoming any more independent, and more factions were forming who thought they should be. Violence in the streets, violence on the continent. Violence at the Post Office, he thought. I must get back to that.

Samson was on duty in the infirmary again that Monday. He had not seen Miss Harper since observing her taking the ridged bottle, but he quickly discovered it was the opium tincture that had been removed. The prisoner Susannah's pains had not recurred over the weekend after he had seen her on Saturday and prescribed Dr. Collis Browne's chlorodyne. The combination of peppermint and morphia had calmed her stomach and her mind. So why did Miss Harper need opium?

He would have to confront her, or report the missing bottle to the governor. Perhaps she was addicted to the substance and was suffering without easy access? Or perhaps she was experiencing some kind of pain? Samson at least wanted the opportunity to diagnose her trouble. But her stealth could mean something more sinister. It was not unheard of for prisoners to steal and sell all sorts of things to other prisoners. People detained here were allowed to keep belongings, including their money in some cases, and he knew there was trade in books, tobacco, and alcohol when the warders weren't looking.

Deciding that the matter couldn't wait, Samson went in search of Conner, and found him marking a roster on a stand near the entrance door. He looked up with a frown. "Why might you be out of the infirmary, sir?" He trusted Samson but was aware that he shouldn't, and it was his job to know where all prisoners were at all times.

"I'm sorry, Conner. I was wondering whether Miss Harper could spend some time in the infirmary today?"

"She's due there shortly, doctor. You're supposed to be cleaning the infirmary this morning."

Samson remembered the jug of vinegar that had been left by the infirmary door. Right, it was Monday, and the infirmary should be cleaned before noon. He thanked Conner and returned just as Miss Harper arrived.

"Cleaning day, doctor," she said with a friendly smile, fetching her apron and the mop.

"Yes, it is, Miss Harper. Could we have a word first, though?"

"Of course," she said, and sat down at the table. "What's it about, then?"

"Well, first I want to ask about Susannah. Is she still feeling well?"

"She is. Thank you so much for seeing her. I don't think Mr. Warner could have done better for her."

Samson looked into her eyes. There was no sign of guile, no portent of secrecy.

"Excellent. Miss Harper, I need to discuss with you something very serious, something I saw you do on Saturday."

Fiona blinked, and Samson saw her lips purse slightly. "Oh?"

"Yes, Miss Harper. I saw you take a ridged bottle from the cabinet and put it in your pocket. I believe it was opium tincture."

She glanced toward the door, but the hallway was silent. She stood, and he saw she was considering whether to leave, then realize there wasn't anywhere she could go. She stared at Samson, her eyes narrowing as she considered her options.

"I am trying to decide whether to take you into my confidence," she said, and he saw the look in her eyes get steely, and her face take on an expression he'd never seen before. Determination, intelligence, with a core of something that, if he didn't know her so well, he might call ruthlessness. He had the feeling in his stomach that it had been a bad idea to have said anything.

"We will talk of this later," she said, her tone dark. "Not now. Let's get our cleaning done. Friday night, O'Brien is on duty. He'll come fetch you when I'm ready, about one in the morning. Will you come?"

Samson agreed, although he had a feeling he would regret it.

Jo hurried to catch the omnibus, aware that she shouldn't be spending the money. There had been plenty of work available at *The Illustrated London News*, but she had not felt right going into the studio there all day, every day. Most mornings she was able to leave home in plenty of time, but George left too, and Hortense had Sally to care for all day. Were the men she worked with, mostly younger illustrators without family responsibilities, moving on more quickly with their careers? She was sure they were, especially because they were willing to travel: Ireland, India, America. Jo had not been offered those assignments, although she knew if she insisted, no one would stop her. Instead she was relieved at not having to refuse them.

She had developed a new talent. Instead of staying at a location and completing an entire drawing, fully drawn with shading and scenery, she had learned to sketch places as quickly as she sketched people, filling in the details later. She'd need that skill this afternoon, when she went out on assignment. She'd arrived at the ILN offices early to do the shading for drawings sketched by Herbert Cox who, despite his dislike of machinery, was very good at drawing foreign scenes based on descriptions sent in by reporters. But she had to leave the studio at twelve. Visiting hours were short at the Clerkenwell House of Detention, and she didn't want to be pushed for time. As she paid for her ticket on the omnibus, she reminded herself that George was now contributing to the household money, even if he did eat quite a bit of it.

She had brought no food or packages with her to the gaol, so she was admitted quickly into the corridor. Since it was not an infirmary day, Samson was in his cell. She saw through the metal door that he was writing something at his small table.

"Samson?" she said.

He turned, not recognizing her until he moved closer to the opening.

"Why, Jo Harris!" he said. "How nice seeing you here."

They had not seen each other in quite some time and had never known each other well. Samson had been tutoring Tommy when Jo was spending much time with Ellie Slaughter and the Women's Reform Club several years ago. Their paths had crossed, but they had little time for conversation. He knew about her and Hortense primarily through Tommy Jones.

"Samson, it is good to see you, but it's horrid that you're in here. Has there been any progress on your case?"

"Not much yet," Samson said, trying to sound optimistic, "but Tommy's hard at work up north to bring back the witness, and I'm sure Inspector Morgan is working on the case."

"Ellie said you had a good barrister?" It was difficult to converse like this, standing in a corridor. Even squeezed next to the door, only possible because Jo wore a simple dress rather than the more voluminous fashion, she felt she was shouting.

"Yes, I do. Perseverance Stone. He's been to see me."

Through the bars on the opening, Jo could see that he looked as tired as Hortense. It must be difficult to sleep in a place like this. Even now, every sound from the cells seemed loud in the high-ceilinged corridor. Sounds of scraping metal openings, turning locks, and creaking cell doors echoed.

"That's good," said Jo, then wasn't sure how to proceed. "Samson, I am here on a very selfish errand."

"You are?"

"Not for me. Well, yes, for me, but more for Hortense. She is quite ill."

"Do you need me to recommend something for her? I could give you a note for an apothecary."

He was such a generous man, Jo thought. It was a shame. This whole thing was such a shame. What on earth was he doing here?

"No, thank you. We have seen a physician. He's recommended surgery." Jo told him everything, the diagnosis, the need for surgery, the potential for recovery, and the recommendation on anesthesia.

"Dr. Wallace says that Mr. Spencer Wells could do the anesthetic himself, but that's not the safest way. And I want a second surgeon who knows about hygiene and will keep Hortense safe if at all possible."

"Spencer Wells is a good man," Samson said. "I have seen him work at St. Bart's. He's an expert in women's medicine, was a pioneer using anesthetics, and follows Florence Nightingale's recommendations on ventilation. You couldn't make a better choice."

He could see, even through the bars, that Jo's expression was somewhat reassured, but still worried.

"But Dr. Wallace is quite right. It would be much better to have a second surgeon attending to the anesthesia and the carbolic, or whatever Spencer Wells wants to use."

Jo looked at him, and she tried to stop the tears from coming, but he heard her sniff them back.

"Obviously there is nothing I can do while I'm detained in here," he said. "How soon did Dr. Wallace think the surgery needed to be? Have you seen Mr. Spencer Wells yet?"

"Not yet," said Jo. "Dr. Wallace thought no more than a month's delay would be safe."

"My trial is May 2. With any luck," he said, then stopped. "With a lot of luck, I will be acquitted, or the actual murderer will be found. If that happens, I'll be honored to tend to Hortense's anesthesia. I don't think Spencer Wells is at St. Bart's anymore, but wherever he is, I'm happy to go there."

This made Jo feel even more miserable about coming. She was talking to a man in gaol, about to go on trial for murder, about doing her a favor if he happened to be released. He saw her expression.

"Please, don't feel badly. I am a surgeon, and if there is justice here, I will continue to be one. I know what it is like to care deeply for someone, and to want what's best for them."

They both heard the warders starting to come around, asking visitors to prepare to leave.

"But I want something from you, Jo. Please go see Prudence? There's just the other doctors in the offices at home, and they aren't there at night. She's distressed and looks very tired. I'm not sure she's eating properly."

"Yes, of course. I'm so sorry about all this, Samson. Thank you so much for offering your help."

It was already two when she left the gaol, but she still had her assignment and couldn't return home until she'd gotten a start. Daniel Maclise, the famous history painter and illustrator, had died the day before in Chelsea. *Punch* was planning a tribute poem, but Mrs. Ingram thought *The Illustrated London News* could go one better. Jo had been assigned to go to his home and, since it would be untenable to ask for anyone's portrait, she was to draw the house and perhaps its surroundings. His Chelsea home was reputed to be lovely and could be used to portray his importance.

It was quite a distance from Clerkenwell to Chelsea, over four miles through Bloomsbury and St. Giles, through Covent Garden and Westminster. Walking would take almost two hours, and a cab through these areas would be caught in afternoon shopping and delivery traffic. She considered trying to get down to the river, but the thought of the smell appalled her. In the end she decided to spend money again. A cab might be able to select less trafficked areas. Either way, she knew she'd be too late to make dinner and would have to rely on George's good nature and cooking skill.

Tommy knew he wasn't going to manage it. The jobs he had undertaken were as much as he could do, and the money simply wouldn't be available in time. He would only be able to pay for Donald Fowler to travel to London alone, and he knew that wouldn't happen. He hadn't even convinced him to go. To get himself back to London in time for the trial, he'd need to leave in the next day or two, taking cheaper coaches and begging lifts on dray carts. He'd ask Donald Fowler to sign something, a statement. Maybe he could get Andrew Rutherford to sign it too, as a constable. Maybe if he presented a document in court, it would count for something.

The letter from Prudence was in his pocket, inviting him to offer Fowler a place to stay above the surgery in Wilderness Row. He'd collected it from the Post Office during his lunch time. She was so sure Fowler could help, thought Tommy, that she'd offer him hospitality even though she was a woman home by herself. Prudence's confidence in Fowler, and in him, was unjustified. He had found the man, certainly. He had even discovered he might have important information. But he couldn't follow through by bringing him into the courtroom.

Melancholy was a new feeling for Tommy, and he didn't care for it. It was after a day of carrying bricks, and he was heading across Framwellgate Bridge. The old man was sitting near the peninsula side, clubbed foot out in front of him, the yellow dog asleep by his side. He was humming a tune, his chin down low on his chest. Tommy glanced in his cap and saw only two pennies and a farthing. The dog raised his head, and Tommy went over to scratch it behind the ears.

"Poor thing," he said. "You're all skin and bones."

The old man raised his head too.

"His name's Robbie," the old man said. "And I'm Callum. And you're the young man wot's working all over town. Working to forget your sorrows?"

"No," said Tommy, smiling, "just aiming for the moon when I can't reach the treetops."

He looked up toward the cathedral tower, glowing orange in the lowering sun. "It's so beautiful here."

"Aye, 'tis," said Callum. "But not so much when it rains." He laughed, and started to cough.

Tommy's pocket was full of coins. Not enough for bringing three people to London. Not enough to marry Maggie and take her away. Not enough to save Samson. Tommy felt tears coming to his eyes. He reached into his pocket, taking out a couple of shillings for a few days of food and moving them to his other pocket. Everything else he put in the cap lying on the stones.

"Oh, young man," said Callum. "Ya canna do that. You need yer money."

"I don't," said Tommy, feeling lighter in pocket and a bit in spirit. "It wasn't enough for me, but it might be enough for you." He rubbed the dog's ears, tipped his cap at Callum, and headed up Silver Street to the Market Hotel.

"Are you sure?" Hortense had asked George on Monday. "I don't like asking you to take time away from your job."

"I know you don't, love," he'd said. "But you must see the surgeon, and I'd enjoy it so much staying home with Sally."

Wednesday morning dawned bright, the straw-colored sunlight shining on Red Lion Street. Sally had been quite content to be left home with George; he had promised to spin the top for her for as long as she wanted, then they would make boiled rhubarb pudding with suet and flour.

Jo hailed a cab when they were just a few steps away. Hortense frowned as it pulled up.

"I'm not incapacitated yet," she murmured, "and the cost—"

"Yes, I know, but this could be a tiring day, and you should be fresh, not bedraggled with riding an omnibus and walking." She helped her into the cab, then gave the driver the address in Portman Place. As the cab clattered down Holborn and then Oxford Street on the way to Marylebone, Jo held Hortense's hand and chatted to her about Sally.

Mr. Thomas Spencer Wells did not look at all like a surgeon. His eyes were widely spaced and twinkled with intelligence. His oval spectacles enhanced the roundness of his face, and his light hair was pomaded on the top but curled down over his ears into his muttonchops, and he had bushy eyebrows to match. He looked like a kindly uncle, the sort who would say he was taking you to the shops, but you would end up at the zoo, watching monkeys and eating chestnuts from a bag. Jo itched to draw him.

"Mrs. Smith," Spencer Wells said kindly, shaking her hand and pulling up a chair for her across his desk. Then he turned to Jo. "I am Mr. Spencer Wells," he said.

"I'm Jo Harris," she said, taking the chair next to Hortense.

Spencer Wells took a seat at his desk and looked at the papers in front of him.

"I have notes here from Dr. Wallace, Mrs. Smith. I understand you have been bleeding heavily for some time?"

Hortense nodded. Jo noticed her skin was taut across her cheekbones.

"And that the cause is fibroids. Removal of the entire womb is recommended. I don't have to tell you that this would be a serious operation."

Hortense shook her head.

"Without it, however, you will simply lose too much blood." He shook his head, as if the idea caused him some distress. He folded the papers into a folder and set them aside. "So that is where things stand, I'm afraid. I would like to examine you, if you are amenable? It would help me greatly to know how large your womb has become."

Hortense nodded and rose. Spencer Wells asked Jo, "Do you mind staying, Miss Harris? Or I can call in a nurse if you would prefer to wait outside."

"I'm happy to stay with her, Mr. Spencer Wells, if it won't disturb you."

"Not at all, Miss Harris, not at all," he gave her a small smile. "On the contrary, having a close friend nearby can be good for the patient."

He guided them to the corner of the room, where a small screen was set up, with a thin high bed behind it.

"Have you been examined before?" he asked Hortense gently.

"Yes, Mr. Wallace was quite thorough."

"If you're comfortable removing your skirts, you may. But it isn't necessary if you are able to grant me access for my hands."

Hortense sat up on the table, and Jo held her hand as she lay back, helping her down. Mr. Spencer Wells went over to the basin and washed his hands carefully, front and back, then dried them on a white towel. Jo stood by Hortense's head and did not watch as Mr. Spencer Wells removed the pads and carefully inserted a hand inside Hortense's body. Hortense clutched Jo's hand, whether in pain or fear she wasn't sure. Wells took only about a minute, then he removed his hands and gently replaced the pads.

"Excellent," he said, as he walked back to the basin to wash, and Jo helped Hortense sit upright. "The fibroids are not too large, and they have not misshapen the womb. We should be able to accomplish this very well." He returned to his desk and Hortense rose. Jo helped arrange her skirts before they returned to their chairs.

"Is the bleeding continual, or do you have respites?" he asked.

"Only for a few days," she answered. He nodded.

"Dr. Wallace mentioned that your husband was not available to sign with you for permission to operate?"

Out of the corner of her eye, Jo saw Hortense sit up more stiffly.

"Actually, he has returned from the business that took him away. But he may be off again soon."

"It would be helpful to meet him. Would that be possible?"

"I don't understand," interrupted Jo. "Mrs. Smith is ill. What does her husband have to do with it?"

Mr. Spencer Wells was looking less kindly now. "It is important that the husband be apprised of the situation, particularly since this surgery will make it impossible for Mrs. Smith to have more children. And, I'm sorry to be blunt, but we also need to talk about costs."

Jo could feel herself getting angry. This wasn't about George knowing in case she could die, or that she might never recover if a mistake were made. It was about the patient's function as a birther of children, and money. She spoke through gritted teeth.

"Mrs. Smith and I run a household and are raising her daughter. Mr. Smith is a good man, and he gave Hortense enough to live on when he left. But since then he has provided no assistance, financial or otherwise, for three years. I work and earn money, although Hortense has been unable to do so. How great is the cost?"

Spencer Wells looked down at the papers but did not answer the question. "I believe I have a solution," he said. "I perform women's surgeries at several hospitals in London, including St. Bartholomew's. But in this case, our best option may well be the Samaritan Free Hospital for Women and Children. It is very close to here, on Lower Seymour Street." He waved out the window behind him to indicate the direction. "However, in my experience, married women of means are sometimes concerned that being treated at a Free Hospital would mean loss of social status among their set."

Jo and Hortense scoffed simultaneously, and Mr. Spencer Wells smiled.

"As I thought, you are not concerned about that. Let me assure you that the Samaritan Free Hospital is as safe and hygienic a place for surgery as anywhere in London, and there is far less attention paid to the patient's marital status."

Jo looked over at Hortense, who nodded. "That sounds very acceptable," said Jo. "But we have another request."

Mr. Spencer Wells put down his pen and looked at her with bland interest.

"We have come to you not only because Dr. Wallace recommended you, but because we were told that you are expert in anesthesia and hygiene. We know a surgeon whom we would like to assist with the anesthesia for the surgery, so you don't have to accomplish two tasks at once."

Spencer Wells looked surprised, unsure what to think. He looked up at the ceiling for a moment, then started to smile.

"I'm delighted with your request," he said. "I will seek out another surgeon to assist me."

Jo and Hortense exchanged a glance.

"If it's possible," said Jo, "and we're not sure yet whether he will be available, but would you find it acceptable to ask Mr. Samson Light? He is a friend of ours."

"Ah," said Spencer Wells, as if several questions had just been answered, "I see! Yes, of course. I have heard good things about Mr. Light at St. Bart's, although I have never worked with him. That would be most acceptable." He turned to Hortense. "Now, Mrs. Smith, I must ask: are you aware of the risks?"

"I understand," said Hortense, her voice hoarse, "that the chances of my survival are roughly half."

Spencer Wells nodded seriously. "That is true, according to the numbers. But the numbers are general. My own numbers are significantly better. But you should consider the risk seriously nevertheless. There are people who would prefer to accept the bleeding and be treated as an invalid until the end comes, quietly and painlessly."

Hortense reached across and took Jo's hand. "We have discussed this together," she said quietly. "I do want the surgery."

Spencer Wells looked at them both. "In that case," he said, "we should schedule within the next few weeks." He looked at his notebook. "I would be able to operate on Friday, May 6. Shall I inform the hospital and send a note to Mr. Light?"

Jo looked startled. "The date is fine, and yes, do inform the hospital. But seeing as he's a friend, we will be happy to speak with

Samson Light. In the event that he is unavailable, however, we'd like you to have another surgeon standing by if possible."

10

Tommy wrote a note to Perseverance Stone, although there wasn't much to say except that he was sorry, that the situation with the Durham miners made it impossible for Fowler to leave, and that he would be returning soon by the slow route on carts and carriages as best he could to Darlington, then train to London. He would depart the following morning, giving him four days to return before the trial. He would bring a signed statement and testify if he were allowed.

The post office at Elvet Bridge was busy that morning, but his days at the fever ward had been reduced since they were laying floors. Henderson had excused all temporary workers in the mornings for the rest of the week. It was raining hard, and Tommy wondered whether the floor layers had been able to get their materials under cover. Since the London mail didn't depart until 10:30, he decided not to wait in the queue, and instead kept the letter inside his coat and walked up Saddler Street to visit St. Cuthbert. He stayed on the pavement to provide a bit of cover under the shop awnings, then stayed under the trees in front of the Castle, skirting the edges of Palace Green. He was nevertheless quite wet when he arrived, and stood on the mat for a while just inside the cathedral door.

Few people were inside, and although the air was cold, Tommy found his heart slowing and a peace descending as he walked slowly up the side aisle to behind the altar. St. Cuthbert's shrine was empty, and he kneeled directly in front of the stone marking his tomb.

He had become somewhat better at praying, or at least it had become easier. He first asked protection for the people he loved, his parents in heaven and his friends, then Maggie and Donald Fowler. He asked blessings for the people who annoyed or bothered him, including his flighty young pupil, Gerry and his boys, and those who had treated him unkindly in the workhouse. He thanked the saint for his health, his abilities, and the contentment he had since he'd given his money to Callum the day before. And he prayed for guidance upon his return to London, and one last time that a way might be found for Donald Fowler and Maggie to come with him. Last he said goodbye, knowing that he might never be able to return to Durham again, and of all his prayers this brought the deepest sadness.

By the time he left the cathedral, the rain had slowed, so he skirted the Green then went back down the hill. With the pause in the rain, the narrow pavements on Saddler Street were crowded with people going in and out of the businesses, and he found it more convenient to walk in the cobblestones of the street. There were only two people in the queue at the post office, an old man in clothing that marked him as a professor at the university, and a woman he recognized as Kath, the woman who had lured Gerry and his friends away from him. She smiled as he took his position in the queue, her eyebrow raised. Tommy knew this meant she was asking whether she should acknowledge him in public, so he spoke immediately.

"Good morning, miss. Out in the wet weather?"

"Yes, hoping for a letter from my cousin Fred. You?"

"Sending one back to London." The old man was busy with the person at the desk, so Tommy lowered his voice and said, "I want to thank you for helping me get away from Gerry and the boys on Saturday. I was in a bit of a pickle."

Kath smiled, and he saw that one of her front teeth was chipped. "'Sawright," she said amiably. "You're a good lad." He didn't know how she knew this, but he gave her a grateful smile.

"They'll have at you again, you know," she said, as the old man started to leave. "They don't care for you."

"I know," said Tommy, shaking his head. "But I'll be gone soon enough. I'm leaving tomorrow."

"Back to London are you?" But the attendant was ready for her now, and she turned.

"No letter today, miss," said the man in a flat tone, his brow knitting in disapproval. Kath smiled at him anyway, "That's all right, Charley. Thank you for checking." She nodded to Tommy and went out.

"Now you I have something for," said Charley, turning to his pigeonholes and pulling out a small parcel, handing it to Tommy. "Anything to send today?" Tommy noticed it was from Perseverance Stone.

"Thank you, yes. But I'll want to open this first."

By now there were three people in the queue behind him, so he went over to the tall table at the side of the office, where there was pen and ink for people to address their letter or write a quick note. He opened the parcel and found a letter wrapped around—

Tommy gasped, and a woman in the queue turned toward him so fast her hat ended up askew on her head.

"Sorry, ma'am. Didn't mean to startle you," Tommy said with a small bow, as he turned back toward his small stack of banknotes. Stone had sent money, more than enough to cover train fare back for all three of them, with plenty left over. He read the letter quickly, an update on the progress of the case. Stone explained that he had struggled to extricate himself from Foreign Office work, had spoken with Morgan and found him unhelpful, had seen Prudence, and had visited Mr. Henry at the General Post Office. He also included a short list of what had been found on Horace Wright's body. Finally he had talked to a friend who worked at St. Giles and discovered the reasons for Morgan's resentment toward Samson. He apologized for the delay in sending funds, which were enclosed.

Tommy practically danced onto Elvet Bridge. Maggie. He must talk to Maggie. Where would she be at this hour? Cleaning and baking at the Market Hotel? Shopping for food? Wednesday, it was Wednesday. Fowler had told him she'd be returning late last evening. Would she still be home?

The Market Hotel was closest, so he tried there first. The burly man was stacking cold pies in the kitchen and didn't know where Maggie was. Tommy then crossed Framwellgate bridge and looked for Callum to say good day and tell him the good news, but he didn't see him or the dog. He found the door open at the house in Neville Street.

"Maggie?" She was scrubbing the counter in the kitchen, humming to herself. When she heard Tommy's voice, she stopped and turned, her face suffused with pleasure.

"Well, Tommy Jones, there you are."

"Welcome back, Maggie. How is your cousin?"

"Fairly well. The baby came early but seems to be feeding all right." She noticed the excitement in his face. "What have you been doing while I was gone?"

"Maggie, look," he said, showing her the packet of notes. "Perseverance Stone sent it, the barrister I told you about. It's enough for all three of us to go to London."

She smiled and her eyes sparkled. "Oh, Tommy!" Then he saw a cloud pass over her face. "But father," she said, shaking her head. "He won't come. The Durham Miners' Association . . . "

"He will, Maggie. He must. Because I love you and we're going to London and then we're going to get married and come back and get you the tavern you want to run." And he kneeled before her, all his desires pouring out of him. "Maggie Fowler, will you marry me? I have no certain job, but many skills, and I can work anywhere. We can stay in London after the trial, or get married there and return here, and we will make our way, Maggie, we will!"

"Well, Tommy Jones—" and she stopped, her eyes wide and her mouth in a smile. Then she knelt in front of him, kissing his forehead and his cheeks. "Yes. We will."

He kissed her fervently, laying her back on the flagstone floor. She returned his passion, then stopped and laughed.

"A wedding, Mr. Jones. A wedding first, afore we start making babies."

Tommy laughed too, kissing her cheeks and eyes and neck.

"Yes, Mrs. Jones." He looked down seriously at her face, her hair splayed out on the floor. "I promise to protect you and help you, to be a good husband to you."

"And I promise to protect you and help you and be a good wife, after—" she paused, turning her head to the side.

"After?" Tommy held his breath.

"After I go to work, you fool. Now let me up."

Donald Fowler came home that night to find Tommy Jones sitting in the parlor, reading his *Railway Times*.

"Evening, Tommy," he said. His eyes looked bleary. "Is Maggie at home?"

"No sir, she's at the Hotel working. She's left a cold supper for you in the larder if you don't feel like cooking."

"Ah," he said, putting his satchel on the table. "Then you're here on your own. Did you work today?"

"Yes, sir. I worked the afternoon at the fever ward."

Fowler noticed he was being called "sir" a great deal more than usual. "I see."

"Yes, sir. I'd like to speak with you after you've had your tea, if I may. I'll start the kettle while you wash?"

As Fowler took his usual trip to the privy, he couldn't help but wonder what was amiss. He knew Tommy wanted him to go to London, and he had been speaking with the leaders of the Durham

Miners' Association. Could he be spared for a week, even a fortnight, now that the officers were all slated? When he'd explained about Samson and the murder at the Post Office, there had been murmurs and considerations.

They sat down quietly together at the kitchen table, listening to the rain resume. Although he had served them both, Fowler noticed Tommy was eating very little.

"I am reminded," said Fowler, "that less than a fortnight ago, I found you outside my door. You seemed like an earnest and honest lad, if a little afraid of me. I later realized it wasn't me, but what you thought I'd done. You thought I had murdered Horace Wright."

"It was possible," admitted Tommy, "but as soon as we talked I felt it was most unlikely. I have known a murderer, Mr. Fowler, and I didn't recognize it at the time. I just didn't want to be fooled again."

"I understand." Fowler pushed his empty plate away. "And now, you want to talk to me. Which topic will be first?"

Tommy was confused. "What do you mean?"

"I'm a fairly intelligent man, young Mr. Jones. I enjoy your company. But in the time I've known you, I've only seen two things that interest you: getting me to London to testify, and my daughter."

Tommy could not keep the shock from showing in his face. He decided that there was nothing for it; he would brazen it out. Everything he'd planned to say, all the elegant phrases he'd been rehearsing in his mind all afternoon, were completely forgotten.

"Yes, sir," was all he could manage.

"So, on the first topic: London," said Fowler. "I am willing to travel to London to do what I should have done before: say what I saw, what I knew, and what I didn't see. It's the right thing to do. Money, however, is a problem. So I have arranged to borrow—"

"There's no need!" Tommy interrupted joyfully. "The barrister, Perseverance Stone, has sent me enough money for all of us—"

Fowler's eyebrows were raised so high they threatened to disappear underneath his hair.

"All of us?"

"Sir, I beg your pardon, because I should rightfully have asked you first, but I have asked Maggie for her hand."

There was a long pause, as the rain beat down harder outside.

"Have you?" said Fowler, his face expressionless.

"I know I'm not what you expected for your daughter. But sir, I will put her needs and wishes first. Always, for as long as I live. I don't have a set job, but I can do all kinds of things. And if she wants to run a tavern, I'll do all I can to make that happen."

Fowler stared at him.

"Young man, you've been here less than two weeks."

"Yes, I know, sir, and I've come from the south. I'm a Londoner. If she chooses to have us live there, I know the streets and the way the city works and breathes. If she wants to live here, I will find a way to stay here with her. I have felt that this place was special since I arrived."

"You've fallen in love with both my daughter and this city?"

"I have, sir. But again, I'll always put Maggie first."

Fowler rose and slowly walked over to the family things near the window. He looked down at the picture of Maggie's mother.

"We always did too," he said quietly.

Jo intended to work through the morning at *The Illustrated London News* studio, filling in the sketch of Daniel Maclise's house in Chelsea. She hadn't wanted the house to look too plain, so instead of an architectural rendering, she had created a scene. The house was framed by trees, the view drawn from across the street, all the way down on the riverbank. It had been muddy, and her boots had stuck, but the perspective was just right. The iron fence added visual interest above the edge of the shored-up bank, and a picturesque horse and cart were crossing the drawing near the center. The contrast between the rough river bank and the smooth house in tree-lined Cheyne Walk was just perfect.

She was just drawing the house windows more carefully when Mrs. Ann Little Ingram came breezing into the studio, her bustled skirt whisking on the floor.

"Miss Harris!" she called, coming swiftly to Jo's table.

Jo jumped and almost dropped her pen. "Yes, Mrs. Ingram?"

Ann Little Ingram was the proprietress of *The Illustrated London News*, having taken over after the death of her husband and son in a collision on Lake Michigan in America. She had hired Jo seven years before.

"Getting better at drawing horses, I see," she said sharply, looking over Jo's shoulder.

"Yes, ma'am," said Jo.

"Don't ma'am me." Her tone was good-natured. "You're needed down at the engravers, quickly. They must go to press, and there aren't enough heads in the drawing of the Easter Volunteer Review."

"The Easter what?" said Jo, getting her things together.

"It was at Brighton Pavilion. The artist who did the drawing has been taken ill, and Miss Dalziel says it doesn't look right without more heads." Mrs. Ingram handed her coins for a cab.

Jo left for the Dalziel Brothers office, almost a half hour's ride to Camden High Street. She was ushered down to the engraving room, and, with one eye on the clock, began drawing heads. Samson had told her that Prudence took lunch at the bookshop at one o'clock, and Jo had promised to go see her. She was needed to help at home in the evenings, so now was the best time. Jerusalem Passage was another twenty minutes and another cab fare, but there was nothing for it. On the other hand, it was close to home, so perhaps afterward Jo would end her workday.

Jo arrived at C. Herbert, English and Foreign Booksellers, at half past one and was told that Prudence was out in St. John's

Square, eating her lunch. The day had turned warm, and she found Prudence sitting on a low wall near the church. All round the square she heard the sounds of industrious work: clockmakers, cobblers, and stay-makers all had workshops there. Prudence was just packing up her satchel when she saw Jo.

"Jo Harris!" she said. "What are you doing here? Making drawings of the activities of Clerkenwell for the magazine?"

Jo sat next to her. "Good afternoon! I hope I'm not interrupting your lunch. Samson told me to come by around one."

"You've seen Samson?" Pru's face lit up.

"I went to the gaol on Wednesday. He asked if I'd come by, make sure you are all right." Pru looked very pale, thought Jo. Not pale like Hortense, just undernourished. She saw a mild sheen of sweat on her brow, but it was a warm day.

"That's very kind. I hope to visit on Saturday."

"I'm not a nurse," said Jo, "but you do look a little ill. Have you been feeling well? Are you able to get enough sleep with Samson away?"

Prudence looked at Jo, her head tilted slightly and her eyes narrowing. She knew Jo from years before, when Pru worked for Ellie Slaughter and Jo was Ellie's friend and fellow reformer. But they had never become friends, and she wondered for a moment whether that might be precisely the type of person she needed.

"May I tell you something, if you promise to keep it between us?"

Jo thought a moment. She had just asked Samson a special favor, to do Hortense's anesthetic, and he had asked her to look in on Prudence. She wanted to be honest with him. But if Pru had a secret and needed to share, perhaps that was more important?

"Yes, I think so," said Jo.

Pru put her hand on her belly and leaned in toward Jo. "I'm with child," she said quietly, as if the clockmakers of Clerkenwell might shout out the news. "Not far along, though, so it wouldn't be right to tell people." She gave Jo a wan smile.

"Samson knows?"

"Yes."

Without thinking, Jo took Prudence's hands in hers. "That's wonderful," she said. Her mind flooded with her love for Sally, combined with a twinge of sorrow that she would never bear her own children.

"Not so wonderful yet," said Pru ruefully, "I'm sick quite a bit. To be honest, I hope I'll be able to keep down the lunch I just ate, although it tasted good at the time. But I've heard that's a good sign."

"I'm sure it is," said Jo.

Prudence's face went from smiling to serious, then Jo saw tears form in her eyes.

"I'm sorry," said Pru. "I keep crying, too."

"That's fine. You have things to cry about, certainly." She reached into her bag and pulled out a handkerchief. Pru took it gratefully, the tears starting to fall. Jo looked away. There were people in the square, people who worked in the surrounding workshops. Two women passed them and looked sympathetically at Prudence. One had a deformity of the jaw. Must be a match factory around here, thought Jo. It looked like phossy jaw, caused by the white phosphorus used on the strike-anywhere matches. Jo gave her a smile, trying not to look as sick as she felt that people had to tolerate such unspeakable work.

"Jo," Pru sniffed, "do you think there's a chance that Samson will be able to come home? I'm waiting for a letter from Tommy. He's supposed to bring back that witness, Donald Fowler. But we don't know what Fowler would say, and Inspector Morgan seems to be doing nothing."

"But Samson has a barrister, doesn't he? What does he say?"

"He is a very busy man, but he sent me a note last week. He thinks he may have discovered why Inspector Morgan is being so unhelpful. Something about a case at the hospital. But Jo, if the police won't help, and the witness won't come, what chance is there for Samson?"

"There must be something that's been overlooked."

"I think so too. A fortnight ago, I even tried to do some investigating myself. I went to the Pneumatic Railway Company offices, to try to learn about the machinery. I thought maybe if I could understand how the railway worked, I could see why someone who worked with it might be killed. Do you know," she said confidentially, her tears dry now, "I pretended I was a reporter for the *Illustrated Police News*!"

Jo grinned. "That's very brave! What did you find out?"

Pru sighed. "Nothing. The thing works with fans and engines."

"I know," Jo said. "I've drawn them."

"Oh, that's clever of you! I didn't understand them. I did get a list of the board of directors. I've been looking up their names at the bookshop."

"Anything?"

Pru shook her head. "But then, I don't know much about business." A trio of workers passed by, one in a top hat and two in caps, all wearing the pocketed aprons that clockmakers wore. The one in the hat tipped it at the women.

"I know a little about business, from the illustration work. And we have a house guest who's trying to do it all, making his way by trading in animals."

"Animals?"

"Yes, he's brought marsupials from Australia. At the moment, they're living in my kitchen."

"Goodness," said Pru, then looked away and gazed off into the square.

"Look, Prudence," said Jo, "I want to help you and Samson as much as I can. Will you promise you'll come call on me if you need anything? Anything at all?"

Pru nodded, still looking at nothing. The women sat in silence for a moment, then Pru rose and brushed crumbs off her dress. "I'd best get back to the shop."

Jo stood, too, then impulsively reached out and kissed Pru on the cheek. "Take care of yourself. I won't tell anyone, but you send for me if you need anything, all right? I live just over there, in Red Lion Street. Number 54." She pointed across the square.

"Thank you, Jo," Pru said with a wan smile, and went back across the square to Jerusalem Passage.

The next morning, Tommy got up early because he had so much to do. It had been decided that he, Maggie, and Fowler would leave for London the following morning. That way everything could be arranged today. Maggie would let them know at the Hotel that she would be gone and would persuade her friend Jane to work in her place. Fowler would arrange for leave with John Marley in Darlington and let the miners know when he would return. Tommy had letters to write, to inform Perseverance Stone and Samson that he was coming with Donald Fowler in tow. Although it was not a bakery morning, he would stop by so Mr. Gowland would know he would not be there as usual on Tuesdays and Saturdays. Simon Henderson needed to be told that today would be his last afternoon of brick carrying, and in the evening he would set type for the *Durham County Advertiser* and tell Mrs. Duncan he wouldn't be returning. But this morning, he needed to find Gerry.

Tommy knew Gerry worked at Henderson's Carpet Manufactory. This huge place was operated by a branch of the same family as Simon Henderson, Tommy's supervisor at the fever ward. John Henderson, who owned the manufactory, was away in London, representing Durham as the Liberal Member of Parliament, but the factory operated efficiently without him. The building was in Back Lane, where cloth manufacturing had been centered for as long as anyone could remember. Before he left the boarding house, Tommy apologized to Widow Hutton for his sudden departure. She was sorry to see him go. It wasn't often you had a boarder who was willing to be so helpful, she said, and how lucky he must be for his rent to be paid up exactly.

"You arrived on a Friday, and you're leaving on one. Couldn't have planned it better!" she smiled. "Of course, to find another boarder will take some time . . ."

Tommy understood and gave her sixpence. "For my food," he explained, when she looked embarrassed. Then he wrote his letters and took them with him for when the Post Office opened later in the morning. He walked up through Market Place, the gray sky drizzling as he went past the church into the warren of streets behind the big indoor market, which he knew had also been built by a Henderson, although he couldn't remember all their Christian names. Upon arriving at the factory, he found the main door, but there was no desk inside, nor anyone about. He heard machines running, loudly clacking a rhythm on the floor above, so he found a flight of metal steps and went up, following the sound.

A supervisor, a young man his own age, was walking among the looms, checking the work of the weavers running them. The looms were threaded with thick carpet yarn, and each were several feet across, with hole-punched cards hanging from one end. As the end of the shaft turned, the cards clicked through, determining which warp threads were lifted to make the design. The noise was deafening. Large pulleys and straps ran from the engines in the next room, which powered all the machines. As he neared the end of the row, the supervisor spotted Tommy and came over, a frown on his face.

"May I help you?" he said loudly, speaking close to Tommy's ear. "I'm Hugh Mackay, weaving supervisor."

"Yes," Tommy yelled back, cupping his hand to his mouth. "I'm looking for Gerry."

"Gerry who?" Mackay said. Tommy realized he wasn't sure of Gerry's surname. Perhaps it was the same as Maggie's?

"Fowler, I think?"

Mackay thought for a moment. "Oh! You mean Gerry Walker. His mother is related to the Fowlers, but his dad is a Walker."

Tommy smiled, remembering what Maggie had told him: anyone named Fuller, Tucker, or Walker had been fullers in earlier times, treading cloth with their feet or using waterwheels. It occurred to him it must have been much quieter back then, before these noisome machines.

"I'll fetch him. But don't keep him long, mind!"

Tommy promised, and Mackay pointed back to the stairs. Tommy waited on the ground floor, gazing out the open door onto the rainy road. He told himself not to be nervous, that Gerry would hardly beat him here, now, in daylight, when he might lose his employment. It was, he comforted himself, a good idea to meet him here. The machines above were still loud enough that he didn't hear Gerry's boots on the stairs, but suddenly he was there beside him.

"Oh, it's you, Londoner," he said in what Tommy chose to interpret as a neutral tone.

"Yes, it's me, Gerry. Good morning."

"Good morning yerself. What did you come for?"

"I came to bring some news, and I hope that you won't strike me for bringing it."

Gerry's face looked stern, then he smiled briefly. "No promises. What is it, Londoner?"

"It's Maggie."

Gerry's brows knit in a look of concern. "What about her? Is she hurt?"

Tommy spoke quickly. "No, not at all. She's fine. But Gerry, I've asked her to marry me, and she's said yes."

Gerry's mouth opened slightly, but he said nothing, just stared as Tommy hurried on, the words tumbling out.

"I know you don't like me because I'm a Londoner, but I love her and will care for her. I'm traveling to London with her and her father tomorrow to help me save one of my friends, a man who's very important to me. We may well return here, Gerry, if she wants to live here, or we may remain in London. Either way, I don't want enmity between us. I believe you're a decent man, and I always want to believe so. You want what's best for Maggie, and that happens to be me." He felt every muscle in his body stiffen, waiting.

A moment passed, but Tommy didn't take his eyes from Gerry's face. He saw emotions pass swiftly across it: anger, confusion, thoughtfulness, then finally a wary acceptance.

"What about her dreams?" Gerry asked, his jaw tense.

"She wants to run a tavern or public house. I'll help in any way I can."

Gerry thought for a minute, turning to stare out across the road. Then he nodded firmly.

"That's that, then," he said, his jaw relaxing. He extended his hand. "We'll be family now, Tommy. And I protect my family. Take care of our girl."

Samson heard a whisper at the opening in his cell door. "Mr. Light?"

He was fully dressed, waiting for the clock to strike one in the morning. The halls of the Clerkenwell House of Detention were quiet at this hour; just a few coughs and snores broke the silence. He rose and showed his face at the opening.

O'Brien opened the cell door as quietly as possible, but a squeak could still be heard in the hall.

"Bring your notebook, sir."

Samson chose his small notebook and the stub of a pencil and followed O'Brien down the hall to the far end. The warder took out his key and opened the last cell, pulling it open for Samson to step inside.

The cell was the same size as his own, but with no furnishings except one oil lamp and a chair. On the chair was a man Samson hadn't seen before, a man with dark wavy hair and a full beard. He was secured to the chair with leather straps, his head drooped forward onto his chest. He seemed insensible. Fiona stood beside him and appeared to be running a hand down his hair. She turned as Samson entered, O'Brien closing the cell door behind him.

"Mr. Light," she said. The lamplight made a halo around her head, but she looked anything but angelic.

"Miss Harper," he replied.

"I was not planning to share my activities here, Mr. Light, but I've decided it is best to take you into our confidence."

He noticed the plural. "Our confidence?"

"Yes, me and Mr. O'Brien. He and I provide services, shall we say secret services, to certain members of Her Majesty's government."

Samson's mind raced. She was a spy? Fiona Harper and Mr. O'Brien. Ireland. It must be about Ireland. He looked at the man in the chair and instinctively approached him, lifting his head gently with one hand while tilting his face toward the lamp. The eyes that opened were awake, but glazed. The man saw Samson and gave a small smile. "Evening, sir," he said with a slur.

"He's drugged," said Samson, but of course she knew that.

"Mr. Hofmann, this is a friend of mine, Samson Light. He's a doctor. If it weren't for him, I wouldn't have been able to get you the opium you enjoy."

"Pleasure to meet you, Mr. Light, I'm sure," said Mr. Hofmann. Samson thought the accent was either German or Austrian.

Fiona saw the notebook in Samson's hand and motioned for him to take it out. He flipped to a clean page and readied his pencil. For the first time in his life, he was unsure whether what he was doing was right. Was Miss Harper who she said she was? He had no reason to disbelieve her. But this man was tied to a chair, and she had stolen opium to give him. Was this how espionage worked?

"Mr. Hofmann, now that we're friends and are relaxing together, can you tell me why you are here?"

Hofmann looked confused. "The warder brought me here," he said.

"Yes, he did. But I mean why you are in gaol?"

"Oooooh," said Hofmann, as if this were the answer to an unsolved mystery. "I was drunk, and I hit somebody."

"Yes, you did, Mr. Hofmann. Somebody who called you a name, I believe."

"He called me a Bavarian," Hofmann said, and tried to spit but couldn't quite make that happen.

"But you aren't a Bavarian, are you?"

"No, miss," he said with an exaggerated shaking of his head. "Not a Bavarian. Prussian." He then said a word that sounded like "Pri-seh", with some force, and began to sing:

Lieb Vaterland, magst ruhig sein,
Lieb Vaterland, magst ruhig sein,
Fest steht und treu die Wacht, die Wacht am Rhein!

Then his voice trailed off and his chin sunk to his chest again. Fiona reached for his hair and Samson winced as she pulled his head back up.

"And who do you work for, Mr. Hofmann?"

"*Lieb Vaterland,*" he mumbled.

"We think you work for Wilhelm Stieber, Mr. Hofmann. Is that correct?"

Hofmann nodded vigorously. "*Ja, ja,* Herr Stieber." Fiona looked at Samson, so he made a note.

"And what do you do for Herr Stieber, Mr. Hofmann?"

Hofmann looked confused. Fiona tried again.

"What did Herr Stieber ask you to do?"

"*Die unterlagen,*" said Hofmann.

"Documents?" Fiona asked. "Which documents?" But Hofmann just shook his head and tried to scratch his knees with his hands, looking mystified when he saw his hands were tied together.

"Where are these documents now?" Fiona asked quietly, smoothing his knees with her hands. He looked up into her face.

"*Liebchin*," he said softly. "So lovely. *Schön*."

Fiona smiled. "Where are the documents?" she said kindly.

"*Der kasten*," he said, and Fiona shook her head at him. "The case. At the Gymnasium."

Fiona tensed. "The German Gymnasium? In King's Cross?"

Hofmann raised his head and gave her a sloppy smile. "*Ja, ja.*"

"So if I went to the German Gymnasium and found your locker, I'd find the papers?"

Hofmann shook his head and chuckled. "*Nein.* I had to moooove them."

"Why?"

Hofmann's head eased downward, and he began to hum a tune Samson didn't know.

Fiona shook his shoulder. "Mr. Hofmann," she said. There was more humming. "Heinrich?"

Hofmann raised his head and gazed stupidly at her. "*Ja?*"

"Where are the documents now? *Die unterlagen?*" She reached out and smoothed his hair from one temple.

"Down, down, down." Hofmann stifled a giggle. "I found a better place. Down at the post office." He snorted at his own joke.

"Which post office, Heinrich?" She ran her hand through his dark curls. He leaned his cheek toward her hand.

"The big street. With *der eisenbahn*."

"A post office on a big street, with a railway?" She looked confused, wrinkling her nose. He nodded, transfixed as he gazed at her face. Fiona stood back and thought for a moment.

"I think I know what that is," said Samson quietly. She turned toward him with an eyebrow raised. "The General Post Office, in

St. Martin's-le-Grande. The pneumatic railway is in the basement. They haven't opened the line yet."

Hofmann turned his face, surprised to see Samson still there. "*Ja*," he said in a whisper, looking to either side of the cell. "Down, down, down." And then his head drooped again, and he began to snore.

Fiona took a deep breath and let it out slowly, then tapped on the cell door. O'Brien opened it slowly. She and Samson stepped out into the hall.

"We got it," Fiona whispered to O'Brien, with a grateful glance at Samson. "The papers are somewhere in the basement of the General Post Office. The new annex with the railway."

O'Brien looked relieved. "Well done, Miss Harper. I'll take him back to his cell now, shall I? Then I'll come back and unlock Mr. Light's." He stepped into the cell where she'd been questioning Hofmann and brought out the sleepy prisoner. He smiled when he saw Fiona and reached out to touch her face. She gave him a dazzling smile, and O'Brien took him down the corridor.

Fiona stood in the quiet hall with Samson.

"Thank you," she said.

"For what?"

"For knowing what he meant, for not saying anything to anyone about what you've seen here, and for not reporting my theft of the opium. You have done your government a great service."

Samson stood, stunned, but he managed to nod, then tore out the page of the notebook. It had only "Wilhelm Stieber" and "German Gymnasium, King's Cross."

"Dare I ask what this is all about?" he whispered.

"Wilhelm Stieber is Bismarck's head of espionage. He is planning for a possible war on the continent, likely against France. He doesn't want Britain to interfere. We've suspected for some time he was trying to obtain naval plans, and some secret documents have gone missing. When Hofmann was arrested there was reason to suspect him, and I was sent here to find out."

"So you're not here for forgery?"

Fiona shook her head to the side, as if she pitied his naïveté. "No."

Samson said nothing, but lowered his gaze when he realized he was staring at her.

"Matron O'Brien is waiting for me in the women's ward," she said. "I must go."

It was almost three before Samson could sleep.

It was time to depart for London. This time there would be no carts across the countryside. The three met at Durham Station, up on the hill. Tommy had not realized how far the station was above the town, located high up on the viaduct he'd seen from below in North Road. Fowler was dressed for travel, in a dark gray suit and tall hat, with a leather satchel. But it was Maggie who caught Tommy's attention. She wore a green traveling dress, plain but of good sturdy fabric, and a matching cap with lace streamers trailing down. Her hair was done up with sweeping swirls. She carried both a basket and an intricately woven carpet bag. When he caught his breath, Tommy asked if he could carry one for her.

"I can manage both, thank you, Tommy Jones." Her color was high in her cheeks, and Tommy caught some of her excitement.

"What a serviceable bag," he said.

"Made of Henderson's carpet manufactory scraps, of course," she said, her eyes crinkling at the corners.

"She hasn't ridden in a train since she was a wee girl," explained Fowler, tipping his hat to Tommy. But it was only an excuse. Maggie looked like a woman set on a great adventure, and it wasn't only about the train. Tommy gazed into her eyes, heedless of her father, but then remembered he needed to purchase their tickets. He managed to return only minutes before the train arrived from Newcastle.

The journey home was long, but uneventful. They changed at Darlington and managed to find seats facing each other in the carriage on the London train. Maggie opened her basket, and they had a lunch of cold beef and potato pie she'd brought from the Market Hotel.

"How did Mr. Burns react when you told him you'd be gone awhile?" Tommy asked Maggie.

"Oh, he wasn't pleased at all. Wiped his greasy hands on the apron he always wears and gave a grunt that sounded like a great boar. But then he started talking to me."

"Talking?" scoffed Fowler, who knew Burns' taciturn nature.

"Yes, I've never heard him string so many words together. Said as how he was going to retire soon himself, how instead of cooking pigs he wanted to raise them. His uncle died in Copmanthorpe, left him a croft. He said his wife, God rest her soul, had loved Durham, but he'd never liked it much."

"Did you ask him who would run the place if he left?" An idea was forming in Tommy's head.

Maggie understood immediately. "I didn't! Oh, Tommy, I should have, shouldn't I?"

"We could write him from London," said Tommy.

"If he reads," grumbled Fowler.

"Oh, I'm sure he reads. He must, to do the books. Well, at least I think so. Though he does have me write the menus—"

Fowler gazed out the window as Tommy and Maggie chatted and planned. The green fields rolled by, the trees looking identical in the distance. Sheep grazed here and there, and as they passed little towns and villages, he could see the occasional church spire pointing up out of the trees. He missed Emmy so much. She should have been here, sitting with Maggie and her lad, chatting about when the wedding might be. He could almost see her there, sitting across from him, the way her eyes would crinkle at the corner when she smiled, just like Maggie's were doing now. God, bless my

Maggie, he thought, but why couldn't you have let her mother stay a little longer with us?

He fumbled in his jacket pocket and, not finding what he wanted, began rummaging in his leather bag, keeping his head low so the young people couldn't see the tears in his eyes.

"What do you need, Dad?" said Maggie.

"Oh, just looking for my pipe. Thought I'd go to the end of the carriage and see if I could have a smoke."

When he'd left, Tommy's eyes glinted at Maggie. "Come, sit on my lap," he said, beckoning her to come across. They were alone in the carriage, and he wanted to take advantage. She snuggled into him, and he could smell her warm body, then he kissed her and felt happy and possessive and scared, all at once. When she kissed him back, he felt something else entirely, and set her down firmly beside him, taking a deep breath.

"What?" she said huskily, smoothing his hair back over his ear.

"Well, Maggie, we can hardly be intimate in a railway carriage—" He caught his breath as she started nibbling his ear lobe. "Not with your—um—father—ah—returning from a smoke in—oh Maggie—just a few minutes—"

The door swung open, and the conductor stepped in to collect their tickets. Tommy quickly took off his cap and put it in his lap. The conductor gave them a look over his large brown whiskers but said nothing. Fowler returned to see the heightened color in both their cheeks, and laughed. "It's all right," he said. His breath smelled like tobacco. "I wasn't always this old, you know. How do you think our Maggie got here?"

The arrival at King's Cross was hectic, people pouring off the various trains on the platforms, porters piling baggage onto carts, young travelers running to catch an omnibus. Tommy had been a helper here, had worked for coins, and was grateful that neither Maggie nor her father had brought a trunk. So much more practical to carry just one bag. They went out in front of the station and caught a cab to Wilderness Row. It was well past time for an evening meal, so Tommy had decided if Pru wasn't at home they would find a pub. But she answered the door even before Tommy knocked, and when she saw him came out the door and threw her arms around him.

"Oh, Tommy," she said. "I got your letter, and I'm so glad you've come!"

She looked up at her guests and caught the bemused expression on Maggie's face.

"I'm Prudence," she said with a smile, holding out her hand first to Fowler and then to Maggie. "Welcome! I don't have much room, but Maggie can sleep upstairs, and I've set up a bed in the surgery for you, Mr. Fowler. You must be hungry—I've made some stew. Put down your things, go on back to the kitchen and eat. I'll be out here by the window. Just need to put my feet up for a bit. It was a long day at the bookshop."

If they thought it strange to eat without their hostess, the three didn't say so. Tommy left for home, walking along Wilderness Row, a little ways down St. John Street, then through Passing Alley to the Gate. The night was cool and the air damp, his room cold. His room was always cold but tonight, without Maggie, it felt even colder.

The opening of the new tube between the central station at 245 Holborn and the General Post Office at St. Martin's-le-Grande was far less exciting than the opening of the first line from Holborn to Euston. William Wilson was relieved. That day five years ago had been a bit much for everyone. The Duke of Buckingham, the board, and their hangers-on had not simply inspected the cars, posed for sketches, and thanked all the engineers. They had insisted on actually riding in the cars.

Wilson wasn't sure where the idea sprang from originally, but he had been appalled. It started with a joke made by one of the

Duke's friends, that surely the speed would be too much for a man to tolerate. Mr. Rammel, the engineer in charge, had taken offense at this. Thomas Webster Rammel had been the man behind the Crystal Palace pneumatic railway, which ran in a 10-foot diameter tunnel and carried passengers. He had built it the summer before, in 1864, and it had been a wonder. The cars could hold 35 visitors and ran between the Sydenham entrance and the armory near the Penge park gate, with a timed journey of just under a minute. The carriages had proper seats and visitors reported the journey was quite comfortable. It cost six pence to ride. Although dismantled at the end of the summer season, the Crystal Palace railway had proven that pneumatic technology was feasible.

But the Holborn to Euston mail train was a very different affair, meant for business rather than pleasure. The tunnel here was deep underground, and the diameter of the tube was only four-and-a-half feet. The cars were low and long, intended to carry mail bags and parcels. No one had ever ridden in them, nor should they. After smiling politely at the joke about it being too fast for passengers, Wilson had been shocked to hear Mr. Rammel say, "Gentlemen, my pneumatic railway can carry people in perfect safety! Certainly it was not intended for passengers, but if Your Grace would like . . ." Wilson stopped listening and began, as was his habit, to prepare for the crazy ideas of his betters. He strode over to one of the mechanics, asking him to fetch candles, matches, and cloths to cover the gentlemen's clothing. When he returned, the Duke and several gentlemen were gleefully climbing into the cars, determining themselves how many men could fit in each of the three. The answer was two, albeit uncomfortably.

The telegrapher, who had thought he was there to explain the telegraph system to the visitors, was pressed into actual service. He was to telegraph to Euston that the gentlemen were coming, so they would be ready at the other end.

The six men were quickly covered in cloths and given lighted candles. As soon as the tunnel doors were closed and the engines began to start up the fans, furtive glances were exchanged among the engineers and mechanics. The machine was not built for this. Were they about to mutilate or kill Richard Grenville, 3rd Duke of Buckingham and Chandos, the director of the Pneumatic Despatch Company? Would he and his friends die of suffocation during the five minutes it took to reach Euston? Nobody knew. They just knew that if anything bad happened, they were all out of a job. Wilson didn't think he drew breath for the full five minutes.

The telegraph signal had been sent, and there was a substantial sigh of relief as they received word: the party had arrived safely at Euston, their candles blown out but their spirits high.

But that had been five years ago which, Wilson had to admit, was an absurdly long time without the main line opening. What was exciting in 1865 was long overdue five years later. No nonsense today, thought Wilson. No dukes hurtling through tubes. Just Mr. Faber and the engineers, and Mr. Henry from the General Post Office. It was the same telegrapher as back in 1865, and he shot Wilson a glance relaying humor and irony. The police had not confiscated the car in which Horace Wright's body had been found, so it would be used. Jenkins lugged the mail bags into the cars, the doors were shut, the lever pulled, the telegraph tapped. The sound of the fan got louder and louder, and Mr. Henry, who preferred the quiet of his office, had to stop himself from covering his ears. Wilson waited at V.G. Faber's elbow in case anything was requested, and he prayed that the whole thing would work. The test runs had been fine, although no one mentioned that one of these runs had carried a dead body. He listened for any sound that might indicate a problem, but he wasn't an engineer. They heard a clunk, the vacuum formed, and a whine indicated strain on the engines; they knew that the cars were in motion. A few minutes later, the telegrapher notified them that the bags had arrived safely at St. Martin's-le-Grande. There were handshakes and congratulations all round. V. G. Faber shot Wilson a look of profound satisfaction. Mr. Henry went out to catch a cab back to the General Post Office, the workers joking that he should just ride back in a pneumatic tube car and avoid the traffic. Wilson followed Faber back to Victoria Street.

11

Donald Fowler rose early on Saturday morning, intent on filing a report at St. Giles Station. Tommy had told him that Detective Inspector Joseph Morgan was in charge of the case, and he wanted to make things right. It was a very long walk, but the morning was fine and he strode the pavements, admiring the newer buildings. He walked because it was London and he knew the way, avoiding the heavy foot traffic on Holborn and skirting through the Inns of Court, bypassing 245 Holborn as he went by way of the British Museum, where the neighborhood had more trees.

The Clark's Buildings looked hideous, situated among bulky tenements on dingy gray streets. He came up to the desk and removed his hat. A young constable with a chiseled jaw approached the desk on the opposite side and asked if he could be of assistance.

"I've come to see Inspector Morgan, please."

"The Inspector is out on a case, I'm afraid," said the constable. "Can I be of any service?"

"I don't believe so," said Fowler. "I've come as a witness for the case of Horace Wright's murder. I've been up north and have come to testify at the trail. I want to make a statement."

"Is that so, sir?" said the constable, his eyebrows rising. "Well, that's very important. Allow me to take your name and your London address, sir. As soon as Inspector Morgan returns, I will alert him, and I am sure he will want to speak with you."

Annoyed by the delay, Fowler wondered momentarily whether he should ask to have his statement taken by someone else. But police procedure was what it was, and he wanted to speak directly to Morgan. He gave the constable his information and asked when the Inspector might return.

"Cases take time, sir. Sometimes the Inspector is gone most of the day."

"But the trial starts Monday!"

"I understand, sir. I will make sure he knows you've called."

Fowler hesitated outside the station, then began walking toward New Oxford Street. Two children approached, their clothes a size too big and their shoes worn through. They were silent, but each held out a hand, hoping for a coin. Fowler said nothing, but reached into his pocket and gave them each a two-penny piece. They ran off into a courtyard where he heard other children playing a game, likely Prisoner's Base by the sound of the shouts. Curious, Fowler walked over to watch almost a dozen children in a washing yard, making home bases of some of the tubs and prisons of others. Two larger children were obviously the guards, and the boys, plus one girl, tried to capture prisoners. The children took no notice of him, and he turned back and walked past the police station.

After crossing New Oxford Street, Fowler realized he was headed toward 245 Holborn. He wasn't sure why. Maybe to say hello to Jenkins, if he was still working there. To be honest, he thought, he wanted to look at the dispatch room again, to remember that morning and what he saw. Maybe to just have something to do before Morgan returned to the police station, for Fowler had every intention of going back there after an hour or so.

He was relieved that he didn't see anyone on the ground floor and was able to go down the stairs without attracting any attention. It was almost eleven, and sure enough, Jenkins was sitting on the edge of the control platform, enjoying a cup of tea. Next to him, Fowler saw a man he didn't recognize, with a rosy face and blond hair. This man was laughing at something Jenkins had just said.

Jenkins saw Fowler and jumped to his feet, almost spilling his tea.

"Why, if it isn't Donald Fowler! Come down from the north? You're back in a hurry."

Fowler shook his hand, and Jenkins looked over at the other man.

"George, this is Donald Fowler, the engineer who ran off to the north what, a month ago? He left the day we found poor Mr. Wright. Mr. Fowler, George Smith. Your replacement, after a fashion."

"Can I pour you a cup of tea?" said George, smiling. "We have plenty."

"No, thank you," said Fowler. He turned to Jenkins. "I'm back in town for the trial. I've come to testify."

"Testify?" Jenkins looked confused. "But you didn't see anything that I didn't. I'll be saying how we found Mr. Wright in the rail car."

"It's about what I didn't see, earlier that morning."

"What you didn't see?"

"The argument between Mr. Wright and the man they're saying killed him, Samson Light. Didn't happen. I was out front waiting for the cart at the time."

Jenkins nodded, thinking. "Who was it again who said there was a fight?"

"Teach."

Jenkins grunted. "I see," he said.

"And I need to tell the Inspector what Mr. Wright said about those seals," said Fowler.

"What seals?" said Jenkins.

"The seals on the pneumatic railway cars," said Fowler, nodding toward the metal doors. "He said they leaked."

"Now, I said at the time, if they leaked, I'd have known it," said Jenkins. His jaw twitched, and he looked like he might get angry.

"We should have," said Fowler. "I never bothered to look that closely."

"But you're an engineer, man!" said Jenkins expansively, "You would have known! What would a clerk like Horace Wright know about seals? He was just a fancified mail sorter."

Fowler frowned, his bushy eyebrows knitting, and looked over at George, who'd been listening attentively.

"I thought I'd have a look round, see if I'd forgotten anything before I speak to the Inspector."

George nodded. "Good idea."

Fowler walked over to the rail car waiting to be loaded. "Is the line open now to St. Martin's-le-Grande?" he asked.

"Yes, opened only yesterday," said Jenkins. "Works like a charm."

"St. Giles is just up the road, isn't it?" said George. "Were you able to find Inspector Morgan?"

"No, he's out. I'm going to go back there every couple of hours until he returns." He looked up at the clock. Time for the next run, if the schedule was still the same.

Jenkins and George set the teacups on the shelf at the edge of the room, then George pushed the cars into the new tunnel and closed the doors. Jenkins went up to the platform, pulled the lever, and tapped the telegraph. After the whoosh of the outgoing mail, the Euston tunnel began hissing, the telegraph bell sounded, and Jenkins pulled a different lever. He jumped down from the platform.

"Give us a hand, as long as you're here," Jenkins said to Fowler. "There's cuffs over there."

Fowler had nothing else to do, so he put on the sleeve protectors and helped bring in the mail from Euston Station.

Saturday wore on, with Fowler going over to the police station every couple of hours, only to be told each time that Inspector Morgan was out. He had lunched with Jenkins and George Smith at the Gordon Arms, where they'd agreed to walk so that Fowler could be halfway to the police station.

"I ate here once with my wife. That would be three, four years ago," said George, enjoying a steak and kidney pie.

"That would be shortly before I was hired on," said Jenkins, sipping a beer.

"I have happy memories. She was a ray of sunshine." His voice was wistful.

"Is she still with us?" asked Fowler, cognizant of his own pain at being a widower.

"What?" George looked bemused. "Oh, yes, she's with us. Well, not with me. I left, you see, to make my fortune in South Africa. Only I went to Australia instead."

"Gold?" Jenkins asked, and when George nodded, shook his head. "Thought of doing that myself," he said. "Figured that mining must be in my blood somewhere."

"I've become an exotic animal dealer now," said George proudly, sopping up the gravy with a piece of crust.

"When he's not working in the engine room," said Jenkins, laughing. "Do you transport tigers?"

"No, not tigers. Smaller animals. Soon to be much smaller."

"There are so many stories about tigers," Jenkins continued, as if George hadn't spoken. "Did you hear about the one that got away from that dealer, Charles Jamrach, back in '57?"

Fowler shook his head. George shook his head too, deciding now was not the time to mention that Jamrach was the buyer for his animals.

"It was right after the Mutiny, when we all feared that every Indian in London would murder us in our beds. It was a Bengal tiger, straight out of Oudh, where the uprising began. All those sepoys, working for the British East India Company, rising up because of the rifles."

"The rifles?" said George.

"The rifles, the Enfield Rifles. The ones that had to be breech-loaded in the wet, with the greased cartridges. But was the grease pig fat or cow fat? And were the sepoys Hindu or Moslem? That's what started the mutiny."

Jenkins took another sip of beer and continued.

"So everyone in London was on edge, then this Bengal tiger gets away from Jamrach. Attacks a boy in the street, pulls him up in its mouth. Nine years old, the boy was. And that's where the story gets interesting."

"Did it kill the boy?" asked George, horrified.

"That's why it's interesting. Some say it killed the boy outright, then a bystander attacked the tiger with a crowbar. But others say that the bystander saved the boy. And there's also a story, which I've seen printed in several places now, that Jamrach himself saved the boy, by hitting the tiger with the crowbar brought over by the bystander. Others say Jamrach wrestled the tiger to the ground and that there was no crowbar. But the boy must have survived, because it was reported that his family sued Jamrach for three hundred pounds. Some stories say he wasn't badly injured, others say he was. So the moral of the story is—"

"Lock up your tiger better," said George.

"No, the moral is to watch out for testimony. Everyone has a different story."

By the end of the day, Donald Fowler had visited the police station four times, and Inspector Morgan was not there. He had worked hard at the 245 Holborn helping Jenkins and George, more for the exercise than anything else, and had enjoyed it. He hadn't realized he'd missed the whoosh of the pneumatics or the simple labor of hauling and lifting. George and Jenkins left at six, shaking their heads when Fowler insisted on staying another quarter hour to check a squeak on one of the doors.

As soon as the two men were gone, Fowler grabbed a lamp and got down on his knees to peer into the new tunnel and look closely at the rails on the lower edges. Everything looked shiny and new, as it would, having been used for only a day or two. He got back up and pushed the first car in, then aimed the lamp at the lower edges, flattening himself against the floor so he could see where the wheels contacted the rails. But he needed to see the other side, too. So he pulled out the car, bent over at the waist, and backed himself into the four-foot tall tunnel, holding the lamp in front of him. He grabbed one of the two round bumpers and pulled the car in after him. There was a circle of light all around the car from the room, but that was normal—a small gap was necessary to make sure the pressure didn't build too much. He pushed the car out and came back into the room, turning again to see it from the outside.

This time he noticed that the gap around the rails was wider than the gap around the whole car. This was the leak. It wasn't a leak of water or oil, but of air. The iron wheels would only increase this leak as time went on and they pressed the rails over and over. He also noticed the rubber flange had ragged edges; it looked like it had been chewed. Horace Wright was correct; this was not a sustainable system, nor a good investment. It would be worthless within a year, losing pressure and slowing to a crawl. He sat back on his heels, looking into the tunnel and thinking what to do. He heard a quick footstep behind him, felt a horrible pain between his neck and his shoulder, and then everything went black.

Samson awoke with a start. He'd had the dream again, the one with the child.

It had been three years ago, and he knew it hadn't been his fault, but the guilty feelings remained. It had been a case where no amount of medical knowledge would have helped, one of those horrible street accidents that was so avoidable and yet so common. Young Patsy Morgan had been struck by an omnibus near Holborn Viaduct, her ribs broken and her legs crushed. Rushed to St. Bartholomew's, she had been brought into the accident ward. Her father, the newly promoted Detective Inspector Joseph Morgan, had rushed into the hospital as Samson Light had been evaluating her for surgery. Morgan had bullied the staff and hollered at Samson that his daughter must be saved, at all cost. The child was unconscious, and so was not subjected to the scene.

At the time, it was clear from the extent of her injuries that she could not survive. Samson had done his best to keep her comfortable and free from pain, but operating would have achieved nothing. The senior surgeon had agreed, shaken his head, and walked away to make the report. Samson had held the girl's limp hand, and in his dreams sometimes he saw her pale round face, her blue lips drawing their last breath. She had expired a mere two hours after arriving at St. Bart's. It had been Samson who had to explain to her father. Inspector Morgan had not taken it well. He had even filed a formal complaint, but as he refused to allow a post-mortem examination, the hospital board was only able to issue their condolences. There was no cause for anyone at St. Bart's to take the blame.

The morning of Samson's arrest a few weeks ago had been harrowing, so he hadn't recognized the Inspector right away, despite the disdain with which he questioned Samson the next day. He had said little, but now Samson understood what he had sensed, Morgan's hatred and his smugness at being able to catch Samson as the murderer he thought he was. Of course there had been no help from that quarter, no real investigation. If anything, Samson thought, Morgan would have been trying to prove he had committed the crime. He got out of bed in the cold cell, lit his candle with a shaking hand, and began penning a note to Perseverance Stone.

"We'll just have to find him is all," said Tommy, staring into his cup of tea.

He had been awakened at dawn by a banging on his door in St. John's Gate, to find a distressed Maggie and a troubled Pru just outside. Donald Fowler had not been seen since the previous morning, when he left Prudence's house, muttering something about a statement. Tommy took them downstairs to Mrs. Wren's kitchen. She had clucked at their troubles and made some tea.

"Should we go to the police?" said Pru. "He said he was making a statement. Do you think he would go to the station near Wilderness Row, or to see Inspector Morgan?"

"My guess is Morgan," said Tommy.

"I agree," said Pru. "We should start there."

They left without breakfast because Maggie couldn't sit still. Mrs. Wren handed Tommy a cloth wrapped around some buns as they went out the door.

"Don't let that one get hungry," she whispered to him, nodding her head toward Pru. "In the family way, she is."

Tommy was too surprised to say thank you, and ran after the women.

"The St. Giles station is a fair distance, and it's Sunday," he said. "I have money for a cab—"

"Yes, yes," said Maggie, as they approached the alley for St. John's Street. They hailed a cab and were in St. Giles within a quarter of an hour.

Maggie rushed up into the station, leaving Pru and Tommy behind to pay the cabbie. "We need to see Inspector Morgan, right away," she said to the young constable at the desk. Tommy came in as the constable explained that Inspector Morgan wasn't there, as it was Sunday.

"We'll go to his house, then. Where does he live?"

The young constable blinked. "I'm sorry, miss. We cannot give out that information. If you will leave a note, we can see that Inspector Morgan receives it. Then he can call upon you."

Tommy could see Maggie was about to lose her temper and stepped in front of her. "Thank you, constable." Pru helped usher Maggie outside.

"What did you do that for?" Maggie snapped, pulling away from Pru.

"It's no use if he's not here," said Tommy. "What we need is someone who has a directory."

They stood there for a moment outside the station as Maggie's temper subsided and they thought what to do.

"We could go see Jo," said Pru. "I'm sure she'll have a directory, for all those assignments they send her on. But we'll need another cab, since she lives back in Red Lion Street."

Tommy still had some of Stone's money, and he figured this was just the sort of thing it should be spent on.

It was only nine o'clock, and Jo, Hortense, George, and Sally were in the kitchen eating breakfast. George had made toast and sausage. He answered the door with a big smile, and Pru stepped back a bit in surprise.

"Hello," she said, "we've come to see Jo."

"She's here," said George. "Come in, come in."

"I'm Tommy," he said to George as they entered, "and this is Prudence and Maggie."

Jo was rising from the table to greet them. "My goodness, this is an entourage! Come have some coffee." Then she caught the look on their faces. "What's happened?"

Sally was sitting in Hortense's lap, sucking her thumb and taking in the visitors. She took her thumb out long enough to yell, "Tom Tom!" and Tommy went over and picked her up.

"Hello, sweet Sally," he said, giving her a squeeze. "We've come to see Jo. It's very important." He put his finger over his lips. Sally nodded and put her thumb back in her mouth, learning her head on his shoulder.

"I'm Hortense, Sally's mother," Hortense said to her guests. "Welcome. Do sit down. If you'll excuse me? I'll be back in a moment." She went upstairs.

Prudence explained to Jo about Maggie and her father, and that he had disappeared. They needed to find Inspector Morgan at home, and did she have a directory?

"Yes, of course," said Jo, and went to the parlor to fetch it.

"She did have one!" Maggie said to Tommy, impressed.

"Wait a minute," said George, who was scraping bits of sausage out of the pan and onto a small plate. "What's your dad's name?"

"Donald Fowler," said Maggie.

"I thought I heard that accent," he said. "He's the man who came by the station yesterday. Helped us out all day."

"He what?"

"He came by 245 Holborn, to call on Jenkins. Said he had come to London to testify about poor Horace Wright. I told Jo and Hortense about him last night."

Jo had brought the directory and handed it to Prudence. As she went toward the table to lay it out, her foot kicked a wooden box, and there was a snuffly sound.

"What is that?" asked Prudence.

"One of the animals I mentioned," said Jo. "It's a quokka. Quite friendly."

Sally took her thumb out. "Good kitty," she said.

Pru put the directory on the table and began looking in the section of public names.

Maggie was getting impatient. "When did he leave? Did he say where he was going?"

George thought a moment, looking at the ceiling. "We all left at six. No, wait, he didn't. Said he wanted to check one of the doors. Jenkins and I left without him. He'd spent the day going back and forth to the St. Giles station, trying to find Inspector Morgan, but he never did."

"So he might have gone back to the station after six," Tommy said. "We need to find Morgan."

"I have him," said Pru. "Gilbert Place, number 27. It's near the British Museum."

"Back across," said Tommy with a sigh. "Let's find a cab."

The three of them arrived at Gilbert Place in a hopeful mood. Surely once they alerted Inspector Morgan, the police would be involved and Donald Fowler could be found. At the same time, Tommy had met Morgan before. He didn't want Maggie's hopes dashed, but he felt he should warn her.

"I must tell you, I didn't find him helpful about Samson's case at all," he told her. "Just so you know."

Maggie got a determined look on her face and rang the bell. It was opened by a parlor-maid with light brown hair curling under her crisp cap.

"Good morning. May we see Inspector Morgan, please?" Maggie asked.

The parlor-maid began to reach for a salver, then realized they had no cards.

"I shall see if he's at home," she said, taking note of their clothes and shoes. "Whom shall I say is calling?"

"Tommy Jones, Maggie Fowler, and Prudence Light," said Tommy. "It's a matter of some urgency. A man has gone missing."

"If you'll wait out here, please," and she closed the door.

"Wait out here?" said Maggie. "What the blazes for? We're not good enough to come in?"

Tommy looked up at the house, with its two tones of brick and its new windows. "Probably not."

The door opened. "I'm afraid the Inspector is not at home," said the maid.

"Like hell," said Maggie, pushing her way past into the house. Tommy gave the maid an apologetic look and ushered Pru inside.

"What's all this then?" said Morgan, coming in from the morning room with a serviette tucked into his collar.

"I'm Maggie Fowler," she said, standing in the hall. "Daughter of Donald Fowler. We've come all the way to London to testify at the trial of Samson Light. And now my father's gone missing."

Morgan looked over her shoulder and saw Tommy. "I remember you from the station," he said. "And I saw you there too," he said to Prudence. "You're Mrs. Light, aren't you?"

Pru nodded. She was feeling a little lightheaded.

"Very well, Miss Fowler, and company. Come into the morning room and sit down. You look like you're going to fall down, Mrs. Light." He pulled a tapestry rope by the mantle. A woman appeared, plump and wearing an apron.

"Tea for our guests, Mrs. Hobbes," he said. She nodded and left.

"Now," he said, facing Maggie. "You say your father has gone missing? When was this?"

"Yesterday," she said, speaking calmly. "He left to go to St. Giles station to find you. Then it seems he went to the railway dispatch room in Holborn and worked all day in between visits to the station, hoping to see you. He said something about making a statement. He didn't come back."

Morgan nodded. "So you last saw him yesterday morning?"

"Yes," said Pru.

"Do you have any idea what he was going to testify about?"

Tommy answered. "He told me that he was in front of the Post Office at the time the argument supposedly took place between Samson Light and Horace Wright. He said there was no such argument."

"You don't say?"

"He also said that Horace Wright had told him something about the train cars. He'd also mentioned it to some of the people he worked with at the Post Office."

"Indeed? Well, this does sound serious," said Morgan, removing his serviette and folding it carefully. Then he rose and went to the table near the window. "I'm writing instructions for the sergeant on duty today at the station. I am giving him all the information on Mr. Fowler's movements yesterday, just as you've told me. I'm instructing him to have our top constable join him on a search of the area."

"Can we help?" said Maggie, jumping to her feet.

"No, I would not recommend that. The area around the station is not safe. The people are poor, and thefts take place on a daily basis. You'd be a target. The sergeant and constable are known there and will ask the right questions. Could you describe your father, please? His appearance, and what he was wearing yesterday?"

After taking down the details and sealing the note, Morgan was about to pull the bell when Mrs. Hobbes came in with the tea.

"Oh! Yes, I'd forgotten about the tea. Please, you three enjoy a cup while I make sure this gets to the station and contact a runner who might be helpful. He's informed for us before. Polly will show you out when you're finished."

"Well," said Pru when he left the room. "I suppose that's all we can do." She took a sip of tea and tears came to her eyes.

"Is it too hot?" asked Tommy, concerned.

"No," said Pru, with a sniff. "It's just that I didn't go visit Samson yesterday, like I should have. And the trial starts in the morning."

Tommy went and sat next to her. "It will be all right, Pru. Morgan will find Mr. Fowler, and we'll help as best we can."

But as they left Morgan's house to find yet another cab, Tommy's mind was busy. Morgan had promised to help, but he wasn't sure he believed him. Notes and informers didn't feel like action to him. When Pru fell asleep in the cab, Tommy leaned near Maggie's ear and whispered.

"I want you to stay with Pru today," he said. "Mrs. Wren thinks she might be with child, and her husband goes on trial tomorrow. Will you do that for me?"

Maggie looked at him, and her eyes narrowed. She whispered back, "You want me to just sit while my father could be in danger?"

Tommy took her hand in his. "I want you to help Pru today so she'll be strong for tomorrow. You're always strong, but she's not."

"Hmmmph," said Maggie. "And what are you going to do, may I ask?"

"Some investigating of my own."

"So it seems I've made everything worse," said Tommy, sitting in Inspector Slaughter's study.

He'd successfully hidden his despair from Maggie and Pru, who were already worried. He hoped they would comfort each other. But there'd been no comfort in his own mind. He had offered to help Stone, gone up to Durham, and finally brought back Donald Fowler. And now Fowler had disappeared. The trial was tomorrow, and Samson was sure to be convicted. So all he had done was bring hope in order to have it dashed. And now there was Maggie to disappoint as well. No, not just disappoint, he thought. He may have gotten her father killed.

He wasn't worth a cab, he decided, as he walked to Farringdon and watched for a cart he could jump on, as he used to do when he was a boy. But every cart was full, and some now had rails on the back. He walked through Smithfield Market, which was as cold and miserable as he felt inside, then down Farringdon, but the bright red Holborn Viaduct gave him no joy today. Eventually the road became Blackfriars Bridge. He crossed and returned to Southwark, where he had spent his childhood, and realized his feet were heading west to Inspector Slaughter's house in Palmer Street.

Cuthbert Slaughter was still in his dressing gown when he opened the door to Tommy.

"Come in, my boy, come in," he said. "Ellie's gone to do the shopping." He noticed Tommy's face and said, "It's not going well, is it?"

He offered Tommy a chair and a cup of tea, trying to find biscuits and failing. Tommy had explained everything that had happened, and by the time he was done the tea was gone.

Slaughter listened, but he didn't take notes or interrupt. He rose now from his wing-back chair and went over to the desk. In the drawer was his pipe and tobacco. He filled a pipe, glancing up at Tommy as he did so. The morning gloom outside was clearing, and the study was becoming lighter, the dark colors of the sofa, chairs, and curtains becoming more clearly forest green and maroon. He took out a second pipe, a small clay one, from the drawer and held it up to Tommy, raising a questioning eyebrow. Tommy nodded.

Returning to his chair, he handed Tommy the pipe. Never a smoker, Tommy watched Slaughter carefully as he tamped, lit a match, and drew. Then he did the same. He inhaled carefully, holding the smoke in his mouth as he saw Slaughter do, then exhaling it slowly. It was somehow soothing.

"Well, Thomas. It sounds like you're in a right pickle. What's best to do?"

Tommy looked up, perplexed. Had he thought he could just come here and the Inspector would solve all his problems? That seemed rather childish, now that he thought about it. He leaned back in his chair, smoking the pipe. What was best to do?

"I could go out now and try to find him."

"You said Inspector Morgan was already doing that."

"I could go see Samson and ask if there's anything he hasn't told me."

"It's Sunday. They don't allow visitors on Sunday unless it's a holiday."

"I could find Perseverance Stone."

"You haven't seen him since you returned?" Tommy shook his head.

Slaughter nodded and drew again from his pipe.

An idea occurred to Tommy, and he sat up straighter. "I could map out everything I know so far and see where things stand."

"Ah!" said Slaughter. "Now you're in my territory. I'll get some paper." He rose and went over to the desk.

"Can we work in the kitchen?" said Tommy.

"Certainly."

The kitchen table was soon covered with squares of paper, each representing a person or place. Tommy wrote down everything he could remember from his visit to Wright's flat, to the General Post Office, and from what people had said to him.

"I should have one for Inspector Morgan, too," he said, laying that out. "Oh!" He still had Stone's letter in his pocket, wrapped around the money. "And here's the information of why Morgan hates Samson, and what was found on Horace Wright's body."

He wrote down on a slip of paper: handkerchief, key, six shillings, pocket watch.

"All right," said Slaughter, looking at the papers. "Now what?"

"I'll draw connections," said Tommy, taking up a pencil. He drew lines for awhile, then stopped.

"What?" said Slaughter.

"That's odd. I saw a pocket watch in Horace Wright's flat. Would he have had two? On his salary?"

"That doesn't seem likely." Tommy made a note, then stopped again.

"What?" said Slaughter.

"This doesn't make sense," said Tommy. "It's too big."

"What's too big?"

"The whole thing. It's too big to be personal. It can't be just that someone hated Horace Wright. We have no evidence that anyone hated Horace Wright. And even if someone did, that doesn't explain the disappearance of Mr. Fowler."

"What do you mean?"

"If it were personal, or an accident, then it's just to do with Horace Wright. Why do something to Mr. Fowler?"

Tommy started turning some of the pieces over to the blank side.

"In addition to the pocket watch, there are two problems here," he said. "One is Edward Teach. He claims he saw something Fowler should have seen and didn't."

"The argument with Samson."

"Right. And the other problem is: why get rid of Donald Fowler?"

"Because he knows something? What does he know?"

"Something Mr. Fowler said. That Horace knew about the trains, a leak or something. But the real question is," said Tommy, decisively, "who cares that he knew it?" He began pointing at the pieces of paper. "Edward Teach, who might be lying? Who would tell him to lie? Mr. Henry, who runs the section of the Post Office that has the railway? He might be in trouble if something doesn't work right."

Tommy stood up and started pacing the kitchen.

"How far up does this go? To the company? The board?"

"Or all the way to Mr. Faber?" asked Slaughter. "He's in charge of the board."

"Yes!" said Tommy. "This is about money." He turned to Slaughter. "Thank you, Cuthbert."

"What did I do, Tommy?"

"Helped me to think, like I always helped you. I may not know where Donald Fowler is, but now I know what to tell Perseverance Stone."

Tommy had walked for hours after talking with Cuthbert Slaughter, down past Waterloo Station, across Westminster

Bridge, up Horse Guards Row. Whenever a man passed him who had Fowler's build, he looked at his face, hoping for bushy eyebrows. He continued past the Foreign Office and over on Pall Mall into Trafalgar Square. He had been here with Samson before, to the National Gallery. The Gallery was closed on a Sunday evening, of course, but sitting in the square Tommy thought through the various possibilities. Cabs and carriages clattered around him, taking wealthy couples to dinners and house parties. Omnibuses came by almost continually, packed with Sunday night workers returning to their homes in less fashionable areas of the city. He forgot to eat supper, and it was nine o'clock before he realized he should return to Wilderness Row, that Maggie and Pru would think he'd disappeared too.

By the time he'd stopped by Pru's house, kissed Maggie goodnight, and assured the women that he was all right, he had formed a plan. It was too late to go to Perseverance Stone's house; the barrister would need his rest for tomorrow. But the next morning, Tommy woke at six in his cold room in St. John's Gate. He dressed quickly and went downstairs. Mrs. Wren was already awake, baking bread.

"You're up early, Tommy," she said, pushing back her damp hair from her forehead. The smell of bread suffused the kitchen. Tommy realized he was starving.

"I need a favor, Mrs. Wren," he said. "It's the first day of my friend's trial at the Old Bailey, and there are things I must do. I have a bit of money, but no food. If I succeed, I'll need enough for two meals at least."

Mrs. Wren's face lit up at the opportunity to be helpful

"Then it's a lucky thing I did my shopping yesterday." She began bustling round the kitchen, packing a basket with rolls, cheese, and oranges. She thought and added two bottles of beer, serviettes, and a knife. Tommy reached into his pocket for some coins, but she stopped him.

"Go on then," she said, handing him the basket and touching his cheek with the palm of her hand. "Good luck."

Pounding on the door in Gate Street, Tommy realized that the hour was very early, but he had no choice. He had to lay out what he knew before Perseverance Stone in time for court that morning. It was a full minute before Mason answered the door, his eyes bleary but his morning clothes neat and trim and protected by a white apron. Tommy saw him snatch off his sleeping cap as he opened the door.

"Mr. Jones, is it?" asked Mason. "Mr. Stone is upstairs, dressing. I'll tell him you're here." He stepped back to let Tommy in.

"I'm sorry, but there's no time," said Tommy, dashing up the stairs.

"Tommy Jones!" Stone was surprised but not disturbed that Tommy was in his bedroom. "You must have information for me." He moved his robes and wig off the chair in the corner and motioned for Tommy to sit down.

"Not necessarily information, sir, but a map, if you like, and some ideas."

"Proceed," said Stone, fastening his collar.

Tommy explained everything he had worked out at the kitchen table in Palmer Street. By the time he had finished, Stone was dressed and was going downstairs to breakfast, with Tommy trailing behind.

"If you're correct," said Stone, as Mason silently served two cups of tea, two boiled eggs, and two plates of toast, "then there are only two places Fowler could be, assuming he's alive."

"Yes," said Tommy.

"And I assume you will go look while I go to court?"

"I will. I have brought some food, because if I find him I suspect he'll need sustenance if I'm to get him to the courtroom."

"Have you a weapon?" asked Stone.

"No, sir. I have never carried any. I've always used my wits and my speed."

Stone smiled. Tommy smiled back, but it was a mirthless smile.

"Do me a favor, Mr. Stone?"

"Of course, Tommy."

"Tell Maggie and Prudence I'll be there as soon as I can."

High Holborn in the early morning was bustling with carts and coaches in the road, and workers, bankers, lawyers, and gentlemen jostling for position on the pavement. A baker's boy pushing a wagon filled with bags of flour tried to weave his way through. The gray light made everything look ghostly. Tommy hovered next to the Music Hall, just out of sight of the entrance at 245 Holborn. He didn't want to be seen by anyone on the ground floor, but if Mr. Fowler was in there somewhere, he needed to be quick. He walked in quietly, relieved the area was empty, and headed directly to the archway leading onto the gallery, his basket bouncing on his hip. As he came down the stairs into the railway room, he saw Jenkins finishing a cup of tea and turning toward the tube for the new line to the General Post Office in St.-Martin's-le-Grand. "Hello, Mr. Jenkins," Tommy said. He looked around the space, but there was nothing unusual.

Jenkins saw the basket. "Young Mr. Jones! Brought me breakfast, have you?"

"No, this is for later. I'd be happy to give you a hand, though, if you like." He put the basket down and walked around the edges of the large platform. Nothing there of interest.

Jenkins grinned seeing him near the platform. "Hoping to run the train again, eh?"

Tommy forced a smile and nodded. "May I?"

"Of course! I'm about to pull in the first car from Euston. You can run it back out on the new line." Jenkins checked his pocket watch, jumped up on the platform, and pulled the lever. A deep humming sound began. The noise became louder and louder as the two Cornish engines in the adjoining room revved up and turned the huge fan disc. A few minutes passed as the disc turned faster, and Tommy was just as fascinated as when he'd seen this the first time.

A low roar was starting in the Euston tunnel. "Here it comes!" Jenkins said. "Stay back from the rails!"

With a groan the tube doors opened, triggered by the approaching cars. They rolled into the room on the tracks in tandem, gently hitting the bumper. Jenkins powered down the disc.

"Give me a hand, then," he said over the subsiding noise. "George went to take the oil pans upstairs."

Tommy helped Jenkins transfer the double car to the other track, rolling it across the recessed wheels mounted in the floor. They pushed the cars into the new tube, the one going to the General Post Office. Jenkins then closed the iron doors and latched them, then went up to the platform. As Tommy turned to go with him, he heard a metallic clink above the chugging engines.

"What's that?"

"What's what?" said Jenkins, from the platform.

"A sound. From inside the tube."

"Which tube?"

"That one," said Tommy, pointing to the doors he had just closed.

"Probably just an air pocket. I didn't hear anything." Jenkins turned to the controls and began powering up the disc.

"Wait!" Tommy said, and went over to the iron doors, unlatching them and swinging them open. The disc powered down. He looked inside. Just the cars. He pulled them toward him until both cars were completely out of the tunnel, and leaned over to peer in. The clinking sound came again.

"Don't you hear?" Tommy said, his voice more urgent now. "Have you a lamp?"

"Of course," said Jenkins, coming off the platform and getting a lamp that was hanging on the stair rail. "Must be rats or something."

Tommy crouched at the tunnel's entrance and shined the lamp in.

"I think I see something inside. Can you hold the lamp while I go in?"

"Certainly." Jenkins held the lamp, and Tommy ventured into the tube. He heard the sound of a rat skittering away as he approached. He stepped over the rubber flange and noticed the smell of animal fat. Must be for lubrication, he thought as he crawled a bit further. The lamp's light could not shine in far, however, and he bumped against the object before he saw it. The unmistakable scent of human waste accosted him.

"Mr. Fowler?" Tommy asked. He patted the bundle and could feel Fowler's body inside. There was a grunt, and a foot kicked out weakly, but that was all. Suddenly Tommy heard the sound of the cars moving on the track behind him, and the lead car pushed at him, the two bumpers knocking him over onto Fowler's inert form. Tommy started to apologize to Fowler, then yelled to Jenkins for help.

All went dark, and Tommy heard the doors slam shut. He was trapped in the tube with Fowler. He heard the lock engage, echoing into the tunnel. Then, from far down the track ahead, he heard a hum. The hum got louder. Tommy realized the disc was starting up. He felt the air start to pull from deep in the tunnel. When the pressure got high enough, the cars would be pulled into them with incredible force. They would certainly be killed.

Tommy exhaled and squeezed his body to turn around, careful not to kick Mr. Fowler. He pushed on the bumpers and heard the cars bang against the doors. He did it again, the sound reverberating in the tube, but nothing gave. In desperation, he reached under the car nearest him and tugged at one of the wheels on the track. If he could dislodge it from the track perhaps it might help. But the wheels were fixed fast.

He banged the cars against the doors again, hoping that either he would be heard or that the doors might give. But he knew there was nothing he could do. He began to pray to St. Cuthbert, and to apologize, to Mr. Fowler, to Maggie, as the hum became a roar. What had he done? He'd been trying to help, help Samson, help Prudence. And now he was going to get Maggie's father killed, and get himself killed, because he hadn't thought things through.

And then suddenly there was silence. Tommy heard the doors swing open, and the cars were pulled out on the rails smoothly, in a whoosh. He looked up to see a lamp shining and a ruddy round face with a halo of blonde hair smiling into the tunnel. "You in there, Tommy?" said George.

12

The gallery in the courtroom was filling, as it often did when the charge was murder. Maggie sat with Prudence, who looked pale and terrified in her sky blue dress. But she kept looking around for Tommy. Jo arrived shortly before proceedings began, and Maggie waved at her to come over.

"I must go—I can't stay here," said Maggie. "Will you look after Pru?"

Jo sat in Maggie's seat and took Pru's hand in hers. "Of course," she said. Pru saw Samson come into the dock, and her hand came to rest on her chest. Jo thought she was barely breathing.

Maggie heard the judge calling the court to order as she left the courtroom. She ran out the front of the building and up to Holborn Viaduct, looking up and down the street. It was noisy and crowded here, but at least she was outside. The room had been stifling, with the heat of the bodies and the smell of everyone. Where was Tommy? Where was her father? She stood on the corner, unsure where to go. London was so chaotic compared to Durham. Roads and buildings went on for miles, and the countryside seemed far away.

A cab rattled up and as it passed she heard Tommy's voice call her name out the window. Her heart racing, she ran back to the courthouse as Tommy helped her father out of the cab. Donald Fowler was strangely dressed, wearing a bright red waistcoat and trousers too big for him, but Maggie didn't care. She threw her arms around him and he staggered a bit.

"It's all right, Maggie girl," he said. "I'm still weak is all. Help me into the courtroom?"

She asked no questions but took his arm and helped him up the steps as Tommy paid the cabbie.

"You smell like flowers and spice," she said.

"Bathhouse," said Fowler.

"I couldn't have brought him the way he was," said Tommy apologetically, and Fowler grunted in agreement. "Have they started?"

"Just now," Maggie said. "They already sentenced a case about a robbery and beating. Now it's Mr. Light's turn."

They brought Fowler into the lower seats of the court. A tall man, whom Maggie assumed was the prosecuting barrister, was finishing his introduction, explaining the argument witnessed by Edward Teach and promising further evidence shortly. The man at the other table must be Perseverance Stone, Maggie thought.

Stone was turned to face the other barrister and saw out of the corner of his eye Maggie and Tommy helping Mr. Fowler to his seat. His face didn't change, but he exchanged a glance with Tommy. Then he stood and made his introduction, promising to convince the jury that Samson Light did not commit the crime, and that he would prove it. As the judge instructed the jury to listen carefully to all the evidence, Tommy stepped down to the front rail and handed Stone a note. As the prosecutor rose to call the first witness, Maggie saw Stone read the note. His expression changed from one of concern to one of deep satisfaction. He nodded at Tommy and began making notes on his papers.

Maggie looked up at the man in the dock, who must be Samson Light. She could tell he was relieved to see Tommy.

Samson saw a strangely dressed man being brought into the courtroom by Tommy and a woman. This must be the witness Tommy had told him about and he gave Tommy a grateful nod. But he avoided looking up at Prudence because it might make them both cry, and he didn't want to appear weak. Instead he looked around the courtroom, diagnosing in his head. Creased earlobes on the bailiff meant he was a bad surgical risk. The judge had a sallow complexion that might indicate liver problems. Mr. Stone was remarkably healthy for a man who had little opportunity for outdoor exercise.

Although he had intended to listen carefully to the testimony, Samson was unable to concentrate on everything that was said. He watched as the judge called in the policeman who had been first on the scene at 245 Holborn. The constable testified to finding the body lying on the floor with Mr. Jenkins guarding the dispatch room. Jenkins had told him the dead man was Horace Wright from the Post Office. It looked to the constable as though Mr. Wright had been strangled.

The coroner gave evidence as to the results of the inquest, that death was caused by strangulation, and that a chain of some kind had been used to crush the larynx. Nothing appeared to have been stolen from the victim's person.

Then Inspector Morgan was called to give evidence. Samson could not resist the urge to look at him, if only to make sure he was the same man whose daughter had died in St. Bart's three years before. The look Morgan gave him was a combination of suppressed loathing and calm satisfaction. He testified to the contents of Horace Wright's pockets, his understanding of the coroner's report, his unsuccessful search for a chain. The arrest of Samson Light had been made after he had asked questions of the staff at the Post Office, and Edward Teach had reported the argument. When asked by Stone why he had taken over a case that should have rightly been investigated by City of London police rather than the Metropolitan, Morgan explained that since the body was found in Holborn, he believed it would be in the force's best interest for him to command the investigation.

Samson leaned forward slightly in the dock.

"Inspector Morgan, did you know the accused before the death of Horace Wright?"

Morgan looked confused, his brows knit together. "I don't believe so."

"I regret bringing up a family tragedy," said Stone kindly, "but did your daughter not meet with an accident three years ago?"

Morgan nodded, his voice choking. "Yes, she did."

"And was not Mr. Light one of the surgeons who treated her at St. Bartholomew's Hospital?"

"He might have been. I don't recall."

Samson looked at the jury and saw confusion on some faces, stony placidity on others. Stone presented the jury with the records from the hospital, suggesting that Inspector Morgan might have a grudge against Samson Light, but stopping short of saying so.

Edward Teach was called, and Samson was quite certain he had never seen the man before. The prosecution elicited the story of the argument Teach claimed to have seen at half past eight the morning of Wright's murder. Samson couldn't help shaking his head as the man reported events that had never happened. Stone rose and asked Teach why he hadn't reported the argument to the constable on the scene, but had only relayed the story two days later, when questioned by Inspector Morgan.

"I hadn't thought it important at the time," said Teach, his eyelid twitching.

"But you did two days later?"

"Yes, when Inspector Morgan asked if I'd seen anything unusual that morning."

"And had you spoken about the matter to anyone in the meantime?"

"I don't know what you mean, sir."

"Mr. Teach, between the discovery of the murder and the interview with Detective Inspector Morgan, were you in fact offered money to tell this story about an argument?"

Teach did not reply as a murmur went through the crowd in the room. Stone spoke again. "I remind you that lying in court is called perjury, and that you would, if convicted of perjury, spend time in gaol."

And thus it came out that Teach had been contacted by a man, a man he didn't know, and offered forty pounds to tell the story of the argument. Teach had a sister who was ill, and he needed the money. His pay as a senior clerk wasn't enough to buy her medicine. Samson looked at the jury and saw sympathy, but he also saw some of their minds working, putting together what was being said.

Donald Fowler was then called, and he testified that he had been at the General Post Office on the morning of March 31, preparing the terminal of the rail line. He had been in front of the Post Office awaiting a delivery at half past eight and had seen no argument take place. The cart had brought the wrong items, oil for engines instead of grease for flanges, and he had returned on the cart to 245 Holborn, where he and Jenkins discovered the body. The prosecution made much of him leaving after the body was discovered the next day at 245 Holborn. He explained why he left, but to do so he had to admit that he'd been afraid, afraid that he might be next to be killed.

"Why did you think that?" asked the prosecutor.

"Because Horace Wright had told me he had doubts about the pneumatic railway, that it wouldn't work properly, or wouldn't work for long. He said the seals leaked and would always leak, that the design was wrong. He told me, and I told him I'd check the seals."

"Wasn't Mr. Wright just a sorting clerk?"

"Yes, but he was very observant and very precise."

Being questioned by Stone, Fowler admitted that he had not shared Horace's concern with the other engineer, Jenkins, because he hadn't thought it a serious matter. But after Wright had been found dead, he realized things were deadly serious, and he didn't want to be involved. He had the opportunity to leave and he left.

That had been wrong, he realized now, which is why he had returned. But it appeared he had been right about why Horace Wright was killed, and right to be concerned for his own safety. He had recently been attacked.

The prosecution objected, saying that the evidence being given was beyond the scope of the murder. But the judge asked Fowler to continue, as Samson listened in astonishment.

"I arrived in London on Friday. Saturday morning I went to find Inspector Morgan at St. Giles to make a statement. But he wasn't there. I spent the day at 245 Holborn, helping Jenkins and George Smith load the trains. After they went home, I investigated the track."

"And what did you find?"

"It was leaking air and didn't seal properly, just as Horace Wright had said. But as I was looking, I was struck from behind. When I awoke, I was inside the new line's tunnel and was tied up with cord. The doors to the tunnel were closed and latched."

"How long were you there, sir?"

"Two nights. Until just a few hours ago."

The spectators gasped and began talking so loudly that the judge had to use his gavel to ask for order. A blond man with a round red face, wearing a worker's overall, came in the door of the courtroom and sat down at the back. The judge turned to Fowler.

"How do you come to be here now, Mr. Fowler?"

"I was able to reach a coin in my pocket, and I used it to tap on the side of the tunnel. But no one came, and I was sure I would die there." The courtroom was very quiet now.

"This morning, I heard the tube doors open and the cars being pulled out, and I thought I was dreaming. Tommy Jones, the man who brought me here from Durham" —he pointed to Tommy in the courtroom—"came inside. But then we were both trapped, and the engines started. The pressure was about to build to where the rail cars would crush us, when the engines stopped and George Smith opened the doors. He told us he had—"

The prosecution objected vociferously that this was hearsay evidence. What George Smith said would have to be his testimony, not Fowler's.

"Is George Smith in the courtroom?" the judge asked. George stood from where he'd been seated at the back and came forward.

Stone relinquished his time for questioning Fowler, and George took the stand. He told how he had come back from upstairs to find a horrible scene. Jenkins was lying just inside the doorway unconscious, with a trail of blood running down from his forehead. A man he didn't know was on the platform, pushing the lever on the machine to start the train.

"Now, I've been in Australia, your lordship, and lived a rough life. I've seen things a man shouldn't have to see. And I may not know much about business, or being a good husband, but I know when a man is committing a heinous act."

"What did you do?"

"I'm afraid I attacked him, your lordship. Punched him in the face, then the stomach, then the jaw. Knocked him out cold. Then I ran over to see to Jenkins. He was just coming round and pointed toward the closed doors on the tunnel and said Tommy's name. He started to point at the engine lever, but fainted again. I figured I'd better turn it off. When I did I heard a banging from the tunnel, so I opened the doors and pulled the cars out. They were in there, Mr. Jones and Mr. Fowler."

He then explained how he tied up the attacker with the cord he cut off Donald Fowler, who was soiled and starving. At Mr. Jones's request, he gave over his clothes to Mr. Fowler, putting on the overall that was kept there for the men who stoked the engines. Mr. Jones had gotten Fowler bathed and come here, and he had followed after fetching the police.

"Where is this man now? The one who attacked them?"

"At the police station in Marylebone, where I took him," said George. And he beamed a satisfied smile at the judge.

Samson sat and stared when the case was dismissed. Had he heard correctly? Then he looked up at Prudence's face, beaming out from among the noisy crowd in the gallery, and knew he had.

Perseverance Stone accompanied Samson, who was taken back to Clerkenwell Gaol to collect his things.

"I'm not sure I understand," said Samson, as they rode in the police van. "It all happened so fast. Don't murder trials take days and days?"

"Not typically," said Stone. "A few hours is usual, especially on the first day of a session."

Samson drew a deep breath out the open window of the cab.

"You'll be all right," said Stone. "Justice can be swift."

"I confess I wasn't able to follow everything that was happening."

"You were in the wrong place at the wrong time," said Stone. "You happened to be walking in front of the General Post Office as the murderer was leaving. He discovered who you were and paid Edward Teach to give false evidence."

"So it wasn't even about me?"

"Well, it became about you—oomph," said Stone as the van hit a bump in the road. "It became about you when Inspector Morgan discovered you'd been accused. He simply wasn't interested in having anyone else considered a suspect."

"And Horace Wright was killed because he knew the seals leaked on the railway?"

"Yes, indeed. And that was why Donald Fowler left London. Or it was partly why he left, at any rate. He had a job waiting in Durham."

"So Fowler knew because Horace Wright told him. The poor man," said Samson, shaking his head. "He was just a postal clerk, trying to do the right thing."

"And you are just a surgeon, trying to help people. Bad things happen. If they didn't, I would have no career."

The police van jostled again as it slowed in front of the gates of the Clerkenwell House of Detention.

"I shall leave you here," said Stone. "I'm sure you'll wish to say goodbye to the governor. And Miss Harper." His eyes twinkled.

"How did you—?" asked Samson as they alighted from the van.

"I have good investigators." Stone began walking toward the corner to catch a cab back to Gate Street.

"Wait—who is the murderer?" But the police van rattled as it turned around, and Stone didn't hear.

Shaking his head, Samson walked in the front gate of Clerkenwell Gaol, and as he passed through the courtyard, he almost ran into Fiona Harper. She had her bag in her hand and was clearly on her way out.

"Miss Harper," he said in surprise.

"Mr. Light," she said with a smile.

"You are leaving?"

"My case was suddenly and mysteriously dropped," she said. "I hear you have had great success in court. Congratulations."

Samson was still mystified.

"Miss Harper, I must ask—why did you take me into your confidence? And," he said quietly, looking around to make sure he wasn't overheard, "what happened to the papers?"

She lowered her voice too. "They were in the Post Office, behind a cabinet of cubbyholes that were being installed."

"How did you obtain them?"

"I sent a note to headquarters that night, through Mr. O'Brien. They sent someone to, as you say, obtain them." Her eyes sparkled with amusement. "And I trusted you because I am an excellent judge of character. You're spectacularly easy to read. I knew your honor would demand reporting my theft of the opium to the governor, and we'd worked very hard to ensure that he knew nothing of what we were doing."

He took a deep breath, then smiled back at her.

"I wish you the very best, Miss Harper."

"And I you, Mr. Light."

The rain was slow and steady. The group was comfortably ensconced at Jo and Hortense's house in Red Lion Street, with George making tea in the kitchen. The wet things had been deposited near the kitchen door. Pru, Maggie, Tommy, and Mr. Fowler had returned to Wilderness Court to get Fowler changed out of his ill-fitting clothing, which they had brought to return to George. Sally was sitting on Hortense's lap in the parlor, having just awakened from her nap, when there was a knock. Jo rose and looked through the window pane, then motioned to the kitchen door around the corner. Samson came in to a round of cheers. He shook off his coat just outside the door and hung it on the rack, wiping his feet on the kitchen mat before coming into the parlor.

"I'm still confused," said Hortense, whom they'd been regaling with the events of the day. "Who killed Horace Wright?"

"The chap I hit at Holborn," George said. "The police took him. Don't know his name."

"What did he look like?"

Everyone listened as George described him as slight and wiry, with pomaded hair and a pinched face.

"Did he wear a pince-nez?" interrupted Pru.

George frowned. "Dunno. But I did hear something crunch in his waistcoat pocket when I punched him."

"Oh my Lord," said Pru.

"What?" said everyone.

There was another knock at the door, and Perseverance Stone was waved down to the kitchen door. He smiled as he was brought into the parlor. Introductions were made all around, but as soon as Stone was seated he was barraged with questions.

"It was Mr. Wilson, wasn't it? The secretary of the Pneumatic Despatch Railway Company?" demanded Pru.

"Yes, Mr. Wilson of the company," said Stone, as he was handed a cup of tea.

"But why?" asked Hortense.

Tommy said, "I know why." All eyes turned to him.

"Horace Wright discovered that the pneumatic railway leaked air. Now I've seen the device up close, so I know there's a gap around the cars, so they can move. The India rubber flanges cover that gap to get the vacuum. I noticed when I crawled inside that the flanges smelled of animal fat, and one was ragged at the edges. I heard a rat running when I crawled into the tube. It's possible that rats chew the flanges, making holes. And the rails themselves don't make proper contact, so soon the whole system would either stop working or the cars would become so slow as to be useless."

"So the pneumatic idea doesn't work?" asked Jo.

"Oh, it works. It's in use all over London, just small tubes to carry notes and things. Nothing of this size."

"But I thought they tested it all, at Battersea. My mother had a friend who rode on it back in '61," said Pru.

"I think testing it lying on the ground at Battersea is not the same as running it under the streets of London," said Tommy.

"Is that why the line to the General Post Office didn't open until now?" asked Hortense.

"No, that was because of the failure of Overend, Gurney & Company, the big bank. The company had a lot of trouble getting it going again after that. Mr. V. G. Faber and the board have a great deal invested in it working properly," said Tommy.

"They must have," agreed Pru. "There's even a Duke on the board. I have the list of members."

"Is that the V. G. Faber who has all the book stalls at the rail stations?" asked Maggie. Tommy nodded.

"And Mr. Wilson is very loyal to Mr. Faber and to the company," said Pru. "I could see that when I met him."

"You met him?" said everyone at once. Sally squeaked, as she'd been trying to fall back asleep with the hum of adult conversation. Samson's face was creased with concern.

"Yes, I went to the Pneumatic Despatch Company office to see what I could find out about how the railway worked," said Pru, squeezing Samson's hand reassuringly. "I thought him an officious prig."

"An officious murdering prig," said Jo, getting up to wind the clock.

"Oh!" said Stone suddenly. "The pocket watch."

Tommy grinned. "Mr. Wilson put it on Horace Wright's body, didn't he? I've been thinking about that."

"But why?"

"To make us suspect Mr. Henry if his choice of a bystander didn't work. He took his pocket watch somehow, off that chain he's always fiddling with. Must have been a pickpocket before becoming a secretary."

"And he paid Edward Teach to lie?" asked Hortense.

"Yes," said Tommy. "He was trying to hide what he had done. And he got very lucky that Inspector Morgan hated Samson so much he looked no further."

As the evening drew to a close, Perseverance Stone warned the group. "Be sure to write down everything you know or have done in regards to this case," he said. "It may be needed for the trial of William Wilson, which would be next session, the beginning of June. Someone should investigate the company's investments, and inform the investigating detective at Marylebone." He shook out his still damp coat and put it on. Jo handed him his hat.

"You're not defending him, are you, Mr. Stone?" asked Maggie.

"No," said Stone firmly. "I have work to do at the Foreign Office."

Samson and Pru had agreed to pull the wagon with the picnic basket and folding campaign chairs. It had been tricky getting the wagon on to the boat, but Pru had chosen Cremorne Gardens for the engagement picnic. The Chelsea Steamer at threepence for each of them was the best way to get there.

"Where on earth did you get those chairs?" Pru asked Tommy.

"I used to know a man at the workhouse, and he knew a man who'd been stationed in India, and—"

"Goodness! You do know everyone, don't you, Tommy?"

"Only in London." Tommy grinned, looking over at Maggie. They dragged the wagon across the lawn, until Sally insisted on a ride, then George joined them pushing from behind. The day was fine, and the lawn was damp, but it was Wednesday, so they knew the bandstand would be free and they could picnic there.

Hortense took Jo's arm, and they walked more slowly behind.

"I hear it gets quite wild in the evenings here now," she said to Jo.

"That's what I hear too."

"I wonder if there's a toilet here?"

"There should be, near the dining rooms. But if not, I've brought your things, and I can tell you there are many bushes and places to hide."

"Don't tell me how you know that," said Hortense, smiling up at Jo.

"A lady never tells her secrets," said Jo. Hortense's face in the sunlight glowed, but beneath she looked positively gray. The surgery would be Friday, in just two days time. Both of them knew these could be their last days together, and Hortense's last days with Sally. The others knew too, but no one mentioned it. It would sadden a day made for happiness, the happiness of Tommy and Maggie getting married.

"Have you decided, Maggie?" asked George as they laid out oilcloth on the grass near the bandstand and set up a chair for

Hortense. Maggie had been trying to make up her mind where they should get married, and where they should live.

"It's Tommy's decision too," said Samson stoutly. Everyone laughed.

"It's Maggie's decision," said Tommy, handing out bottles of beer from the basket.

"It's been Maggie's decision since she was two," grumbled Donald Fowler, but he was smiling as he said it. Regardless of her decision, he would be returning to Durham on the Saturday train.

"When are you leaving, George?" Samson asked. "Off to the wilds of China, isn't it?"

"Yes indeed," said George. The sun peeked out from behind a cloud and made his blond hair glow like the gold in his brocade waistcoat. "Mr. Jamrach has paid for the animals, and I'm off on the Sunday boat to discover the world of marketable insects."

"Mo' kitties?" Sally asked, eating the pieces of tart Jo handed her.

"No, my little miss, no more kitties." Sally frowned. She missed the creatures living in boxes in the kitchen.

The sky was graying again, a dark cloud coming in over the Gardens. They all felt a hint of a cool breeze and then large drops started to fall. "Rain!" cried Sally, and she began running in circles on the lawn. Jo, Samson, and Tommy began gathering things and dragging the wagon up onto the bandstand. George and Maggie lifted the oilcloth and held it over Hortense's head to keep her dry as she moved, too. The rain was getting heavier. Jo fetched a still circling Sally off the grass and handed her to Donald Fowler, then went out again to get the camp chair for Hortense. The meal was reassembled under the cover of the bandstand roof as hats were removed and shaken out, and shoes stamped away from the oilcloth. A place was found for everyone to sit.

"I've decided," said Maggie suddenly over the sound of the rain. "I want to run the Market Hotel and be married at the Durham City Register Office." She said it strongly but looked over at Tommy and raised an eyebrow in question. He nodded.

"Everyone," announced Tommy, standing and raising his beer bottle. "I'm announcing my decision to be married in Durham at the register office and join Maggie in running the Market Hotel, which will be the finest tavern in the best town in the world." Everyone cheered and sipped their beer. "Except London, of course," he said as he sat down. Donald Fowler was smoothing the water out of Sally's curls with his fingers, and smiling to himself.

"Maggie replied to my letter," said Pru.

"Did she?" said Samson, squeezing her hand. They had taken the brown line omnibus, alighted at King's Road in Chelsea, and were now walking along Marlborough Road.

"I had written her that Hortense was fully recovered, thanks to your consummate skill," continued Pru.

"Thanks to her own ability to heal."

"You're too modest, Samson."

The surgery had been difficult, but Mr. Spencer Wells had been able to operate quickly because Samson was attending to the anesthesia. He'd even declared that he would prefer a separate anesthetist from now on and had invited Samson to join him when he could. Samson had more work at the hospital now, with the friends and family of his patients coming to consult him.

"I also told her what Perseverance Stone told us, about Inspector Morgan retiring suddenly and moving to Swansea."

"May he never have a day's luck there."

"And William Wilson being sentenced to Coldbath Fields."

"Likewise. And what do you hear from Maggie?"

"She says she's signed the papers to take over management of the Market Hotel."

"Good! And what's Tommy doing?"

"She says he's helping enormously, but that he's also working at the Mechanic's Institute Library."

"Oh, that's good. Plenty of use for his knowledge there."

"That's two days a week. And he works for a barrister named Maynell on Fridays, doing research."

"Really?"

"And he has a job in the office of the *Chronicle*." They looked at each other and smiled. Tommy was a man of variety.

Suddenly there it was: Thomas Crapper's Sanitary Showroom. The Marlboro' Works was a two story building with shop windows on the ground floor. An array of pedestal toilets shone in the window.

"My goodness," said Pru. "I've certainly never seen toilets displayed like that."

"They say," said Samson, a gleam in his eye, "that women have fainted on seeing this very window."

"More likely fainted from their stays being too tight. How funny!"

They entered the shop and followed the signs upstairs to the showroom. Pru gasped in delight. Toilets, bathtubs, basins and taps, organized both by type and arranged together in neat model rooms, gleamed in the open space.

"How may I assist you today?" asked a bearded man in a white apron.

"We're looking for a matching toilet and basin," said Samson. He felt foolish asking about toilets, although he didn't know why he should. A more comfortable income should mean a more comfortable bathroom.

"Excellent, sir," said the man, and was just about to begin an explanation when a sophisticated gentleman with neat gray hair and beard entered the showroom, checking his watch.

"Mr. Crapper," said the salesman with a tone of deep respect. "A very good day to you, sir!"

The man looked up, then saw Samson and Pru and smiled. "And to you, Paul. You are assisting this young couple?" His hearty Yorkshire voice carried through the showroom.

"Yes, sir. I was just about to tell them about the benefits of the Self-Rising Seat—"

"The Self-Rising Closet Seat is an innovation," explained Crapper to Samson and Pru. "One of my earlier patents. It raises and lowers on its own from here, with counterweights. Gentlemen," he said, lowering his voice, "need not use their hands to lift the seat. Do let Paul here know if you need anything. I must get back down to the foundry. Cisterns, you know."

As he went downstairs, Paul's face was still a bit pink.

"Mr. Crapper seems very energetic," said Pru.

The assistant nodded. "He's an amazing inventor. You've been to Westminster Abbey, yes? We did the new drains—you can see the big round covers with our company name near the school. And he's going to design the plumbing for the royal family, at Sandringham."

"You see, Pru?" said Samson. "Our bathroom will be palatial."

After showing them the options for seats (mahogany or walnut would be best; pine was for servants), Paul invited them to look around on their own. Pru took Samson's arm as they walked through the staged rooms, comparing models.

"I used to clean these," said Pru. "Now I'm shopping for my own." Samson could hear the smile in her voice.

They weren't buying a bathtub, but they looked anyway. Some had claw feet close together, and Pru thought she might tip the tub getting in and out. Others had decorative edging that matched the toilet and basin. They came upon a toilet with a dark mahogany seat and base, which contrasted with the white tank above. They looked at each other and grimaced.

"About Jo," said Pru. "I think you've only caused trouble there."

"Don't worry. Jo will get used to it," said Samson. "It's only a kitten. Hortense seemed to like it even if Jo was skeptical. Sally will grow up with a little feline companion. They'll be adorable together."

"You're a soft touch, Samson, and that's a fact."

"Well, little Sally was so sad about George's animals disappearing. Her tears were hard for me to bear."

"Oh, Samson. Our baby is going to be so very spoiled."

"That is the idea," said Samson.

Author's Notes

As a historian writing fiction, my first note is to acknowledge the help given me as I researched the history from across the pond: Barry Attoe and Gavin McGuffie at the Postal Museum, Liz Bregazzi and Pete Bradshaw at the Durham County Records Office, Adam at Thomas Crapper and Company Limited, and Sally Collins at University College London.

As in the other books in this trilogy, it is important to remember that Victorian life was not as stodgy as is assumed. Many of the sources we have on the era are prescriptive, describing what the author thinks *should* be, rather than what actually is. Even without the vote or property rights (and married women gained these in 1870, shortly after the events in this book), women held considerable political, social, and economic influence.

Clerkenwell Gaol, or the Middlesex House of Detention, is frequently confused with Coldbath Fields, or the Middlesex House of Corrections. Coldbath Fields was a prison where inmates worked at demeaning and dangerous tasks such as picking oakum or marching on treadwheels to make power. Clerkenwell Gaol was as portrayed in the novel, with visiting hours, decent food, and good treatment. It was reserved for people awaiting trial.

Clerkenwell was an Italian neighborhood in 1870, known for its clock factories. Many ice cream vendors were Italian, and they served the ice cream in small glass "penny lick" cups, which were rinsed in a bucket of water before being used for the next customer. These were eventually outlawed due to concerns about the spread of disease, especially tuberculosis.

The use of anesthesia for surgery was becoming more common by 1870, but there was still conflict over germ theory and the best way to reduce the high mortality of surgery patients. Hortense is indeed facing a 50% chance of survival, and few hysterectomies were attempted. Her surgeon, Thomas Spencer Wells, was a highly respected doctor who advanced the use of both anesthetics and hygienic practice, and his success rate for the removal of ovaries was excellent. Anesthesia and medicine during this era is covered more fully in *Murder at Old St. Thomas's*, the first book of the trilogy.

The Old Jerusalem Tavern did have an Urban Club that met in the room over the arch and celebrated Shakespeare's birthday. The Tavern itself has moved several times over the years, but in 1870 was attached to St. John's Gate.

The Post Office service throughout the country was highly convenient, delivering mail within the city of London between six and twelve times a day. The General Post Office in St. Martin's-le-Grande, originally providing large and well-lit workspace for sorting, became more and more crowded and dismal as the population expanded, and workers were not paid well. In 1870, when the government nationalized the telegraph, expansions were already planned for across the street, as well as a new building for telegraphers, who were predominantly women. The Post Office had never been enthusiastic about the pneumatic railway.

The London Pneumatic Despatch Company was quite real. It was established in the 1860s and due to the Duke of Buckingham's influence was able to obtain an Act of Parliament allowing it to tear up streets. The line was laid using cut-and-cover for the western portion between Holborn and Euston, while deeper work was needed to approach the new Holborn Viaduct to the east on the way to the General Post Office. The first part was opened in 1865, and the entire venture was abandoned by 1874. The tube was rediscovered in 1900, and again more recently—two of the original cars are now on display in the Postal Museum in London. Edmund Clark, Thomas Brassey, John Horatio Lloyd were all real board members. While there was no female member of the board to my knowledge, it was not at all unusual for such a place to be occupied by a widow if her husband was a deceased member.

The collapse of Overend, Gurney & Company causes problems at several places in the novel. This was the "banker's bank", the most secure market bank in England, and its failure caused ripples throughout the economy.

Ann Little Ingram was the wife of Herbert Ingram, managing editor of *The Illustrated London News*. When he died on a boating excursion with his son in America, Ann took over the magazine. Despite the fact that she ran the paper for nine years, until one of her sons took over, there is almost nothing written about her life, and nothing about her management of the most popular paper in London.

All of the sketches described as drawn by Jo actually appear in *The Illustrated London News* but were drawn by real artists.

Arthur Otway was Under Secretary to Lord Clarendon, who would die in July, leaving him to manage the Foreign Office response to the Franco-Prussian War. He was also chairman of the Brighton and South Coast Railway Company, which just shows how many important people were invested in railways. And yes, there were spies, "secret services" provided to governments. Stieber's network under Bismarck was one of the first to become organized.

Samuel Graham's treatment for tuberculosis, provided to Pru's mother in a private hospital, was part of the new movement for treatment based on open air and meaningful work for patients. At this time, the approach was just getting started in Britain, although such small hospitals were already popular on the Continent.

Coal mine explosions were common, due to the presence of firedamp (primarily methane gas) and the use of open lamps, even after the invention of the Davy and Geordie lamps. The Durham Miners' Association was formed in November 1869 and met on the dates in the novel at the Market Hotel.

The song the old man sings on the Framwellgate Bridge in Durham is called "The Collier's Rant" and was written many years before and was a local song in Newcastle. The lyrics were published in 1827. *Cushy Butterfield* was a popular bawdy song of the day.

The Market Hotel in Durham has undergone a few name changes but is in the same location, currently as Market Tavern. It had a female proprietor in the 1870s.

Hugh Mackey was a real person; Durham born and bred, he started working at Henderson's Carpet Manufactory at age 12 and worked his way up to manager, then went on to establish his own carpet manufacturing company.

Toileting was tricky for women who were out and about in London, or anywhere really. Some refer to a "urinary leash" which kept women at home when there were no public facilities. While it's true that after the debut of flushing toilets in cubicles at the 1851 Crystal Palace Exhibition there were no public conveniences built until the 1880s, both men and women were accustomed to finding a semi-private location in an alley or by-street to do their necessary business. Women's underwear was separated at the crotch, which made this easier to manage with skirts. It's also quite likely that once men's conveniences became available, women would use them in pairs with one keeping watch, much as is done today. The provision of public toilets in London would increase as a social good after 1890, but by the mid-20th century declined again to the horribly low levels we have today.

The Old Bailey routinely held murder trials lasting only a few hours. "Giving evidence" was all verbal; physical evidence was only introduced as part of someone's testimony, usually a police officer's.

Perseverance Stone is noted as a prosecutor for the Müller case, where a German immigrant was hanged for murdering a man in a railroad car. At the time, all cars opened onto the platform and had no connection with each other, thus people in a car were isolated from the rest of the train. The case frightened people in the early days of popular rail travel and may have led to peepholes being cut between cars.

Thomas Crapper opened the first showroom for bathroom fixtures in Chelsea, and by the 1860s was contracted to help with plumbing for the royals. While there were rumors that women fainted at the site of toilets in the front window, this is unlikely.

Dedication

This book is dedicated to my family: David, Sarah, Taylor, and my mother, who encouraged and read; my wonderful readers, Jane and Jenny; my editors, Payton and Erika; and the many scholars and clerks who helped put so many resources and documents online and accessible.

Bibliography

"Another Pneumatic Railway in London," *Scientific American* 13, no. 2 (July 8, 1865): 18–19.

Alfred E. Beach, The Pneumatic Dispatch, New York: American News Company, 1868.

Durham Directory 1869 and 1870, Archives, Durham Records Office.

Henry Mayhew and John Binny, *Criminal Prisons of London and Scenes of Prison Life*, London: Griffin, Bohn, and Company (1862)

"An Old London Inn and Tennis Court," *The Gentleman's Magazine*, July-Dec 1906, pp 543-547.

B. Penner, 'A world of unmentionable suffering: women's public conveniences in Victorian London,' *Journal of Design History*, Vol.14 (2001).

British Postal Guide; Containing the Chief Public Regulations of the Post Office, with Other Information, London: George E. Eyre & William Spottiswood, 1870.

William Brockie, *Legends and Superstitions of the County of Durham*, Sunderland: B. Wiliams, 1886.

C. J. Cornish, *Life at the Zoo: Notes and Traditions of the Regent's Park Gardens*, London: Seeley and Co. Limited, 1895.

John Hawkins, "Report of Society Meeting: The Evolution of Pneumatic Railways and the World's Second Underground Line." London Underground Railway Society, August 9, 2016, https://www.lurs.org.uk/.

"Holborn Viaduct Subways," *Scientific American*, November 15, 1873.

"In Parliament - Session 1864: The London Pneumatic Despatch Company," *London Gazette*, November 22, 1863.

"Infected Ice Cream," The Lancet, September 19, 1885, p. 537.

Ian Mansfield, "London's Lost Tunnel." *IanVisits*, July 11, 2009, https://www.ianvisits.co.uk/blog/2009/07/11/londons-lost-tunnel/.

Sarah McCabe, *The Provision of Underground Public Conveniences in London with Reference to Gender Differentials, 1850s-1980s*, Institute of Historical Research, University of London (2012).

"New General Post-Office Buildings," *Illustrated London News*, February 7, 1863.

"Opening of the Pneumatic Despatch Mail Service," *Illustrated London News*, February 8, 1863.

Michael Richardson, *Durham Cathedral City from Old Photographs*. Stroud, Gloucestershire: Amberley Books, 2013.

"Pneumatic Despatch Co." in *Grace's Guide*, n.d., https://www.gracesguide.co.uk/Pneumatic_Despatch_Co.

"Pneumatic Despatch Company (Limited)," *Saturday Review*, June 9, 1860.

"Pneumatic Dispatch Railway, from the Pall Mall Gazette, Oct. 12," *New York Times*, October 29, 1865.

Ian Steadman, "London's Victorian Hyperloop: The Forgotten Pneumatic Railway beneath the Capital's Streets," *New Statesman*, December 18, 2013.

Julian Stray, "The Beginnings of the Pneumatic Railway" and "The Pneumatic Railway's Second Chance" (11 June 2020), Postal Museum Blog, retrieved from https://www.postalmuseum.org/blog/the-beginnings-of-the-pneumatic-railway/.

Syken, J. M., "Underground: How The TUBE Shaped London," PDH Online, Fairfax, VA, 2013.

"The Pneumatic Despatch," *Illustrated London News*, August 24, 1861.

"The Pneumatic Despatch Company Having Laid down a Tube…" *Illustrated London News*, February 7, 1863.

Harry Thompson, "London's Lost Tunnel," *Windsor Magazine*, Volume XI, 1899-1900, pp 617-625.

"Underground London: Its Railways, Subways and Sewers," in *Old and New London*, V:224–42. London: Cassell, Petter & Galpin, 1878, https://www.british-history.ac.uk/old-new-london/vol5/pp224-242.

Robin Weir, "Penny Licks and Hokey Pokey, Ice Cream Before the Cone," in *Oxford Symposium on Food and Cookery 1991: Public Eating*, 295–300, Prospect Books, 1992.

John Wilson, *A History of the Durham Miners' Association 1870-1904*, Durham: J. Veitch and Sons, 1907.

Ingram Content Group UK Ltd.
Milton Keynes UK
UKHW040952240323
419106UK00004B/516